Pamela Hart is an award-winning, bestselling author of more than 35 books. Her historical novels are set in the first half of the twentieth century (although she has been known to write an occasional Regency romance). Her last full-length historical novel was *The Desert Nurse*, which concluded the ANZAC series (which started with *The Soldier's Wife*, *The War Bride* and *A Letter from Italy*). In 2020, she also saw the publication of *Song and Dance* which, like *The Charleston Scandal*, is set in London in the 1920s.

As Pamela Freeman, she is well known as a beloved children's author and fantasy writer. Her most recent children's book is a non-fiction picture book, *Dry to Dry: The Seasons of Kakadu*. Her adult fantasy series, The Castings Trilogy, ended with the award-winning *Ember and Ash*.

Pamela lives in Sydney with her husband and their son, and teaches at the Australian Writers' Centre. *The Charleston Scandal* is her 37th book.

To find out more about the true stories behind *The Charleston Scandal*, and to sign up for Pamela's newsletter, visit:

www.pamela-hart.com
f pamelahartbooks
🐦 @pamelahartbooks

D0185294

ALSO BY PAMELA HART

The Soldier's Wife
The War Bride
A Letter from Italy
The Desert Nurse

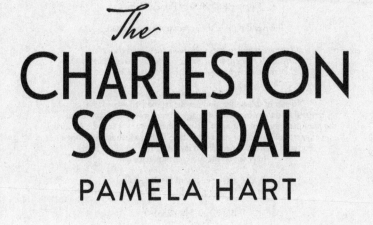

The CHARLESTON SCANDAL

PAMELA HART

PIATKUS

PIATKUS

First published in Australia and New Zealand in 2020 by Hachette Australia
An imprint of Hachette Australia Pty Limited
First published in Great Britain in 2020 by Piatkus
This paperback edition published in 2021 by Piatkus

1 3 5 7 9 10 8 6 4 2

A CIP catalogue record for this book
is available from the British Library.

ISBN 978-0-349-42561-0

Text design by Bookhouse, Sydney
Typeset in 12.8/16.5 pt Adobe Garamond Pro by Bookhouse, Sydney

Printed and bound in Great Britain by Clays Ltd, Elcograf S.p.A.

Papers used by Piatkus are from well-managed forests
and other responsible sources.

Piatkus
An imprint of
Little, Brown Book Group
Carmelite House
50 Victoria Embankment
London EC4Y 0DZ

An Hachette UK Company
www.hachette.co.uk

www.littlebrown.co.uk

For Doris, the best mother-in-law ever

'And a five, six, seven, eight!'

Kit launched into the tap routine with all her enthusiasm and that special smile pasted on her face. This was her edge on the competition – she knew she was one of the best dancers the director had seen, because she'd been sneakily watching the auditions of the other girls from the foyer. There were better singers, and a couple of real beauties, but none of them had been good at tap. Ballet types.

As always, the sheer *fun* of tap dancing took her nerves away and she could feel that professional smile shift to real enjoyment. Jack Bernes, the director, and the producer – the legendary André Charlot! – sat up a little straighter in their mid-stalls seats, and she burned into the last sequence with extra oomph, and landed in the final position, arms out as if to embrace them both.

This was it. She'd done the read-through pretty well, she'd sung in tune and strongly . . . now the verdict. The nerves flooded back. It was impossible to believe that she could land a job in the West End – that she'd be *good* enough for the London theatre. A few years on stage in Sydney wasn't really enough. She was just a country cousin.

'Thank you, Miss Linton. Just one more thing . . .'

Oh, no . . . her energy was draining out, but she pulled herself into 'listening to the director with careful attention' position, her stomach knotting. 'Yes, Mr Bernes?'

'This role requires ballroom dancing as well. We'd like you to go through a waltz with Mr Gardiner.'

More dancing! Excellent. None of the other girls had been asked to do this. Energy surged through her again. She grinned at the thought that her mother's insistence that she 'learn to dance like a lady' would be paying off here, of all places.

'Of course, Mr Bernes.'

A tall young man emerged from the wings. Dark brown hair, the bluest of eyes, and a congenial smile. Yes, classic second-string leading man, just as she, with her blonde bob and green eyes, was the classic ingenue. The two of them together made the youthful pair who had the main subplot in just about every musical comedy. Their job was to give the stars some time off the stage, and to carry the lighter elements of the plot.

Let's hope he's a singer, she thought. *And that he can lead.*

Gardiner smiled at her and held out his arms for her to step into dancing position. The way he held her showed he wasn't a professional dancer – his grip wasn't quite tight enough. Damn. Without a good partner, how could she show herself off? But when the music started, he swept her away competently enough, and he knew the steps, so she put everything she had into being graceful – a completely different body shape to tap dancing, submissive and yielding.

He *was* rather dishy.

They ended with a dip and a twirl that had Charlot and Bernes nodding with satisfaction.

'Very good,' Charlot said, his voice unexpectedly deep. 'I think we have our second leads. A pair of colonials, eh? We might make something of that in the publicity.'

Her heart almost exploded. She was *in*. She *had it*. A joy so intense swept over her, as if she were dissolving from the inside. Hah! Take that, Father! She couldn't wait to write home and let them all know that they'd been *wrong*. She could make it in the theatre in London. She would.

'*Thank* you, sir!' she said.

A moment later, doubt hit her. Could she act well enough? Could she stay the distance?

Gardiner squeezed the hand he still held.

'Yes,' he said, his voice rich and deep enough to explain why they'd cast him. 'Thank you very much.' He had the faintest trace of an accent. American? No, if he was a 'colonial' he was probably Canadian.

'Go and see Francis in the office next door,' Bernes said, 'and he'll sort out your salaries and so forth.'

Charlot cut in, smiling. 'Congratulations, children. You're part of the family now.'

They ran offstage, still hand in hand, laughing, and as soon as they were out of sight Gardiner picked her up and swung her around, then plopped her back on the floor.

'We did it!'

She grinned up at him. 'We did!'

He held out his hand. 'Zeke Gardiner.'

'Kit Linton.' They shook, mock-solemnly. 'I'll just get into street clothes. I'll be right back.' Tap shorts were considered decent on stage, but they'd cause a riot on the street, coming as they did halfway up the thigh.

She raced to the girls' dressing room and scrambled out of her audition clothes into her stockings and dress, a lovely peacock blue dropped waist with a shawl collar. Nice tan shoes with a French heel. Tan gloves. A smart cloche in a darker blue. For a moment she looked at herself in the mirror – she could be any well-dressed girl going out for the day. But she wasn't. She was the new ingenue in a London West End musical.

A deep sigh came out of her.

It had been a long road to this moment, and she had no confidence that she would make it any further. She'd just have to carry on without confidence. If she worked hard enough, she wouldn't have time to worry.

◆

Zeke Gardiner went through the lodging house door and hung his hat on his assigned hook on the coat rack.

'Good lad,' Mrs Coward said to him, smiling as she took the post he'd gathered from the letterbox on the way in.

Mrs Coward dealt with having lodgers in her home by having a place for everything; superficially, she was a flustered, flighty woman, but underneath she was as organised as an army drill sergeant. And a lady by birth, if not in circumstances.

He smiled back at her, uplifted by success. 'I got the part, Mrs Coward.'

'Oh, that's wonderful! Noël! Noël! Mr Gardiner got it! I'll just put the kettle on.'

He followed her to the kitchen where she made tea. It was a homely, sunlit room in the mornings, but in late afternoon the shadows were drawing in. He knew better than to turn the light on even one minute before sunset – the Cowards had to watch their pennies. As she was pouring the water into the teapot, Noël came out of his ground-floor room, yawning, in a silk dressing gown he'd bought cheaply from the wardrobe mistress of the last show he'd been in.

It was purple, with turquoise peacocks, and it suited his dark good looks, besides proclaiming loudly that he didn't even try to be a 'manly man' – at least, not at home.

'What's this I hear?' he asked, arching an eyebrow at Zeke.

'I am now gainfully employed. On the bill.'

Noël smiled, genuinely pleased, and shook his hand. 'Well done, old chap! I knew Charlot would like you. You'll be the hit of 1923!'

Noël had tipped him off to the audition, which hadn't been advertised in *The Stage*. Charlot relied on his network of contacts, not advertising, to find his casts.

'I owe you one.'

'Pshaw!' Noël flapped his hands dismissively. 'Mama dearest, are those *crumpets*?'

'No, they're drop scones. In honour of Mr Gardiner's success.'

'Delicious! I'll be Mother.' Noël poured tea into delicate porcelain cups, being 'Mother', and handed Zeke his tea. This was the moment where Zeke always felt just a little uncomfortable. Before coming to London, he'd never drunk from cups like this, and he was still unsure of the etiquette. The handles were so *tiny*! There was no way he could get even one of his fingers into them. But did you stick your little finger out, or not? He observed Mrs Coward carefully. Her pinkie wasn't tight against the cup with her other fingers, but it wasn't held out deliberately either.

He tried to copy it, but he wasn't sure how successful he was. At least he knew not to slurp his tea – or pour it into his saucer to cool off, as his father used to do. Canada had its class system, like everywhere else, but the English had so many rules of etiquette. And breaking even one of them made you 'not quite'.

Mrs Coward was a good person to study; but then, the women's rules were slightly different to the men's . . . he'd be a fool to copy Noël, though. God alone knew what trouble that would get him into. Things Noël could get away with through sheer force of personality would make him *persona non grata* in an instant.

'When do you start?' Mrs Coward asked.

'Rehearsals start next Monday in rooms, and we move to the theatre in two weeks and open a week later.' A short rehearsal time was normal in London, he'd found. Managements relied on their cast and crew's professionalism.

It was the dancing that worried him. Thank God that Linton girl seemed to know what she was doing!

Noël took a bite of scone. 'Who's in it?' Zeke went through the cast, Noël nodding and making shrewd comments about each of them, until he got to Miss Linton. 'Linton? I don't know the name.'

'She's new. From Australia.'

'Oh, *Orstralia*,' Mrs Coward said. 'How nice for you two colonials to be working together!'

He didn't say anything, although the term, as always, set his teeth on edge. Mrs Coward had grown up with the British Empire being the greatest power on Earth. It would take her generation time to see that things had changed.

Noël caught his eye, and grinned, reading his mind easily. Too sharp by half, that lad.

'Oh, yes,' he mocked, 'I'm sure the *colonials* will just love each other!'

CHAPTER 1

The applause seemed to lift her up, like shooting the surf at Bondi Beach. But higher, much higher than any wave could take her.

One, two, four curtain calls. Another. One more. Charlot in the wings, smiling benignly. Bernes clapping them each on the back as they came offstage, kissing the women, shaking hands with the men.

'Well done. Well done all. Party at the Riviera Club.'

The Riviera Club! Charlot wouldn't have sprung for that if he'd had any doubts. They were a hit.

Susan Maxwell smiled at her as they went into their shared dressing room to change. Susan had clearly given up all ambition to play the lead: she was happily plump and her shoes were chosen for comfort rather than fashion. But she was a lady, and by God she could act. Kit had realised at the first rehearsal that she could learn a lot from watching Susan, and she had.

'It went well, do you think?' she asked her now.

'Very well, pet.' There was no trace of Susan's New Zealand background in her voice, but she'd taken Kit under her wing, saying 'we antipodeans have to stick together'.

'Any notes?'

'You might wait just a beat more before you say, "Maybe I do".'

Kit nodded. That was a big moment in her character's story, just after a romantic dance with Zeke. A beat would add more uncertainty and tension.

'Thanks, Susan.'

They changed swiftly, Kit tucking a souvenir program in her purse. Susan had been going home, instead of to the party, but Kit talked her into changing her mind. 'It wouldn't be a celebration without you.'

'Oh, you don't need me.' But she came anyway, pleased to be wanted.

Zeke grabbed Kit's hand as she came out of her dressing room in her new dress and they went out to the street together, Kit arm in arm with Susan, surprised to find so many people clustered at the stage door. The pre-War days of the 'stage-door Johnnies' were long gone, but there were still fans; waiting for the real stars, Marguerite Ritchards and Basil Elliot, no doubt. But no, the earnest shop girls and a few middle-aged matrons thrust their autograph books at Kit and Zeke as well as Susan.

Kit beamed at them. 'Our first autographs! Thank you!'

'Oh, thank *you*, miss!' a girl answered, and simpered at Zeke. 'And you, Mr Gardiner.'

He bent down and gave her a kiss on the cheek.

'For luck!' Grinning, they got into a cab that the stage

doorman had called. Behind them, the girls chattered, 'Ooh, isn't he nice!' 'You lucky thing!' 'I think I'm in love!'

'You've made a hit,' Kit laughed at him.

'We both have!' They were buoyed up by that very special potion: successful performance. The play had gone perfectly – but more than that, they had danced and sung better than ever before, moving together in a synchronised balance that was in itself intoxicating. And then, the applause!

Kit sighed in pure satisfaction. Supper at the Riviera Club, where the highest high of London society mingled!

It didn't seem possible. She pinched herself, just in case.

Zeke's hand closed over hers. 'It's real,' he said. In the shadowy cab, with slabs of light flicking over his face as they went past streetlights and shop displays, his voice seemed deeper and darker than before. But it was full of a comforting solidity.

Real. She really was a successful actress.

She tucked her hand in his. 'Let's hope for real *and* a long run.' He laughed out loud, the joyous sound making the cabbie turn and grin at them.

'Let's go dancing!' Zeke said. 'Susan, you're first on my dance card.' Kit could have hugged him.

Susan beamed at him. 'Oh, you're a lovely thing, aren't you, but these shoes aren't made for dancing.'

But hers were.

◆

The Riviera Club . . . oh, my.

It looked so staid from the front; no different to all the other Georgian houses in Pimlico. The line of taxis outside the door, letting off couples arrayed in black tie and furs, was the first hint it wasn't so; Zeke handed Kit out of their own taxi with a flourish that made her smile. Susan was collected by her counterpart in the play, Percy, so that was all right.

Marguerite, head high and smile wide, went in on Basil's arm, Susan and Percy followed them, and then it was their turn.

All this success was still hard to believe. Kit shook her velvet evening coat around her shoulders and smiled up at Zeke, aware of a photographer's flash somewhere nearby. He smiled down at her. The flash went off again, and then they moved on, into the portico, through the doors. Zeke took her coat off to the cloakroom, and Kit checked her hair in the big mirror to one side of the entrance.

She'd do. She didn't have anything like the money some of these women had – not yet – but she'd show them what a 'colonial' could do.

Zeke came back, looking good in a tuxedo. The fashion was a few years old, the collar a bit too wide, but she knew a man's evening dress was very expensive. He'd probably update it now they were getting full pay. At least his shoes were shined.

They went into the ballroom, arm in arm, following Charlot and the stars of the show through the Doric columns at the entrance. Small round tables skirted the room; in a corner a few had been pushed together for a larger party. The lights were low, and a jazz band was playing a syncopated beat. Not Paul Whiteman at the Grafton Galleries, but not bad. Kit found herself walking in time as they threaded their way around the dance floor, following the maître d'.

On the floor, couples danced – some trying unsuccessfully to foxtrot, others simply jigging in place. Feathers were in, it seemed; Kit smoothed down her dress, which had cost a whole

4

week's salary, adjusted her own ostrich feather headdress, and smiled, her heart almost bursting with excitement.

In Sydney, she'd never dared to go out dancing like this – the daughter of the Dean of St Andrew's Cathedral was allowed to be up to date but not in the forefront of fashion. And certainly not *fast*. But here . . . here she could be herself without worrying she'd bring her family into the gossip columns.

The maître d' showed them to a table near another large party. 'That's the Prince of Wales,' Zeke said as he pushed her chair in for her. She snuck a quick look over her shoulder. Royalty! If only her mother could see her now! That familiar feeling of acting a part crept over her, and her momentary confidence deserted her. Could she really carry this off? Next to *royalty*? Her dress suddenly felt much too revealing.

The Prince of Wales was part of a laughing group. She could identify some of them from the Sunday papers – that was the Duke of York and his fiancée, Lady Elizabeth someone-or-other. The youngest man could be Prince George . . . and there was –

'Miss Linton!' an American voice called, and a dapper figure threaded his way lightly through the chairs to her side.

'Mr Astaire,' she said, smiling. Astaire and Zeke shook hands, the American smiling genially. They had met the Astaires, Adele and her brother Fred, at the BBC, when they had both been doing radio broadcasts promoting their respective shows, and had hit it off immediately.

'Well now, I guess we know each other well enough that you'd better call me Fred,' he said, with a jerk of his thumb over his shoulder at the princes. 'Just about everyone else is.'

He winked drolly, and they both laughed. 'Kit and Zeke, then,' she said.

Astaire made the rounds of the big table, congratulating Charlot.

'I've already heard it's going to be a hit,' he said, indicating the royal table. 'Prince George was very taken with it.'

'Let's hope he tells all his friends!' Charlot said, and there was general laughter.

Adele Astaire popped her head under Fred's arm and dimpled at them. 'Come and join us.'

'Delly, you can't invite people to join the Prince of Wales' party,' Fred remonstrated.

'Oh, pooh!' She turned and waved at the larger group. 'Look, sir, it's our friends! Kit and Zeke from *Dance Crazy*.'

'Then we should definitely join the parties together. It would be divine to have some more dancers in the party.' The voice was almost comically upper-class, but it was good-humoured. Trust Adele. She was the kind of person who could get away with just about anything through sheer charm and force of personality. No wonder she was a star.

Kit stood, uncertain, her heart fluttering with ridiculous nerves. Here he came. Zeke had straightened beside her and pulled down the back of his dinner jacket. Charlot rose, looking suitably respectable, and bowed, as did all the men. The women curtsied, a wave travelling around the table as the prince turned his head and acknowledged everyone.

The prince was in a tail-coat, perfectly tailored, naturally. Fair, not as tall as she'd thought he would be, a slight man rather of the same build as Astaire. In his late twenties, he seemed older.

6

He smiled down at her and put out his hand. *Curtsey. Curtsey.* Her debut training came back to her and she achieved an elegant bob.

'Miss Linton,' he said.

'Your Royal Highness,' she managed.

'Oh, none of that stuff here!' He waved her words away. 'Sir is fine.'

She wanted to laugh. He thought he was being so magnanimous, but calling a man his age 'sir' seemed almost as stuffy to her. Like he was a schoolmaster. Or a grandfather.

'Yes, sir,' she managed, and he smiled again before shaking hands with Charlot and then with Zeke, who performed a rather shaky bow, as if he wasn't sure how low he needed to bend.

'Sir,' he said.

'That's the ticket. Join us, won't you?'

'Thank you, sir.' Zeke looked pale. A bit overwhelmed. She suspected she looked like that herself.

The real stars of the show, Marguerite and Basil, came up and were presented. Marguerite did the most beautiful curtsey imaginable and the prince nodded in approval. They began to chat, and Kit and Zeke moved thankfully into the background.

Adele Astaire slipped her arm through Kit's. The waiters were hurriedly moving the tables together. 'I'm so glad you're here,' she whispered. 'They're all very sweet but oh! so dull!'

Kit bit back a grin and Adele winked at her.

They weren't introduced to anyone at the royal table, and Kit realised they were expected to know the others on sight. Because they were all royal. Someone called Maud, another called George (he *was* the young man), Bertie and Liz (Prince

Albert and Lady Elizabeth), and some others she could only guess at.

Champagne appeared at her elbow and she drank. Rather nice, but one glass would do her. Best to keep a clear head. And then she was on her feet, dancing with the Prince of Wales.

He was a good dancer, for an amateur. Fit, and knew how to lead, which was the main thing. But what was the etiquette for talking to him? She had a vague feeling that she was supposed to leave it to him to make the first remark, so she concentrated on the fine-sewn seam of his shoulder and gave herself over to the dance.

'By Jove, you do dance well, don't you!'

Emboldened, she smiled up at him. 'Well, it's my job, sir. It would be a worry if I didn't.'

'You colonial girls are all so sporting,' he said, nodding in approval.

She had no idea if that were good or bad – it was clear that *he* thought it was good, but she'd met a few young British lads who thought 'sporting' meant that she'd race into bed with them. His hands on her didn't have that feel, though – he held her very correctly, his right hand high up on her back, where he could guide her most easily. It never strayed downwards.

'You're a long way from home, eh?'

'Yes, I am, sir.'

'It's hard to miss the ones one is fond of, isn't it?' This time, his voice was positively melancholy, and his expression matched. A thread of gossip awoke in her memory – something about a relationship with a woman who was in America.

'It *is* hard, sir.'

He nodded, his attention withdrawn, his thoughts some-where far away. They finished the dance back at their table, and he handed her off to his younger brother George, who danced energetically and whose hands were not quite so proper. But she could handle George with one hand tied behind her. The older prince went on to dance with Marguerite, and then with Charlot's wife Florence.

Then Adele said, 'Freddie, show us what you and Miss Linton can do.'

Kit and Fred took the floor, her stomach a little nervous as the others watched. But then he swung her into the first movement and they were away. Now this was more like it! The song was a waltz, Paul Whiteman's 'Three O'Clock in the Morning', but with a swing beat, and it was too complex for most of the revellers, so they had a good clear space to fill. Kit grinned as they twirled, and Fred grinned with her. He tried a couple of steps she'd never done before in her life, but she followed him into them as naturally as if they'd practised all day.

There was a hill near where she lived that led down to Sydney Harbour, and as a child she had rolled down it, the green of the grass and the blue of the water flashing around her in circles until she laughed and laughed and laughed. That was what dancing with Fred was like.

By the end, the other dancers had crowded to the edges of the floor to leave them to it, and as the music finished everyone applauded. Fred bowed, so she curtsied, and then they bowed and curtsied to each other before returning to their tables, flushed and triumphant, Charlot gazing at her approvingly. Zeke was about to say something, when Adele jumped up. 'Now it's our turn!' She grabbed his hand and, before the other dancers could take the floor, dragged him out into the middle.

Smiling, he bowed elaborately to her and she made a full court curtsey. Then the band launched into 'Stairway to Paradise' and they floated around the floor in a quickstep. Adele was as light on her feet as a feather in the wind, with a charm that made it almost impossible to take your eyes off her to look at her partner.

Fred leaned one hip on the table next to her and watched critically. 'That boy of yours is pretty good, Kit, but he's not as good as you.'

'He's a good actor,' she said, tucking that compliment away for later perusal. 'But I've been doing the choreography.'

Fred nodded. 'Delly's better than me on the dance front, but I do our choreography, too.'

She grinned up at him. 'Don't listen to your big sister, Fred. You're pretty special yourself.'

They smiled at each other. Well. She hadn't expected to make a friend tonight, but she rather thought she had. Fred Astaire needed to come out of Adele's shadow. But that probably wasn't going to happen any time soon. Not when the girl had that ability to draw all eyes. There was just *something* about her. A sharp pang of envy hit Kit. No matter how hard she worked, she'd never have a tenth of Adele Astaire's charm.

She straightened her spine. She'd just have to make do with great dancing and singing – and some pretty good acting, too.

The applause for Adele and Zeke was double what she and Fred had got. *One day*. One day she'd be as famous and as loved as Adele Astaire.

'Good show,' the Prince of Wales said. 'Let's have another drink on the strength of that.'

A while later, they all took a turn on the terrace overlooking the Thames. It was an intermittently cloudy night, so that the moon flashed out and was covered over and over again. A night when things seemed uncertain. Zeke and Adele leaned over the balustrade together, watching the late boats on the river.

'Don't worry about them, Kit,' Fred said. 'She's got her head screwed on straight. She's sworn never to marry anyone in the theatre.'

'Marry? She doesn't seem like the marrying kind.'

Fred crossed his fingers. 'Let's hope you're right.'

Waiters came among them, distributing more champagne. The crisp breeze off the water, the wandering moonlight coaxing glints from the women's jewels, the shiver of chiffon and silk, the dark blots of men's suits, the precise British accents now a little slurred from drink, and there, the actual in-the-flesh Prince of Wales, with whom she had danced . . . and the two of them, from so far away . . . Kit leaned against the wall and lifted her glass. 'To London, who welcomes visitors so well.'

Fred clinked solemnly. 'To London.'

CHAPTER 2

The next morning, Kit stood on the corner of Eaton Square under a pale blue English sky. The trees were in leaf in the park at the centre of the square, there were actual English daffodils blooming around their roots, and the air was full of a particular scent she'd never smelled before: earth coming back to life after a frozen winter. It was a heady, uplifting smell, and it called to something in her blood, proclaiming 'Home'. This was what her mother had meant when she'd said, sighing, 'I do miss proper seasons.' Easter, which was next week, made so much more sense when it was celebrating spring instead of autumn, and the world was coming back to life around you.

Enough of that. She couldn't stand here all day. There was her uncle's house, just across the square. An imposing five-storey Georgian mansion, complete with a columned portico over the front door. All she had to do was go up to it and present her letter to whomever opened the door. The butler.

She couldn't do it. She couldn't go up there like, like a *servant* or a poor relation, even if she *was* a poor relation. She wasn't going to wait on the doorstep while his lordship decided if he'd see her.

The letter had her address in it. If he wanted to see her, he could send a messenger.

Which was an excellent idea. There was a newsboy on the opposite corner, just down from her uncle's house. She crossed over to him.

'Would you like to earn a shilling?'

'Lead me to it, miss!' he said, trying to salute despite his armful of papers. She showed him the envelope and pointed out the house.

'Just go up, knock on that door, and hand over the letter. That's it. Then come back here and I'll give you the shilling.'

'Right you are, miss!' He reached out to take the letter, but his hand was grubby with ink from the newspaper.

'Just a moment.' Kit took out a handkerchief and tried to rub the ink away, but it was ground in; she wrapped the handkerchief around his hand instead so that the envelope would stay clean. How embarrassing it would be for her letter to be covered with dirty fingerprints! 'Off you go.'

He dumped his papers at her feet and raced off. Knocked on the door. It opened. From this angle, she couldn't see inside, but whoever it was took the letter and closed the door sharply. A long sigh escaped her. It was done. She'd kept her promise to her mother, and what happened next would be up to her uncle.

The boy ran back and received his shilling. She let him keep the handkerchief. It was ruined now, anyway.

'Fanks, miss! Easiest shillin' I ever made. *Plus* a nose rag!'

She smiled at him. 'Thank *you*.'

On the bus back to Charlotte Street, she realised she didn't know what she wanted: for her uncle to ignore her, or for him to contact her and welcome her into the family.

Right now, she was free, if alone . . . well, it didn't matter, not really.

Because tonight she would be back on stage, singing and dancing in a new London musical. That was what had given her the courage to write the letter. It was one thing to say, *I'm in London trying to be an actress.* Quite another to say, *I'm in the new Charlot production in a major part.*

She smiled to herself, ignoring the stares from the man across the aisle. Rude. *So* rude, the way men always stared. It was why she preferred getting cabs to buses. From now on, though, they'd be staring up at her from the stalls.

And that was the way she liked it.

♦

A reply came by messenger in late afternoon the next day, when everyone at the Theatrical Girls' Boarding House (otherwise known as the Cats' Home) was having tea before they went off to their theatres.

'It's for you, Kit,' Mrs French, the owner, said, handing over an envelope.

'Oooh!' Perry, her roommate, raised her perfectly plucked eyebrows. 'Is it a billet-doux from an admirer?'

'Wish *I* was getting billy-doos by messenger,' Brenda said.

'Just from my agent.' Kit waved off their interest, which died away immediately. Agents weren't interesting unless they were offering you work.

The girls of the Cats' Home were a dazzling mix: an Indian girl who claimed to be a princess and did a snake-charming act at the Tivoli; a flaming redheaded magician's assistant with a broad Yorkshire accent who shared a room and a bed with a blonde contortionist; a pair of twins who both played violin in a Lyons tea shop orchestra; an Italian soprano studying for the opera. And then there was Val, auburn-haired, blue-eyed and willowy.

A well-known female impersonator, her ad in *The Stage* said, but it seemed to Kit that Val was less a female impersonator than . . . a female. Mrs French had declared her an honorary Theatrical Girl after a heavy at her last boarding house had beaten her up.

And Perry, her roommate, a black-haired, red-lipped girl who danced in the chorus of *Let the Fun Begin!*

They all stuck together, lending each other stockings and hair grips and frocks, straying in and out of each other's rooms with no respect for privacy. Kit had two sisters, but they had never acted like this. It made her vaguely uneasy, but she didn't let it show. If this was what being a Theatrical Girl took, she'd do it.

'I wish I was a bit bigger in the knocker department,' Sally mourned. 'Larger headlights would get me more dates.'

Rude responses flew around the room.

They really were *very* vulgar. But so funny. If only she could have joined in, and laughed and joked. But Kit sat mute, not knowing what to say or how to say it. Some of the words they used she'd never even heard before.

Up in their room, washing her stockings at the sink, Perry said, 'You think we're all pretty low class, don't you?'

She didn't sound upset, but Kit felt panic sweep over her. How was she supposed to answer that without alienating Perry forever? She tried so hard not to stand out; she wanted so much to belong here. Perry glanced over at her and laughed.

'You don't need to look like a kid who's had her lolly stolen. It's okay. We *are* pretty low class. Except Val, maybe.'

'It's just . . .' Kit pleated the bedspread under her fingers and tried to find the words. 'If I'd said *any* of those things, my mouth would have been washed out with soap.'

'How did a proper young lady like you get onto the stage in the first place? It's as likely as a Derby winner pulling the baker's cart!' Perry laid her stockings over a hand towel on the rail next to the sink while Kit sought for a way to explain.

How could she describe her own frustration, her internal railing at the narrow world of the Deanery? Her passionate need for something wider, wilder . . . Dance was the first thing that had promised something *more* than obedience and social conformity, and she'd clung to it like a lifeline.

'I was started on ballet because of poor posture,' she said at last. 'And I *loved* it. We all learnt ballroom –'

'For your *debut* –' Perry cut in, gently mocking. Kit flushed. If she knew that Kit had actually *been* a deb, the teasing would never end.

'Well, for social occasions. And then we did amateur theatricals at school. Shakespeare, you know. And . . . and I liked it. I liked being someone else – stepping into someone else's life. Mine was so *boring*.'

Boring, confined . . . stultifying. A double pressure on her: the same social conventions that all young women of good class were expected to follow, but then also the conventions of a church family, always on show, always held up as models of behaviour. How she'd hated sitting in the front pew, all eyes upon them!

'But *tap*? You're not telling me your posh school taught tap!' Perry propped her hip against the chest of drawers and waited.

Kit leaned back against the bedhead and laughed. 'Not on your life! But some of the theatre in Sydney is a mixture of amateurs and professionals. The amateurs pay some real actors to come in and make them look good. And there was a girl. Jane Burns.'

'Jane and Jonesy? They played on the bill at the Palladium last year!'

'Yes. That's the one. She came over in '21, but she's in New York now, on Broadway. Gosh, she's nice. She taught me, just for fun. And then I paid for lessons later. And there we were.'

'Your parents wouldn't have liked you being a professional, though.'

Kit jumped up and dusted down her skirt. She wasn't going to be drawn into reminiscing about *that* horrible week. 'No, but they adjusted. I had to change my name, though, so as not to bring scandal on the family.'

Perry laughed out loud. 'So what's your real name?'

Kit dimpled. 'Honestly? Katherine Agatha Scott. But everyone's *always* called me Kit.'

'*Agatha!*' Perry howled with laughter, and Kit threw a pillow at her, which she caught and threw back.

'I suppose I can't laugh,' Perry confessed. 'My real name is Persephone. My mum didn't even know what it meant – she just liked the sound of it.'

Kit tried not to laugh. Persephone would be a burden of a name. 'And your parents didn't mind you going on the stage?'

'Mum was all for it!' She eyed Kit with sympathy. 'Your parents wouldn't have wanted you to come to London, I suppose?'

Kit winced at the memory of that fight, the biggest one of all. 'I was twenty-one. They couldn't stop me.'

Looking back, she was amazed at how brave she'd been. But it hadn't been bravery. It had been desperation. She'd just *had* to get out of Sydney, where everyone who was anyone had known her – and mostly disapproved of her. She had pinned her hopes on London being somewhere she would *fit*.

Maybe she would, some day. She smiled at Perry.

'They were rather cross that I used my own money, too – I don't think they'd realised how much I was earning!'

Perry grinned at her. 'Hah! An independent woman, right under their noses.'

So that was all right.

'Well, go on,' Perry said, waving at the letter Kit still held in one hand. 'Open it!'

She used a nail file to slit through the heavy cream fold, and pulled out a simple piece of paper.

Her uncle's crest was at the top.

'Oh, it's nothing,' she said, pushing it back in. 'Just a reminder about rehearsal times.'

'Gosh, *I've* never got special notes about rehearsals.' Perry eyed her uncertainly for a moment. 'Don't go and do anything stupid, will you?'

She thought it *was* a note from a lover! Kit almost gasped, but turned it into a chuckle. Should she tell Perry the truth?

No. The girls here already thought of her as too posh. An uncle who was an earl would just make them uncomfortable. 'You can trust me, Perry.'

Kit watched, amused, as Perry fixed her Dutch bob and made up her eyes heavily. She tied her garter below the knee, so that the ribbon dangled seductively below the hem of her satin dress, and slid a headband on instead of a hat.

'Very swish.' Kit worried, just a little, that Perry was going at it too hard. There was hardly a night in the week when she was in bed before the sky started to pale.

She blew Kit a kiss and sailed out the door, a black shawl trailing over one elbow. She'd be cold out there. It wasn't summer yet. But probably her escort after the theatre would spring for a cab. In fact, if he didn't, he wouldn't be coming back. Perry had no time for 'making-do'. She liked the best of everything, and why not? She was so beautiful, with her bobbed black hair and dark eyes, there was no reason she couldn't get it.

The door closed behind her. Kit took in a long breath; it felt as though she hadn't breathed at all since Mrs French had handed her the letter. The paper was thick and slightly rough under her fingertips as she pulled it out again. Expensive. And *not* from her uncle. From her aunt, her uncle's wife.

My dear Katherine,

Please forgive my delay in returning your letter. At the moment, we are staying at Barrows, and it was forwarded to us here. We're delighted to hear that you are in London. Your mother had informed us that you were coming Home, so we are very glad that you chose to contact us.

Cecil and Daphne, your cousins, are having some friends over for a house party, next weekend. Daphne tells me that you'll be performing on Saturday night, so perhaps you could be with us for Sunday and Monday?

Your uncle and I would be delighted if you could come down. Of course, it may seem a little strange to you, meeting relatives you've never known, so you should bring a friend to keep you company. We heard you and Mr Gardiner on the radio and were most impressed – Daphne wondered if perhaps he would like to accompany you?

There were some details about how to get there.

Just drop me a line confirming your arrival, my dear, and we'll send a car to the station.
We're very much looking forward to meeting you.
Regards,
Your aunt,
Sylvia Dassington

A house party. Lord, it had been more than a year since she'd been to a house party! A vista of tennis matches and walks on the terrace and possibly even riding opened up before her. The room seemed abruptly too small and rather dingy.

Zeke. Would he come? Should she ask him? It would be good to have a friend with her, and she certainly couldn't take Perry. Perry was lovely, but the odds on her knowing which fork to use at dinner were pretty bad. Zeke was a better choice.

She'd ask Zeke today, and send a note to her aunt tomorrow, either way. Warmth filled her, along with quite a lot of apprehension. That line about her mother . . . she wouldn't put it past her parents to enlist these unknown relatives in their campaign to wean her off the theatre. Well, they'd learn, just as her parents had.

◆

They always warmed up before each performance – a must if you were going to be injury-free for the whole run. Zeke loved the calm of the empty theatre.

Theatres were old friends. He'd been working in them, one way or another, since he was fourteen. This theatre was grander than the ones in Vancouver or Victoria, but it had the right *smell*. The new wood and house paint they used to make the sets, greasepaint warmed on light bulbs in the dressing rooms, Lysol in the toilets, and a general tang of old wool and rope. Perfect. He shared a dressing room with Percy Hopkins, the 'character' male lead. A big step up for him, to have a dressing room with his name on it at all, even a shared one.

Lightning changes were part of the business. Zeke slid easily out of his street clothes and into his warm-up gear.

He could hear the murmur of the director talking to the lighting riggers as he walked to the wings.

Kit was standing upstage, behind the star of the production, Marguerite Ritchards, a blazingly handsome woman with immense presence. Next to her was Susan, who alongside Percy carried the comedic thread of the story.

Basil and Marguerite had the drama, Percy and Susan had the comedy, and he and Kit had the story of young love. A standard arrangement, but one he was more than happy with. It meant he and Kit had a couple of good songs and three solid dances, including one with the chorus, and enough lines to show what they could do with a better part.

The older actors didn't do more than a cursory warm-up. They didn't dance much. After they left the stage, the chorus came on, in a flurry of tights and practice skirts.

'Zeke?' Kit joined him in her tap shorts. Her foot tapped out of rhythm, which wasn't like her. 'I've been invited to a house party at my uncle's and told to bring a friend. Would you like to come?'

He started to stretch, and she joined him, blonde curls bouncing as she leant over.

'A house party?' What the hell was a house party? Was that one of those all-weekend jaunts he'd read about in the magazines? High life in the country.

'A nice couple of days in Suffolk, with my cousins and my aunt and uncle. I've never met them. Please do come. I'm a bit anxious about meeting them alone.' It sounded horrible; family life wasn't exactly his strong point. But he should support Kit; they'd become good friends over the rehearsal period, and she did look a bit nervy.

'I suppose.'

'Thank you! And it will be a chance for both of us to see real English life.'

Zeke grinned and began the simple tap routine they used nightly to loosen up. Kit followed him into it. 'I suspect that "real" may not be the right adjective for a house party.'

'Oh, you!' They picked up the pace, the chorus following them.

Ten minutes later, the callboy shouted, 'Twenty minutes, beginners, please!' and they all scurried back to their dressing rooms.

He was lucky she'd been cast. Going to a house party, whatever that entailed, was probably a small price to pay to cement their friendship. A professional, that was Kit, but a nice girl as well. And gorgeous, which helped the show. There'd be men coming back a second and third time, just to get a look at her.

But he couldn't afford to think about her like that. No relationships. No entanglements. No chance of following in his father's footsteps.

CHAPTER 3

'Novello's having some people over, and Noël said we should come along,' Zeke said, leaning against the doorjamb of her dressing room. Kit greeted the suggestion with a mix of anticipation and nerves. A party was just what she needed after the stress of opening night and the three subsequent performances (they were doing eight a week, because of the two matinées).

But she'd never been to a London theatre party. She'd never actually been to a party at all by herself before. Even at theatre parties in Sydney, her mother or her married sister had come with her, to chaperone. It had been awkward at first, but her fellow thespians had become used to it, and they'd always left early, so as not to be wet blankets.

There *had* been dinners and dances on the ship over, but she'd been at the Captain's table because of her parents' contacts, and he'd kept quite a close eye on her.

It hit her that there was no one she had to answer to. Mrs French didn't care when you got in – too many of her girls worked late for that. Perry certainly didn't care.

She could go to the party and stay *all night* if she wanted to. And have a drink, now she was over twenty-one. It was a heady thought. And Zeke looked so nice tonight, in his tuxedo. He deserved a party, too!

'What a lovely idea,' she said. 'Noël', she supposed, was Noël Coward. He was an actor and playwright, and a songwriter, and his parents ran a boarding house in Ebury Street, which was where Zeke lived. Coward was becoming well known in the theatre scene. Nice of him to invite Zeke along. Nice of Zeke to invite her.

Excitement bubbled up in her stomach, along with nerves. Would she fit in with these most sophisticated of party goers, or would she seem like a *colonial*? She wished she'd had more practice at this.

Saturday night was *the* party night for theatre people, because the theatre was dark on Sundays and Mondays. And Ivor Novello, film star and composer, was the bee's knees of theatrical party givers.

He lived, for a start, on top of the Strand Theatre, in a place known only as 'the flat'. To get to it, you crowded into a rickety old elevator which bumped and jumped its way upwards, shuddering and bouncing.

'It's like getting a massage!' Gertie Lawrence, star of another of Charlot's productions, declared as they tumbled out into Novello's foyer and surged as a group towards the bar set out on a side table.

'I'll give you a massage any time you like, Gert!' some wit yelled, and Gertie grinned.

'Get me a cocktail first, darling. After this I have to go home to the baby and husband, and I deserve a little fun first!'

They piled their coats on a couch and mingled.

When Kit had been a rebellious teen in Sydney, dreaming about an unlikely career on the stage, this was the second half of the dream. The first half had already happened that night – there she'd been, on a real stage, in London, with real 'Name' actors and actresses, getting thunderous applause from an English audience. She'd never really believed she could get there, but she had. It put a warmer glow under her heart than the white wine that Zeke wangled for her from the crowded bar. He himself, she noted, was drinking orange juice. Or perhaps that was some kind of cocktail? She was so ignorant about these things. So new to it all.

But here she was, living the second half of the dream, which had evolved in those long, dreary stretches of listening to her father's sermons (he'd insisted the whole family come to every service on Sunday, and he gave the same sermon at each). Then, she'd put the straitjacketing boredom out of her head by imagining *fun* – laughing and singing and dancing and friends. Now it was right in front of her, complete with fashionable clothes and Noël Coward on the piano, singing one of his risqué songs which would make a sailor blush.

She wished she felt more of a part of it. That sense of standing back and observing came over her. All these people seemed so comfortable in their own skins. If only she was.

Ivor Novello (she had to remember to call him David, his real name) came over to them and shook Zeke's hand, gave her a kiss on the cheek.

'David,' Zeke said. 'Thanks for asking us.'

'Lovely to see you!' he said warmly. 'I did like the way you put over that number on the BBC.' How nice of him. Their broadcast at the BBC had been a week ago tonight, but it seemed so much longer. At his elbow, Bobbie Andrews was almost as handsome as he was – which was saying something, since film audiences had been known to literally swoon at Novello's profile. So handsome! Such a matinée idol! If only his fans knew . . . David and Bobbie made such a lovely pair.

And this was also something she'd dreamed about while she'd pushed the tea trolley around the Women's Institute meetings and polished the brass vases under the strict, judgemental eyes of the Altar Society. She'd yearned for a world where people could be themselves, even if it was only here, behind closed doors, among friends. But if she were herself, would they like her? Or would she be too dull and respectable for them? She was probably the only virgin in the room.

'Come on, Zeke, give us a song!' Noël Coward bellowed across the room. Swept up in the crowd, they were pushed over to the piano and she laughed up into Zeke's face as they began to sing Coward's rude version of 'Have You Ever Seen a Winkle Wink?' Performing, she could be anyone, and tonight she let loose, and so did Zeke.

The crowd was in fits – Coward himself was mugging at the piano, David and Bobbie were dancing, Gertie Lawrence steadied herself against a dark-haired vampish girl and laughed so much she cried. Kit grinned. At least when she was singing, they liked her. That was a place to start.

They finished with a flourish and a bow and Gertie took over, sitting on the baby grand with her skirt up over her knees, singing 'After You Get What You Want'.

Zeke slung an arm around her shoulders as they listened; she leaned into him and he glanced down at her, his eyes alight with laughter. He really was very attractive.

The girl in the song accused her boy of not wanting her after he finally got her.

So easy for that to happen; a good reason for not getting in over her head with Zeke, especially while they were working together.

Sometime after midnight, she was chatting on the red chaise longue with the dark-haired vamp. She was an American named Tallulah Bankhead, who was opening with a new play at Wyndham's Theatre later in the year, and she was both outrageous and charming, and made Kit feel like a country cousin. Zeke slid in alongside her and said, 'Might be time for us to be off.'

Kit looked a question at him, and he nodded his head towards the inner door. Their hosts were in the main room, laughing and dancing, but she could smell that distinctive odour of reefer coming from the patio. She made a face. This was part of the theatre world where she *didn't* belong.

She wasn't interested in doing reefers or cocaine – the smell of reefer, in particular, made her feel ill. Besides, it ruined your complexion. That was what she'd say if anyone asked. It made her a bit nervous, the idea that the others might think she was . . . a wowser, they'd call her in Sydney. A wet blanket. Her foothold in this world was so very new, and seemed so precarious.

And yet there was something in her that rebelled against being pushed into behaving as they did. Why should she?

Tallulah laughed, sliding a hand up Zeke's arm. 'Oh, darling, you're very straitlaced. I do like a strong, *wholesome* man.'

'That's useful to know,' he said, and gently detached her hand.

She laughed again, throwing her head back, and Kit was conscious of a kind of magnetism. She'd do okay, this one. She had that 'star quality' the Americans were always talking about, and she'd done well in New York. It remained to be seen if she could act to the level a British audience expected. Du Maurier would whip her into shape, no doubt.

'*So* devoted, my dear!' she said to Kit. 'A real triumph for you. I'll have to settle for a bit of Mary Jane.' She left, waving a thin hand as she went towards the patio.

Was he interested? Kit peeked up at Zeke's face, to find it full of amusement.

'It'd be a brave man who would take up that invitation,' he said.

'Oh, *hundreds* have,' Noël's voice replied. 'I swear, my dears, that one goes through men like a barber goes through hot towels. And girls, too.'

He took the place that Tallulah had left on the chaise, sitting cheekily upright with his legs crossed. 'Noël!' Kit chided him.

'I'm not saying anything she wouldn't say herself. Ask her!' He winked at them.

She had to laugh, but they left soon after, descending in the decrepit old lift. How good Zeke was! There weren't many men who'd turn down an invitation from Tallulah Bankhead.

And she never saw him drunk. In fact, she'd never even seen him tipsy.

'You don't drink much?'

The walls of the theatre passed them in jerks as the lift made its way down. Zeke was silent for a moment.

'The occasional beer.'

She didn't like to ask, so she said nothing, just tightened her hold on his arm. Maybe that was the right thing to do, because he sighed.

'My father . . .'

He didn't need to say more. A whole life story was behind that phrase. She didn't need to imagine it – she'd seen it, often enough, in the settlement work she'd done with her mother and the Ladies' Aid Society.

'I understand.'

He cleared his throat and said, 'You don't drink much either. No gin fizzes.'

'I drink champagne. Wine with dinner. But not hard liquor. Gin can get a girl into situations she's not keen on.'

He nodded and, as the lift ground to a stop, pulled open the brass concertina door and then the wooden sliding one. They emerged onto Catherine Street, almost deserted except for a laughing couple trying to find a non-existent taxi.

◆

It wasn't that far to the Cats' Home, so they started walking down Bloomsbury Street. An English spring night, but more like winter in Sydney; the low clouds reflected the London streetlights so everything had a faint glow to it.

When they reached the Cats' Home, Zeke hesitated. The chill March wind had reddened his cheekbones, and under the golden light from the parlour window his blue eyes were in shadow. He looked like a matinée idol, all of a sudden. Almost a stranger.

In a matinée, this was the point where the man would kiss the girl. Nerves spiked up through her stomach.

'Kit . . .'

She looked up at him, not sure what she'd do if he tried.

'We'll be working very closely together. The press will try to make a romance out of it.'

'Oh, God, yes. They always do.'

'This is my first big break. I can't afford to get distracted by anything like that.' He was hesitant, as though he didn't want to insult her.

Clear relief broke over her. 'Oh, I'm so glad you said that! It's exactly how I feel. This is my chance, and I have to concentrate on it.'

'So, brother and sister?' he suggested.

'Like the Astaires!' She grinned and held out her hand.

'You can be Fred, and I'll be Adele,' he said, batting his eyelashes at her as they shook to seal the bargain.

Kit went up the steps lightly, feeling as though the conversation had set her free of something – other people's expectations, maybe. She glanced back at him once, before going in, and he was still standing there, looking up at her as if there was something special about her going through a door.

'I'm lucky to have you,' she said, honesty breaking through, and then she went in hastily. What had got into her tonight?

She *was* so lucky to have him backing her up like a big brother. He was one of nature's gentlemen, even if not quite a gentleman in the usual sense. It was grand for her that he wasn't a drinker, but it made her guilty that she felt that way. Poor boy. His father must have been horrible.

She went up to bed to find that Perry was still out; chasing sensation, no doubt. Kit hoped she was being cautious; there were reasons why girls were more likely to say 'no' than boys, and they mostly had to do with pregnancy looming as a threat over every encounter.

Too late for a bath; she'd have one in the morning, when the banging of the pipes wouldn't wake everyone. She washed in the basin and brushed her hair in front of the window, her view of London streets mysterious and grey under the clouds.

She was glad that they had come to an understanding. As though they were joined together, like chums, on an adventure.

◆

Despite the late hour, Zeke decided to walk to Ebury Street, as he did after a performance. It was a long walk back every night, but it kept him fit. And it gave him some time alone. The drawback of a lodging house, even one as home-like as the Cowards', was the lack of privacy.

The English air was cool, but not as cold as it would be at home, this time of year. He hoped his mother was all right; that the coal supplier had dropped off the monthly delivery on time. He'd paid a neighbour's boy to shovel it into their bay in the cellar for her, but he still worried.

Thank God Kit wasn't much of a drinker. She'd nursed that one glass of wine for an hour, and then switched to ginger beer.

That made things easier. He didn't like standing out from the crowd, but he wasn't going to drink to fit in. Not with his heritage. Asking for trouble. These things ran in families, they said, and his temper was bad enough without it being made worse by drink.

He grimaced, crossing over The Mall, almost empty at this time of night.

Kit hadn't been quite at home at David and Bobbie's. Nerves, probably. She hadn't seemed judgemental about them; no one lasted in the theatre who was, not for long. It was just part of the world they lived in. Odd pairings, odder tastes, drink and drugs and too much sex had too easily.

Not his style.

He went around Buckingham Palace, the guards on duty as still as stone. Boring, it must be. The opposite of tonight's party. Poor bastards.

To entertain them, he did a quick soft-shoe along the pavement, twirling a few times and finishing with a 'ta-da!' They didn't even blink. He raised his hat to the nearest one and went on down Buckingham Palace Road.

A good lie-in tomorrow.

What a great life he had. If only he could bring his mother over to share it with him. He'd do it, even if he had to take another job during the day. If he got her out of Canada, she'd be safe.

CHAPTER 4

'Mr Gardiner, if you'd spare me a moment?'

Charlot stood in the door of his office, waiting as if patient – but Lord knew he wasn't. On his way out after having collected his weekly pay – fifteen pounds! – Zeke pulled the hat from his head and stopped.

'Yes, sir?'

Charlot withdrew into the office and Zeke followed him. Like Charlot himself, the office announced 'restrained English gentleman' in a definite cut-glass accent, despite the fact that André Charlot was undeniably French.

Standing behind his desk, Charlot hesitated but didn't sit down. That was a worry.

'Sir?'

A cough, more a clearing of the throat. Staring down, rather than at him. What was going on? If he didn't know that nothing put Charlot off-stride, Zeke would swear he was embarrassed. Oh, God. What if he was getting the boot? Panic climbed in his throat and clutched his bowels.

'Mr Gardiner.'

'Yes?' Take it like a man. Chin up and all that rot. Don't show how much it hurts.

'I'm not quite sure how to broach this subject . . . but it's your clothes.'

The relief was almost as much a punch in the gut as the sack would have been.

'My clothes?' What on earth?

'It's been brought to my attention . . .' *That dresser, Marty. The little weasel.* 'That your, er, attire leaves a little to be desired. You must understand that you're representing The Company, my boy. We can't have you going around looking like an out-of-work tramp.'

Looking at his one and only 'decent' suit, Zeke had to admit it had seen better days. Out of date, a bit baggy at the knees. And his shoes did need reheeling. But comparing him to a tramp was a bit much.

'Surely we pay you enough to buy a decent suit – even a ready-made one?' Charlot said 'ready-made' as someone else might have said 'typhoid'. His own clothes were Savile Row.

'Well, um . . .' How to explain?

'Because if you can't dress properly on the salary you're earning, Mr Gardiner, that must mean that something else is consuming your funds. Gambling, for example. Or drugging. And I don't allow that kind of thing in The Company. It never *does*.'

'Oh, no, sir, nothing like that!' Humiliation burned through him; he could feel his face turning red. 'It's –' He had to come clean. 'It's my mother. I send money back to her every month, to – to pay her rent and so forth.'

To pay her rent so she didn't have to go back to the farm and his father. To pay off the cops in her neighbourhood so they wouldn't act on any request from his father to haul her back. To build a nest egg so that one day he could buy her a house, free and clear, and she'd never have to worry about money again.

Even on a West End salary, that took most of his pay.

'I see.' Tapping his finger on his moustache, Charlot stared at him, and then smiled slightly. 'The mother, that is important.' He'd never sounded so French. 'Very well. We cannot have you walking around London bringing down our reputation. Go to Annie in Wardrobe and tell her to fit you into that grey suit from the last production. And to find you a dinner suit. That should tide you over for now.'

This was even more humiliating. For a second, he was possessed by a blind hatred of his father, who made all this – yes, this degradation in front of a man he admired – all this necessary.

'Thank you, sir,' he made himself say. 'You're very good.'

'Off you go.' Charlot waved him out the door. 'And, Mr Gardiner – get your shoes heeled, please.'

'Yes, sir.'

He managed to get out the door without making more of a fool of himself. Tight under the breastbone, churned up, sick with the indignity, he threaded his way through the flats backstage and went downstairs to find Annie.

Charlot, though – what a man. The kind of man one wanted to be. Clever and successful and still kind. He hated *having* to be grateful, but he couldn't escape the feeling of gratitude.

And the suit was very nice. He looked rather like a gentleman in it. He wished his mother could see him. At least he had something decent to wear to this dratted house party.

◆

'I don't think I can afford this place,' Kit said. The shop – no, the boutique – was so exclusive that all it had in the window was an artfully draped silk scarf. Over the door, 'Dernier' was written in gold. That was all. She definitely couldn't afford it. But she did so need something to wear at dinner at her uncle's . . . She had all the clothes she'd brought from home, but compared to what the London women were wearing, they were so stodgy she couldn't bring herself to wear them. Even the day dresses went down to her ankles!

'Oh, honey, we're not going to *buy* anything!' Adele Astaire said, tucking her arm into Kit's. 'That's not how it works. Come on, now.'

She swept Kit into the boutique – bigger inside than it looked, taking up two storefronts, and decorated in the latest jazz colours. The walls were pale grey, but the settees and chairs were upholstered in bright pink with scatter cushions of black and gold. Very luxe, ultra-modern. Kit felt decidedly out of place in her art silk frock she'd bought off-the-rack. At least it was from Harrod's. But she did need new clothes; she didn't want to feel unfashionable at Barrows.

A young woman, dressed in the latest style, came to meet them.

'Oh, Miss Astaire! Just take a seat and Monsieur Dernier will be with you. Would you like tea? Coffee?'

'Coffee would be grand, thanks, Maudie.'

They sat. A tea lady in a wraparound pinafore brought them petit fours, and coffee in tiny cups.

Only a few moments later, a concealed door at the back of the store opened and a man came through.

He was – rather surprisingly – dressed in the most conservative suit Kit had ever seen. No tan with brown shoes here. Not even light grey. This was a proper navy pinstripe, complete with black shoes and a regimental tie. Surely that couldn't be right? Although so many men had the right to regimental ties now . . . She wished she understood military insignia, so she would know which regiment, because inside the suit was a man with dark skin. The combination, of what looked like Indian descent and upper-class British clothes was striking.

And then, bizarrely, he spoke in a French accent.

'Mademoiselle Astaiiiire! *Je suis enchanté!*' He took her hand and kissed it.

'Oh, come off it, Benny,' Adele said, dimpling. 'Kit's a chum.'

He grinned up at her and straightened. 'Fair call, Delly.' *This* accent was just as strange – pure Cockney. He held out his hand to Kit and they shook. Strange to see such a dark hand against her white gloves. Her mother wouldn't approve. She felt a quick thrill of being almost as cosmopolitan as Adele.

'This is Kit Linton.' Adele looked from one to the other with satisfaction. 'She's an up-and-comer, Benny. In Charlot's show at the New Theatre.'

'Now that *is* useful. Let's see what we can do, ducky. Would you mind standing up, Miss Linton?'

'Please, call me Kit.' No, her mother definitely wouldn't approve, but Adele did. She nodded briskly as though Kit had passed a test.

'Kit . . .' He drew her to her feet and turned her around with a professional hand, surveying her figure. What if he didn't like the look of her?

'An English rose!' he said at last, falling back and staring at her, assessing. 'Yes, I can do something with that.'

'Australian.' She felt she had to say it. He grinned, his brown eyes lighting up.

'Even better. Do they call you a colonial? They do me. As well as – well, no need to sully your ears with it. That's why I went French. Born in Bombay, but I came back here when I was two.'

'Oh, yes,' she said bitterly. 'They call me that.'

'All the more reason to knock their socks off! Wait here for a minute.'

He disappeared into the back of the store and they settled back into their chairs and sipped their coffee.

'He'll have something special for you,' Adele said. 'He's a genius.'

'But I can't *afford* him!'

Benny arrived soundlessly next to her. 'Don't you worry about that, ducks. No bread and honey involved.'

'That means money,' Adele whispered.

'That's it. No money changing hands. Just one mate helping out another. You wear my dress, and when the nice journalists ask you where you got it, why then, you say, "But of course, I get all my clothes from Monsieur Dernier!" Better yet, tell Lady Mountbatten. I do *so* want the dressing of her!'

'You don't get to keep it, though,' Adele said practically. 'It has to come back, so try not to spill anything on it.'

'I'd be terrified!' Kit exclaimed. Benny patted her hand.

'There's always dry cleaning. This first time, just to be nice, you can keep the dress. After that, loans only.'

That seemed almost too generous . . .

'You've got a new style and you want to promote it,' Adele said, her dark eyes sparkling with interest. 'Show us!'

Benny clapped his hands and the young woman who had greeted them came through the back doorway, clad in an extraordinary creation.

It was pale green, long and figure-hugging – *very* figure-hugging – with sequins in silver creating intricate patterns in an Egyptian style. From the hips, long strands of sequins hung free, creating the illusion of a full skirt over the slender material underneath. Would she be able to dance in this? Then the model walked across the shop, posed and turned. There were slits in the skirt on the side . . . she could dance, but gosh! they went up high. And the back dipped almost to her waist. What would Charlot think if he saw her in this dress?

'It's a bit . . . daring,' she said. 'I'm an ingenue.' Actresses who played ingenues in the theatre – the 'innocent young woman' roles – were expected by their managements to maintain that reputation in public. There had been more than one young actress let go for 'conduct unbecoming'.

'Damn,' Benny said, with no apology for the bad language. 'Maudie, try the blue.'

The girl went out and came back a very short time later in a more demure piece. But oh! it was pretty. Pale blue, with white beading instead of sequins, a higher neck and back, the whole thing cut on the bias so that the skirt swung gloriously as she turned. Now *this* was a frock to dance in!

'It's beautiful!' Kit said.

'Mh-hmm,' Adele agreed. 'You'll look a peach in that, kid.'

She did. She looked so good, in fact, that she was pathetically grateful to Benny. Not just for giving her the dress, but for . . . for showing her to herself. The woman in the mirror was so *right*. So fashionable and poised and really not at all bad-looking. Someone who could belong in the chic London theatre crowd.

'Bang up to the minute,' Adele said. 'I might try that green one, Benny.'

Adele looked even better than Kit had in the blue, but she was resigned to Adele Astaire outshining her. Even so, she loved that blue dress. She hoped, fleetingly, that even her aunt would approve of it.

'Bee's knees,' Benny said, nodding approvingly at Kit in the mirror. 'The absolute cat's pyjamas.'

'A real *look*.' Adele twirled gracefully, the sequin strings swinging out and falling with a series of muted clicks. 'I like this, Benny. I might even pay you for it.'

'That'll be the day!' Monsieur Dernier said.

CHAPTER 5

The Dassington house, Barrows, was a mansion, set in a large park. It shouted 'money' to Zeke, as did the chauffeur-driven car Kit's aunt had sent to meet them at the station.

Huge. How many bedrooms? he wondered. Twenty or thirty? He asked Kit as the road looped around to an enormous portico.

'Oh, at least twenty, I should think,' she said vaguely. 'Not counting the servants.'

Well, naturally. Not counting the servants.

He was nastily aware that, under any other circumstances, his type would be going to the servants' entrance, not the front door. God help him at dinner! He knew the basics, thanks to Mrs Treece, his mother's friend back in Victoria, but the subtleties . . . He hoped he didn't embarrass Kit too badly.

The chauffeur drew up in front of the portico and got out to open Kit's door – and Kit, whom he'd seen jump nimbly out of cabs, stayed primly waiting for him.

'Thank you, Mason,' she said. Had he introduced himself? Zeke shrugged. He must have missed it in the flurry at the station. Not that he'd feel comfortable calling a man twice his age by his surname.

Should he help Mason get the bags out? But Kit was walking confidently towards the front door, so he followed her. The door was opened before they got there by a proper English butler. Just like in the books, complete with grey hair and a slight paunch. And shrewd eyes.

Kit nodded to him with perfect poise, and he bowed slightly. 'Miss Scott?' he asked.

She frowned, but gave a small movement with her shoulders, as if shrugging something off. 'Yes, and Mr Gardiner.' Kit had warned him on the train that they would likely call her by her 'real' name, but it was still odd to hear.

'Lady Dassington is in the green drawing room, miss.' He indicated a door in the left wall of the enormous, rather dark hall. A double staircase, suits of armour – it was almost too storybook to feel real. As though fiction had come to life.

Kit followed the butler to the door and waited for him to open it. Was that what you did? Apparently, because the man seemed to think it was normal. They went in to a burst of sunlight, streaming through long windows facing the south. A big room, with sofas and chairs surrounding an enormous fireplace. Mirrors and paintings climbed the walls. A baby grand piano in one corner – and the room was so huge it didn't seem to take up any space at all.

A woman rose from an armchair and came towards them. Not what he'd expected. No pearls or soignée clothing; she wore sensible shoes and a tweed suit, and had a sensible, tweedy kind of face. The sort of face he'd imagine riding to hounds.

'Katherine! Jolly good to meet you!' She and Kit shook hands.

'Aunt Sylvia.' Kit smiled, looking a little relieved, and her aunt turned to Zeke.

'Mr Gardiner, is it? Splendid! Nice of you to come.' She had a handshake like a man's, strong and decisive.

'Lady Dassington,' he said. Thank God the butler had used her proper name. He'd had no real idea what to call her.

'Your uncle's around somewhere – probably in the greenhouse,' she said to Kit. 'He's obsessed with getting those blasted pineapples to flower! And the young ones – oh, here they come.'

A door Zeke hadn't noticed on the outside wall opened and two people came in.

'Cecil and Daphne,' Lady Dassington said with satisfaction.

These ones looked more as he'd expected. Like something out of a magazine. The boy was slender and dapper, although his face was somewhat haddock-like, with bulging eyes. The girl definitely soignée in terms of clothing, although she looked nervously at Kit and him, as though at animals in the zoo. They were both younger, he thought – the girl no more than eighteen, the boy perhaps twenty-one.

They shook hands all round, and sat down on chintz sofas. 'We'll have tea,' Lady Dassington said.

'It's a bit early for tea, Mumsy,' Daphne protested. 'Why don't we take Katherine and her friend out for a walk? Moffat's bitch has just whelped and I'd rather like to choose one of the pups.'

He jolted a little at the 'bitch', but realised she was using the term in a veterinary sense. About a dog.

'Sound idea,' Cecil said.

'You just want to ogle Moffat's daughter.' Daphne looked disdainfully at him.

'She's worth ogling.' He elbowed Zeke. 'You'll see, old man.'

'We'd love to see more of the place,' Kit said, intervening before it became an argument. 'But I'll just have to run up and change my shoes.'

'What about you, Mr Gardiner?' Daphne looked at him expectantly. Should he change? But what did he have to change into? He only had two pairs of shoes – these and his dress shoes, to wear with his dinner suit. Not counting his dancing shoes, which he hadn't brought with him.

'I'm fine, thank you.' Was she Miss Dassington or Lady Daphne? He'd wanted to ask Kit, but had been ashamed to reveal his ignorance. Too proud. Pride goeth before a fall. Well, there was a Canadian way out of that. 'But please call me Zeke.'

'Oh!' Daphne blushed and looked at her mother for guidance, and got the tiniest of nods. 'Well, thank you. Then I shall be Daphne, and this is Cecil.'

Hah. Scraped through that one. But how many other traps would there be this weekend? The next two days stretched out before him like an obstacle course.

◆

Kit ran up the stairs lightly, but halfway up, where the light from the stained-glass windows over the central landing reached her, she paused.

How beautiful it all was! The windows showed country scenes in the four seasons. William Morris, perhaps? Nineteenth century, anyway, which made them newish, in this house. She breathed it in: lemon, furniture polish, old wood, the faint trace of wood smoke, and something else. Sheer age, perhaps. And under it all, the smell of the nearby sea.

Her mother had told her stories of growing up here, of nursery treats and climbing trees and being taught to ride on a fat old pony. Of snowy Christmases and carol singing. All the storybook things. Kit had never thought she'd *be* here. It made her a little weepy, which was silly.

Everything was so *new* in Australia, by comparison, except the Aboriginal heritage, with which she'd had nothing to do. Something about the age of Barrows called to her; the feeling seeped into her bones and put a tight hand under her heart, a kind of yearning.

She had fought to get out of the narrow confines of vicarage life, but this place didn't feel constricted in the same way . . . Outside the stained glass, the flat fields of Suffolk swept down to the sea, an unbounded invitation.

Slowly, she went up to her room, moving through the varied colours of the stained-glass light as though through fairyland.

She'd better not get to like it too much; this wasn't her home, and never would be. She shook herself out of the mood and walked quickly to the room the butler had indicated. At least she had the right clothes.

◆

The puppies were sweet. The walk to the Moffat farm and back was delightful. In fact, everything was lovely, Kit thought, except perhaps her family's insistence on calling her 'Katherine', despite her commenting more than once that she preferred 'Kit'.

She suspected they were in an unspoken conspiracy to ignore her life in the theatre. She was just there as a relation, Katherine Scott, and that was all. Daphne's clear fascination with Zeke was the only explanation for why they had invited him; her aunt wasn't impressed, clearly.

Perhaps her uncle had sanctioned it.

They met at lunch, and he was like an exaggerated male version of her aunt: hearty and kind and not at all fashionable, unlike Cecil.

'Katherine! Lovely, lovely.' Lord Dassington – Uncle Joseph – kissed her cheek and pumped her hand, and then shook Zeke's with equal vigour.

Lunch was in a secondary dining room at a table that could seat twelve. Conversation was general. She was glad for Zeke's sake that it wasn't formal; she had a twinge, wondering if he *knew* the rules for formal dining. Her uncle lost no time interrogating him.

'So, Mr Gardiner, you're from Canada?'

'British Columbia, sir.'

'Hah! Jolly good. And your father?'

'He's a farmer, sir.' Zeke looked like a rabbit in the headlights, but he was holding up. It was slightly funny, really.

'A tenant farmer, eh?'

'Oh, no, sir. We own our farm.'

'Hmph. How many acres?'

'A thousand acres, sir.'

Uncle Joseph blinked. That seemed smallish to her – Australian properties tended to be bigger, but English farms *were* much smaller. The farms she'd seen from the train had tiny fields.

Zeke seemed to realise he'd said something noteworthy. 'Mind you, a lot of it is grazing.'

'A pastoral estate, then?'

'I suppose so . . .'

There was a subtle shift in the room. An actor was one thing, but the son of an estate owner . . . Kit almost laughed aloud, it was so obvious that Zeke had moved up at least one rung on the class ladder in a couple of sentences. It made her a little angry. *He* hadn't changed; only the way the others looked at him.

After lunch, as they moved into the hall, Cecil said, 'Tennis, cuz?' He was trying for an air of sophisticated boredom, but it didn't quite work. He clearly wanted to play tennis. And so did she. It had been *months* since she'd had a game.

'Oh, lovely!' she said. 'But I'll have to borrow a racquet. I'll just nip up and change.'

'Jolly good. How about you, Zeke?'

She paused, a foot on the first step, waiting for him to join her, but he shrugged. 'Sorry, I don't play. I'm happy to watch, though.'

Good Lord. She went up the stairs feeling rather sorry for him. Fancy never having learned to play tennis! Perhaps farms didn't have tennis courts? Her friends' families who owned cattle or sheep stations all had courts . . . it must be different in Canada.

She hadn't realised how different their upbringings had been . . . she hoped she hadn't made him uncomfortable by agreeing to the tennis. She would have to make sure she didn't put her foot in it like that again.

But when she went down and joined the others, Zeke seemed fine. He settled into a deck chair and smiled whenever she looked at him. Maybe she was being too sensitive on his behalf.

It was a wonderful game, and she trounced both Cecil and Daphne soundly.

They flung themselves on the slightly damp benches near the court and waited for Baxter, the butler, to bring them lemonade. Cecil pulled out a cigarette case and started to smoke, without offering either Kit or Daphne one, from which Kit concluded that her uncle and aunt didn't approve of women smoking. Zeke refused politely as he got up and joined her on the bench, being rather careful of his suit.

His care contrasted sharply with the way Cecil lounged casually over his bench, smears of moss on his tennis whites. Of course, Cecil would go up to change in a moment . . . was it possible that Zeke didn't have anything else to change into? That older suit of his was hardly suitable.

Her stomach tightened at the thought, and she avoided looking at him. There wasn't anything she could do to help, anyway.

Better to concentrate on what a marvellous day it had been. Apart from her deep satisfaction with Barrows itself, the new relations had been welcoming, the setting superb, and the tennis just smashing. Not to mention the food! She hadn't eaten so well since she'd left the ship. *Proper* food, with several courses, rather than one solid plate with perhaps a pudding if Mrs French was feeling generous.

◆

'Let's go in,' Daphne said, shivering in the breeze that had picked up. 'I'm freezing.'

Back to the house they went, where Baxter had anticipated everything and set out hot chocolate and cake in the green drawing room.

Kit sighed with happiness as she sipped her drink. The rich chocolate seemed to represent everything about Barrows: delicious, luxurious, warming. Like her room, with its fire ready-laid for tonight, and its gleaming bathroom. A far cry from the Cats' Home.

A far cry even from the Deanery in Sydney.

Daphne cut the cake and served it, handing out pieces and cake forks. Zeke hesitated, casting a quick look at her as if unsure. Surely he knew how to use a cake fork? Maybe he didn't. Poor lamb. She picked hers up and used it to slice off a mouthful of cake. His gaze flickered as though he realised she'd done it deliberately, for him; was there a slight flush of embarrassment on his cheekbones?

But he managed the cake and fork all right. A quick study.

The whole incident made her deeply uneasy. She pushed away a memory of an argument with her mother. 'Etiquette is just outdated! It went out with the War!' she'd insisted, and her mother had smiled infuriatingly.

'You'll learn,' she'd said. It was true that, at Barrows, all the ridiculous gradations of manners which her mother had drilled her in seemed more . . . appropriate. Even right. But she did feel sorry for Zeke, whose mother, clearly, had been nothing like hers.

◆

He didn't fit. It was as simple as that. He was ignorant, probably boorish, certainly lower class. His father's son. Goddammit! He was as angry with himself for caring about their ridiculous rules as he was, sneakingly, ashamed.

Time to get ready for dinner. The thought made him sick with apprehension. What else would he get wrong? If he picked up the wrong fork, would he be totally ruined in Kit's eyes? If he wasn't already.

That look she'd given him! It would have been better if it had been pure disdain; he could have got mad at that. But that *pity*. He concentrated hard on tying his bow tie so his gorge didn't rise at the memory. No girl looked at a man she was interested in with *pity*. Just as well they'd agreed to be brother and sister, because he'd be out of the running with her, that was for sure.

The class system was pernicious, and unfair, and all the rest of it that the Bolsheviks shouted on street corners.

But when you were in the middle of it, it was so easy to start judging yourself by their standards, to be beaten into shape with shame. Well, not him. He'd take anger over shame any day. It filled his veins with satisfactory energy.

He'd try his best, so he wouldn't embarrass Kit in front of her relations, but he'd be damned if he was going to think worse of himself because he hadn't known how to use a bloody cake fork. He was as good a man as Cecil Dassington.

At dinner, he was put on Lady Dassington's right hand. An honour, but also a wonderful place for him. He just waited until she picked up the relevant piece of cutlery (he suspected he was supposed to wait, anyway), and then followed suit. And took exactly as much from the servant's proffered platter as she did. If he ended up a bit hungry, too bad. At least he wouldn't look like a greedy pig.

The conversation was formal, as there were several other guests, including the local doctor and vicar. So predictable. So very *English*. The vicar clearly disapproved of him and probably of Kit, but they were insulated from his comments by the fact he was in the middle of the table, so the rules of formal discourse meant he couldn't speak directly to them.

One good thing about these blasted 'manners'.

He was sweating by the time dinner was over, and then there was the dreaded port and cigars after the ladies had withdrawn.

What kind of society *preferred* to segregate the sexes? The kind where the men had gone to all-male schools, he supposed. It was odd to a Canadian – and boring, since he neither drank nor smoked.

'What? A tipple of port, man, surely?'

'No, thank you, Lord Dassington. I don't drink.'

'Not at *all*?' The man frankly goggled at him. '*Never*?'

'I'm in training,' he said. 'Dancing is an athletic business.'

To a man, they looked dubious, but decided to accept it. The vicar accosted him from the other side of the table.

'Don't you realise you are leading youth astray by these pernicious performances! Tap dancing! Chorus girls!'

Zeke leaned back in his chair and surveyed the company. Every man, bow tie precisely tied, had turned to look at him. They formed a 'story picture' that the Victorians would have loved: *The Question* would be a good name for it.

'No, Reverend, I don't realise that at all. Musicals are very wholesome.'

'Chorus girls!'

'Have you been to Brighton lately? They're wearing less on the beach than the girls do on stage.' That just sent the vicar – and the doctor – off on tirades about modern manners and the degradation of girlhood. Flappers came in for particular vitriol.

Gosh, they hated women!

'At least Katherine isn't a flapper,' the uncle said soothingly.

'She's on the stage!' the vicar snapped. 'She might as well –'

'Vicar . . .' Lord Dassington said, a warning clear in his voice. And just like that, the reverend shut up. Perversely, Zeke was annoyed by that. A man shouldn't keep quiet about his beliefs just because a lord told him to.

But it was time to join the ladies, apparently. Zeke rose with a sigh of relief and waited for the older men to precede him. Lord Dassington paused by his side and regarded him with a shrewd eye.

'You think we're a lot of old fogies, I suppose?'

'I think the world is changing,' Zeke said, as diplomatically as he could.

'Hmph. But is it changing for the better?'

He didn't wait for an answer.

Zeke trailed after them, girding his loins for the next section of the party. At least Kit would be there.

And yes, as far as he could see, the world *was* changing for the better. Less pull, more merit to get ahead, for one thing. Fewer women ground down into the dirt, like his mother had been because there was no job available for her; he'd seen what poverty did to women, and he was all for women's work.

The new world couldn't come fast enough for him.

◆

Monday was more of the same. More tennis, with him sitting on the sidelines. He managed to thrash Cecil at billiards, which was satisfying, but otherwise it was just one damn test after another, and he failed too many of them.

Mostly in the clothes department. Even the men seemed to change clothes every five minutes. Whereas he had two suits: day and evening. No 'flannel bags'. No 'shooting togs'. No 'tennis gear'. Unlike Kit, who seemed to have an outfit for everything. It showed him what her life back in Australia had been like. You didn't have tennis clothes and riding clothes and walking clothes if you didn't need them. Not to mention that astonishing blue dress she'd worn for dinner last night. Thank God Charlot had given him the dinner suit.

Kit was meshing into this family as though she belonged there. As though she'd never set foot on a stage.

It wasn't good to see. At dinner on Sunday night, she chattered to Daphne about fashion with as much insouciance as any deb.

'Are you making your debut?' Lady Dassington asked.

'Oh, I've already done that!' Kit smiled. She flicked him a friendly glance, her blue eyes laughing as though that idea were funny. 'Several years ago now, Aunt Sylvia.'

The aunt simply nodded, but Daphne beamed. 'Then you can chaperone me! Mama never likes going to parties.'

'Steady on, Daph,' Cecil said. 'I don't think – no offence, cuz, but I don't think Daphne's chances are going to be enhanced by being chaperoned by an actress!'

The table fell silent.

Daphne's 'chances' were her hope of making a 'good' marriage. These people treated marriage like they were breeding horses, and they wanted a strong pedigree for a son-in-law. Any scandal – like an actress for a cousin – would put the kibosh on that. He only knew that from reading Jane Austen, and it was ridiculous that the same rules still applied a century later.

Zeke had to step in. 'Besides,' he said, 'we actors don't have time to go gallivanting. We work every night! I can just imagine Charlot's face if you tried to get the night off to go to a party!'

He pulled a mock-threatening face and the others laughed. Kit smiled at him gratefully. It had shaken her, he thought, being reminded that she didn't really belong.

Good. She was too grand a girl to get caught up in this society nonsense.

◆

They went back to Town by the early train on Tuesday morning, over Aunt Sylvia's objections. As they waited in the hall for Mason to bring the car around, she made a last effort to dissuade them.

'But surely you don't have to rush away?'

Kit smiled at her and kissed her on the cheek.

'I'm afraid so. The director will give us notes this afternoon, before tonight's performance, and God help us if we're late for that!'

Aunt Sylvia regarded her with a tolerant but not approving eye. 'Your poor mother's worried sick about you! This mad start of yours –'

'It's not a start, Aunt. It's a career.'

Behind her, she could *feel* Zeke listening. He'd had a less-than-wonderful weekend, she feared. She wouldn't invite him again; it wasn't fair on him.

She was sad to go. The time here had given her a glimpse of what her mother's life had been like, and a sense of continuity, of belonging, which stretched back into the distant past.

It would be easy to belong – and luxurious, too! But too much luxury was bad for a working actress; better to become a star so she could afford her own nice house.

Though she really wasn't looking forward to her cold, dingy little room at the Cats' Home.

They said all their goodbyes and left.

As they settled into their seats on the train, Zeke gave a heartfelt sigh, and then looked embarrassed.

'I'm sorry,' she said. 'I shouldn't have pushed you into coming with me.'

'Happy to help,' he said, still looking flushed. 'But I can't say I covered myself in glory.'

A rush of affection warmed her right to her fingertips. How kind Zeke was. Always making things easy for her.

'Oh, that kind of life is on the way out!' she said briskly. 'All very well for old fogies like that, but not for us.' She didn't mean it, deep down. But she *wanted* to mean it, and that counted for something, surely?

Zeke relaxed and tapped his hat against his knee. 'Really? I know I let you down.'

'Oh, don't be silly!' She could hear a note of annoyance in her voice, which wasn't what she'd intended. The warmth in her veins drained away. 'There's no need to even *think* about it!'

A wry smile twisted his mouth, as though he heard all the things she wasn't saying. All the embarrassment she'd felt on his behalf at the small gaffes and obvious uncertainty over manners. All the pity and regret. Should she offer to *teach* him how to go on? No. That would be too shaming.

'Okay, then. Do you have your script? We might as well run lines while we're travelling.'

Back to business. She was genuinely happy that it was just business between the two of them. It was wrong of her. She *knew* it was wrong. But the sight of Zeke floundering in those social situations had dampened down any attraction she'd felt towards him. So *blinkered* to think that way. But she wasn't going to talk herself out of it; it was safer like this. Besides, she couldn't help how she felt, could she?

'Yes, let's. Would you mind if we start at Scene Three? I'm having trouble with the timing there.'

'*En avant, mon ami!*' Zeke smiled at her, but it was all business.

Gosh, his French accent was atrocious.

◆

Coming back to the Cats' Home that night after the performance was dreary. But after she'd unpacked and washed her smalls in the hand basin, she went down for a boiled egg supper, and there were all the girls, chattering about how some songwriter named Feldman had taken out a full-page ad in *The Stage* newspaper – 'For a song no one else can even get a licence for, so what's the *point*?' as Perry put it.

She had no answer to that, but was ensnared in the conversation as if she'd never been away; still, she wondered if she'd ever really fit in here.

She loved being on stage, but the rest of an actress's life was distinctly unglamorous. There was a part of her that yearned for the cool beauty of Barrows, for the ordered and lovely life it offered.

It wasn't as confining as the life of a Dean's daughter . . . although, laughing at her own romanticism, she wondered if Daphne would agree. Perhaps it was only attractive because she knew she could leave it.

CHAPTER 6

'Message for you, miss.' Sam handed her an envelope as she came in the stage door.

'Thanks, Sam.'

It was from Adele Astaire.

We're off with the Prince of Wales tonight – he says you and Zeke should come with us! Meet us at the stage door.
Delly and Fred

Well! That sounded like fun. Out on a Saturday night with royalty – British royalty *and* theatre royalty! She waltzed into Zeke's dressing room with the invitation in hand, but he shook his head.

'I'm feeling a bit under the weather, and I don't want to make it worse.'

He did look a bit pale under his makeup. Green, even.

'Nothing serious?'

'Had a bad pie for lunch.'

She made a face at him. 'Easy to do.' Poor lamb. She hoped he'd make it through the performance.

He did, but only just. He spent the interval in the bathroom, heaving, dragged himself back on stage for the final act, and rushed back there afterwards.

'Can I do anything?' Kit asked, outside the door.

'Kill me,' he groaned. 'Oh, go on. Go have your night out.'

There wasn't anything she could do, really, so she changed into Benny's blue frock, tipped Sam on the way out to get Zeke into a cab complete with a bucket, and went off to meet the Astaires, bubbling with excitement. It was one thing to bump into the royals at a club and have a dance. It was another thing entirely to be *invited by the Prince of Wales*.

For a moment, she was filled with an unholy satisfaction, imagining her mother's and sisters' reactions when she wrote to them about it. Hah.

Especially her oldest sister, Violet, who had been very snobby indeed about her being an actress. Petty to plan out the letter to her, but oh! so satisfying.

Delly and Fred were at their stage door, surrounded by eager fans. It took them a while to sign all the autograph books and programmes, but they didn't seem to mind. They were generous people.

Kit made Zeke's apologies.

'Poor guy,' Fred murmured. Then they were off, arm in arm with Kit in the middle, down the lane and into a cab.

'Where are we going?' she asked.

Delly and Fred glanced conspiratorially at each other, and Delly giggled.

'We thought it was time the royals had a taste of America,' Fred said. 'Some pals of ours are over from Paris. *Real* jazz players.'

The cab slid into Soho; a less than salubrious district, her mother would have said. It was notorious for its prostitutes and 'gentlemen's clubs'. Where could they be going?

They drew up to a red door in a brick wall. No signage, no doorman. What on earth? It couldn't be bad if Fred was prepared to let Delly go there. He was a most protective brother. But tingles of nerves crept up and down Kit's spine.

As they emerged from the taxi, a group across the road got out of theirs. The Prince of Wales, the Mountbattens, and Prince George. They were a bit light on for women. Perhaps just as well Zeke hadn't come.

The prince bounded across the road, hand held up in greeting.

'Well met!' he said. 'And the lovely Miss Linton. So glad you could join us. I'm looking forward to this.'

Fred shook his hand. 'You'll enjoy it, I'm pretty sure, sir.' He opened the red door, and immediately the sound of 'hot' jazz came up the stairwell inside. Fred grinned. 'The sound of home.'

They traipsed down the none-too-clean stairs to find a smallish club with a surprisingly large dance floor which was full of well-dressed couples – and a few who were less so but who showed all the signs of being professional dancers. Chorus girls and their boys, here for the dancing, just as they were.

The brick walls were saved from bareness by theatre posters and occasional mirrors, which reflected the low lighting and the long mahogany bar to the right of the stairs. Swirls of smoke filled the air – but less so than in a normal club, because everyone was on the dance floor.

On the stage – more a dais, really – was a band. Ah. Now she understood what Fred had meant by *real* jazz players. They were all black Americans, elegant in white tie and tails.

The band struck up at that moment and she was swept away by the music. This *was* real jazz; extraordinary syncopation combined with a deep beat which set her hips swaying.

'The Jazz Kings,' Fred said. 'They usually play at the big hotels when they come to London, but they couldn't get a licence this time from the Department of Labour. So this is on the down-low.'

'Just like an American speakeasy!' Edwina Mountbatten exclaimed.

'That's it, doll.' Delly put on a gangster's voice and they all laughed.

'We're incognito tonight,' the prince whispered in her ear. 'So call me PW.'

'Oh. Um. Yes, certainly, sir. PW.' She was blushing for sure. She must look so gauche. But that music claimed her attention again. She'd never heard anything like it.

'The band's just over from Paris for a week,' Delly told her as they were shown to a large table, already reserved. 'That's Louis Mitchell leading.'

They ordered drinks from the decidedly British waiter (what a Cockney accent!), but she couldn't wait to get on the dance floor. Fred grabbed her hand.

'Come on, Kit!' he said. They slid onto the floor and into a foxtrot, smooth as silk. She let the music take her over and simply followed where he led. The rhythm got into her very bones and she wasn't dancing like an ingenue. Not at all.

By the time the drummer crashed the last cymbal of the number, she was sweating and exhilarated.

'Now *that's* jazz!' Fred said, grinning.

They went back to the table for a drink. Delly propped her face in her hands and examined Kit while Fred chatted with the princes.

'If you weren't sweet on that Zeke Gardiner, I'd have to have a word with you about Freddie.'

'Oh. No. I mean . . .' What to say? Deny she was sweet on Zeke? *Was* she? 'I *like* Fred. He's very charming. But . . .'

''Zactly.' Delly nodded. 'So we can all be friends together. It's a relief, I can tell you. I have to warn girls off so often.'

Kit laughed. 'What does Fred think about that?'

'Oh, all Moaning Minnie thinks about is choreography.' Delly waved a hand in pretend exasperation, and then went suddenly serious. 'But I can't take the risk of some floozy breaking up the act.'

'What happens when he falls in love? Or you do?'

Adele took a big swig of her cocktail and blinked as it went down. 'May that day be a long time coming!'

'Let's dance!' Fred held out his hand again, and Kit jumped up and straight into his arms. 'It's a pleasure to dance with someone who knows what they're doing,' he said, 'and who *isn't* my sister!' Adele stuck her tongue out at him and linked arms with the Prince of Wales. They all swung into a two-step.

Around them, the rest of the royal party gathered. Prince George had picked up a partner from somewhere, a pretty girl with red hair. Kit and Edwina Mountbatten smiled broadly at each other, filled with a shared sense of adventure and of doing something risqué. Nice girls didn't dance the way they were dancing.

Another couple approached them as the dance came to an athletic end.

'Hello all!' the man said.

'Henry! Good man,' Prince George hailed him. 'Join us, why don't you?'

Louis Mitchell took the microphone. 'Ladies and gentlemen,' he said in a southern US accent, 'take the floor for the Charleston!'

The Charleston was more infamous than famous – its origins in jazz dives made it quite scandalous. It had been banned at a lot of clubs, partly because of its unsavoury reputation, and more because at some clubs the floor had collapsed due to the coordinated stamping the dance required. But here they were safely on solid ground. And it was so much fun to dance!

'I don't know how to,' Edwina Mountbatten said.

'It's easy!' Delly replied. 'Just follow me.'

They lined up, along with the other dancers, across the dance floor, facing the band. The prince was on Kit's left, the new man, who Prince George had called 'Henry', on her right. On the Prince of Wales' other side was Edwina Mountbatten, and beyond her, her husband Louis. Fred and Delly were in the line in front, with George and his partner, so they could all follow their movements.

'One, two, and a one, two, three, four!' Louis Mitchell shouted.

Kit knew the basic moves – the hands, the knees, the stamping. She'd danced it before, to records. But that was nothing like this. The deep bass of the music took hold of her and swept her up, and watching the Astaires dance together was, in itself, like a drug. She devoted her entire attention to following Delly, as if she were in a dance class. There was a special way of watching and dancing simultaneously that every professional dancer developed. Vision turned itself into movement without any apparent intervening thought, as though her body was only a function of her eyes.

It was so much *fun*. Fast, intense, the beat underscoring every move, and quite, quite different to dancing in a couple. This was a group effort, everyone in the club united in a grand, sweaty, exhilarating frenzy. Next to her, the Prince of Wales flailed wildly, happily, a smile right across his face, his hair whipping out of its neatness and his coat tails flapping. They grinned at each other.

And then the flash of a camera went off.

CHAPTER 7

The Prince and the Actress!

Palace shocked!

Romance in the air for the POW?

Royal affaire with a stage darling?

The Charleston Scandal!

Star of *Dance Crazy* in shady relationship with POW!

Secret Romance with Chorus Girl!

'*Chorus girl*?' Kit shouted. She threw the newspaper across the dining room, her stomach churning.

Perry laughed quietly in the corner. 'They could at least have said "ingenue".'

Kit shot her a fulminating look. Just like Perry to make light of this. The other girls gathered around, not sure what to say, but riveted by the articles. It was a moment of excitement, she guessed; other people's scandals always were riveting.

On Saturday night, the prince had shrugged off the photographer's actions; the club servants had hurried the man out of the room immediately, and they'd gone on to dance and laugh some more.

But the way the newspapers were reporting this – the photograph had come out in the *Sunday Post*, showing only her and the prince in full, freewheeling Charleston. By Monday morning every newspaper in London had picked up the story, and the tabloids had run with it. They were making her out to be no better than a whore. And the fact that they'd been dancing the Charleston just made everything more shocking. This would kill her mother.

Thank *God* she didn't use her real name – Daphne's 'chances' wouldn't be affected, and her aunt and uncle could pretend not to know her.

What on earth would Charlot think?

That made her go cold. Damage to an actress's reputation could be fatal to her career. Particularly a young one like her. No matter what went on behind the scenes, actresses were supposed to have blameless reputations.

She had to get to the theatre. Perry, sitting by the window writing a letter, looked out onto the street.

'There's a bunch of reporters out there.'

How had they found her? *How?* Blast. Someone at the club must have heard the prince call her by name, and then it wouldn't have been hard to track her down. Or possibly the photographer had been one of the ones at the Riviera Club on opening night. She was in the public eye in Charlot's show as she'd never been before.

Mabel grinned. 'Let's doll you up. I've got a red wig.'

'Ooh, yes!' Val said. 'I can lend you some falsies. Make you bigger than usual.'

Exasperated but grateful, five minutes later she was 'dolled up'. It turned out that she and Val were the same size; perhaps Val would like some of the dresses she'd brought from home. She was so much taller that they would look quite fashionable on her, the hems just the right length.

'Your own mother wouldn't recognise you,' Mrs French said. 'Off you go, in a crowd. Perry, you distract them.'

'Righto!' Perry said with gusto. They went out the door in a scrum, Perry in front. 'Hel*lo* gentlemen!' she said, posing on the bottom step as the others streamed past her. 'Who wants a scoop about the girl in the photo?'

They all pressed in, half a dozen reporters and three photographers. 'What's she like?' 'Is it true the prince is in love with her?' 'How long has it been going on?'

Perry laughed. 'It was all a joke, lads. You've all been taken in. No romance there . . .'

They yelled and shouted more loudly. Kit slipped around the corner. She owed Perry a pair of silk stockings for this.

Her stomach was churning with anger and resentment. How *dare* they? A simple dance and they were building it up to a major scandal.

She had to get to Charlot and make sure he knew the truth. Val put her fingers in her mouth and whistled loudly to a passing cab. Kit hopped in gratefully.

'Thanks, thanks to you all,' she said, and the cab drove off as Mabel said to Val, 'Nicely done, but really a lady doesn't whistle like that.'

'This lady does!' Val said.

◆

She slipped in through the stage door, winking at Sam as he stared at her in astonishment.

'Wouldn't have recognised you, miss.'

'That's the idea, Sam. Is Himself in?'

'Aye. Up in his office.'

Kit went to her dressing room and whipped off her disguise, brushing her hair out, straightening her clothes. Looking respectable was particularly important today.

Charlot's secretary, a young spotty man with a bow tie, waved her through.

'He's expecting you.' That was ominous. She swallowed, called up all her stagecraft, and walked into the office as though there was nothing in the world bothering her. Charlot was behind his desk. His manners as impeccable as always, he rose as she came in, and helped her into a chair.

His desk was covered with newspapers. She cast a swift look over them, and blanched a little. There were even more than they'd had at breakfast.

'Well, Miss Linton.' Charlot's voice was smooth and silky. Dangerous. Or was that a slight hint of humour underneath the silk?

Oh, bother this act! It wasn't fooling him, anyway.

'Am I in trouble, Charlot?'

He laughed. 'For getting your name and the name of our little show on every newspaper in London? Hardly! The box office is reporting that we're selling out every performance.'

She gaped. It had never occurred to her that Charlot could be *pleased*.

'My dear,' he said, patting her hand. 'A scandal where you were found *in flagrante delicto* with some commoner would be bad. But a scandal where you're dancing with the Prince of Wales? No one but the Palace is going to object to that.' For once, he sounded like a Frenchman. They were supposed to take these things more lightly, weren't they?

'But . . . my reputation . . . what they're *saying* about me!'

'They're implying, rather than saying. Staying just on the right side of the libel law. But I'm afraid that, the world being what it is, a woman's reputation is *less* damaged by a liaison with a royal prince than you might think.'

That made her a little sick, even as relief swept over her.

'But this is enough,' Charlot said. 'We don't want to *confirm* any rumours, do we?'

'Oh, no!' He couldn't think . . . 'It *was* just a dance. Adele Astaire invited me to join the party.'

'*Parfait!* Off you go to warm up. You must perform *à merveille* tonight. We have a full house!'

◆

Marguerite and Basil were less sanguine. 'Let's hope it's not a bubble that will burst as soon as this all dies away,' Basil grumbled.

Susan patted her shoulder as they waited in the wings. 'You'll survive it, dear,' she said, as though it were a disease, and Percy smiled sympathetically.

Zeke slung an arm around her shoulders. 'Enjoy it while it lasts!' She scowled at him. He *would* take it lightly, like Perry. Men had it easy. No one was going to think worse of the Prince of Wales – at least, no one outside a vicarage. Her father, for one, would thoroughly disapprove of anyone going dancing with an actress. Especially the Charleston.

She made her first entrance with a heavy heart, but an excited whisper spread across the audience as she came in and, despite herself, it buoyed her up. At least they knew who she *was*. She smiled her best smile at Zeke, and prepared to perform *à merveille*.

CHAPTER 8

The knock at the dressing room door came just as Kit was taking off her gloves the next morning. At least she was decent. She'd taken more trouble than normal with her appearance, in case the photographers were there again. And they had been, though she'd come in early for the director's notes session. Susan wasn't even here yet, and she was normally first in.

'Yes?' she called through the door. If it was another reporter, she'd give them the side of her tongue.

'Miss Linton?' The voice was educated. Did reporters sound like that? Cautiously, she edged it open. The man outside was no reporter. An actual top hat and morning dress! And quite good-looking. He stood like an ex-military man. Stiffly, he took off his hat as their eyes met. She opened the door a little wider, but not all the way.

'Yes?'

'My name is Wilfred Berkhof. I'm His Royal Highness' aide-de-camp. The Prince of Wales', that is.'

How odd. She stood back and let him come in. At least the room was tidy. It looked quite nice in the morning sunshine coming through the small high window, although his quick, dismissive look around made it clear he didn't think so.

'Won't you sit down, Mr Berkhof?' She sat herself, conscious of moving smoothly, like a lady. Her mother would be proud of her. She silently offered to take his hat, but he shook his head as if surprised. In fact, he seemed to be reconsidering her, a frown between his brows.

'Well, Miss Linton.' He sat in Susan Maxwell's chair and smiled suddenly – a practised smile, a diplomat's smile. She gave him back the smile of an actress suppressing boredom, just for fun, and was pleased when he looked puzzled.

'Well, Mr Berkhof?'

'We seem to be in a pretty pickle, Miss Linton, thanks to your little dancing escapade.'

'*My* escapade? The prince is a grown man and he makes his own choices, Mr Berkhof.'

He fidgeted with the hat on his knee. 'Well. That's so. But the fact is, the papers are making a terrible hullaballoo about it, and the Palace is not pleased.'

The Palace. He meant the King. The King himself knew what had happened. She pushed down a small thrill that the King of England knew her name. *Not the right attitude, Kit.*

'So . . .' Berkhof went on. 'We've come up with a solution we think might do the trick.'

'We?'

'The Palace and I.'

'Not His Royal Highness?'

For the first time, he avoided her eyes. 'The prince is less concerned about public perception than, perhaps, he should be.'

Berkhof didn't like the prince. There was a nugget of gossip she'd never be able to use. But it was true. She could see it in the tight mouth below his military moustache. In his set jaw. Poor man, given the task of supervising a prince who just wanted to raise hell. She took pity on him; she could understand that job might be very hard indeed.

'What is this plan, Mr Berkhof?'

He laid his hat aside and leaned forward in his chair. The light from the window struck his head and she realised he was younger than she'd thought. Probably chosen by the King so he'd 'get on' with the prince. Poor, misguided man, if he thought he could control that prince.

'In the photograph, one can just see Lord Henry Carleton next to you.'

'Yes?'

'The Palace has issued a statement that Lord Henry was your actual partner, not His Royal Highness, and that the prince was, in fact, dancing with Lady Edwina Mountbatten.'

'So you're throwing Lord Henry's reputation to the wolves?'

'Well, Miss Linton, it's a far less serious thing when the third son of an earl dances with —'

He stumbled as he realised that there was no way he could finish that statement without insulting her. Her stomach tightened with anger. It was growing stronger and stronger. Was being an actress so terrible? Did that wipe out all the other things she was? If the papers had thought she was the niece of Lord Dassington, there wouldn't even have *been* a scandal!

It made her sick, being classed in with, with – she couldn't even finish the thought. But she forced herself to.

'With whom, Mr Berkhof? With an *actress*? With a *woman of low repute*? Times have changed, you know. We're not all Nell Gwynnes now!'

He spread his hands on his knees as if resigned to her tirade, which just made her angrier.

'You've just parcelled me off to a sprig of minor nobility like you'd pass around the port after dinner, is that it?'

'Oh, no, not *minor* nobility! Lord Henry is the son of the Earl of Carleton! It's a very old creation!' There was something ridiculous about his instinctive response.

'Oh, well then, as long as he's not "minor" . . .'

'You're making fun of me, Miss Linton.'

'And why shouldn't I?' She sprang to her feet and paced to the door and back. 'You're treating me like a – like a –' There was no word for what she felt that wouldn't immediately make him think less of her. Nothing a real lady could say that was bad enough.

'Not at all, Miss Linton. The Palace merely asks your assistance in reducing the adverse publicity this event has inspired.'

Oh, that sounded so reasonable.

'By publicly coupling me to a man I've barely spoken two words to!'

'But you *have* spoken to him. So it's entirely possible you were dancing with him. All we need to do is make that clear.'

'That's it? You put this release out without my permission, and now you want me to back you up.'

Berkhof looked down at his hands. 'I do regret you've been placed in this position, Miss Linton.' That sounded sincere, at least. 'But there is more to it than that. In order for the press to *believe* the response from the Palace, you'll need to be seen in Lord Henry's company in the future.'

Anger burst through any attempt to be ladylike. How dare he treat her like a common harlot? How *dare* he! Her voice went low and she spoke through her teeth.

'I'm not a prostitute, Mr Berkhof. You can't just organise my time and my life to suit the *Palace*.'

'I should have known we couldn't expect a colonial to understand their duty.' He spoke as if to himself.

'A colonial? Perhaps you'd better remind the Palace that Australia hasn't *been* a colony since 1901, and I was born a citizen of Australia, not Britain!'

'You're a citizen of the Empire!' he retorted sharply.

'Take a look around, Mr Berkhof. The Empire isn't what it used to be.'

He got to his feet, ramrod stiff. 'You have a duty to your monarch.'

Did she? To her monarch, maybe, but not to the bloody Prince of Wales.

'Fine. I won't contradict the press release. You'll have to be satisfied with that.'

They stared at each other for a long moment, his expression a mixture of fury and surprise, as though he *had* expected her to cower at the very mention of the Palace and promise to be a good little girl.

'I think you'd better leave, Mr Berkhof.'

'This is not the end of the matter, Miss Linton.'

'I daresay not.'

After he left, she stood there, clutching the chair back, appalled at herself. She'd let her anger get the better of her. She shouldn't have done that. But to be treated like – *like an actress*, her mother's voice in her head said, dryly. *Which you are.*

She wanted to kick the chair and scream. But ladies didn't do that. And, actress or not, she was a lady.

◆

'Message from the guv'nor, miss!' Billy, the messenger from the office next door, handed Kit a folded piece of paper as she came out of her dressing room, freshly made up and ready for the street. The weekly notes session with the director had been brief today, and she'd been hoping to get in some quick shopping before she had to come back to the theatre for the performance. She desperately needed toothpaste and soap. Oh, well, she'd just have to get up early tomorrow.

Charlot's office was in the theatre, but The Company offices were next door, including the room known as 'the Boardroom' even though there wasn't a board. Charlot was waiting for her there, along with – oh, no. The man from the Palace.

Blast.

She could just see how this conversation was going to go. She would say she didn't have to comply with Palace requests if she didn't want to, it was a free country, etc etc, and Charlot would say it was in The Company's best interests . . . she would come off looking like a sulky schoolgirl if she protested. Charlot would insist . . .

Bother and blast. She couldn't win.

If she couldn't win, she wouldn't fight.

'Fine,' she said, as soon as the door closed behind her. 'Tell Lord Henry to pick me up after tonight's performance.'

Both men blinked, and Charlot hid a smile.

'Uh, yes, well then. Excellent,' Mr Berkhof said.

'Is that all?' Kit held her head up. She wouldn't give them the satisfaction of seeing her annoyance, although she suspected Charlot had a very clear idea of it.

Berkhof cleared his throat. 'Yes, yes, thank you.'

'Gentlemen.' She nodded at both of them, and winked at Charlot as she turned away from Berkhof to the door. His mouth twitched with laughter, but he held it back.

She even managed not to slam the door on her way out, which took real restraint. Outside, on the footpath, she turned sharply on her heel and went to the nearest shops on Shaftesbury Avenue. How ridiculous!

Here she was, going off to buy toothpaste, and tonight she was being escorted on the town by the son of an earl, in order to safeguard the reputation of the Prince of Wales. That familiar sense of being hedged-in hit her.

How did a girl get *into* this situation? And how could she get out of it?

Her parents' daughter, Katherine Scott, wouldn't be in this situation. This was all about Kit Linton.

A few dates with Lord Henry, she supposed, and then the whole thing would drop.

She pondered Lord Henry as she picked up supplies. She only vaguely remembered him. Not bad-looking, at least, but not her type. Too hearty and rugger-playing and full of exuberance. That blond, blue-eyed look, which screamed 'English'. At least he had a chin.

She'd better get her good blue dress dry-cleaned. Tonight she could wear the new eau de Nil satin which Benny had sent around as a loan, but if she was out with Lord Henry she'd need to vary her 'look'.

Blast! She should have asked the Palace for a clothing allowance!

CHAPTER 9

That night, after the performance, Kit took a little more care than usual with her makeup. She needed to be ready for the photographers, because the Palace would undoubtedly have tipped some off. Making a face at herself in the mirror, she closed the little case of mascara and braced herself for the ordeal.

She didn't know why she was so appalled at the idea of her face splashed across the gutter press, coupled with a man, given that Charlot didn't seem to be worried, but the very thought revolted her.

'Where are you off to?' Zeke asked as they headed together to the stage door.

'I'll tell you all about it tomorrow,' she said. She didn't dare tell anyone else – Perry was a dear, but a terrible gossip. Zeke, on the other hand, was as silent as the grave. She needed *someone* to confide in if she was going to get through this farce successfully.

Because right now she felt like smashing Lord Henry in the mouth and saying, 'To hell with the Palace.' The sense of being pushed into a box that was too small for her, so familiar from her girlhood, overcame her and she felt a constriction in her chest.

Take a breath. Another.

'Have fun!' Zeke said lightly. Was there something else behind that tone? She smiled up at him. No. He was just being neighbourly.

Lord Henry swept up, loudly exclaiming, 'Kit!'

Yes, there were the photographers' flashes going off. He slid an arm through hers and ushered her into a waiting car – a Rolls-Royce. Long, low and beautiful, she had to admit.

The door closed her inside as another round of flashes went off. She smiled her best stage smile.

Then the car moved off.

'That would be "Miss Linton", thank you very much.' Glaring at him, she removed his hand from her shoulder and leaned back against the soft leather.

That was *not* what he had expected, clearly.

Oh, the reputation of an actress. It was beginning to really irk her. He recovered his poise and smiled, trying for urbane and failing.

'I'm so sorry. I understood . . .'

'What you should have understood is that I'm doing this under protest and only because my management wants me to.'

'Oh. No. No, that wasn't how it was explained to me.' Rather put out, by the look of it. Well, this was going to be a jolly outing if they were both out of sorts.

'I suppose we have to make the best of it,' she said, trying to smile. 'But calling me by my first name in front of strangers . . . no, really, Lord Henry, it won't do. You may not think much of an actress's reputation, but I care about mine.'

'Awfully sorry. One just wanted to give the impression . . .'

Oh yes. The 'impression'.

'I'm sure me getting into your car gave that impression quite adequately.'

'Such a jolly impression, though!' He smiled, and this time managed a fair degree of charm.

He really wasn't much older than she was. Less a hearty rugger player than a big puppy. An ungainly puppy who hadn't learnt the rules yet. Always had everything he wanted. She knew his type. They always got handsy. Best to set the boundaries firmly and early.

She stared intently into his baby-blue eyes and said, 'This is purely business, Lord Henry. That's all. We go out a few times, we're *seen*, we're photographed, the gossip dies down, and then we're back to where we were.'

'Yes, quite. But there's no reason we can't have a good time doing it, is there? Bourke? The Riviera Club, if you please!'

He pulled the glass up between them and the chauffeur.

'No.' She made her tone as firm as possible.

'But –'

'I am *not* dining alone with you, Lord Henry. Not after that little display. I'm happy to be seen with you in a group, or at a party, but dining alone? No. I'm sorry. It's just not done.'

He looked ready to argue. Women *did* dine alone with men, sometimes – advanced women, who had independent incomes and didn't have to worry about their public. But the rules for a debutante and the rules for a young actress were surprisingly similar. No being found alone with men; no dining alone with men in public; no drinking alcohol in public; no scandals; no risqué clothing . . . The only thing an ingenue actress got to do which debutantes didn't was wear makeup.

She smiled her best smile at him and softened her voice. 'I'm an *ingenue*, Lord Henry. My job, if you like, is to be a professional virgin.'

He blinked at her forthrightness. 'Er, yes.'

'This scandal about the Prince of Wales is bad enough. You know *his* reputation with women.'

For a moment, she thought he was going to explode, but then he put his head back and laughed.

'God, yes!' he gasped. 'Poor PW. He does get around. But I assure you, Miss Linton, you're safe from him. He prefers them . . . more experienced.'

Her mouth twitched. They shared a conspiratorial smile, and he gave a last chuckle. 'All right, then. We'll go to the Bridlinghams' ball. They're pushing out their youngest gel. Bingo's sister, y'know.'

'I can't go to a debutante's ball! Not dressed like this!'

He assessed her shrewdly. 'Nonsense. That's a nice pale colour. Kind of thing all these gels wear. Rub off the lipstick and you'll be fine.' He pulled the glass down. 'Bourke, we're going to Grosvenor Square, to the Bridlinghams'.'

Well. She took out a handkerchief and mirror and 'rubbed off' the lipstick, and tried to downplay her eye shadow. Lord Henry lent her his own hankie, far more durable. By the end of the ride, she'd managed to achieve a 'natural' look. She hoped. The low light didn't help. She'd probably be shunned by everyone there. An actress at a deb's ball – it sounded like the beginning of a rude joke.

◆

But when they got to Grosvenor Square, she couldn't help but feel a tingle of anticipation, much as she'd felt when she'd arrived at Barrows. This was the real high life. A Georgian mansion, red carpet laid down from the curb, footmen ready to hand one out and light one's way, a blaze of lights and warmth streaming from the open front door, the scent of gardenias and the sound of dance music . . .

As she walked in, she could feel herself slipping back into being Katherine Scott, leaving behind the somewhat slapdash manners of the theatre. She even walked differently; the dancer's lithe grace settling into something more sedate. Perry's voice saying, 'What a laugh!' echoed in her head, but was drowned out by the sounds of the discreet orchestra playing a waltz.

She'd been a debutante herself, when she was seventeen. Made her curtsey to the Governor of New South Wales. Her mother had insisted. But it was in the middle of a run of *A Midsummer Night's Dream*, and she'd had to let her understudy go on for her for that performance, much to the management's disgust. So there had been no 'season' for her, and she'd thanked God for it at the time. Her three sisters had all gone through the mill, done their duty and been married off.

Not that a season in Sydney could compare to this. The society matrons in their villas around the Harbour would like to think so, but she'd been to enough parties there to know the difference.

Lord Henry gave her his arm and they went in, surrounded by the flash and glitter of real jewels, of couture gowns, of impeccable tailoring . . . of those high and rather harsh voices of the English aristocracy.

There was a receiving line at the door: an older couple, a young girl (no doubt the debutante) and a young man. They all greeted Lord Henry with familiarity, and looked her up and down with a mixture of surprise and ingrained politeness. The mother, Lady Bridlingham, looked rather closely at her face, and her eyes hardened. Kit winced internally – it was so hard to get mascara off without smudging it. No doubt she'd reinforced whatever prejudices the woman had against actresses.

The young man, Lawrence Bridlingham, shouted, 'Henry! Good Lord, man, I thought you'd have enough sense to stay out of this clishmaclaver!' and grinned openly at her.

'Oh, do go away, Bingo,' the girl, Sarah, said. 'You're just holding things up.'

'Right you are,' Bingo agreed. 'Come on, you two.' He led them towards a pair of open doors.

'I say!' Bingo looked at her more closely. 'You're that gel in the papers.'

'Miss Linton is –' Henry started, but she cut him off. This was why they were there, after all.

'Yes. I'm that girl.'

'What a brouhaha over a little dance!' Bingo chortled. And that was that.

◆

Tomorrow, Kit vowed, she would write a note of thanks to Benny. Every woman in that room, she instinctively felt, would have known a ready-to-wear frock at first glance. As it was, she could hold her head high.

And dance.

Like most men of his class, Lord Henry could dance well enough. At least he *led*, and his clasp on her back was neither amorous nor tentative. She could work with that.

They waltzed, and then stopped for champagne. At least, Henry had champagne. The waiter clearly thought she was a deb, as she was handed lemonade. Better that way. No need to rub her outsider status in. She danced with Bingo, who hopped around the room like a kangaroo and trod on her toes. She danced again with Lord Henry, who said, 'Please call me Henry or no one here will believe we're really a couple,' and then with Henry's friend who was apparently called 'Squibs', and then they went into supper and ate crab cakes and drank more champagne, after she'd informed the barman that she was over twenty-one, thank you very much.

Cecil and Daphne weren't there, thank goodness. The other guests shot her sidelong glances and spoke quietly to each other while they did so. Gossip making the rounds. The older women sneered covertly, the older men ogled. But Henry's friends were very welcoming, so she put her chin up and smiled.

Squibs turned out to be a Marquess. Bingo a Viscount. Sarah, his sister, was a Lady.

'I'm only a third son,' Henry mock-mourned. 'Nobody, really.'

'Wish I were a third son,' Bingo said. 'You'll never have to take your seat.'

'Half your luck,' Squibs added.

For a moment she was puzzled, and then realised they were talking about a seat in the House of Lords. It was an odd thought. These men, these silly young fellows, would one day take up their role as part of the government.

She felt, briefly, as if she were part of something bigger than herself. The Empire, perhaps, that Mr Berkhof felt so strongly about. Or merely the inner circle of wealth and influence to which her family had belonged before her parents had left this country.

Her father planned to be a bishop. Her mother, an earl's daughter, was certain he'd achieve it. Which was why having an actress in the family was such a disgrace; and why her stage name was Linton, her paternal grandmother's maiden name.

Perhaps she ought to change it by deed poll.

'Miss Linton?' Lady Sarah said her name as though repeating it. Kit paid attention to her surroundings again with a start.

'Oh, sorry.' Too much champagne after a long working day.

'We're going on to the Riviera. Will you come with us?' She was a nice girl, a couple of years younger than Kit, but very poised and friendly.

Kit had done her duty – and enjoyed it, she admitted. But –

'I have to work tomorrow,' she said. 'If I don't get my beauty sleep . . .'

They protested, gallantly, but escorted her out. She insisted on saying goodbye to her hostess, and thanking her for a lovely evening.

Lady Bridlingham smiled graciously and without any real kindness. 'Perhaps we shall see you again, Miss Linton?'

'I do hope so, Lady Bridlingham,' she answered smoothly. Her hostess's eyebrow rose; surprise at her bravado, or at her correct accent? One thing Kit was sure of: she had no trace of Australia left in her voice or manner.

'Well. We shall see. Henry is a lovely boy, but he does tend to . . . get excited about things.'

Translation: he'll drop you as quickly as he picked you up. Although that was exactly what she wanted, there was no reason to let this harpy know it. 'Oh, I find it's best not to let men get *too* excited. It's bad for the little dears.'

That was as good an exit line as she could hope for, and she sailed off feeling momentarily on top of the world, until she recalled Lady Bridlingham's curl of the lip. No matter who her escort or how nice her frock, that curl said she didn't belong there and she never would. But what if she'd mentioned her aunt and uncle? Would Bingo's mother have been quite as dismissive of Lord Dassington's niece?

◆

In the Rolls-Royce on the way home, Lord Henry – Henry – smiled lazily at her. 'Now, tomorrow night . . .'

'Too soon. We're trying to put out a scandal, not start another one.'

He sighed theatrically and patted her knee. Just as theatrically, she picked his hand up and placed it back on the seat between them. He laughed.

'All right, then. Squibs' sister is having a garden party on Sunday, out near Windsor. They've got a little place there. One of those dos where women wear big hats. I'll pick you up at two.'

A garden party. Despite herself, anticipation bubbled up. But what would she wear?

As they drew up on Charlotte Street, Bourke came around to open her door. It was her first good look at him, and she saw with a little shock that he was foreign – Italian or Egyptian.

It made her realise how *British* everyone was in her new life. Australia was far more varied in race.

'You fitted in very well tonight,' Henry said suddenly, as if the sight of the Cats' Home had reminded him she wasn't one of his usual dates.

Stepping out of the car, she turned and looked back at him. How much to tell him? Better to protect Cecil and Daphne, and give him the bare minimum.

'My father is in the Church.'

He fell back onto the squabs dramatically, clutching his heart. 'A vicar's daughter! I'm doomed.'

She couldn't help laughing, and Bourke's mouth definitely twitched.

'Good night, Bourke,' she said.

'Good night, miss.' He closed the door behind her.

She had to admit, it was nicer to come home this way than to walk or catch a bus.

◆

At breakfast, Perry and the other girls bombarded her with questions while Mrs French gave out the post.

'The *Bridlinghams*?' Sally yelped. 'That's the ball of the *season*! Who was there? What did they wear?'

'Was the Prince of Wales there?'

'Did you dance?'

'What did they have for supper?'

'Was there champagne?'

'Did he *kiss* you?'

'No, he certainly did not kiss me, and he's not going to, either!' She dumped her bag on a chair and sat down at the dining table. 'Why are you all so excited about this fellow, anyway? You weren't this het up about the Prince of Wales!'

'Oh, the Prince of Wales,' Sally said, waving one hand. 'Nothing's going to happen with a *prince*. But a lord . . . *anything* could happen with a lord!'

'Here,' Mrs French said, handing over a letter.

'Just my mother,' Mabel said. 'What I wouldn't give to get a billet-doux from a lord!'

Perry laughed as she took her own letter from Mrs French, and tucked it into her purse.

'Daisy Danvers married a lord!' Mabel added.

'Nothing's going to happen.' Kit couldn't tell them the truth – the girls were darlings, but they gossiped ferociously. There'd be no point to the masquerade if she let them in on it. The news would be all over London in a day. 'He's nice enough, but nothing special.'

As one, the girls sighed. Except for Perry. 'Do you need special, if he's rich?' she asked, her mouth twisted in a wry smile.

She already knew the secret. Kit gave her a long-suffering look. 'Money isn't everything.'

'No, but it's a blessed lot,' Mabel declared, and the others murmured agreement. Not for the first time, Kit realised how different her background was from the other girls'. Hardly any of them had somewhere they could go home to. None of them had anyone they could ask for monetary help if things went bad; not because they didn't have family, but because their families were struggling themselves. She thought of her own stash – a bank account with enough money to get her home safely, plus a bit. She'd never had to dip into it, but she knew it was a real luxury to have a nest egg like that.

She wished she could help all of them, but she was a working woman herself now, and no better off week to week. Which was why she needed their help.

'I have to go to a garden party on Sunday. With a big hat.'

Silence fell. None of them had that kind of outfit. A big hat meant a longish, flowing dress. Something flowery and summery. Silk, for preference. And sweet kitten heel shoes. She might get away with her French heel beige ones.

'No one?' Kit asked. Every head was shaken.

'Ask your wardrobe mistress,' Mabel advised. 'For an occasion like this – it's good publicity, right? The social columnists will be there. Let the management help out.'

That was good advice – better than Mabel knew, given that it was Charlot's fault she was in this position.

'Right,' Kit said. 'I will.'

The girls trailed out – the ones who were working went off to their rooms to darn stockings until it was time to go to the theatre; the ones who weren't pulled their coats on and set out to audition or besiege their agents.

'What was with the no-makeup last night?' Perry asked as they walked down the road to the bus stop.

Kit grinned. 'I went to a debutante ball, I had to look like a debutante. So very, very ingenue!' Suddenly, it seemed so funny, and the two of them laughed until they cried.

The rules that governed debs seemed ridiculous now, although they had felt constraining when she had been one. Only wearing pale colours, no drinking, no smoking, no *anything* without a chaperone. She was glad she'd put those days behind her.

'Still,' Perry said, wiping her eyes and pulling her hat on

more firmly. 'You have more claim to it than anyone else around here. Being a debutante, I mean.'

Should she tell Perry that she really had made her debut? Perhaps not. There was already a little gap in their friendship because of their different upbringing. She didn't want to do anything to make that gap grow.

'Oh yes,' she said. 'I'm such a shrinking violet!'

Perry laughed again. 'A blushing rose.'

If she was going to go to a garden party, she'd have to try to remember what it was like to be an actual blushing rose. God help her. She didn't want to embarrass Henry, who'd been pushed into this just as she had.

Lord, look at the time! She'd better get a move on. They were making a change to the chorus choreography, and she had to be on hand.

CHAPTER 10

After the show, Kit headed into Wardrobe to ask Annie, the wardrobe mistress, for help.

'A garden party?' Annie put her hands on her hips. She was a stout woman with extraordinarily beautiful pale skin and silver hair. A long history as a dresser had led her here, and there wasn't much going on in the theatre world that she didn't know, but she never gossiped. 'And what would Mr Charlot say about you borrowing finery?'

'It was his idea for me to go out with Lord Henry,' Kit disclosed. 'But that's a secret.'

'Hmph!' Annie eyed her, walking around and inspecting her the way a judge looked at a dog in a show. 'I suppose you could wear that pink silk from *Flying Doughnuts*.' *Flying Doughnuts* had been a revue that had only closed a month ago, so the frocks would be still in fashion.

'Thank you, Annie.'

The pink silk was beautiful. The fawn hat with a pink scarf around it was beautiful. Her own French heels would be fine. Her own ivory silk stockings would be fine.

Annie regarded her when she was dressed with a benign eye.

'I have to say, you look better in that than Mandy Carter did. Like a lady.'

Well, that was something to hold on to. Annie had a keen eye for a lady.

◆

Squibs' sister's 'little place' near Windsor turned out to be a mansion. Naturally.

Buoyed by the pink silk frock and the big hat, Kit strolled into the party on Lord Henry's arm as if she belonged there.

In a way, she did. This was the life her mother had trained her for. Fashionable women, rich men, history and culture and tradition. It was the life her mother had lived, before she'd fallen in love with Kit's father and followed him to Australia. She claimed that she'd never regretted it for herself, but she wanted better than a draughty vicarage and a Church stipend for her girls.

All those hours of her posture being corrected, her manners dissected . . . finally, they were paying off, even more than they had at Barrows or at the ball. Kit sent an unspoken 'Thank you' to her mother and smiled up at Lord Henry.

'Now, Henry, who do we have here?' A youngish woman, dressed in a deep red that on a debutante would create a scandal, confronted them, looking Kit up and down without shame.

'Patsy, I'd like you to meet Miss Linton. Miss Linton, this is Lady Patricia Morley. Our hostess.'

'How d'ye do, Miss Linton. I don't think we've met before?'

Lady Patricia's shrewd brown eyes were assessing her, searching for flaws.

'No, I don't think we have. I've only recently arrived in England, from Australia.'

'Oh, a colonial,' Lady Patricia drawled. 'And an actress, I believe. Lady Bridlingham tells me you're a *friend* of the Prince of Wales?'

There was a bite to that question, the 'friend' implying that she was his mistress.

'I have met His Royal Highness,' Kit said smoothly, 'but I wouldn't dare to claim friendship.'

'Come off it, Patsy,' Henry said. 'Patsy's' nose twitched. She was angry at Henry for foisting an actress onto her nice party.

'Well then,' Lady Patricia said. 'Do enjoy yourself, won't you? Henry, I think Sarah and Bingo will be here later.' She walked off. Not quite the cold shoulder, but icy enough.

Henry fetched them drinks, then led her through the crowd to a pavilion where food was set out as a buffet. A small group of young people were in a corner, sipping champagne and laughing.

Cecil and Daphne were among them. She had to warn them. Didn't she? Oh, this was so complicated! She let her eyes wander over Cecil without recognition. He frowned.

'Henry, why don't you introduce me?' she said.

Henry performed the introductions while Daphne blinked at her in bewilderment. But she kept her mouth closed. After a few moments of chat, Henry hailed another friend and she managed to get Cecil and Daphne to herself.

'I say, Katherine, should you be here?' Cecil asked. His prominent eyes goggled, rather. 'Were you *invited*?'

The words were like a blow. She didn't belong, no matter what her birth was. As Lady Patricia had made clear, an actress had no pretensions to respectability. She could only do harm to poor Daphne and really, what was the point of her being here if there were no reporters? Although Lady Patricia would give a list of the guests to the society columns, she would probably leave Kit's name off.

She fought back unexpected tears. No sense giving them the satisfaction of seeing how it hurt.

Henry appeared at her side, glasses of champagne in hand. He gave her one while Cecil gawked at him.

'Ah, there you are! Hullo, Dassington. Dassington and I were at school together, Kit. Terrible humbug of a chap, aren't you, Cecilia?'

'Don't call me that! We're not at school now.'

She should probably tell Henry the truth. It was his life she'd been inserted into, after all. 'Cecil and Daphne are my cousins.' Kit surveyed them, surprised at how much calmer she was, now Henry was here. She had felt, for a moment, very isolated and unsure.

'Lucky for them.' Henry looked down his aristocratic nose at them, and Daphne gaped. She wasn't plain, exactly, but she was so pale – hair, eyes and skin – that she seemed to disappear inside her dress. The pale colours debs had to wear were hard on girls of Daphne's colouring. Poor thing.

'Carleton,' Cecil said with a forced smile. 'I would take it as a kindness to Daphne if you didn't bandy about that Katherine is our cousin.'

'You're an idiot, Cecilia. You should be proud to know Miss Linton.' This was a side of Henry she hadn't seen. Automatically arrogant. High and mighty. If he hadn't been acting in her defence she would have found it repellent.

'But Daphne –'

'Daphne's a very nice gel –' Daphne simpered '– but if she had a bit more of Miss Linton's poise she'd do much better. She'd do well to take Miss Linton as a model, not be ashamed of her.'

Kit blushed. That was possibly the nicest thing *anyone* had ever said about her.

'Come on, Kit,' Henry said. They walked away, Kit merely nodding goodbye. 'Gosh, he's a weed,' Henry added. 'Harry hated him.'

'Harry?'

'Prince Henry. We were all in the same year at Eton. He was Harry, I was Henry. He's off big-game hunting in Africa right now. Shocking blighter, that Cecilia. Harry and I were in the rugger team together. And cricket. Cecil just loathed sports. Well, a fellow can not like to play, but Cecil never even cheered on the school. Just sat there trying to look superior. Harry and I soon knocked that out of him.'

That was Empire talking. Arrogant and cocksure. She wanted to feel sorry for Cecil, but instead, to her shame, felt a quick surge of satisfaction that he'd had his comeuppance, even if it were years ago.

'Even so.' She took his arm. 'It wouldn't be kind to Daphne to spread the news of our connection.'

'Humbug. But if that's what you want.'

Henry's support buoyed her up so much that the rest of the afternoon was much easier. She didn't exactly feel she belonged, but she didn't *not* belong. She was in a curious position: Kit saw

Lady Patricia whispering to a couple of people while casting glances her way, and it was clear that her status – or lack of it – had quickly done the rounds of the party.

◆

There *was* an air of talking down to her. No 'colonial' could quite measure up, it seemed, let alone an actress. But on the whole, the event was much easier than she'd expected, except for Lady Bridlingham.

She appeared halfway through the afternoon, with Bingo and Sarah in tow. 'Oh, Lord!' Henry said. 'They've brought the dragon. M'mother's best friend, don't you know. Nothing I can do but turn her up sweet.'

Lady Bridlingham greeted Henry civilly enough, and then inspected Kit from head to toe, looking faintly disappointed when she found nothing to criticise. But that didn't stop her.

'I see you've abandoned your rouge for this occasion.' She raised supercilious eyebrows. Kit smiled sweetly at her.

'Oh, at my age I don't need rouge. Or hair dye.' That was a low blow, but if The Bridlingham's pale gold hair was natural, Kit would eat her very large hat.

Lady Bridlingham turned away sharply, muttering something about upstarts under her breath.

Bingo rolled his eyes, and Sarah immediately tucked her arm into Kit's in apology.

'Don't mind her,' Sarah said. 'Sometimes I think she cares more about Henry's prospects than about ours.'

'It's the countess,' Bingo said. 'She feels responsible because the countess is on the Continent. Feels she has to keep an eye on Henry for her.'

'M'mother's not one for town life,' Henry said, almost apologetically. 'She prefers Carleton.' The countess would be Henry's mother, then. As once before, Kit felt rather breathless at the company she was keeping. Which was silly. It wasn't like her own family weren't well bred. That knowledge didn't seem to help.

Sarah was so happy and kind, though, that she soon relaxed. Plus, the food and drink were divine.

And the house . . . she could get used to a house like that. Slipping in to use the bathroom, she'd been astonished at the *lushness* of it. Yes, the rooms were huge and echoing, but the gilt and the carpets and the voluminous drapes, and the modern artwork glowing from the walls! If you grew up here, you'd expect the very best, no matter what, no matter where you were.

It was different from Barrows, which had an air of aged, solid comfort. This place was newer, and far more luxurious. And Henry thought this was 'a little place' in the country. The sooner the two of them parted company, the better, or she'd be losing all sense of perspective.

But she arrived back at the Cats' Home far more in charity with him than she had been. His complete support of her had been unexpected and . . . heartwarming. When he said, 'Perhaps I could take you to lunch tomorrow?' she was happy to say, 'Tuesday would be better.'

'Jolly good!' He'd smiled at her, apparently genuinely pleased to make the arrangement.

At least one person valued her just as she was.

CHAPTER 11

It was a slow news week. Nothing much was happening, either in Britain or abroad – so the story about Kit and Lord Henry stayed in the news for several days.

The reporters at the stage door were a thorough nuisance. Even Sam was annoyed.

'I will arrange an exclusive interview for you, then it will stop,' Charlot announced before the performance. 'You're *une Australienne*, yes? There's an Australian journalist at the *Evening News*. I'll contact the editor. It will seem natural that you give the exclusive to them.'

Sure enough, the next day Kit was asked to come in early to meet the reporter. When she opened the door of her dressing room (carefully made up and ready for questions), she was startled. The Australian journalist was a woman – a very beautiful blonde, backed up by a dark-haired, strong-looking photographer, with a tripod over his shoulder. A woman reporter! Gosh.

'Come in,' she managed to say.

'Rebecca Yates,' the woman said, holding out a hand to be shaken. 'And my husband, Sandro Baker.'

'So you're like an actress!' Kit exclaimed. 'Keeping your own name.' She bit her lip – not everyone would appreciate being compared to an actress.

Rebecca smiled. 'That's right. My professional name.'

The photographer – Sandro – began setting up his tripod and grinned at both of them. 'The only one who calls her Mrs Baker is my mamma.'

Was that a trace of an Italian accent? Was Sandro an Italian name? He was certainly attractive in that dark, Italian way. What a smile.

Rebecca Yates. There had been a Rebecca Yates at school with her eldest sister. She had been –

'You're Amelia Yates' daughter!' Amelia Yates was a leading Australian proponent for women's rights. She had even stood for Parliament. What would it have been like, Kit wondered, to have had a mother who positively *encouraged* you to break the rules society set down for women? Perhaps she could ask Rebecca one day.

Rebecca laughed. 'Yes, that's me. And you're Sophia Scott's little sister.' Kit made a face and Mr Baker grinned.

'It's like an Italian village. All the Australians in London know each other's families!' he said.

'That's a class thing,' Rebecca said absently. 'It takes money to get to London.'

They sat in the visitors' chairs and Rebecca took a notebook out of her smart handbag. She was dressed in a navy suit, with an ivory silk shirtwaist which Kit immediately coveted. It was a very good style for a woman who wanted to look professional. She tucked that idea away and paid attention.

'You understand, normally I don't do, er, "society" stories. I'm a straight news reporter.' Rebecca smiled encouragingly. 'But my editor was very pleased to get an exclusive on this.'

She asked a standard series of questions: how Kit had come to London, how she got the part in the show, what her background was. Easy; those answers were automatic. She described her father as a vicar, rather than a dean, and asked Rebecca not to use her real name.

'Oh, naturally,' she said. 'Our secret.' Then Rebecca put the pencil down and leaned forward.

'Let's cut to the chase: were you dancing with the Prince of Wales or with Lord Henry?'

'Well, neither, really. We were all just dancing in a big group.' Rebecca went back to making notes.

'But you were with the prince's party, not with Lord Henry?'

Thank God for Prince George's *bonhomie*, she thought. If he hadn't invited Henry to join the party, she'd have no answer to that.

'Lord Henry was *with* the prince's party. We all were.'

'Had you met the prince before?'

'Once. At the Riviera Club. Miss Astaire introduced us – and *she* was the one who invited me the other night.'

'Ah.' Rebecca's face lit up with interest. 'So you're friends?'

'I hope so.' She *did* feel that Delly and she were friends; but she had a strong suspicion that everyone felt like that about Delly. It was part of her charm. 'She's certainly been very kind to me.'

'And *Mr* Astaire?'

'Oh, Fred's a chum.' That was easy. Who wouldn't like Fred?

'Now, Lord Henry . . . you've been seen in public with him several times now.'

'Yes. He's a friend.'

Rebecca sighed and exchanged glances with her husband, who was still fiddling around with his camera. 'I'm sorry, Kit, but I *have* to ask this. I'm on orders. "Just friends?"'

Kit set her mouth. It wasn't Rebecca's fault. She let out a long breath. 'I can assure you that Lord Henry and I are *only* friends.'

'And likely to remain so?'

'I like to stay on good terms with all my friends.'

'Lord Henry's friends tell me that he's far more serious about this relationship than others he's been involved in.'

Because the Palace told him to be. 'I wouldn't know about that. But I'm concentrating for the foreseeable future on my career. I'm not interested in becoming *seriously* involved with anyone – prince, lord or pauper!'

'That's a good quote,' Rebecca said with satisfaction. 'We'll just get some shots and be on our way. Sandro?'

'No. The light is terrible in here. Can we go on the stage?'

◆

On stage, Sandro had her stand in the middle of the dressing. The set was a forest scene, ready for a 'picnic' in the first act. He got the stage manager to bring up the lights and the curtain, took a couple of close-ups, and then went up to the dress circle to get some longer shots.

'This is probably for his own work,' Rebecca said from the wings. 'He has a one-man show opening next month. You should come.'

'Just move forward one step,' Sandro shouted from above. She did so. 'Now, look up at me and make your face blank.'

It was like working with a director. She wondered what image would come out of this, but she made her face blank.

She'd never done that for a photo before. Had always smiled. She rather liked this.

While Sandro packed up and came down, Rebecca shook her hand and gave her a card. 'If you ever need a friendly reporter,' she said, and then hesitated. 'Or just a friend. I'm happy to chat off-the-record, too. It's nice to talk to another Australian woman.'

Was it silly to feel a little teary? She didn't care. Rebecca felt like ... not like home, but like the promise of a home that might exist, someday. Another Australian who wasn't following the path prescribed for women of their class. Who was making her own way in the world, and successfully, and who hadn't had to give up love to do it. Pressing her hand, Kit nodded. 'I would very much like to catch up again soon.'

'Call me,' Rebecca said. 'The paper will always take a message if I'm not there.'

'*Cara mia*, we have to be at the German embassy in fifteen minutes!'

'Darn it!' Rebecca waved as she ran off after Sandro. '*Ciao!*'

◆

A letter from her aunt was waiting for her when she got home.

My dear, we're very grateful to you for safeguarding Daphne's reputation as you have, but of course this imbroglio with the Prince and Lord Henry does, unfortunately, mean we can't invite you to Barrows when we have company. Not now that your status as an actress is so well known.

Perhaps during the winter, when we are free of company . . .

The front door of Barrows slammed shut in her face. Her hands clenched into fists.

How *charming* of her aunt. How *well-mannered* to write to her about it.

Anger and a kind of grief filled her. She had loved Barrows; had found something large and good and almost noble there.

And for what? So the reputation of a prince could be safeguarded?

'Pshaw!' she said aloud, and then laughed at the ridiculous sound. She'd have to do without Barrows, that was all. It had never been hers anyway, not really.

CHAPTER 12

Going to Novello's flat sounded like a bad idea to Zeke. He knew the crowd there would be avid for details of Kit's royal adventure and its lordly aftermath. But they had to be faced sometime and, really, underneath it all they were kind. He hoped.

Kit shone in a new frock of dark green velvet. The kind of thing she couldn't wear out with her lordling. Far too daring for a society party. And she moved like a dancer, willowy and lithe. How could anyone not see that?

'Do Lord Henry's friends know you're an actress?' he asked as they went up in the shuddering old lift.

'Oh, yes.' She hesitated, as though embarrassed. 'That was the whole point, for people to know.' A quick glance at him. Boy, she was unsure about all this. He patted her shoulder. He hoped she didn't get caught up in all that aristocratic nonsense. Lot of bunkum. But when they'd left Barrows, she'd seemed reluctant to go. As though part of her wanted that life. 'His mother's friends are not happy about it, so I'm trying not to embarrass him any further. It's not his fault this whole thing happened.'

'So you're playing a part?'

She turned to him eagerly. 'It *does* feel like that, Zeke. But sometimes, I feel like I've turned into one of my sisters!' A half laugh. He bit back a wry comment. She didn't need aggravation from him.

The lift clanked to a halt and they went out to join the party.

Novello's flat was an odd shape. You funnelled through a longish hall to another hall and then out into the big room – a combination of music room, lounge and rounded patio, beyond which the advertising lights of the theatre shone in. It was a large, congenial space, with lots of lounges and chairs and a bar in the corner behind which, at the moment, Noël Coward was dispensing cocktails.

Zeke went over to deposit their offering of Gordon's gin and a bottle of tonic.

'Ah, the classics!' Noël said. 'Never go out of style. How's our little ingenue?' They both glanced over to where Kit was being besieged by questioners.

'Be kind, Noël. She's had a rough time with this.'

'Oooh, I didn't know the prince went in for *rough*!' he said archly, but he went over with a glass of white wine for Kit and slung his arm around her shoulders, waving the questioners off with his other hand. 'Away, away, children! I shall interrogate her myself and bring you all the scandal.'

The flappers and chorus boys drifted off, but Gertie Lawrence stayed.

'Are you all right, dearie?'

'I am now,' Kit said, taking the wine. 'Thanks, Noël.'

'But my dear, I meant it. I need *all* the scandal!'

'There's no scandal. Except that the prince keeps odd company, I suppose, if you think I'm odd, and evidently the Palace thinks so.'

'Oh-hoh! The Palace! Tell all!'

'Nothing to tell. Wrong place, wrong time. I was there with the Astaires.'

'Who will be here any minute, so I can interrogate them as to the verash-verak-damn it, truthfulness of your statement!'

Noël, Zeke realised with some amusement, was just a little bit drunk already.

'How's the play going?' Noël was in the final stages of writing a new revue – *London Calling*, which would be produced by Charlot later in the year.

'Do. Not. Ask. Which is why I'm off to France as soon as it's finished! I need *stimulation*, my dears! And some sun.'

'We'll miss you, Noël.'

'Darling, of course you will!'

Off he floated, tucking Gertie under his arm despite her protest that she needed to 'get back to the baby'. Tallulah slid in to take his place.

'Darling,' she said to Kit, while absent-mindedly rubbing her hand up and down Zeke's arm. 'I *do* so want to ravish a prince. Can you introduce me?'

Kit laughed. 'Any prince?'

'Any prince at all, darling!'

'Well, here's my advice.' She leaned close, the two cropped heads almost touching. Zeke watched with deep amusement.

Tallulah unbalanced most people, but not his Kit. 'Find out where Prince George is going to be, and then just smile at him.'

'That's all?'

Kit straightened up and grinned. 'That's all. George is one of your persuasion, Tallulah – he has *wide* tastes, and doesn't mind indulging them.'

Noël, passing by, stopped to say, 'I can vouch for that. *Very* wide tastes, and lovely manners. He sent me flowers the next day.'

They laughed; somehow, Zeke wasn't surprised. George had had an equivocal air about him when they'd met at the Riviera.

'Ooh, how delicious!' Tallulah shivered all over. 'What a treat. Thank you *so* much, Kitty-kat.'

The crowd of sensation-seekers came back, now Noël was gone, and bombarded them both with questions. What they thought *he'd* know Zeke couldn't figure out.

'Is he in love with you? The prince, I mean.'

'Is Lord Henry as dreamy as he looks?'

'Did you sleep with him?'

Kit just stood there, shaking her head, and finally held up one hand.

'Nobody slept with anyone!' she said firmly. 'It was all a misunderstanding.'

'That's right, honey. That's a good story and you stick to it.' Adele Astaire's voice came from behind them, and they all whirled around to look at her. She stood in the doorway, one hand on her hip, the other with a shawl draped over it. A classic entrance, claiming all eyes and the attention of the whole room. He had to give her credit, she was a pro.

'Delly!' Kit said with pleasure.

As usual, Fred was just behind Adele. Poor man's whole life was being just behind his sister. He didn't look like it bothered him, though. He nodded at Zeke and they went over to the bar together.

'Sorry we let Kit in for all that bother,' Fred said. 'Came out of nowhere. You Brits really do like a royal scandal.'

'I'm Canadian,' Zeke reminded him. 'Gin and tonic?'

'You don't have a beer back there, do you?'

There was some beer, and he got the bottles out, flipping the caps off with a coin. They made a satisfying pop. He and Fred clinked bottles and took a long swig. Beer was a strictly occasional treat; if he kept to one, he reckoned he'd be safe. But no more than that; and no more than once a week.

'Can't get used to you boys over here drinking it warm.' Fred made a face, but took another swallow.

'Hey, I'm with you. But these blokes say you can't taste it when it's cold.'

'Huh.' They watched the gaiety around them for a while: Bobbie was on the piano playing a tango and there was a lot of dancing going on, some of it close to obscene. Kit was standing with Adele, the two of them laughing at something Noël had said.

'Quite a scene. You don't seem to join in much, though.' Fred tipped an enquiring glance at him.

'Not to my taste.'

'Nor mine.' Pausing, Fred tapped his foot to the beat. 'Music's fine, though. And it's nice for Delly to have a friend like Kit. Not many have the . . . confidence to be friends with her. It's usually hangers-on or leeches.'

'Not Kit. She's true blue.'

'Take care of her, then. These girls . . . they need a bit of cosseting. Not when they're working, of course. But there are too many wolves out there.'

That was as clear a message as he'd ever heard. Who was the wolf Fred was warning him about? The prince? Surely not. Maybe this Lord Henry . . .

'The prince's set . . . I wouldn't like Delly to be going around with them if I weren't there.' Fred shrugged as if settling his shoulders, and went off to the piano. 'Play something we can sing!' he demanded, and Bobbie laughed and complied, swinging into 'If You Were the Only Girl in the World'. Everyone sang along.

> *Sometimes when I feel bad*
> *and things look blue*
> *I wish I had a pal . . . say one like you.*

He couldn't help but look at Kit. Nope. No siree. That was a bad idea. Fred's warning, though; he'd have to keep an eye on her. There was no way he could squeeze himself into these outings with the lord, but . . . he'd just make sure she was all right. She was too precious to let some jumped-up aristocrat spoil her.

CHAPTER 13

'I 'm sick of this place,' Kit said. She threw her jacket over the single chair, where Perry's navy woollen coat already hung.

'Me too,' Perry agreed.

Down the hall, shrieking laughter bounced from room to room, along with the clink of glasses. Kit made a face, and tugged off her shoes, sitting on the side of her bed. She didn't even need to stretch out her arm to be able to touch Perry's bed. The Cats' Home wasn't known for being spacious – just cheap.

She'd pushed down the yearning for better digs after visiting Barrows, but spending time with Henry was reminding her anew of the better things in life. And she couldn't invite him or his friends back here. The mind boggled at the thought of them in the parlour, being inspected by all the girls.

Kit thought with longing of her old room in Sydney, with its high ceilings, solid brick walls and views of the ever-changing

Harbour. The smell of the sea. The whisper of wind in the gum tree outside her window.

The corridor party barged into the room next door and half a dozen voices started singing 'The Whichness of the Whatness'. Most of them off-key. Wincing, Kit shrugged at Perry. 'Even the single rooms have walls made out of cardboard. No point in moving into one. Let's get out altogether. Let's get a flat together.'

Away from the smell of kippers and cabbage. Somewhere quieter. Somewhere *bigger*. There were times she felt like she was suffocating in this tiny room. She could afford it, surely? They were getting second billing now, had a regular salary, and the play showed no signs of losing its popularity. Houses were full for every performance.

'Oh, *yes*,' Perry said. 'Let's.'

◆

One thing about working in the theatre – you had all day to do things most people needed to take time off work for.

They went flat hunting, copies of *The Stage* and *Daily Mail* tucked under their arms.

The list wasn't long – at least, not for them.

'I'm not living in bloody Hammersmith or Shepherd's Bush,' Perry declared.

New to London as she was, even Kit knew how far away those suburbs were from the West End.

'There's one in Russell Square,' she said. 'And another in Haymarket.'

'Don't want to be taken for tarts, dearie.' Perry pulled her brown felt hat down more firmly across her brow, and gave its dark green feather a flip. 'Actresses already have a bad reputation.' She grinned, and Kit grinned back. There wasn't anything they could do about that – and besides, that reputation was mostly deserved.

The Russell Square 'flat' was a room with a toilet attached, share bathroom. A bedsit, more like. Kit could smell mould, and the ceiling showed evidence of past floods. These old buildings had bad roofs, most of the time.

The rest of the day was just as frustrating, but at the theatre the assistant stage manager said, 'How much can you afford? My chum is going on a world tour, performing on the *Arcadian* for six months. He's looking for a sublet. But it's a two bedroom, up in the Sicilian Avenue mansion block, and it won't be available for a few weeks.'

That meant nothing to Kit, but Marguerite, who was listening, made an O with her mouth. 'Pricey!'

'Maybe if you let him use the second bedroom to store his gear, he'd give you a break on the rent.'

'Wonderful!' Kit said. As they waited in the wings to go on, Zeke raised an eyebrow at her. 'Perry and I are getting out of the Cats' Home. Can't stand it anymore.'

'Are you sure you can afford it?' She knew Zeke was careful with money – much more careful than she was. It was as though he didn't believe in their success. He was boarding at Noël Coward's family lodging house in Ebury Street, but in an attic room, no less, as though he were one of the chorus. And he wore his one good grey suit everywhere.

'Guess we'll find out!' Kit flicked him a grin and a wink as their cue came, and he smiled back, as he always did, shaking his head a little.

She peeped up at him from under her lashes, flirting a little. It wasn't that she was *seriously* thinking of romancing him. But there was a part of her, which she preferred not to think about, that was piqued by his apparent lack of interest.

His hand on her back pulled her closer, and his breathing picked up a little. A spurt of satisfaction hit her, and made her ashamed at the same time. She shouldn't tease him. Not when she didn't, couldn't . . . wouldn't.

But her body knew what it wanted. All through the dance, through the long sequence of moves which they performed so perfectly, through the lovemaking so delicately sketched out in the choreography, her body yearned towards his as a flower towards the sun, and he grew stronger, more masculine, more virile, as he inevitably reacted.

The audience went crazy afterwards and they had to do a bit of 'business', pretending to be breathless, to allow themselves time to settle.

Immediately afterwards, in the play, Zeke's first line to her was, 'You see how we dance together. Why don't you love me?' and hers was, 'Maybe I do.'

It was best to play these kinds of scenes by looking just to the side of the person's nose, so there was no chance of laughing. But she couldn't help taking a quick peep; he was gazing at her as ardently as the young fool he was playing would have, until they were interrupted by Marguerite and Basil making their star entrance.

'Well, what have we here?' Basil said, lifting his eyebrows.

Kit wondered the same thing all through the performance. She'd had waves of thinking she was attracted to Zeke. And then the wave would recede, buried under the memory of that awkward weekend at Barrows. But each wave seemed to get stronger.

◆

Sicilian Avenue. A grand name – and, for once, the building lived up to it.

A double mansion block set on either side of an open arcade of shops, it was fabulously ornate, with Portland stone edging red brick, and fewer than twenty years old. No decrepit roofs here! There were even turrets with round glassed sunrooms all down the side, and Ionic marble columns supporting the arcade sign, which was picked out in gold.

It looked far too expensive for them. Kit felt a little spurt of annoyed disappointment; she recognised it as the expectations of her mother's daughter being thwarted, and laughed at herself.

If the building had had a lift she would have turned around and left right then, knowing it was out of their price range, but the stairs were reassuringly ordinary – although made of a lovely mahogany – and the flat was on the second floor at the back; since the place was at the V-shaped junction of two roads, it turned out that 'the back' was also the front, on a different street.

As the door opened to Kit's knock, light flooded out. The living room faced south-east, and pale English sunlight streamed in. A good omen?

The assistant stage manager's 'chum' turned out to be a well-known tenor from the music-hall circuit, Peter Simms, taking the cruise 'for my health, don't you know?'

Kit wasn't quite sure she did know, since he looked as hale as any man who'd clearly been up drinking late the night before, but the flat was *charming*. Pale green chintz and modern furniture, big casement windows, some of them with stained glass, and, amazingly, one of the round sunrooms, which jutted out from the living room like a diving bell, with window seats all around. From it, you could see right down Southampton Row to Holborn, with the bright red double-deckers moving easily through the light Sunday traffic.

Kit fell in love with it at first sight. Perry was more interested in the kitchen, as modern as possible with a gas stove and closed 'built-in' cupboards. The bathroom was black and white, with a big claw-foot tub. There was only one bed in the main bedroom, Simms said, indicating a closed door, but that was all right. She'd shared a bed with her sister growing up, and it had been fine. Perry didn't snore, at least.

'We were four in a bed in our house,' Perry laughed. 'Just two is luxury.'

With some trepidation, Kit asked how much the sublet would be.

Simms took in their clothes with a comprehensive and far too well-informed glance.

'Well, dearies, if you agree to lock up the second bedroom with all the knick-knacks, you can have it for six pounds a week.'

That was a lot for what was effectively a one-bedroom flat, and they'd have to start buying all their own food. She doubted they could do it as cheaply as Mrs French. But they could afford it – at least, Perry would be stretched, but it was a reasonable amount for Kit to pay, on her fifteen pounds a week. It would be worth it for her to put in a bit more, to enable Perry to live with her. She really didn't want to live alone in London.

And besides – Sicilian Avenue was a walk to *all* the theatres, being just up from Shaftesbury Avenue. They would save on taxis.

'You can have it in three weeks,' Simms said. 'I sail on the Friday, so come on the Thursday and I'll have the keys for you.'

'Do we need to sign a lease?' Kit asked.

The chum waved his hand. 'Oh, no. Barry tells me you're more than trustworthy. He'll keep an eye on things for me.'

As though summoned by his name, Barry poked his head out of the bedroom, looking bleary-eyed.

'God, Kit, did you have to come *this* early?' he complained, and disappeared again.

Well, that explained that.

'A rather nasty policeman has me in his sights,' Simms explained. 'He's determined to prove that I'm an invert and slap me in prison. A little excursion to the Mediterranean for a while seemed like a good idea.'

'Don't worry,' Perry said immediately. 'You can use me as a shield, if you'd like. If he comes sniffing around here, I'll give him what for.'

'*Darling*,' Simms said, giving her a peck on the cheek. 'How divine. For that, I'll leave out the good china for you.'

◆

'It's a lot of money,' Zeke said as they limbered up on Tuesday morning.

'I can afford it.'

He considered that as he did a few shuffle steps across the barely lit stage. It was set up for the big finalé scene.

The director, W. Courtney Rowden, was making a film called *Britain Dances*. He had picked the highlights from a number of stage musicals to showcase British dancing talent – or, at least, the talent on Britain's stages, so quite a few American, Canadian and Australian actors as well. Including them! A corking thing, to be in his first film.

Was his own fear of poverty overblown? Kit had had an easy life. Even if she had grown up in a vicarage, as she said, she had the likes of Barrows behind her. He was one hundred per cent sure that if she turned up there and said, 'I'd like to live with you for a while,' they'd take her in with open arms.

Even apart from Barrows, she, unlike him, had a home to go back to. And no one there waiting for that monthly cable of rent money. His mother still taught singing, and having moved her to Victoria when he first started in the theatre, there were more potential pupils, but it was hard work for little pay, trying to make talentless debutantes sound good enough for 'solos' at musical evenings. Being looked down on as though she were gutter-bred. And being blamed when they inevitably hit a flat note.

Too many nights of his childhood, she had gone hungry so that he could eat. He would liberate her from that life if it was the last thing he did.

'From the top, ladies and gentlemen,' Rowden called.

Zeke shook out his legs, held his hand out to Kit, and prepared to go through the dance routine for the eleventh time. He'd keep his digs at Coward's and stash his money away. Who knew how long it would last?

At least they were getting paid extra for this film work. And it would give his mother a real thrill to see him on the screen.

CHAPTER 14

They got to the door of a suite at the Strand Hotel and Kit baulked.

'I can't, Henry.' She stopped him, a hand on his arm. 'It's been quite a week. I just can't face a party.' That was true. But also, it never seemed quite right to drink on a Sunday, even in a private suite. Her vicarage upbringing was sometimes quite inconvenient.

He'd had a couple of drinks in the bar while he was waiting for her, and he smiled good-naturedly. 'Let's walk down by the river, then.'

They went down to the Embankment via Savoy Street, past the BBC studios where the lights still blazed though it was past signing-off time.

It was a pleasant night; chilly enough for her wrap to be useful rather than decorative, but clear and mild. The river held its night-time calm. Barges tied up on the southern side, a lone dinghy heading across the smooth, shining surface towards the Southwark steps. The streetlamps on Waterloo Bridge like a string of pearls. Kit sighed. The Thames, although it was often smelly and dirty, at least reminded her of the existence of sea and ships.

'Why the sigh?'

'I miss Sydney Harbour. A river is all very well, but when you've been brought up by an ocean . . .'

'I'm thinking of taking a cruise,' he said. 'Italy, Greece, maybe Egypt. I never did get to do the Tour.'

'The War.'

He nodded. They walked on together, their steps matching naturally now that they were used to one another. The thought of him going away brought a pang . . . she was accustomed to having him around already.

'So many things were interrupted,' she added.

'My eldest brother, Mark. Died on the Somme. The next one, Stewart, got winged at Ypres. By the time I was old enough, it was over.'

She couldn't tell if he was glad or sorry.

'Me too. My sisters were all in the VAD, but Mother said I couldn't join until I was sixteen, and by then . . .' The Voluntary Aid Detachment had bolstered the nursing services for the military; vital work, and they'd given training to the many girls who'd joined up, but she'd been too young. How she'd envied her sisters, going off to the repat hospitals every day!

'The older chaps,' he burst out, 'they look down on one. As though one's still a child.'

She'd seen that happen. Not a mean attitude. More

indulgent, as if no one, even a man of forty or fifty, was really an adult if he hadn't fought.

'Yes,' she said. 'I've noticed that.'

He paused in the shadow of Cleopatra's Needle, and held her hands, his face vulnerable in the light reflected from the river. 'Do you think they're right? Do you have to have fought to be . . . worth anything?'

'I suppose,' she said slowly, 'it depends on what you do with your life from now on.'

He stepped back and tucked her arm into his, walking back the way they had come. 'Oh, that sounds so *worthy*! I'm anything but, my dear!'

But there was a harsh note to his voice, and she suspected that he was unhappy with who he saw in the mirror.

'Enough introspection!' he declared. 'Let's go back to the party and have a drink!'

She went with him without protest, because she feared that any protest would be a slap in the face to him, and he didn't need that right now.

She'd seen a side of him she hadn't expected, and it gave her pause. A younger, unvalued son. No proper job. No limits on spending or indulgence. No real guidance, if his father and his brothers were off at war, growing up in the horrid boarding school atmosphere of Eton. It was a wonder he'd come out of it as well as he had.

Poor Henry. For the first time, she looked at him carefully, to see the person instead of the title, instead of the Prince of Wales' friend. She wasn't sure what she saw, but it was more complicated than she had realised. In those moments of honesty, he had seemed more attractive; more vulnerable and less facile.

He could do with a friend, she thought. Perhaps he and Zeke . . . No. She couldn't quite imagine that happening.

◆

Instead of returning to the Strand Hotel – 'They'll have moved on by now,' Henry said – he hailed a cab and told the driver to go to St James' Palace.

'PW said to drop in if I chose.'

For an odd moment her mind went blank, but then she remembered that PW was what his friends called the Prince of Wales. Who lived in St James' Palace.

A palace.

As had often happened lately, a sense of unreality overtook her. She seemed to float beside herself in the cab, weirdly disconnected. What was she *doing* here?

Images of her bedroom at home came to her: the blue Australian sky outside the window, the heady scent of saltwater floating up past the masts in Darling Harbour, a haze of jacaranda blossoms floating down to the garden . . .

. . . outside the cab window, the streets were grey and shining as it began to drizzle. The red lights of the bus ahead of them gleamed brightly; the cab smelled of leather and Henry's cologne, lightly musk. And the path to St James' took them past her theatre, and there was her name, up in lights . . .

Was it possible to belong wholeheartedly to two places? To have two homes? Henry was exactly the wrong person to ask. He was, like all these English aristocrats, supremely confident of his place in the world, even as a third son, even with all the vulnerability he'd revealed to her that night. He knew where home was. Carleton Towers, which he spoke of rarely but with great affection.

Perhaps that kind of security only came with family, and generations upon generations of shared history, which no British Australian could have, even in Australia. It must be the same for Canadians. She'd have to ask Zeke.

She deliberately turned her thoughts away from Barrows, now so inaccessible. It had promised that kind of security; had called out to something in her blood and bones. Was there such a thing as race memory? No time to think about that now.

The cab drew up to the gates of the palace, and Henry spoke through the window with the guard, who waved them through.

The way in was under a huge arch in a red-brick tower which looked more like a fortress than somewhere someone – even a prince – would live. The royal coat of arms hung at the top of the arch, proclaiming majesty.

But the courtyard within was more human-sized. If not homely, then not so threatening.

'We're going to York House,' Henry said to the driver. 'Go through that gate there.'

'Right you are, sir.'

York House. The name conjured up Shakespeare: Richard III had been a York king. She shook herself. This distracted mood had to go or she'd make a complete fool of herself.

A servant in livery came out with a big umbrella to shelter them as they moved from the cab to the door. Livery! Good Lord.

She vaguely knew that St James' had been built by Henry VIII. But inside, away from all that exposed Tudor brick, it seemed surprisingly modern. Victorian rather than Tudor, at least.

The prince's apartments were upstairs, apparently. They followed the footman down a long corridor where gilded chairs lined the walls like a guard of honour, and up some heavily carpeted stairs to a set of double doors, where the footman knocked discreetly and then opened for them to go through.

She'd once been told, 'Good servants don't knock,' but clearly the prince's did. She wondered what activities the prince wanted to keep private from his servants.

Once through the door, that was obvious. Music poured over them, and the haze of smoke smelt foreign. Turkish? Or something else?

'Henry!' A shout went up as they entered.

She'd expected opulence, but this was just like any other bachelor's flat in London. A lot like David and Bobbie's place, in fact, although bigger. And it was crowded. Half a dozen couples were lounging around on overstuffed sofas while two other pairs were dancing – the Charleston! – to a gramophone.

She didn't know anyone here except the prince. These were older people than the set Henry hung around with – early thirties or late twenties, like the prince. The women looked her over with experienced eyes, the men openly inspected her.

Oh, she was wrong! There was Prince George, in a corner whispering to a young woman who giggled incessantly and who had tied her garter below her knee. George wiggled his fingers at her but soon returned to his companion, walking those same fingers up the girl's knee. That left her feeling faintly soiled.

'Get them drinks, Bradley,' the prince said to a manservant – not in livery, this one, but in the swallow-tailed coat and white tie common to footmen in aristocratic houses.

She was presented with some kind of reddish cocktail.

'A Hanky-Panky, Miss Linton!' the prince said, waiting for her to drink. Meanwhile, Henry downed his and got a refill.

It smelt of gin and orange juice. Oh dear. She couldn't refuse, could she? A short sip seemed to satisfy him, as he turned away and clapped Henry on the shoulder.

'Glad you could make it, old man.'

The English really were silly. Calling Henry an 'old man'!

'Come and dance, Kit,' Henry said.

Thankful, she disposed of her drink on a side table, careful to put it on a doily; God only knew how much this exquisite antique furniture was worth. The sofas were modern, but the rest was an eclectic mix of styles and ages that could best be described as 'historic'. Every piece was a treasure.

Which didn't seem to worry anyone else; why should it? They had all been brought up in this kind of atmosphere.

Blast it. She would *not* feel inferior. These people couldn't even dance properly!

She threw herself into the music while the rain drummed on the lead-paned windows, seeming to keep time. Henry grinned at her and grabbed another drink, trying to sip it as he moved, dripping it onto the priceless Persian rug.

No matter. Not her problem. She threw her hands up and kicked higher.

'That's the spirit!' the prince said. He relaxed on the nearest sofa, watching them with a mixture of admiration and amusement, as though nothing could be serious for long. She thought that was an act; he might not be a truly serious man at heart, but he wasn't the dilettante he played.

He raised his eyebrows at her and she realised she'd been staring too long.

The music wound down and someone changed the record to a slow waltz. Henry pulled her into his arms; surprisingly, it helped her feel safe. But why wouldn't she feel safe here? She was at the heart of Empire – could anywhere be *more* protected?

Yet Henry's arms felt far safer than being under the prince's assessing gaze. She let her head drop onto his shoulder. He let out a satisfied breath and moved her closer. It *was* romantic. Dancing to the sound of the rain, in a palace, in the dead of night . . .

At the end of the record, the footman presented her with another cocktail and she drank it, because she was thirsty. And how could she ask for water? She would seem so gauche.

Prince George and the girl in the corner had disappeared through one of the doors on the end wall. She refused to think of where they might have gone. That was their business.

It was strange that it seemed somehow more tawdry than Tallulah's frank propositioning. Two of the other couples were entwined on sofas. The prince, oddly, was intently reading a letter, looking wistful.

'Missing his American light o' love,' Henry whispered in her ear. 'He's potty about her. Mind you, if she weren't unavailable, he'd never have given her a second look. He doesn't want to be trapped. Not our PW.'

The prince stuck his letter in a jacket pocket, stood up, and held out his hand. 'My dance, I think, Miss Linton.'

'Kit, please, sir.'

'Kit it is!' he said gaily, and they danced, and danced again before he handed her back to Henry and went into a huddle with a couple of new arrivals – stern young men with rather old-fashioned moustaches. She didn't try to eavesdrop, but the conversation seemed to be about Europe. Someone mentioned Mussolini, whom she was vaguely aware was in government in Italy.

'A strong hand is what's needed,' the prince said, and the other two agreed.

Foreign policy? Did the royal family get involved in that? Perhaps they did, behind the scenes. After all, they were related to just about all the royal houses of Europe, thanks to all those children Queen Victoria had had.

'Let's foxtrot!' Henry said.

One thing she had to say about the Prince of Wales – he knew some interesting people. As the night went on, she was introduced to a mountain climber, a jazz singer from France who belted out a couple of tunes and then fell asleep, she suspected under the influence of morphia, an Italian count who was a racing car driver, and an explorer who'd just come back from South America.

All of them seemed to drink a great deal, but they were clever and interesting in an entirely different way to the theatre folk she usually associated with – and *far* more interesting than Bingo and his ilk. These were people who'd *done* things.

There didn't seem to be much overlap between Henry's friends and the prince's; Henry himself was the only link, due to his long friendship with Prince Harry.

She rather liked being an interesting person in a group of interesting people; that was how the prince treated her, and it was intoxicating. She was more, here, than an adornment on Henry's arm. She was a performer; not aristocratic, but valuable nonetheless.

As she was driving home in a cab with Henry, who was a little the worse for cocktails, she wondered if she was very shallow, to take her value from the opinions of others. It was a perennial problem for the performer: what was an actress worth if no one found her interesting enough to watch?

The thought troubled her, but it was late, and she was tired, so she leaned her head back on the seat and watched the lights of London go past.

CHAPTER 15

Kit's travelling trunk fitted into the cab, but only just. Zeke shouldered it in and stood back, panting. What did she have in there? Bricks?

'You're a trouper.' Kit patted him on the back. 'I'm so grateful.' She peeped at him, a laugh in her eyes. 'I'm afraid the flat is two floors up at the other end. But Henry said he'd come over and help.'

'Oh-ho! So I finally get to meet the mysterious Lord Henry.'

The girls from the Cats' Home gathered at the front door and waved goodbye, Mabel and Val in front. He'd got to know them all through the apparently hilarious process of getting Kit's trunk downstairs. Perry had already gone ahead to open up, her own belongings not needing a man's strength to carry.

Kit waved vigorously. Mabel remarked, as she turned away, 'She'll be back when the run finishes.' He devoutly hoped she wasn't right, but this business was hardly secure. Well, if she needed help in the future, he could dip into his own savings, which were becoming substantial. Almost enough to buy his mother the little London house that would keep her safe and sound in her old age. Soon. He smiled at the thought, and Kit smiled back at him as she climbed into the cab.

There was just room for the two of them and Kit's smaller suitcase, but only if she sat in his lap. An odd sensation. He concentrated on the scenery outside and tried to ignore her perfume; some pleasant rose thing. *Think about bloody Henry*, he told himself.

'How's the lordling, then?'

'Don't be like that. He's harmless, really.'

He twisted his mouth in wry acknowledgement. He had no right to dislike this lord. None at all. But he knew he would.

◆

The building was very posh. Very 'mansion block'. But the stairs were no wider than in the Cats' Home, so he was relieved, if not glad, when a cab pulled up and a nattily tailored, broad-shouldered young man got out and pulled his gloves off.

'Henry Carleton,' he said. 'Call me Henry.'

'Zeke Gardiner.' They shook hands. Damn him, he had a good grip. He'd half expected a wet-fish handshake; it would have been reassuring. 'Let's get this up, shall we?'

They made short work of it, between them.

'Like first day of term at Eton,' Henry said light-heartedly. 'Takes me right back.'

Eton. Zeke controlled his impulse to raise his eyes to heaven.

The door of the flat was standing open, Perry's voice coming from inside.

'Don't you talk to me about immorality! Hounding my poor snookums out of the country on a baseless charge, *that*'s immoral! How dare you! I've got a good mind to write to the papers.'

Kit leapt up the stairs in front of them and popped her head around the door.

'Perry? What's the matter?'

'Oh, Kit!'

Henry slid the end of the trunk down at the door and they stood it up and rested on it, side by side, watching what appeared to be a melodrama play out in the drawing room of the flat. A dapper young man stood next to Perry, confronting a stolid, middle-aged man with a bulldog face. With long experience, Zeke recognised the brown boots of a plain-clothes policeman.

'This, this *person* is the one who's been hounding Peter! And he has the *gall* to come today, of all days, to accuse him again!'

'Oh, that's terrible!' Kit was in full acting swing. 'How could he?' She turned on the policeman. 'Haven't you caused *enough* trouble?'

At first phlegmatic, he seemed to become unbalanced with Kit's entry into the fray.

'Now, you young ladies probably don't know what my suspicions of this young man even *mean* –'

'Don't you give me that! We work in the theatre. We're surrounded by the nancy boys every day. Don't you think I'd know if my own dear snookums was one?' Perry gave him a glassy-eyed stare, which Zeke had last seen on Susan Maxwell's face when she was on stage as the Duchess. What a mimic that girl was!

'Now, Perry, dear, don't get upset,' Peter said.

'You're going *away* and it's all because of this horr-horrible man!' Perry burst into tears. Kit bustled into consoling her, glaring at the policeman over her shoulder.

'You really do have the wrong end of the stick,' she said. 'Men in the theatre *have* to look a . . . a certain way. But that doesn't mean they have to *act* like it!'

For the first time, uncertainty crossed the policeman's face.

'Well, if I've been mistaken –' He didn't look convinced.

'Oh, you *have*!' wailed Perry.

Henry gave Zeke a small 'pay attention' slap on the arm, and walked into the room.

'Lord Henry Carleton,' he proclaimed. 'And you are?' He looked down his nose at the policeman, who seemed bemused. Zeke bit his lip to stop from laughing.

'Detective Sergeant Vance, sir.'

A 'sir'. The first sign of respect. Bloody English class system. It made him sick.

'I do rather think you've made a mistake, officer.' Vance blinked at 'officer', but didn't object. Worried, he glanced at the floor, working his hat in his hands.

'All right, then, milord. If you say so.'

'What about me?' Perry demanded. 'Why won't you take *my* word for it?'

'Well, you're an actress, aren't you?' Vance exclaimed, pushed into it. 'No better than you ought to be, any of you.'

At that, Zeke and Henry both stepped forward. 'I don't think you should speak about Miss Linton and Miss Beck that way,' Zeke said quietly.

Confronted with two pairs of hefty shoulders, *and* a lord, Vance backed down. He sniffed and made his way to the door.

'If I've made a mistake, I apologise. But . . .' He fixed Peter with a steely gaze. 'Don't give me any more reason to suspect you, lad.'

He clamped his regulation bowler on his head and stomped down the stairs.

They all looked at each other, biting back grins. Peter slipped to the door and closed it, then leaned back against it and said, 'Oh, my dears! You were *magnificent!*' One by one, they collapsed on the sofa and occasional chairs, helpless with laughter.

'His face when Henry said his name!' Kit gasped.

'Gold! Pure gold!' Peter positively cackled with glee. 'If you knew –' He sprang up, still laughing, to shake Henry's hand. 'It was perfect!'

'I think this calls for a drink!' Henry said.

'You're so right.' Peter pulled out gin and tonic but only he and Henry took the gin. Zeke frowned a little at that. It was only eleven in the morning. Peter had no doubt had a shock, the police arriving at his door, but Henry . . . he knocked it back as though drinking in the morning were perfectly normal.

He grinned at Zeke. 'Hair of the dog.'

Huh. He didn't look hungover – just a little puffy around the eyes. But he was young, yet, only their own age. Zeke had a quick image of him in thirty years, knocking back another 'hair of the dog', stout, red-nosed and baggy-eyed, unsteady on his pins. Like his own father. Once the drink got its claws into you, it didn't let go.

But maybe he was just being what Kit called a 'wowser'. A killjoy. He often felt out of step with other young men, who seemed to him to drink too much, chase after girls too much – was he stodgy and old-fashioned? Kit was directing Henry to drag the trunk ('Carefully, darling!' from Peter) into the bedroom she and Perry would share.

He found it comforting that the girls would be sharing a room; but best not to think why.

Since they were taking the flat furnished, they had no unpacking to do except their clothes and a few knick-knacks, which Kit declared could wait. Perry whipped up a batch of scones in the up-to-date gas stove, and they had elevenses together, around the kitchen table (the only table), where they told stories about schooldays, brought on by Henry reminiscing about unpacking at Eton.

'Nanny always put chocs at the bottom of the trunk, where the other boys wouldn't find them, but of course I brought them out and put them in the kitty,' he said.

'Chocs!' Peter said. 'I was lucky to get humbugs.' He, it turned out, had also gone to boarding school. 'Where did you think I learnt about buggery?'

Henry laughed at that, which Zeke hadn't expected. 'Oh, there's a lot of that anywhere you get boys together. Or men, for that matter. M'brother had lots of stories about the regiment!'

He was easy to like. Zeke half wished he weren't.

'Well, dears, I'm off,' Peter said. 'Train to Southampton and then onboard. Take good care of my doodads. I've left *all* the good china and glasses out.'

'You're a darling,' Perry said, kissing his cheek.

'My dear, even if you break some it will be worth it to have that flatfoot off my back. He won't dare come around again now the *aristocracy*'s on my side!' He fluttered his eyelashes at Henry, who blew him a mock kiss.

Then there was just the four of them, and it was suddenly awkward.

'We'd best be off, Henry. Let these girls unpack.' Zeke picked up his hat and pulled his gloves out of his pocket, sliding them on. Kit hugged him.

'You're the best. Thank you. Thank you both.' She hugged Henry, too, and he hugged back with a bit too much enthusiasm, so that she came out of it mussed and flushed. Did she like it? Zeke couldn't tell.

'Farewell, sweet demoiselles!' Henry carolled as they went down the stairs.

Outside, with the calm Sunday morning traffic sliding past, he glanced sideways at Zeke. 'So . . . you and Kit –'

'She's too good for you,' Zeke said.

'Oh, I know *that*! But she doesn't seem to, yet, and I hope she'll never find out.'

It was a perfect answer, damn him.

'We're partners.' His tone was short, which Henry didn't deserve. 'Look, when you work together, you get close. I look out for her.'

Henry settled his homburg onto his carefully pomaded hair. 'I see that. But there's no romance?'

The world seemed to pause around him. What was the right answer? Which one would keep Kit safe and happy? Could she be both? Did he have the right to stake a claim when he knew she didn't want to get more involved?

'Not while we're working together.'

Henry clapped him on the back.

'Excellent! Then I hope we can be friends.' He walked off with a wave.

Was he that obtuse, not to understand? Was it just that actors were used to parsing text for every possible construction?

Or was he just wilfully ignoring Zeke's tone? Bloody lords. Took what they wanted and ignored what it cost other people. That was his father's voice, echoing down the years, the Irish accent strong with drink. Zeke sighed. Taking counsel from his father was a very bad idea.

He'd have to keep an open mind about this lordling.

◆

Back at Ebury Street, Noël and his mother plied him with fish paste sandwiches and cross-examined him about Henry. He described the day in full, having them in stitches about the policeman.

'Serves him right,' Mrs Coward said, quite viciously. 'I can't abide the police poking into people's private lives.' Zeke had noticed before that she seemed to take Noël's amorous adventures in her stride. Noël could do no wrong as far as she was concerned.

'So, Henry seems okay . . .'

'I've asked around,' Noël said. 'He's not . . . adventurous where relations are concerned.'

'Well, I suppose that's something. He might be a bit of a drinker, though.'

Noël shrugged. 'Who isn't? Apart from you, m'dear.'

'Kit doesn't have much experience with the seamier side of life.' He couldn't help but worry about her, although she wouldn't thank him for it.

'Kit is a darling,' Noël said. 'But too, too pure!' He turned to his mother. 'As the driven snow, I assure you, darling. Not a *whiff* of scandal, apart from that nonsense about the prince. Over a dance photo! No, our Kitty shouldn't be soiled by some grubby little peer. Not unless he's worthy of her.'

But what if he was? Zeke worried over that throughout the afternoon, when he was helping Mr Coward in the garden, shovelling manure. Back to his oldest memories, shovelling dung onto the heap in the barnyard, his father directing him.

What if Henry was on the square? Would Kit be better off with him? He could give her *everything*.

That afternoon Zeke really wanted, for the first time in his life, to drink himself into oblivion.

CHAPTER 16

Kit crossed her legs and settled into the sofa on stage next to Susan Maxwell. It was Wednesday morning – director's notes time. Every Wednesday, before the matinée, Bernes gave them his suggestions for improvements. He'd already gone on to another piece, but he made sure to see the show at least once a week, and to give them some 'tweaks' to bring it back to where he thought it should be, or to bring it to a new level.

The stage was half dressed for the last act, since that had the most seats available for them, but there weren't quite enough; Zeke stood behind the sofa and Basil perched on the arm next to Susan, while Percy stood nearby, leaning on a cane with practised grace. Marguerite, as if by right, occupied the equivalent of a throne – the large red armchair which was the focal point of the set design.

'So,' Bernes said, beaming at them. 'It's all going very well. Sales are good for this part of the run, but we could do with a little fillip to make things fresh for those who are coming back to see it again. Marguerite and Basil, I think we can put some more oomph into the fight scene – Basil, how would you feel about Marguerite throwing something at you?'

Basil put up a hand in mock defence.

'Something soft, I beg you! She has a strong right arm!'

Everyone laughed, and Marguerite made a face at him, but Kit thought she looked as though she quite liked the idea of throwing something at Basil. The gossip was that they weren't getting on; their 'chemistry' on stage was a little lacking, she had thought. Perhaps Bernes thought that also.

'A pillow? Hmm, not very dramatic,' he mused. He produced a cricket pad (from the first picnic scene) and brandished it. 'How about this?'

After a few minutes' discussion, they agreed on Marguerite's handbag as the missile.

'And I *beg* of you, my dear, don't load it up with a brick!' Basil smiled archly and the cast dutifully laughed.

'Now,' Bernes said, turning to Kit and Zeke. 'You two. The dances are fine, but I think we might put a bit more zing in the love scene.'

'Zing?' Kit asked.

'A kiss.'

'I thought *we* were the only ones to be kissing,' Marguerite said icily.

'Darling, of course, that was the plan.' Bernes smiled at her, not at all cowed. 'But now you and Basil are going to be so passionate in your fight scene, and with a *much* bigger emotional load to feed off in your reconciliation scene, these youngsters will look a bit bland in comparison. I do think we need to spice it up just a little. To give you the support you deserve. You don't want the audience to lose interest before you come on for the last scene.' He *was* a good director. All good directors were overly persuasive, Kit had found. Marguerite had a look on her face that said she knew very well what he was doing, but she acceded, settling back in her chair and fixing Kit and Zeke with a sardonic eye, as though she had no hope they could spice anything up.

'A kiss?' Zeke repeated.

'Oh, very chaste, my boy! Just a little moment. Now, Susan . . .' He had a very minor note for Susan about one of her props, and then clapped his hands to dismiss them. 'Thank you, all. Kit and Zeke, could I have you for a moment more, please?'

Bernes took them through their final love scene, the 'Maybe I do' scene. They sketched in the dance, took their final positions, and said their lines.

'Now,' Bernes said. 'A delicate kiss.'

Zeke was so close! He leaned in and she felt the heat of his cheek against her skin. He bent and kissed her. It was over so fast it barely registered.

'No, no, my boy! Slower and longer. You're supposed to be enjoying this! From the last line.'

'Maybe I do,' Kit said, more softly than she would in performance.

Slowly, very slowly, Zeke moved in. Ridiculous for her heart to beat so fast! His breath smelled of . . . nothing. Just Zeke. He placed his lips on hers. She was vividly conscious of both his mouth and of Bernes watching.

'Good,' Bernes said. 'Now, a slow withdrawal. Kit, I want you to sigh when he's back in position.'

Zeke drew back. She sighed, and she didn't know if it was in response to Bernes' command or just because.

'All right. That's a little rough, but you two can practise it again before tonight. Got the pacing?'

'Yes,' Zeke said. 'Line, beat, slow approach, moment, withdrawal, sigh.'

'Perfect. I'll have a look tomorrow night, see how you're getting on with it. Always best to leave a night for you to settle into it before I see if it needs tweaking. Notes on Friday.'

'Thanks, Mr Bernes,' Kit managed. 'It's a lovely moment.'

'It is! You two have It. You'll light up the stage.'

He waved and went offstage, leaving the two of them in an awkward silence.

It. Sex appeal. Chemistry. She'd felt it herself – not just her own attraction to him, but the way the audience reacted when they stared into each other's eyes on stage. There was a hush, a moment, when you could sense the upwelling of emotion in the house. It was . . . erotic. She tried not to give into it, because perhaps it was just a function of the plot, of the situation. But it was there, sure enough. And this kiss would increase it. She was aware of Zeke's tension, next to her, but what could she say? How ridiculous it all was!

Their eyes met and Zeke dissolved into laughter.

'We've got *It*!' he gasped. She wasn't sure why that was funny, but it was. She began to laugh herself, chuckles welling to the surface.

'The stage will light up!' she said, and he doubled over.

For a moment, they stood there, holding each other up, breathless, with tears in their eyes. And then she became abruptly aware of his strength, his scent, his height. Oh, no no no. This would never do.

But those deep blue eyes looked into hers, and his laughter died away.

'We *do* have "It",' he said quietly.

'Best to keep it for the stage.' It was. It *definitely* was, while they were working together.

He nodded, but he let her go, it seemed, reluctantly.

'Do you want to run through it again?'

'I suppose we'd better.'

They put themselves in the last position of the dance.

'Why don't you love me?' Zeke asked, at half projection. A beat, as Susan Maxwell had suggested.

'Maybe I do,' she said, at the same pitch.

Beat. Slow approach. Moment.

His mouth was on hers. Could she breathe? Yes, it was the hammer beat of her pulse that made it feel like she couldn't. Unlike the first time, his lips moved on hers, and she curved her body into his and kissed him back.

Not too long. They were playing the innocent pair of the drama. But it was so *hard* to pull away.

Slow withdrawal.

Sigh.

'Enough for today?' Zeke asked, turning slightly from her.

'Oh. Yes. Enough for today.' She patted her hair down and twitched the seam in her stocking straight. Anything not to look at him.

But then he grinned at her. 'Work's going to be even more fun!' She slapped his upper arm.

'Oh, you!' It broke the tension, though, and they went back to their dressing rooms to prepare for the matinée almost back on their old footing.

But in an hour and a half, more or less, Zeke would kiss her again. And again that night . . .

She took a long breath, and another, and let it out slowly. Old actor's trick for dispelling tension.

Zeke was not for her. As Kit went out to get herself a sandwich for lunch, she made herself remember those difficult scenes at Barrows, when he had been so out of his depth. She tried to imagine him at Lady Patricia's place at Windsor, and couldn't. No. She and Zeke were *not* right for each other.

Much better to be like the Astaires, as they'd promised.

But Adele and Fred didn't have to kiss each other on stage.

Sam the doorman had been stuck on duty over lunch, so she brought him back a sandwich, and gave the props boy tuppence to run and get himself a pasty. After lunch, as she made herself up, she contemplated her reflection in the mirror. Were her lips a little redder, a little fuller than normal? Her lips seemed to remember the feel of his. What would it be like, to be kissed by Zeke Gardiner every night and twice on matinée days?

The sigh this time was deep and heartfelt. Susan's hand came down on her shoulder.

'He's a lovely chap,' she said. 'But it's best not to mix up the play with real life.'

'You're *so* right!' Kit said, suddenly full of energy. 'Don't worry about me!'

Susan was her guardian angel. She was a professional, and

she could kiss any number of actors without getting emotional about it.

'Beginners, please!' the call boy said outside their door.

'*En avant, mon ami!*' she said to Susan.

'Break a leg!' Susan replied, chuckling.

And on they went.

The kiss was fine. She could certainly handle it. Definitely. Surely.

And the audience loved it.

CHAPTER 17

On Friday, when they arrived at the theatre at the same moment, Kit smiled at him with such open affection that Zeke was filled with exhilaration and delight. Those kisses – he was probably imagining that she participated with the same pleasure he did, but there was no denying that there was a new frisson between them, on stage and off.

As they passed Sam at the stage door, he held out a letter. 'One for you, sir.'

A Canadian stamp. His mother wrote regularly, every two weeks, but this was an extra. He thrust it into his pocket, hoping his father wasn't causing trouble again, but he didn't have time to deal with it now. And part of him, selfishly, wanted to enjoy this feeling. Of being who and what he *ought* to be, with Kit at his side.

The performance was magic. The kiss scene had brought them to a new rapport. At the end of the second act, after the waltz number, the house erupted with applause and the stage manager indicated they should take a bow. A rare thing for the junior couple in the play.

He deliberately ignored the letter during interval. Nothing would bring him down tonight. Whatever it was, it had already happened, and he wouldn't be able to post a reply until tomorrow, anyway.

Waiting in the wings for their third act entrance, he and Kit smiled at each other and she slid her arm through his, both of them alight with the enchantment of a great performance.

At curtain, waves of applause washed over him as though cleansing him of all bad things, all the everydayness which stopped life being magnificent. That was it. He felt *magnificent*.

Kit kissed him on the cheek before she went into her dressing room, and the stage manager said, 'Nice job,' as he went down the corridor. Even Basil clapped him on the shoulder and said, 'I'll have to look out, young feller-me-lad, or you'll be taking my spot.'

He took his slap off and changed into his own clothes, feeling the letter crackle in his pocket.

Time to face up.

It wasn't his mother's handwriting, which was odd. Or his father's, thank God. Who else would write to him? And there was money in it – eighty-five Canadian pounds.

He checked the signature quickly – Marjorie Treece, his mother's neighbour. A cold dread sat itself in the base of his gut. He read it quickly.

Dear Zeke,
   I'm so sorry to tell you that your mother passed yesterday.

She went out to church on Sunday and sang a lovely solo, but she was caught in a shower on her way home and came down with a fever.

It was very quick. There was nothing to be done, the doctor said. I looked after her, but you know how weak her chest was.

She asked me to write to you, and to tell you how much she loved you, and how proud she was of your success.

Unfortunately, the police came and found your father's address in her bureau, so they contacted him and he came and took everything away. But before he arrived I got your mother's rainy-day money from her jewellery box, and I'm sending it to you, minus the money for the burial and for a wreath I will buy in your name. I thought you would want that.

Your mother was a lovely woman and I'll miss her. Her students plan to sing 'Oh for the wings of a dove' at the funeral, and I'm sure it will be beautiful. I know it must break your heart not to be there, but I'll represent you as best I can.

Yours sincerely,
Your friend,
Marjorie Treece

He stood, staring stupidly at the letter, the banknotes in one hand.

Percy looked at him with curiosity, but went out without saying anything. English reserve. Thank God for it.

She was dead.

Not by his father's hand.

All that time, all that fear, all that expense to keep her safe from him, and she was killed by a fever.

She had deserved so much more of life than she'd got.

More *time*. Time to be safe in. Time to finally enjoy her days. It just wasn't *fair*.

He wanted to smash things, to break the mirrors and scream. But his legs wouldn't hold him. He sank down, aiming for the small visitor's chair, missing, going straight to the floor.

His lungs hurt. That would be because he wasn't breathing. For a moment, he stayed there. It would be easier, surely, never to breathe again? But his lungs demanded air, and he dragged in a great, deep, ragged breath.

And another.

He could feel his body coming to life, but his mind was still blank. It didn't seem possible, any of it.

The only thing that rang true was 'Oh for the wings of a dove'. She had to be dead if her students planned to sing that song, because she'd hated it. Not 'planned'. Had sung. It would be over by now, the funeral. Horrible to think of that being the last music she ever heard.

But she hadn't heard it, had she?

A quick knock at the door and Kit put her head in.

'Are you ready? I'm going to dinner with Rebecca Yates and her husband, and I thought you could join us.' She paused. 'Zeke? Are you all right?'

He held up the letter, unable to speak. She came in and took it from him, a worried frown on her face, and scanned it quickly. Her expression crumpled. 'Oh, Zeke, no!' She sank to the floor beside him and touched his arm. 'I'm so sorry.'

He just stared at her. What was there to say? But her genuine emotion sparked something deep inside him, which seemed to spiral out in a burning explosion, like a Catherine wheel. As if she sensed it, she put her arm around him, and he turned to her as the burning reached the surface, hit his mind and his eyes, and he began to shake, clinging to her like a little boy.

She held him and rocked him and rubbed his back and, blessedly, said nothing at all.

After the first great storm she left him, his body all cold down one side, where she had been the only warmth in the world. But she came back and shepherded him to the door, to a taxi, to Ebury Street and upstairs to his room.

He knew he wasn't being the stiff-upper-lip man he was supposed to be. But it was as though everything that held him up had disappeared. He was like a puppet with cut strings. For five years, his whole focus had been on success, because that meant he could keep her safe. But he hadn't. She'd died, anyway.

Kit sat him down in the armchair in his room. His hands were still trembling, but he hadn't cried. He rather wished he could, but his grief was a hard knot in his chest, solid and unmoving, cemented in with guilt.

'If I'd been there . . .'

'If you'd been there, you could have said goodbye,' she answered, 'but that's all. You know that once a fever goes to the chest, there's nothing anyone can do. Pneumonia is a killer, and if you'd been there, it wouldn't have changed anything.'

He looked up at her. This was a new Kit; a Kit who'd seen death before, and he remembered that she was a vicar's daughter, that maybe, like many vicarage children, she'd been called in to help the less fortunate. As if she read his mind, she added: 'I nursed people during the Spanish flu. Once the chest is gone . . . I'm so sorry, Zeke, but you mustn't blame yourself. There was nothing to be done that her neighbour didn't do.'

She bent down like an angel, her golden hair highlighted by the lamp, and kissed him on the forehead. 'Noël will help you get to bed,' she said. 'Try to sleep.'

Noël did come in, unusually subdued, but Zeke was already in his pyjamas. He felt obscurely that following the bedtime routine his mother had taught him was important right now. Very important.

He even knelt on the knobbly rug by his bed like a good child, as he hadn't done in more than a decade, and prayed instead of cursing God, because that's what she would have wanted.

◆

Kit really didn't want to go to dinner, but Rebecca's and Sandro's schedules were so full, this might be the only chance for weeks. Right now, she could do with a friendly face from home.

Rebecca took the news about Zeke's mother in precisely the right way.

'Oh, the poor boy!' She covered Kit's hand with her own. 'It must be so hard, when he's so far away.'

'Yes, I think that makes it worse.' Normally, she didn't worry about her own mother. Agatha Scott was tough, underneath all those manners. Kit resolved to write to her more often.

Sandro nodded. 'Look at us, eh? All three of us, far from our mothers.'

'Nothing we can do about that,' Rebecca said briskly. 'None of us are going back any time soon.'

The conversation veered towards work: journalism, theatre, photography. It was so *satisfying*, to be with people who thought a woman having a career was perfectly normal. It was different to being with theatre people. Rebecca was part of a much larger social change, and made Kit aware that she was, too.

'Someone from our background would never have gone on the stage before the War,' Rebecca commented. 'You're forging new ground! My mother would be delighted with you!'

'I wish I'd had your mother,' Kit said ruefully. 'Mine is horrified.'

'Oh, my mother is horrified at me, too!' Rebecca said sunnily. 'She wanted me to be a lawyer.'

That was funny; that even the most advanced woman in Australia could push her daughter towards something uncongenial. It made Kit feel more in charity with her own mother.

'My mamma wanted me to stay in the meatpacking business!' Sandro said, holding up his left thumb, which lacked the top joint. 'Until *this* happened.' He laughed, throwing back his head. 'Lucky, eh?'

One couldn't help but laugh along with him, despite how horrible it must have been.

Time with Rebecca and Sandro was a blessing. She would invite them over for dinner to the flat, but she'd have to get Perry to teach her how to cook first. She'd mastered boiling eggs and making toast . . . perhaps meeting in what Sandro called a *trattoria* was best, for now.

At home, sliding into bed, trying not to wake Perry, her last thoughts were not of the lovely evening, but of Zeke. Poor man. She would have to make sure he was all right over the coming days. She'd seen enough of grief during the War and the Spanish flu epidemic to know that loss sometimes hit you a way down the track. He would need her.

CHAPTER 18

He had to get a mourning armband, and he didn't know how to. Where could you buy one? Zeke asked Kit after their warm-up the next night.

He felt shocking: exhausted, dizzy. But the show had to go on, didn't it? He had an understudy – one of the boys from the chorus – but the lad wasn't the brightest star in the firmament, and he didn't want to let Charlot down. So he warmed up and, as always, the exercise made him feel better.

'An armband?' Kit stretched her left hamstring, bouncing gently. 'You used to be able to buy them, during the War, but they were pretty shoddy. I'll get some black linen from Annie and make you one.'

He raised an eyebrow at her as he changed legs and kept stretching. 'I never thought of you as the domestic type.'

'Hah! I'm a well-bred gel. Of course I can sew.' She used a parody of an upper-class accent. 'Hand-sewing, that is.'

Before curtain, they went in to Annie and asked. Annie patted Zeke on the shoulder. 'I'm very sorry to hear that, Mr Gardiner.'

He nodded. He didn't know what to say. If he wore the armband, everyone would be doing that. Saying they were sorry. Expecting him to reply appropriately. Gazing at him with pitying eyes.

Could he not wear one? Could he just *not*? Swear Kit and Annie to secrecy? Just pretend that everything was all right?

That was so tempting.

But it would be a betrayal.

'I could make it up for you while you're on stage,' Annie offered. Kit shot her a quick look and something passed between them, some female thing he didn't have a hope of decoding.

'I'll do it,' Kit said. Annie nodded and passed over the makings. Black cloth, thread, and elastic. 'Thanks, Annie.'

'Thank you, Annie,' he parroted. He sounded like an idiot, not showing how truly grateful he was to both of them. So he bent and kissed Annie's cheek.

'Oh, get away with you!' she said. She patted his shoulder again, and he fought back the shakes. This was ridiculous. He had to pull himself together.

How would he cope on stage?

But strangely, on stage he was fine. The character slipped over him like a glove, and Kit was there, all the time, making things easy for him, never faltering. While he was on stage he was someone else, and he needed that surcease as an opium addict needs the pipe.

◆

Kit came back with him to Ebury Street and sat in the Cowards' living room, sewing away, her blonde head shining under the lamp. The Cowards were out at some show of Noël's, so they had the place to themselves, apart from another lodger who had long gone to bed.

They talked desultorily.

'Did you always want to be on the stage?' she asked.

'No.' He was surprised by the strength of the memory. 'I wanted to be an engineer.' Oh, how he'd wanted it! To build bridges and canals and railways. To make skyscrapers reach for the heavens. He'd been obsessed with tall buildings, like every boy of his generation. He chuckled, self-deprecating. 'When I was ten, they built the Dominion Building in Vancouver. Thirteen storeys. We made a special trip into town to see it. It was the most astonishing thing I'd ever seen. So tall. The idea that someone had *made* it . . . had imagined it and planned it and designed it and built it . . . I decided that's what I wanted to do with my life.'

She had stopped sewing and was watching him intently.

'But you didn't do that?'

He shrugged. 'My father made me leave school at twelve and work on the farm. We could never have afforded university, anyway. There's no way a farm boy like me gets to be an engineer.'

Kit's face was troubled, uncertain. But then her mouth firmed and her head came up. 'You could do it now. The universities are used to older men coming in now, because of the War. You could save up and go.'

'They'd never take me!' Astonished, he stared at her. That had never occurred to him. Being an engineer was a dream he'd buried long ago. But the skyscrapers had kept on climbing, and he'd kept watching them grow. It was one of the few things he didn't like about London – they had height restrictions on most of the city, so there were few really tall buildings.

'You could take on a tutor to get you to your matriculation. It would be mostly mathematics, wouldn't it, for engineering?'

Wordlessly, he nodded.

'Just a thought,' she said, almost carelessly, and returned to her sewing.

He made himself laugh, but he was tense all through his body. 'Do you want to get rid of me?'

She stilled, her needle poised. 'No,' she said softly. Well. That was all right, then.

'I'd still need to save up a good deal,' he said. 'University's not cheap.'

She bit off the thread and held up the armband, complete. 'So, no need to make a decision yet.'

Relief flowed through him. No need to do anything except keep on. He could do that. The idea of starting something new was too big for him right now.

He could keep saving, though, especially now he didn't have to send money back to his mother.

It was true that show business was a dicey game. Engineers didn't have to go audition for a new job every six months or so.

Skyscrapers.

Best forget about it. Kit motioned for him to stand and then carefully put the armband on his left sleeve, above the elbow but not so high it would be pulling every time he moved his arm.

'There,' she said. She yawned suddenly, hiding it with her hand. 'Oh, sorry! I'd better be going.'

'I'll call you a cab,' he said. 'And I'll pay for it.'

She opened her mouth to object, but he put his finger over her lips. 'Let me do this for you. A small thank you.'

That smile broke over her face. The rare one, completely open and full of affection. As always, it made him catch his breath. 'All right,' she said.

He watched her drive away, feeling calmer than he had since he got the news. Life went on. Kit was there, at his back.

He'd survive. He shook his head as he went back inside and up the stairs to his attic bedroom. An engineer! As if he could. It was just like Kit to think he could do whatever he set his mind to.

But the thought lingered, nonetheless.

CHAPTER 19

A week later, Henry picked her up from the theatre to go to a party. She'd invited Zeke, but he'd begged off. He had been so hard-hit by his mother's death, she couldn't press him. Poor lamb. He was wonderful on stage, but off it he just drooped.

He was all alone now. She couldn't imagine that. Even with her family far behind her in Sydney, they were still *there*.

To have *no one* . . . that must be hard.

So she'd kissed Zeke on the cheek and patted his shoulder. 'Have an early night.'

He'd smiled his crooked smile, the one that said, 'Thanks, but that won't be happening.' He hadn't been sleeping well, she suspected. 'Have a good time.'

There was champagne already poured for her. For once, she accepted it, leaning back and sipping as the car pulled smoothly away.

'Is that fellow hanging around you?' Henry asked. As if it were any of his business.

'What does it matter?'

'Quite right!' He brightened. 'It doesn't matter, because off we go! And it should be divine.'

Half-heartedly, a photographer took a shot of them as they drove off. But they were old news now, and it probably wouldn't make the papers. At some point, she should put a stop to this charade. In the meantime . . . She drank her champagne.

◆

The 'divine' party looked like a lot of others they had been to. Rich young people, a big house overlooking the Thames, champagne flowing, lights picking out jewels and sequins, tiepins and cufflinks.

The hostess was a Lady Penelope, who had gone to school with Sarah and was some kind of relation to Henry. She was tall and good-looking and apparently delighted to have Kit there.

'Lovely, lovely!' she kept saying. 'Have a drink.' But despite being a bit squiffy, she chatted quite knowledgeably about the London theatre until the band started up. Kit felt rather as though she'd made a friend.

The band wasn't wonderful, but it was good enough to dance to (at least the drummer kept time). As Henry whirled her around, she saw Lady Penelope slip off to a secluded spot and raise a hand to her nose; she wasn't the only one taking cocaine in dark corners.

This was the elite of England, apparently.

Henry, unusually, was being very attentive, and it made her a little nervous that she didn't know why.

They sat on the terrace, alone for the moment, as Bingo was waltzing (badly) with Lady Penelope, and Squibs was trying to polka with a couple of girls at once. Cecil was dancing with some young thing, studiously ignoring Kit. Daphne sat on the sidelines, a classic wallflower. But as Kit watched, someone walked up to her, pulled her to her feet and began to dance. Perhaps it was the start of a romance. That would be nice.

Henry picked up Kit's hand and kissed it. It was so odd a gesture for him that she just stared. He grinned.

'Let's have another drink.'

He had more than one. She lost track; she had given herself a three-drink limit at the start of the night, although getting anything other than champagne from the waiter was a herculean effort. Finally, after taking ten minutes to explain quite forcefully that yes, she *did* want lemonade, she returned to the party to find Henry chugging a bottle of champagne, urged on by a circle of his male friends.

Oh dear.

He finished and threw the bottle into the bushes triumphantly, raising his arms to acknowledge the cheers. Then he burped, loudly, and everyone collapsed into laughter.

'Kit!' he called, lurching over to her. He was definitely drunk. Very drunk. It seemed to have hit him quite fast.

One arm went around her waist, the other turned her face towards him.

'No, Henry,' she said. 'You're drunk. Let's get you home.'

'Norrabitovit,' he slurred. 'I'm jussjolly. Gosh, you're pretty.'

'Uh-huh.'

'Give us a kiss, Kitty-cat!' He tried to pull her closer, but she eeled away from him.

'I don't think so, Henry.'

'But I *love* you!' He sounded so woebegone it made her laugh.

'Of course you do. I think we should go.'

'No nonono, 'm staying. Fine party. Verra fine.'

In the moonlight, he stood there, swaying, smiling happily. No use trying to change his mind. He looked ridiculously handsome. He'd relaxed, for one, and that smile opened up his face and made him rather sweet.

At the end of the garden, there was a splash and a shriek. Someone falling in the river, or being thrown in. She looked. Yes, there were half-naked bodies rapidly becoming completely naked, cavorting along the dock and diving or being pushed into the water.

Time to leave.

'I'm going,' she said. 'If you want to come, come.'

'I'm gonna have a schwim.' He turned and wandered down to the garden, weaving gently from side to side. She bit back laughter. Really, it wasn't funny. And yet it was.

In the house she found a footman to get Bourke for her. He turned out to be down in the servants' hall, having a cup of tea.

'Do you mind, Bourke?'

'Not at all, miss. I can come back for Lord Henry. He'll be a while yet.'

She pondered that as the London streets slipped past, the houses dark, only a solitary bicyclist on the roads. It was too late even for buses.

One shouldn't pump someone's servants for information, but –

'How often does Lord Henry . . . party, Bourke?'

'I'm sure I couldn't say, miss.' The perfect answer from the loyal servant. It made her feel rather sordid for asking. Then Bourke cleared his throat. 'But . . . less since he's been seeing you.'

That was a nothing-answer, and yet it was interesting.

She didn't take Henry's declaration of love seriously. She'd had too many drunk young men declare their affection. But if she were affecting his behaviour . . .

Well, she hadn't affected his behaviour tonight. Not in the slightest.

Parties . . . it *had* been fun, in a way. But getting naked and jumping into the Thames? They'd be lucky not to come away with a disease or two, to say nothing of the nip in the air.

Drunk enough not to care.

Theatre people drank, but they couldn't *afford* to drink like that. Either in monetary terms or in terms of their health. If you were performing, singing and dancing every night, you had to stay in good shape. Even at David and Bobbie's parties, there was a limit.

She'd seen no signs of a limit tonight.

As they went through the theatre district towards Sicilian Avenue, she wondered how Zeke was, and sent a quick prayer that his sleep would be undisturbed.

CHAPTER 20

Zeke was astonished by how fast the dancing film would be ready to be distributed to theatres. Courtney Rowden dropped in to the theatre after the Wednesday matinée to update them on the publicity.

'Three weeks from tomorrow, it premieres. We've been booked into the cinemas for months,' Courtney explained. 'Three-month turnaround, that's what we aim for, from first idea to finished film.'

'Three weeks.' Kit looked troubled. 'That's a Thursday.'

'That's general distribution. Don't worry, Kit, we've set the premiere for a Monday night, so you and Zeke and all the others can be there.'

Excitement stirred in his gut. A film premiere, and he was one of the stars. But his mother wouldn't be there, nor ever know about it. No sending clippings from the papers, as he always did. No getting an excited letter back. He slumped in his seat and forced himself to pay attention to the here and now.

Courtney introduced Vickers, the publicity man for the studio. A bumptious young buck, with too-wide lapels on his suit and an unfortunately large pinky ring. Trying to be American.

'This is a compilation film, but we want some romance to sell the punters. And there are only two couple dances in it – yours and Betty Balfour's one – but she's in the middle of filming in Ireland and can't help.'

'So you two should be seen together,' Courtney said bluntly. 'Get rid of that lord of yours, Kit, and go around more with Zeke.'

Neither of them were in on the secret of the Palace dictat. And God forbid they ever found out. Zeke shuddered at the thought.

'That would make a great story!' Vickers agreed. '"Actress prefers love interest to lord!"'

Kit stared Vickers down. Trying not to laugh, Zeke shook his head.

'Gentlemen, I'm happy to spend all my time in Miss Linton's company, but you can't expect her to just throw away her friends.'

Kit smiled at him. 'No, I won't do that. But I suppose I can also be seen with Zeke. It's not like Lord Henry and I are engaged or anything like that.'

Was that a bit of relief in her eyes? It would be grand if she were tired of Henry. He wasn't good for her. The nights after she went out with him, she was always tired. Her performance would suffer if it kept up.

'We should get a friendly reporter or two to do interviews with you,' Courtney said.

'Rebecca Yates!' Kit exclaimed. 'Let's use her. She interviewed me before, and she was excellent.'

'She's good,' Vickers agreed. 'But she's a news reporter. We want someone on the entertainment beat.'

'No.' Courtney tapped a cigarette on his desk, probably holding off lighting it because he knew Kit didn't like the smoke. 'Woman reporter, Australian, and she's got that photographer husband, hasn't she? It's a nice angle, woman-to-woman. Set it up.'

'Yessir.' Vickers scrambled to make notes.

◆

Vickers must have scrambled to some purpose, because when Zeke and Kit turned up at the theatre the next day a little early, as requested, the reporter and her husband were there to meet them. Zeke had heard about them from Kit, but hadn't met them before.

Miss Yates – 'please, call me Rebecca, Zeke' – was very good-looking. Blonde, but stately, unlike Kit's lithe grace.

'This might be my last interview for a while,' Rebecca told Kit, her hand going to her midsection. Zeke could detect a slight bulge.

Kit squealed with excitement and hugged her.

Her husband hovered around her protectively. Good for them.

Seeing them together, talking to Kit, he was struck, for the first time in his life, with the desire to have a family. Maybe it was because his mother was gone. He was cut adrift, with no place to call home. A wife and children . . . that was an anchor for a man, something to keep him strong and steady. A couple of little blonde girls . . . He brought himself up short, realising that the little blonde girls of his imagination looked a lot like Kit. *Steady on*, he told himself. *That's a step too far.*

But he rather liked the publicity man's idea of the two of them spending *much* more time together.

They did the interview on one of the sets, a drawing room with fake French doors showing a backdrop of a terrace.

'This looks okay in the camera,' the husband, Sandro, said. 'Bring the lights up a bit more in the back corner, would you?'

The lights duly came up and he began taking shots as they chatted with his wife.

She went through all the standard questions about the film. Puff pieces were all the same. Kit seemed a little apologetic.

'I know this isn't your normal work,' she said to Rebecca.

'As long as it doesn't give the editor the idea I *want* to do this kind of thing. I'd prefer to get a scoop, if you have one.'

She grinned at Kit and he saw that there was a friendliness between them that he hadn't seen Kit show to anyone else. She relaxed around Rebecca Yates in a way she didn't even relax around Perry. Maybe because they were both Australian?

He watched them chat, putting in the odd answer himself where necessary. No, it was more than that. They were *alike*. Class mattered, in the end, and they were from the same class, the same country, the same city, the same education system. It turned out Kit's older sister had gone to school with Rebecca. And there you were: the old girls' club.

He wondered if Kit held off getting really involved with anyone in London because, in the end, she'd go home to find a man of her own type.

But she didn't *belong* back there, in the provinces! She belonged here, in the bright glare of the London stage. Or on film, moving thousands. Performing. That was the heart of her; he hoped she realised it.

They did some corny romantic photos in poses from the film. Even in this ridiculous situation, he couldn't help but smile with real affection at her; and there was a matching affection in her eyes and in the light touch of her hand on his.

Maybe it was time to admit that he wanted her as more than a friend. This publicity stunt would give him the opportunity to get her away from Henry.

He'd have to get her dancing as often as possible. That was an area Henry just couldn't compete in.

He pushed down the thought that the lord had too many other advantages: wealth, position, good looks . . . Kit was too level-headed to be taken in by those things. She'd want character in her man, and he was willing to bet that, in that area, he could take Henry one-handed.

CHAPTER 21

Benny had come up trumps in the M. Dernier dress department. Kit smoothed the ostrich feather skirt down over her hips and gave an experimental sashay. Every bit of it shivered in time to her steps. What a shame tonight wasn't for dancing! This dress would look smashing in a foxtrot.

She applied her lipstick carefully. A deep red. She wasn't the second string tonight, she was a film star!

A knock on the door of the flat. She heard Perry go to open it. She was in her best dress, too, all primped and ready. A low whistle greeted her.

'You look spiffing, Perry!' Zeke. Suddenly nervous (which was ridiculous), Kit went out to the living room.

No whistle. Zeke just stared at her. He himself was handsome in a new swallow-tailed coat, his hair slicked back with pomade, his eyes brilliant as he gazed at her.

It made her nervous. The whole night was making her nervous. They'd seen the rushes of *Britain Dances*, and she thought they'd been all right, but what did she know? She twirled around, showing off the skirt to distract herself from imagined disasters.

'Well?' she demanded.

'Beautiful.' Stopped in mid-twirl by the sincerity in his voice, she stood, poised, as if ready to take flight. He held his hat in his hands and smiled at her.

'Oh, come on, you two! Stop making eyes at each other and let's *go*!'

They both laughed. Out they went, down the staircase, she and Perry on Zeke's arms.

Off to be in the movies.

◆

A film premiere! It made Kit tingle with excitement to see the lights and the crowds. Premieres were a recent thing, imported from America where they had begun only the year before. The British ones weren't as . . . as *lavish* as the American ones, she was pleased to see. That would have been a bit vulgar.

But they still brought out the fans and the press, and there were quite a few photographers waiting next to a royal blue carpet, which had been laid down for them to walk in on. 'Red carpet's a bit Yank,' Courtney had said. 'Let's go for British blue.'

For once, she was glad to pose for the photographers, even those who had hounded her over Henry and the prince. She and Zeke, this time.

'Give her a kiss!' a photographer yelled out. With panache, Zeke brought her hand to his mouth and kissed the knuckles, his eyes laughing at her. Shivers ran all the way through her, but she couldn't show it. She smiled and then they stood and moved and smiled again, and walked on in the glare of spotlights.

Kit again felt disconnected from herself. The *making* of the film had been grand, if very short. But this . . . it was as though someone else was moving down that carpet on Zeke's arm.

The feeling was even stronger once the film had begun, and her face, grown enormous, took up the screen.

'Odd seeing yourself so *big*, isn't it?' Zeke whispered to her and she nodded decisively. Odd and not very nice, somehow. As if it wasn't her at all, but some double, a monstrous twin who somehow had her own smile. All her faults of looks and movement, impossibly magnified.

But the audience didn't seem to notice. They oohed and aahed at all the dances, and clapped vigorously at the end.

Afterwards, there was applause. Long and loud. Longer than she'd expected. If it were a theatre, they would have managed perhaps three bows to that applause. That was reassuring. One expected applause at a premiere, but it did sound as if they genuinely liked it.

'It's *wonderful*!' Perry said. 'It'll be a hit for sure!'

Adele Astaire reassured her as well, once they'd gone out into the foyer. She bounced up to Kit and gave her a hug.

'Oh, honey, you looked great! It was splendid!'

'*You* should be in films, Miss Astaire,' Courtney said immediately.

'Oh, no, not me!' Adele said with determination. 'I just hate seeing myself on film. *Hate* it.'

Fred looked rueful. 'I've tried to convince her. But no luck.' He slapped Zeke on the shoulder. 'Great job, Zeke. And you, too, Mr Rowden. I enjoyed seeing all the different styles – one drawback of this job is you don't get to see other performers very often. It's a terrific flicker.'

Courtney seemed to swell with pride. 'Can I quote you on that, Mr Astaire?'

Fred laughed and swapped glances with Adele. 'Sure, why not? We usually charge for endorsements, but hell, Kit and Zeke are friends of ours.'

Mortified, Kit tried to protest, but Adele waved her off. 'Oh, Freddie, now you've made everyone uncomfortable. Of *course* you can quote us, Mr Rowden. Here, I'll give you a good one. "A film to send you out dancing in the streets".'

Behind Courtney, Vickers, the publicity man, was hastily writing it down. No doubt it would appear in tomorrow's papers above the ad for the film.

'You're so generous,' she said to Adele.

'Don't you worry about that. Moaning Minnie here is always complaining if we don't screw every cent out of our endorsements.'

'Mom needs dental work,' Fred explained. 'And American dentists – whew! They charge like wounded rhinos.'

Zeke looked wistful. Time to get his mind off mothers.

'The press is waiting.' Kit took his arm firmly and marched them towards the public and the reporters who'd just seen the film.

More photographs, with the Astaires and without, with the other dancers featured in the film – even with Marie Brett, whom she'd idolised for years! – with Courtney and without. This wasn't a 'star vehicle'; there were multiple stars, and they all got attention. And had questions shouted at them.

'How's the prince?' one reporter yelled.

'How's Lord Henry? Have you dropped him for Zeke?'

Kit ignored them. She was getting much better at that. And then the press rushed off to make their deadlines and it was only a matter of signing autograph books on the way to the car.

'Excellent! Let's go for supper at Angelo's,' Courtney said, sitting back in the limousine, grinning widely.

'Oh, *no*, Courtney, I don't think I can.' She was dead on her feet. More public scrutiny.

'Let it go, Courtney,' Zeke said. 'You've even got a quote from the Astaires out of us. Be satisfied with that.'

'Spoilsports. All right then, where?'

'Just let me off at my flat.' She'd never been so grateful to have a respectable address. Fancy having to take Courtney to the Cats' Home!

Zeke got out of the car with her and waved Courtney off. They stood for a moment in silence, the excitement of the night still buoying them up. It seemed tame to simply say goodnight and go to bed.

'Would you like to come up?'

'I would.' They climbed the steps wearily. 'Who'd have thought that smiling could tire you out?' He laughed. 'I feel like I've chopped wood all day.'

That made her wonder about his childhood. He never spoke about it; he'd mentioned 'the farm', but that was it.

As she opened the door, she asked, looking over her shoulder, 'Did you chop a lot of wood back in Canada?'

Perry had turned on a lamp as they left. She had gone on to a party as soon as the film was over. The flat was quiet and calm, a safe harbour. Kit made tea and they sat on the sofa, not too close, and drank it. Ate shortbread and crackers and cheese.

The tension slowly seeped out of her.

'It *was* good, wasn't it?'

'I think so. *You* were terrific.'

She grinned, teasing him. 'No, *you* were.'

'So was everyone else!'

'Yes, no good getting a swelled head over a few minutes of film.' She could keep herself sensible, even if it did feel as though she'd been on a magic carpet ride.

'I wonder if we'll ever be in another . . .'

'Together?'

Silently, they gazed at each other. His hand moved to take hers, lying there on the seat cushion as though it didn't belong to her. But she felt every inch of his palm against her skin.

He looked down, and then up again.

'I did chop a lot of wood.' Letting go of her hand, he stood and paced to the window, looking out through the diving bell of the tower to the street beyond.

Instinct kept her silent.

'I was raised on a farm in Fraser Valley, British Columbia. Not far from Vancouver. My mum was British; she came to

Canada touring with a vaudeville company. A singer. Met my father. Married him. I guess she must really have loved him.'

A quick look at her, and then back to staring out the window. There was something in the set of his shoulders which showed her this was hard for him. Deeply hard.

'He was a drinker. I guess you knew that. He used to . . . to hit my mother.'

Anger rose swiftly in her. That poor woman! And Zeke . . .

'When I was fourteen – by that time I was taller than he was. He was Irish, a little stocky man, full of rage that only came out when he drank. He pushed it under the rest of the time, nice as you please. Charming. I guess that's why she married him.'

He paced the small room, his hands in his pockets. 'Anyway, by the time I was fourteen I was bigger than he was. He came home drunk one night, went to hit Mum and – I went for him. Mad. Just mad with it. I beat him up pretty bad.' As he spoke, his Canadian accent crept back, so that it was as though that young boy were talking to her directly, through time. 'He crawled off to the barn, and I packed us up and got us out of there. I knew, when he was sober, he could take me and he'd nigh-on kill me for defying him. And her, too.'

He looked so *lonely* standing there. She couldn't stay sitting anymore. She went to him and slid her arm around his waist. His hand came up to touch her hair; it was shaking.

'She had some money put aside – to give to *me* to get me away from him, she said. She'd been saving up for more than a year, because she knew I was going to blow up and she was afraid one of us would be killed in the fight. We went to

Victoria. Further away than Vancouver, and he was less likely to look for us there.'

'And you went on the stage.'

'Not right away. Not at fourteen. But Mum still had some contacts in the theatre, and she got me a job as a stagehand at a music hall. She gave voice lessons. She had a wonderful voice. And I swore to her that she'd never have to go back to him.'

Kit moved to stand in front of him, and took his face between her hands. 'And she never did.'

He blinked, as though that hadn't occurred to him. 'No . . . I suppose not.'

'And the years since you left . . . they were good years for her.'

'Yes.' He nodded. 'Yes, they were. She had friends, church – he never let her go to church – her students. It wasn't easy, but it was safe, and free.'

'Then you should be proud. Proud of taking him on, and proud of looking after her.'

'I'm the son of a violent drunk.' So self-accusatory. His eyes were dark with remembered pain. Was he warning her off? Telling her he wasn't a good bet as a long-term thing? She couldn't let him go on believing that.

'You're the son of a wonderful, brave woman.'

His eyes filled with tears. 'I kept thinking, tonight, how excited she was about me being in the film. How she'd never get to see it.'

'She saw it.'

He smiled at that, and gave himself a little shake. 'You sound certain.'

'I am.' Faith wasn't something she thought about often, but this she was sure of. The dead watched over the people they loved. 'Come,' she said. She poured them each a glass of sherry from the decanter on the sideboard. A treat she'd bought out of her film money. 'Here. To your mother – what was her name?'

'Enid.'

'To Enid!'

'To Enid,' he echoed, and drained the glass.

They stood there for two long breaths, neither sure where to go from there.

'I'd best be off,' he said reluctantly.

Oh, she wanted him to stay! She felt every breath he took. But on a night like this, everything they did and said *mattered*. There would be no coming back from tonight if they took it any further.

'I suppose you had.'

She lifted her hand to his cheek and he bent his head to kiss her palm. Lips warm on her skin, her blood rising to meet that warmth, the scent of his cologne encircling them, bringing all her senses alive.

For a moment, they stood there, and then he tore away from her, picked up his hat and coat, and strode off, not even saying goodbye.

As the door closed behind him she let her breath out.

Had that been the wisest or the stupidest decision she'd ever made?

She had no idea.

CHAPTER 22

'Grab a quick lunch?' Zeke asked Kit as they came off after the matinée curtain. His shin was sore. Basil had kicked him in the billiards scene, and he still wasn't sure if it had been an accident, or deliberate. Basil was liking him less and less as the weeks went on and Zeke's applause got bigger. The film's success had made it worse. Marguerite had been noticeably frosty as well.

'Love to,' she said.

'My treat.' It was sadly pleasant to have the money to take a woman out for a meal, even a quick snack. His gut twisted with grief; it came in unexpected pangs, like this, but if he breathed through it he'd be okay.

'Grand,' Kit answered. 'I'll be out in a jiffy.'

He went towards his own dressing room, but Sam stopped him in the passageway.

'Mr Gardiner, there's a gentleman. I've asked him to wait outside. He says he's your father.' Sam had seen every trick in the book from men trying to get backstage to ambush the chorus girls. But he was looking embarrassed rather than annoyed. 'I wouldn't have bothered you, but he's got a Canadian accent. I served with your lot, so I recognised it.'

Ice in his veins. It couldn't be. Surely not. *Surely* not. He'd never have got himself organised enough to make it to London . . .

'Thanks, Sam,' he managed. 'I'll check him out.'

'Right you are, sir,' Sam said cheerfully as Zeke slipped him a half-crown.

Just as well he had to jingle coins in his pocket in that last scene. Should he go out in his stage clothes? No. Annie would be waiting for them. He entered the dressing room and went through the change back to street clothes by rote, sitting at the mirror and getting the slap off his face as if nothing was wrong. Even answered a comment or two from Percy as though his mind could think about something other than the man waiting outside.

Surely it couldn't be him.

As the stage door opened onto the alleyway, Zeke saw that it was – or, at least, it was someone very much like his father, although thinner than he remembered. This man was cleanshaven, though, and in a suit instead of working clothes, and wore a hat instead of a flat cap. A bowler hat. A *bowler*. The height of respectability.

He was shorter than Zeke remembered. But the deep blue eyes matched his own. And the scar on his left cheekbone, from where Zeke had smashed him with a chamber pot the night it had all gone to hell – that was there, sharp white against his tanned face.

'Zeke!' He came forward, clearly intending to embrace Zeke, or at least slap him manfully on both arms. Zeke just stared at him until he stopped a couple of feet away.

Some girls had seen them and streamed over.

'Oh, Mr Gardiner! Could you sign my book?'

He put on his public smile and did his job, signing and smiling and chatting, thanking God that it didn't need any real thought because he'd done it so many times before. When they'd gone, fluttering with excitement, he said, 'You'd better come inside.'

Best not to take him back to the dressing room. Percy was still there, indulging in his usual post-matinée snack of smoked salmon and brown bread.

He led his father to the props room; the props boy had gone, the evening's portable props laid out on their tables, ready to be handed over. It was an oddly shaped room, tucked in between the lavatories and the electrician's booth; cold and fairly dreary, except for tattered old posters on the walls.

But it was a theatre room, which meant it was *his* territory, not his father's. And that, at this moment, mattered.

'What do you want?'

'I wanted to see you! Wanted to make sure you were all right, now . . .' his voice drifted away. Did he realise that any mention of Zeke's mother would get him thrown out, or was he pretending to be tactful? The latter, probably.

'Well, now you've seen me. I'm fine.' What did the old man *really* want?

His father turned to the wall, appearing to look at a poster for Sarah Bernhardt – a lush Alphonse Mucha design, all curves and translucent fabrics. From another time, before the War.

'I wanted to . . . to say I'm sorry.' A quick glance away from the poster, to see how he was taking it. Acting taught you how to control your face, and Zeke had never been so glad of that. He was as expressionless as a shop mannequin. As if discouraged, his father turned back to the wall. 'Since – since I found out about Enid, I've been, well, thinking about it all. I just wanted to – to apologise. Too late to say it to her, so . . .'

Could that be true? A lifetime of disappointed hopes made it unlikely.

'Sorry for what, exactly?'

His father turned eagerly. 'For everything! For drinking, for, for hurting the both of you . . . everything, really. I didn't do right by you or your mother, and I'm sorry.'

It was a big thing, for his father to apologise. He'd never done that before. A small core of warmth started in his belly. He remembered, briefly, those days when he'd thought his father was the best of all men. Before the drink took him.

'All right. I'm glad to know that.'

Immediately, his father smiled broadly. 'That's grand, then. Just grand.' The faint Irish accent which had always been present was a little stronger. That was a bad sign. That accent came out when he'd had a few. Zeke felt his jaw clench. Not very much had changed, then.

'When are you going back?' Zeke couldn't think of anything else to say. The apology had been given. There was nothing else between them, for good or ill.

'What?' Taken aback, his father frowned and then shook his head. 'No, no, my boy. I've come to stay. To be your family, now there's no one else.'

The penny dropped. As if this selfish, mean, arrogant man would come five thousand miles to apologise.

Rage filled him. The kind of rage that had put that scar on his father's face.

'You read my letters to Mum, didn't you? They called you after she was dead, and you went to scavenge her things, and read my letters. About my work here. You read them, and you thought, "He must be onto a good thing, I'll go and get me a bit of that."'

For a moment, his father just stood there, his face showing nothing. And then it twisted in anger and self-pity.

'And why not?' he spat. 'You've already cost me. Not just what it cost to raise you – I had to *hire* a woman to do for me and do the dairy after you abducted your mother away from me! You owe me, lad.'

Funnily enough, he could relax now. This was the father he knew.

He didn't bother replying, just opened the door and waited. But his father dug his heels in.

'This isn't over. I have a lot more to say to you.'

'We have a guard here.' Zeke nodded to the open doorway. 'Go now or I'll call him.'

Slowly, his father walked towards the door, but stopped, his face only a foot from Zeke's.

'I read all those articles about you,' he said. 'Lots of talk about your poor dear old mother, but no mention of your father. Not. One. Word. How would your adoring public like it if the old man came out of the woodwork and told everyone how his greedy, grasping son had stolen all the poor old man's life savings to fund his trip to London? Eh?'

There was a network of red lines on his nose and in his eyes. Bad breath. A smell. It made Zeke sick to think that this was any father of his.

'Who's going to believe you? You're pathetic.'

That surprised him. He took a step back, and then stopped, as if unsure what to say or do next.

'Zeke? Are you back here?'

Kit. Christ, he couldn't let his father get his hooks into Kit.

'I'll be right there!' he called. Then he bent until his eyes bored into his father's. 'Get out.'

But his father smiled nastily at him. 'That'll be Miss Linton, eh? Your sweetheart? Or is she that lord's girl? Bet *she* wouldn't like to hear anything bad about you.'

He managed a sneer in return. 'Just try it. I'll have you arrested for blackmail. And don't think I wouldn't do it. Or worse.'

Fists clenched, he moved forwards. How he'd love to beat the bastard to a pulp. And why not? Zeke raised a fist.

His father backed away.

'Oh, I know you would. You've always had a mean streak. Mean and vicious!' he shouted as he passed Kit in the corridor. She looked at him in bewilderment. With relief, Zeke saw that Sam was waiting at the top of the passage; he took Rory Gardiner firmly by the arm and marched him out.

Kit, in her day clothes, came down the passage hesitantly. 'Is everything all right, Zeke?'

He turned away for a moment, to catch his breath, and then came out of the props room, shutting the door very carefully behind him, to make sure he didn't slam it off its hinges.

'No,' he said. He was supposed to say, 'Everything is fine!' but this was Kit. 'No. That was my father. Trying to blackmail money out of me.'

In some ways, Kit was more canny than he was. 'He heard about your work here,' she concluded instantly. 'Wanted to milk you.'

Shame flooded him; his face turned bright red. Only his father made him feel like this; he struggled to get his anger under control.

'Might be worth paying his fare home,' Kit said thought-fully, tucking her arm in his. 'Just to get him out of the place.'

He hugged her arm against him like a shield. 'Maybe. Let's not worry about it now. You must be hungry.'

'As a hippopotamus!' she laughed. She was a grand girl; so kind, but ready to put worry aside and simply enjoy life. He wondered where she had learned that trick, and if she could teach him.

'Bangers and mash, that's what I want!' she declared. So they went to the Shaftesbury, which did a damn good bangers and mash. He kept an eye out for his father along the way, but there was no sign of him.

That was bad. It meant he had a plan.

The worst was that the mere sight of his father had brought up in him the person he'd tried so hard to bury. The man who solved things with his fists, just like his father. The rage, the violence that lurked just under the surface whenever he even thought about what his mother had gone through . . .

He'd left that man behind in Canada. Or so he'd thought. Perhaps his father was right, and he had always had a mean streak. Just as well he and Kit had agreed to be brother and sister; he wasn't fit to be more than her friend. With his father as his only example, with this rage inside him, what kind of husband and father could he be?

CHAPTER 23

After the Saturday matinée, Charlot asked them all to stay back and come on stage once they were in street clothes.

'Box office is down,' Marguerite said gloomily as they moved down the prompt-side corridor. Kit looked at her in dismay.

The recent surge in full houses which had followed the scandal – she hadn't even realised that was over.

Life had been too full. But Marguerite, a much older hand than she was, always kept a close eye on the box office – 'So I know when to start auditioning.'

Should she be auditioning, too?

'That's not good.'

'No. But perhaps you can do another *fillum*, dear.' The spiky tone in Marguerite's voice cut Kit, but worse was the sudden chill that enveloped her. If this play folded . . . she had another two months to run on the sublet before she could go back to the Cats' Home. That was all right, probably. Charlot would give them at least a couple of weeks' notice, and she had enough in the kitty for the rent. But she still had to eat. The film money had been good, but . . . she'd had to buy so many things to go around with Henry and his friends. M. Dernier only did frocks. Silk stockings alone had been ruinous. Easy for men. They could wear the same suit year in, year out.

On stage, Kit slid through the crowd – *everyone* had been called, from prop man to the boy who ran messages to the orchestra members, as well as the cast – to stand next to Zeke. He smiled down at her reassuringly, but he looked worried. Everyone looked worried, except the electrician and Sam. They belonged to the theatre, and would go on to whatever production came into this theatre next. But everyone else was employed by Charlot.

He stood downstage, facing them all.

'Well, my dears, you probably know what I'm going to say. We've had a good run, but the box office is down. So we'll be folding in three weeks' time.'

A murmur went through the crowd.

'I'm happy to say the management will be bringing in a new show to this theatre – a six-week run of *Romeo and Juliet*. A week's rehearsal only. So props, costume, lighting, you'll all be staying. Actors, you are welcome to audition for it, but I have to tell you that we've cast the principals. Ralph Richardson, a young actor you may not know yet, has been lent to us by the Doran Management, and Nora Swinburne will be Juliet – she's just returned from New York where she did very creditably. We're borrowing a young man from RADA to play Mercutio – John Gielgud. Other roles are still open, but we're looking mostly for older actors, obviously, for those.' He looked sympathetically at Zeke and Kit, and her stomach clenched. Nothing for them, then. 'Susan, I have you in mind for the Nurse.' Susan nodded with a smile of relief. 'And obviously there's no chorus in this production, and we'll need only a very small musical ensemble. Derek, we'll talk about that.'

The orchestra conductor nodded.

'So, I'm sorry, ladies and gentlemen, but this has been a most satisfying collaboration, and you're all to be congratulated on your performances and industry – in every field.' He smiled benignly at the various groups, actors, musicians, and backstage workers, and then nodded a dismissal.

As they were slowly leaving the stage, he called out, 'Miss Linton! Mr Gardiner!'

They turned and went back to him.

'Now, *mes amis*. This will feel like a disaster to you, but it is not, I assure you. It is just the way theatre works.' Zeke nodded, but Kit could only stand there, hoping she didn't look as miserable as she felt. 'And, if you have patience,' Charlot continued, 'I have another production coming up later in the year. Seven weeks for the Shakespeare, and then we have a touring company bringing in a revue from America for a month, and then we will be back here with a new book and new music.' He regarded them with twinkling eyes, and smoothed his little moustache. 'I am happy to say, there are roles in that production that will suit you.' He paused for effect. 'Possibly, I'll be able to welcome you back even without an audition. But of course I can't speak for the director.'

'Thank you, sir!' Zeke said immediately. He shook Charlot's hand enthusiastically. 'What's the show?'

'Something that Wodehouse fellow and Guy Bolton have put together in New York. I'm going over there to see it once *Romeo and Juliet* is bedded in. It's getting very good reviews.'

'I love his books,' Kit said. She didn't know what else to say.

'So. All is well.' Charlot nodded at her and walked off.

'Well, that's a break!' Zeke said. 'We'll just have to make sure the director likes us.'

She started adding up weeks. Seven, four, maybe a week dark . . .

'That's almost three months without pay!'

He looked at her sharply. 'Will you be all right? Have you got enough put by?'

She had her going-home money. She'd promised herself she wouldn't use it, but . . .

'Yes. Yes, I'll be fine – only, when the sublet is up, I'll have to move back to the Cats' Home.'

'Well, there are worse places,' he said comfortably as they made their way to the stage door.

'I feel like a failure.'

'What are you talking about? The show ran for six months! That's *great* box office!'

He opened the stage door for her. Sam was in his little office, commiserating with a mate from the orchestra. They went out into the alley behind the theatre. The autograph hunters had gone home. That seemed to sum up the day. No one wanted them enough. And she didn't have enough money.

'I should have saved more. Bought fewer clothes.'

'It's harder for a woman.'

'It *is*! I mean, if you go to a party where the prince might ask you to dance, you don't want to wear the same dress you've worn twice before. And there's a limit to how many I can borrow from Benny.'

He was silent. She took a peek at his face; it had that blank look, which meant that he was trying not to say something uncomplimentary – not about her, but about Henry and the Prince of Wales' set. But it *ought* to be about her.

'I've been an idiot.'

Zeke's face lit up immediately, with affection and humour.

'Living above your station?' he teased her.

'Living above my means, anyway.'

'Come on, then, I'll buy you lunch.'

Over lunch at a nearby pub, they discussed other ways of making money during the time off.

'Courtney may want us for another film,' Zeke reminded her. The director had dropped a few hints.

'But that wouldn't be for months, either!'

He took a sip of his coffee. 'We should try to get some singing work.'

'The BBC?'

'Have to be after the play folds, or they'll expect it to be for free. And maybe some concerts?'

'As long as it was light operetta. Or modern. Neither of us has the voice for serious music.'

He took a mouthful of mashed potato and nodded agreement, then swallowed and grinned at her.

'We could go on the halls,' he joked. She shuddered. The music halls – she'd done a turn there once, in Sydney. They could be fun to go to as an audience member, but for the performers, it was on, off, wait three hours, do it all again. She'd hated it – hated the shared dressing rooms, the male performers who thought, if she were on the stage, she was easy game. She'd fended off more hands in those three weeks than she had the entire rest of her life.

At least Henry wasn't free with his hands.

'I need to tighten my belt,' she said. 'No more clothes.'

'Well,' Zeke said, grinning, 'no more *new* clothes. I think you ought to keep wearing the ones you have.'

She blushed and for a moment their eyes locked. She watched his darken, and knew he was imagining her . . . No, better not to think about it.

'I'll have to see my agent.'

Her agent had had remarkably little to do since Kit had arrived in London, apart from getting her the audition for Charlot's play. Time he earned his money. Zeke had the same agent, Keith Middleton.

'What if Keith gets us jobs that conflict with Charlot's next production?'

Both of them were troubled by the thought. Working for Charlot – it was such an important management. Well respected. No shenanigans. Paid on time. Nothing expected of his female talent except actual talent, which was rare.

'I'd *like* to come back for it,' she said. Pushing her hair back, she stretched in her seat. If only she didn't have to think about these things! Or about money!

'Me too.' Zeke finished his lemon squash and stood up to pull her chair back. 'Time to get back.'

The walk to the theatre wasn't long, but it seemed to stretch out. Perhaps they walked more slowly. She wished she hadn't had the ham sandwich; her stomach churned it over until she felt sick. The life that had seemed like such a dream come true was revealed to be unsteady and shaky, and possibly even dangerous. An adventure, yes – but adventures were full of unpleasant experiences, weren't they?

'Don't come back crying to me when you're broke and out of work,' her sister had said before she left Sydney. Her mother had cried out against that.

'Of course you can come to us!' she'd said. At the time, Kit had been more pleased that her sister had been scolded than grateful for the offer. But now she realised that both of them had *expected* her to crawl home with her tail between her legs.

It made her feel young. And stupid. Incredibly stupid. Not to have looked ahead, as Zeke had, and saved her money. She should have stayed at the Cats' Home. Too bad if Henry looked askance at it. *He* didn't have to work for his living. Carriage trade, that was Henry.

◆

When she got home, Perry was, most unusually, sitting on the sofa, darning a stocking.

'I heard the news,' she said, sticking her needle into the darning ball and getting up. 'Rotten luck.' She gave Kit a big hug, and Kit clung to her. She was so kind! A shoulder to cry on was exactly what she needed. Tears clogged her throat and the tense knot under her breastbone hurt. Perry patted her arm. 'It'll be okay, Kit. I've been in and out of work since I was eighteen.' She led Kit over to the sofa, sat her down, and then went to put the kettle on in the tiny kitchen. 'You get used to it!' she called through the door.

'I'm not sure I want to get used to it.' Kit shocked herself by saying it out loud.

Perry put her head out of the kitchen. 'Feels like that the first time,' she agreed. 'And the second. But if you want to stay in the business . . .'

'I suppose I do.' Kit ran her hands through her hair and leaned her head back. 'I suppose it's what we do, isn't it? Just keep going.'

For the first time since she'd met her, Perry looked embarrassed.

'Well, actually . . .' She went into the bedroom, and came back with a small jeweller's box. Opening it, she put it on the coffee table. A ring inside. Tiny, but pretty.

'You're *engaged*?' How could she not have known about this? Why had Perry never told her?

'Not exactly.' Perry picked up the box and fiddled with it, taking the ring out and putting it back a couple of times. 'George is back home, in Yorkshire. He always wanted to marry me. Gave me this when I left home. Said – well, he gave me five years. He wanted me to get it out of my system. If I came home in the five years, we'd get married. If not, I was to send the ring back to him, because it was his grandmother's.'

'He's the one who writes to you!'

'That's the one.' Perry meditated over the ring. 'I've been here four years. I'm never going to make it out of the chorus. It's been damn good fun, don't get me wrong, but . . . after my current show folds, I'm heading home. To George.'

'But –' How could she ask her something she had no right to know? 'The men you go out with . . .'

'You think I've been sleeping with them all?' Perry laughed somewhat bitterly. 'No. Oh, when I first came here, a couple . . . but nothing for at least two years. No one really compares to

George, when it comes right down to it. But I do like parties, and I do like to go dancing, so out I go with them.'

Kit sat back in astonishment. She hadn't noticed *any* of this! Was she completely blind? She hadn't suspected Henry's feelings for her were warming; she didn't notice that Perry wasn't the flirt she'd thought. Had she misjudged *everyone*? Even Zeke?

What a short-sighted fool she'd been!

'I'm such an idiot.'

Perry patted her on the knee. 'You've had quite enough to think about – and I put on a good show.' She grinned, tilting her head at a coquettish angle. 'You have more fun if they think you're easy – although you do have to get quite good at slapping hands away!'

They pottered around, getting ready for bed.

'You're not going to leave the business?' Perry asked as they slid between the sheets.

Kit reached over to turn off the light. 'Today has been such a topsy-turvy day, I don't know *what* I'm going to do!'

CHAPTER 24

The Monday morning post brought a letter from Kit's mother. She regarded it with misgiving. The last one, about the film, had been . . . snide wasn't a word she liked to think of in relation to her mother, but . . .

'Oh, open it!' Perry said, passing a boiled egg in an eggcup over to her. Breakfast was an important meal, according to her, even if it was taken at noon. 'Get it over with!'

Kit took the eggcup and put it down next to her plate of toast. *Get it over with.*

'Read it out,' Perry suggested. 'She's always good for a laugh.'

Yes. 'Let's hope so.'

Dear Katherine,

You sly thing, why didn't you tell me?

It does seem rather odd that I have to find out my daughter is keeping company with the Earl of Carleton's son via a magazine, but so it is. The Tatler column was quite an eye-opener.

However I found out, I must say I was very glad indeed to know that you are keeping respectable – <u>more</u> than respectable – company in London. Henry Carleton's mother and I were at school together, and I believe his uncle was in the same cricket team as your father when they were at Oxford . . .

Kit let her voice trail off in dismay.

'Blimey!' Perry said, eyes wide. 'I didn't know your family was as posh as all that!'

She'd only ever told Perry that her father was a vicar.

'Dad is the Dean of St Andrew's Cathedral in Sydney,' she said in a small voice. 'My mother is the daughter of an earl.'

'Bloody hell! You *are* a deb! No wonder Lord High Muckamuck fancies you!'

Why did that make her want to cry? The idea that she was merely an 'acceptable gel' . . . she wanted to be desired for *herself*, not her family. She'd thought Henry did, but with this letter before her, she realised that her lineage would have been important in his mind. Her being Uncle Joseph's niece was just the sort of thing his kind valued.

Perry was looking offended. 'I don't see why you had to keep all this a secret –'

'You didn't tell me about *George*!' Kit said swiftly.

'Oh, George isn't in the same league as –'

'We both kept secrets.' *Please*, Kit thought, *please don't let's fight.* She couldn't bear it. She needed Perry's friendship more than ever.

Perhaps that showed in her face. Perry's outrage softened, and she shook her head.

'I don't know, kid. You're an odd one.'

'Can you imagine how they'd have treated me at the Cats' Home if they'd known?'

Laughing, Perry reached over to squeeze her shoulder. 'Now, that's the truth. All right. What else does Her Majesty have to say?'

Do keep me informed about your activities, and convey my best to Lady Carleton . . . 'The rest is just some stuff about my sister's children.'

She looked at the letter, and then up at Perry, feeling tears gather. 'You know, I don't think she's ever really approved of me before.'

'More fool her!' Perry regarded her with fond exasperation. 'Eat your toast, woman! And tell her to go to the devil.'

'Well, I can't do *that*!' But she laughed, as Perry had intended, imagining her mother's face if she did.

She had a bath and then they did grocery shopping. Mondays were quiet, ordinary days, when the rest of the world went about its business but actors and actresses organised their lives. Shopping, hairdresser, cleaning house. A domestic kind of day, and oh! she needed one.

By dinner time, she felt almost restored to her normal self. Henry rang to ask her out – she said no, she needed a night in. Zeke didn't ring.

She tried not to let that bother her.

Over a delicious fish tart Perry had made, they discussed Kit's options for employment. They were pretty bleak, if she wanted to be available for Charlot's next show.

'Three months,' Perry mused. 'That's a fair old time. Time enough for a quick romance with Zekey boy.'

Was three months off enough to break the agreement with Zeke that they wouldn't . . . wouldn't *do* anything while they were working together? Because they had to come back and work together again, if it all went well . . .

All the arguments for staying just friends still stood. Perhaps they were stronger than ever.

But . . .

'Ah-hah!' Perry teased her. 'You're thinking about it!'

'Oh, you!'

She got up and started to clear away. Her old ideas about Zeke not being 'gentlemanly' enough for her had seemed to wither away lately, especially when she considered how some of the actual 'gentlemen' acted at the parties Henry took her to. But . . . Zeke hadn't made any move towards her, so he must still think their work was more important.

Just once, she wished *she* was the most important thing.

◆

A call came up the stairs. 'Zeke, dear, there's a man for you.'

Mrs Coward had moved to treating him like an extra son some time ago, including not traipsing up the stairs to knock on his door. He bounded down, expecting his chum from his last job, Billy, who occasionally dragged him out for a game of snooker or billiards on a Monday. He had swiftly adjusted his game from pool to snooker, but billiards was still a challenge when he was up against a good player.

But it wasn't Billy. It was his father, standing in the hall, the light from the stained glass coming in and painting his face a patchwork of colours, sickly yellow and blood red. He was in the same suit he'd worn to the theatre, but it looked crumpled.

Zeke stopped in the middle of the flight.

'There's something I need to say to you,' his father began. His voice was subdued; he held his hat in both hands, like a supplicant, his shoulders bowed. The anger he'd shown at the theatre was gone completely, drained away and replaced by something Zeke couldn't identify.

Mrs Coward was in the doorway to the living room.

'Would you like a pot of tea for your guest, Mr Gardiner?' she asked, picking up from his reaction, no doubt, that this wasn't an ordinary occasion.

'No, thank you, Mrs Coward.' He came down the rest of the way and took his hat and coat from the hatstand. 'We'll head down to the tea shop.'

Not to the pub – not least because it was mid-afternoon, and England had those weird opening hours which meant mid-afternoon was a time you couldn't get a drink. He wouldn't take his father to a pub, anyway. Asking for trouble.

There was a tea shop two streets over, and they walked there in silence, his father following his lead in an automatic way which recalled walking the fields with him, as a child, the two of them finding some shared rhythm despite their different heights. He was the tall one, now. He towered over his father by a good six inches.

It didn't help.

He still felt young; too young to deal with this. He didn't even have the stalwart presence of his mother in the back of his mind. She was gone, and left behind only grief.

His father slowed down as they went; he couldn't work out why, but it was annoying.

At the shop, they sat across from one another. Monday afternoon, it was pretty empty. Just a couple of suburban matrons in a booth, comparing stocking purchases.

'Well,' his father said, after they'd ordered tea and scones from a waitress who eyed Zeke in astonishment and then went back to whisper to the other girl behind the counter. Maybe she recognised him? That had been happening more lately, since *Britain Dances* came out.

'Well,' Zeke said. No encouragement. No siree.

His father was pale. Even his red-veined nose was paler than normal. There were bags under his eyes, and his skin had a jaundiced tone. His breath came quickly; he was so unfit even that little walk had puffed him. Zeke was filled with disgust. He'd done this to himself.

'Well . . .' His father fidgeted with the sugar bowl, the little posy vase, the tablecloth. 'There's something I have to tell you.'

'So you said.'

'You're not making this easy!'

'Any reason I should?' He had a damned nerve, expecting anything else.

The waitress came back with the pot of tea, cups and a plate of scones, with jam as well as butter.

'Jam's on the house,' she said. 'Er . . .' She had an order book and pen in her hand, fiddling with them shyly. 'Would you mind, Mr Gardiner?'

He forced himself to give his public smile. 'Not at all. What's your name?'

'Sally. And my friend's Mary. Could you do one for her, too?'

199

He signed two pages, as requested.

'Oh, thanks ever so!' she said, and escaped on a gulp back to the counter.

The interchange had put his father in a bad mood, which he was clearly trying not to convey. He smiled at Zeke ingratiatingly.

'Well. I *do* have something to tell you –'

'Oh, spit it out, for God's sake!'

'I'm dying.'

He did spit it out, as if a curse, and then fell silent, appalled at his own words.

Zeke stared at him. The paleness. The loss of weight. The slow walking. The gasping breath and puffy face. It made a terrible sense, all of a sudden. He was conscious of not feeling anything but surprise. Not a thing. That was shock, surely.

'Of what?' Even to his own ears, that sounded cold as ice. His father's mouth tucked itself in, annoyed. There had been a time when that expression on his father's face would have sent him running for cover.

'Liver disease.'

It almost made him laugh. What else would it have been? The alcoholic's nemesis.

'How long?' It was as though he were a detective, asking questions of a suspect. That was pretty much how he felt.

The older man shrugged. 'Two months, if I'm lucky. If not . . . a few weeks.' He flushed a little. 'I know you think it serves me right, but the drink . . . once it gets its claws into you, it don't let go.'

The echo of his own thoughts about Henry set him back; made him reassess. Had his father been a young lad like Henry, once upon a time? Had the drink got its claws into him, and never let go? Could he condemn him for that?

No. But –

'Being a drunk is one thing. Being a drunk who beats your wife and child is something else.'

'There's a demon in the drink –'

'No.' No. He'd seen enough drunk people now. He wasn't a naïve little boy. Some of those people became *nicer* when they were drunk. Like Noël. 'No. There's a demon in you that the drink lets out. There's no excuse.'

'So you're just going to let me die in the gutter, are you, ya miserable spalpeen?' The Irish always came out when he was angry.

'That's why you came,' Zeke said, mulling it over.

'Acourse it was why I came! You're my only flesh and blood, where else would I go?'

Growling at Zeke, he bit into the scone with angry need. God, the man was actively hungry. Too hungry to stand on his dignity. And there was no odour of liquor around him. He must really be on his last pennies. Silently, Zeke pushed his untouched scone over. His father flushed, but ate it, smothered in jam, while Zeke watched, unmoving.

'Where are you staying?'

He flushed again. 'At a men's hostel near King's Cross station.' He took one of the paper napkins and wrote on it with a pencil he fished out of his inside pocket. 'This is the address.'

Zeke took it. A dicey neighbourhood. Thank God he hadn't taken a flat when Kit had! At least there was no question of him putting his father up at the Cowards'.

'What do you want from me?'

For the first time, his father hesitated. 'I want to . . . to be a father to you, even if it's only for a few weeks.'

'And?'

'I don't want to die in the poor hospital!' It came out in a rush, as though his father couldn't bear the words in his mouth. Then he quieted, and put out a hand as if he really meant it. 'But it's not just that, Ezekiel. I've been a bad father, and a worse husband, I know. But . . . at the end, can't we let the past be past?'

Oh, that smooth tone! He'd heard it before, when this man had talked his mother into staying one more time. Could it be genuine? And even if it was . . . did that matter?

How much did he owe a drunken, violent man just because of blood?

'I'll think about it.' He stood up and went to the desk to pay, and then, smiling tightly at the blushing waitresses, walked out without a backward glance.

To hell with him.

Out on the street, walking away, he wanted to head for Kit. Wanted so *much* to lay his head in her lap and let her cool hands smooth away his troubles.

She was probably with Henry. Goddam all women who chose drunks. They made nothing but trouble for the decent men who loved them.

He walked and walked for hours, refusing to think about anything, until he stopped on Blackfriars Bridge, watching the reflections of yellow lamps ripple on the water as the tide went out. And only then, standing still, did he realise that he'd admitted to himself, at last, that he loved her.

CHAPTER 25

Going back to the theatre for the Tuesday night performance was bittersweet.

Kit just wanted to get on stage, to perform, to let the music and the applause wash away all her unease. And yet she was also sharply aware that the nights were counting down.

'Buck up, my girl!' she told herself. 'Enjoy yourself while it lasts.'

She smiled brilliantly at Zeke and ran on with him for the second act closing. She would *relish* every moment on this stage – acting, dancing with Zeke, *loving* being here and now. Zeke seemed to catch her mood and they performed especially well.

When he said, at the end of their third act dance, 'Why don't you love me?' she felt a frisson go right through her, so that her returning 'Maybe I do' seemed to have special significance. But after the sweet, lingering kiss, he winked at her, with the eye facing away from the audience, and she had to bite her lip to stop herself from laughing.

They kept going, dancing with verve, lifting the audience with them so that the whole theatre hummed with energy.

As they came offstage after their final bows, the applause still going, Marguerite glared at them, Basil smiled cynically, and the stage manager said, 'If you'd done that earlier, we might not be closing.' Which was both uplifting and a kick in the guts.

But too bad. She wasn't going to let anything undermine her enjoyment of these last three weeks.

'Let's go dancing,' she said to Zeke.

'What about the lord?'

'Don't know, don't care,' she said. Zeke had come in tonight with a thundercloud on his brow, but it had gone, washed away by music, by high kicks, by the smooth, graceful turns they had accomplished together.

'That's the spirit.' They changed quickly and raced out, pausing only to sign a few autographs at the stage door (fewer every night, alas). She saw Henry's car pull up as they ran down the alley, but she ignored it. Not tonight. Tonight was for forgetting anything difficult.

She was in a not-quite-evening dress. They went to a Soho café for supper, and then up the street and downstairs to the jazz club she'd been to on the ill-fated Charleston night. She didn't care. There'd be no photographers tonight. Just hot jazz and cold drinks and Zeke to dance with; dancing with him was like a drug.

They talked about nothing and everything. The weather, the latest movie, books, music, their colleagues, theatre gossip, art. But mostly they danced, and listened to the singer, a plump French *chanteuse* who fronted the Italian band with what Zeke called 'a lot of vibrato' with a lift of his eyebrows, which sent her into giggles when the singer's bosom shivered as she sang.

Afterwards, they wandered back to Sicilian Avenue arm in arm, in perfect harmony.

They were walking through Golden Square when Zeke pulled her towards a bench by the side of the road. 'I need your advice,' he said, very seriously.

His father's revelation drowned her in pity for Zeke; to lose *both* parents, to be completely alone! It must be terrifying. But that didn't seem to be what was worrying him. Perhaps it hadn't hit him yet.

'He'll die in the poorhouse – or at least the poor ward – if I don't help him.' Zeke ran a hand through his hair and then let it drop. Only one side of his face was lit by the streetlamps around the edge of the Square. He wasn't letting anything show. She knew that feeling, when you bottled everything up inside because it was all too big to let out.

The moment was full of significance, as though she had to remember everything about it. A bus went past, its lighted windows casting a flicker over the ground, its engine rumbling. The air smelled of exhaust and coal fires, and a faint scent of the Thames at low tide.

'I can help, if you need money,' she offered. For this, she'd dig into her going-home savings.

His hand came up in a swift gesture of refusal. 'No, no. I *have* the money. I just . . .' Rubbing his eyes, he leaned back against the bench as if suddenly exhausted. 'Does he deserve for me to help him out? That's what I can't decide. He's not a – a good man.'

Oh. That was tricky. She let it run through her mind, slowly, thinking it through from as many angles as she could. Then she took his hand, and held it firmly. Did she have the right to intervene? But he had *asked*.

'I think,' she said slowly, 'that it might not be about what kind of man *he* is. I think it might be about what kind of man *you* are.'

Zeke went very still. Silent. For a long moment, she feared the worst. He was offended, he'd hate her, he'd pull away and be disgusted . . .

His free hand came up and he tilted her chin so she looked up at him.

'You are a good person.' He bent and kissed her cheek, so softly it made her want to cry. She blinked back tears. 'Thank you.'

Her own hand touched his cheek, silently.

Without saying anything else, they got up and started walking again, the night-time sounds and sights of London as soothing as a lullaby.

CHAPTER 26

Finding the right nursing home was easy – he asked Marguerite, whose mother, he knew, had died a few years before.

As with everything Marguerite did, it was expensive, but what the hell. He was either doing this or he wasn't.

So he made arrangements by phone, called the hostel and then went to pick his father up on the Thursday morning.

He didn't have much luggage. A single suitcase plus a Gladstone bag. Zeke hailed a cab and they set off for Croydon.

His father looked worse than he had on Monday, but he was more cheerful. Not surprising. Zeke didn't want to talk, but there was no shutting him up.

'Last time I was in this city, it was just before I went to Canada. Came over to get the boat from Southampton, so I thought I'd have me a spree in London first.' Zeke winced at the word 'spree'. That was how his father had always described his drinking jags. 'Before I met your mother, that was. Oh, she was –'

'Don't talk about her.'

His voice, he knew, was harsh. Good. Let the old bastard hear that he meant it. How he had the *nerve* to talk about her!

'Now, son . . .' The tone was placatory, but also paternal. As if he had the right.

'No. You don't talk about her. Not one word. Or I take you straight back to the hostel. And don't call me "son".'

'I thought –'

Zeke turned his head and simply *looked* at him. All his training went into it, every moment he'd spent on stage or in rehearsal. He called up all the contempt, the anger, the scorn he felt, and he funnelled it into that look.

'No.'

He could see his father swallow nervously. Would he try to sweet-talk his way out of it? Would he try to be convincingly loving and parental? Part of Zeke – the small boy who never quite went away – half hoped he would. Hoped that this relationship was worth enough to his father that he'd risk his nursing home to say words of love.

His father sat back on the cab seat and said nothing.

At the nursing home, which was a converted manor house, he said to the cabby, 'Wait for me,' and took the bags in to the reception desk, his father trailing behind.

A nice motherly woman with an Anglo-Indian cast to her features greeted him. 'Mr Gardiner? I'm Mrs Moncrieff. And this must be your father. How d'ye do.' She shook his father's hand and gave a practised smile. 'This way.'

She led them to a room down a long corridor and opened the door. Nice. Too good for him. It looked out over a rose garden and, beyond that, the river. Expensive furniture, thick green carpet that reminded him of the BBC studios.

His father surveyed the room in astonishment. The nicest place he'd ever set foot in, probably. 'Son . . .' he said in amazed gratitude. That gave Zeke a sour satisfaction; at least he'd shown the old man that he'd made good, despite everything.

'Right,' he said, depositing the bags at the end of the bed. 'I'll be off.'

Mrs Moncrieff tactfully took herself out of the room. His father looked around again, and visibly swelled with satisfaction.

'So, when will I be seeing you?'

'You won't.' Zeke regarded him coldly. 'This is it. I'm paying for you to die here, but you won't see me again.' He paused. 'Don't worry. I won't tip you into a pauper's grave. I might even spring for a headstone.'

Was that real pain on his father's face? Strangely, it didn't give Zeke any satisfaction. He just wanted to get away. To draw a line under this, under every moment he'd spent in his father's company, and walk away.

Maybe his father saw that in his face. 'Goodbye, Ezekiel,' he said, standing stiffly at the foot of the bed. He didn't hold out his hand, but Zeke felt impelled to do so – he had to be able to tell Kit that he'd acted right.

They shook. For a moment, his father's hand clung to his, but then it loosened, and they separated.

At the door, his back to the room, Zeke stopped. 'I hope it's easy, when the time comes.' Then he walked out; stopped in the corridor to get control of himself. No room for tears here. Why should he feel so *much* about this man? It wasn't fair.

He organised payment by cheque with Mrs Moncrieff, paying for the first two weeks, and giving her his contact details.

'I imagine you'll want us to let you know when the time comes?' she asked delicately.

What could he say? Something plausible. 'Yes. By telegram. But I may be out of the country, so don't be surprised if I can't get back in time.'

'A new film?' she asked, her face lighting up.

'We may be in another soon,' he confirmed. Courtney had been hopeful, but it all depended on getting financing, like everything in this business.

'With Miss Linton, I hope?'

'Yes.' A wave of excitement went over her visibly.

'Oh, I do *love* seeing the two of you together! Tell me –' she dropped her voice confidentially '– *is* there a romance there?'

'If there were,' he said, 'I'd be the luckiest man alive.' He winked and went out, hearing her sigh romantically as he left. What a bastard he was. What a lying, manipulative bastard. No better than his old man. But that was his job, wasn't it? To lie for a living.

He was a bit jaded with this acting thing.

Except for Kit.

CHAPTER 27

The waiter took their order and slid away. Kit hoped that he'd be back soon; she was hungry, and the Riviera did a wonderful saddle of mutton for Sunday lunch.

Henry slapped a newspaper down on the table between them. A photo of her and Zeke laughing, gazing into each other's eyes, was uppermost. It was one of the ones Sandro had taken.

'It's just publicity,' Kit said. She looked around – where on earth had Henry *got* the paper from? The Riviera was hardly the place to carry the *Daily Mail* around, even at lunchtime. Besides, it was a week old – from a follow-up piece by Rebecca on how well *Britain Dances* had done at the box office.

'Lady Bridlingham gave it to me,' he said bitterly. 'Full of false sympathy about your betrayal.'

'The old cow!'

'But she's *right*!' Henry picked up a glass of champagne and knocked it back, then glared at her. Outrage stiffened her spine. He had no claim on her. None at all.

'Kit –' Henry's voice was low and tense. She looked at him more closely. He seemed genuinely upset.

He swore softly. 'We can't talk here. Come outside.'

He led her to the terrace, where several other couples were walking in the soft summer air. The scent of lilacs and roses floated up from the garden below, and the low hooting of tug boats on the Thames sounded mournfully.

In the corner of the terrace, Henry turned and took her hands. She wanted to pull them away, but she was conscious of a sharp, sudden desire not to hurt him. Because he *was* looking hurt. She hadn't expected that.

'You're my girl.' For a second, she was keenly aware of her surroundings. The exquisite house, the beautiful grounds with the river flowing past, the silk and linen dresses of the women, the men in their perfectly tailored suits, with their perfectly tied ties. And her, standing there in her borrowed dress.

She pulled her hands free. Silently. Henry looked away, his mouth working. She *had* hurt him.

'I'm sorry . . . Henry, I feel as though I hardly know you! This –' She gestured to the party. 'This isn't a good way to learn what someone's really like.'

'Then spend some time with me!' he said eagerly. 'Come to Carleton. Mother's having a get-together for m'birthday. Come and stay for a week then.'

'Does your mother know I'm an actress?' She had made some friends among Henry's group, but only among the young ones. Henry had never taken her to another ball or garden party, and she was fairly sure that was because the hostesses had made it clear she wasn't welcome. 'Does she know I'm not "suitable"?'

'Hang suitability!' Henry set his mouth. 'I want you to come. And Mama wants to meet you! She doesn't care about that actress rot.'

By next month she'd be out of a job and back at the Cats' Home. She was filled with a piercing distaste for the small, drab rooms, the boiled eggs, the endless chatter of women in too-close proximity. Carleton, whatever else it was, would be big. She'd have a room of her own, for the first time since her visit to Barrows.

Just a week. And during that time, she could lay this relationship to rest. Or else . . . Henry looked at her hopefully. He was a nice boy, really, and he'd woven himself into her heart in a way she didn't quite understand. What had started as a smokescreen had turned into something else without her really noticing. Would it be so bad to see if a relationship between them could work? She owed it to him not to dismiss it out of hand.

Didn't she?

'All right,' she said. 'I'll come. In a month, we can spend time together. As long as your mother knows the truth about me and still wants me.'

'Wonderful!' He laughed and picked her up, swirling her around.

'Henry!' But she laughed, too. It was nice to be wanted.

They had a lovely lunch, and Henry seemed high-flown on happiness as well as champagne. She'd never been the

PAMELA HART

cause of such happiness in another person before. It warmed her through.

Bourke was waiting with the car when they left. As he opened the car door for her, Henry said, ignoring his presence, 'And you'll drop this actor fellow, of course.'

She bit her lip until they were in the car.

'Henry, I thought you understood. That's work. Publicity for the film. I certainly can't drop him.'

'You're turning your whole life into a lie just for money!'

A slap in the face. She jerked back as if he'd really hit her. His voice was slurred, his eyes too bright. As the car moved off down the street, his face fell into shadow, disguising his expression.

The accusation worried her. Was he right? Was she lying, cheating, playing her audience for fools?

The idea shook her deeply. Her hands clenched in her lap, the seams of her gloves biting into her fingers.

'That actor fellow –'

'Zeke,' she said sharply.

'The colonial. He needs to get himself a girl of his own. Or is he an invert?' Henry's eyes lit up at that thought. She was tempted. It would be such an easy way out of the looming fight. But she *wasn't* a liar.

'No. He's very manly.'

'Then he needs to stay away from you. And you need to stop pretending you're in love with him. You're my girl, dammit!'

'I'm no one's girl.' She could hear the hiss in her tone, and she didn't care. 'I'll go out with who I want, when I want, how I want. Don't you *dare* tell me what to do!'

214

She braced for anger in return but he put his hands over his face. 'Oh, Katherine. Can't you see? That's why you're wonderful! You don't care what anyone else wants. You're just *yourself.*' He raised his head and stared at her. The car stopped at a traffic light and his eyes showed up clearly. 'That's why I can't stand to see you lying about this colonial! It taints you. You're so, so, so pure. So straight and true.'

'Oh, I wish I were,' she sighed. He took her hands, and she let him.

'You are. The only girl I know who is.'

'But I'm not *your* girl, Henry.'

'Not yet. I'm not worthy of you, I know. But I'll try to be.'

She might be able to do some good here, even if she couldn't give him what he wanted. 'If you want to be worthy of a nice girl – even if it's not me – you should drink less.'

He regarded her hungrily. 'I will. I will. I'll toss it. Truly.'

'Good.' They were at Sicilian Avenue, so she detached her hands gently. 'Henry, I'm not your girl. I'll still be spending time with Zeke.'

'Don't sully yourself for money,' he pleaded. But he let her get out and threw himself back on the seat as Bourke opened her door and handed her out.

'Goodbye, Henry.'

'Goodbye, my love.'

They waited until she had let herself in and then drove away. Behind the glass lobby door, she watched them. The big, beautiful car, and inside . . . poor Henry. Her heart twisted with affectionate pity. Could she love him? She had no idea. The life she lived with him had never seemed *real*, so she'd never truly considered it.

What if she could?

The lunch hadn't gone at all as she'd imagined. She smoothed her hand down over the pink linen and was glad, at least, that she hadn't spilled anything on it. She could send it back to Benny tomorrow unharmed.

She was maundering on to avoid thinking. Slowly, she walked up the stairs. It wasn't the possibility of love which bothered her. Either she would come to love Henry or she wouldn't. Time would tell.

But the accusation that she was giving her life over to lies . . . for a girl from the vicarage, that cut deep. It was one thing to act on stage, but in her private life . . . Perhaps Henry was right; perhaps she ought to stop all this publicity nonsense. It had seemed no more than a game to play-act before the photographers; Henry's comments made her feel it had all been a tawdry pretence.

As she let herself into the flat, she had a quick vision of Zeke kissing her knuckles at the premiere. The warmth of his lips, his mischievous eyes, the strength of his hand on hers . . . she could feel it all as if it were happening right now.

If that was a lie . . . did she *hope* it was a lie? Or hope it wasn't?

Perry was still out. Kit took her dress off and folded it neatly into the box from Benny's, then sat at the dressing table and brushed her hair, following her normal routine in a daze.

My love. No one had ever called her that before. Except Zeke, in the play. But not in reality.

What did she want to be real? All of it – Henry, Zeke, *everything*? Or none of it, which would leave her free to belong to no one but herself? Whoever that was.

CHAPTER 28

'You're an idiot.' Perry stared accusingly at her and smacked the teapot down on the breakfast table, spilling a few drops. 'You've got Zeke Gardiner on a string and you won't reel him in!'

Kit glared back. 'That's a horrible thing to say. On a string! I do not. We're friends.'

She didn't even know why they were fighting. One minute Perry had been laughing over her going to Carleton ('Oooh, posh!') and the next – why was Perry so scratchy this morning?

'Have you heard from George?' Kit asked.

All the air went out of Perry and she sank into her chair, sighing.

'He wants me to come home right away.'

'You'd made up your mind to go back.'

'When the show ended. A couple of months. I wanted to *finish* it.'

'Are you sure you want to leave?'

Perry stared at her helplessly. 'I want George. But . . . he's a baker. He has his own business. He wants me to come work with him. Me. In a *bakery*!'

'You love to bake . . .'

'Oh, it's not the work.' Perry poured herself a cup of tea and listlessly buttered her toast. 'I'm not sure what it is, to tell you the truth.'

They ate in silence for a few minutes. Was she an idiot? Kit wasn't sure. She definitely didn't like the idea of having Zeke on a string, though. That was the old way of thinking, where a girl's job was to hook a husband by any means necessary.

'I think,' she said slowly, 'I know why we're both idiots.'

'This'll be good.' But Perry sat back to listen.

'Everyone's trying to recreate the "normal" life from before the War. And part of that is trying to get women to go back to the house. Out of public life, out of working for themselves. Back to being a helpmate to a man.'

'You've got that right.'

'And we *can't*. We just can't. At least, *we* can't. The kind of girl who goes on the stage, the kind who leaves home and strikes out for herself – how can we just slide back into the old ways? We know we don't need men to put food on our table, so . . .'

'So we want something more. More than being secure. More than being looked after.'

'Yes!' Was that why she never felt that she fitted in anywhere? Because everything was changing so fast? Did *anyone* feel as though they fitted in anymore?

Perry's eyes were bright. 'That's *it*! I can't just slide back into being George's helper in the shop. I want something more. Something of my own. It's not that I don't want George. But I don't want *just* George!' She jumped up and hugged Kit. 'You're a genius!'

Kit laughed and hugged her back. 'But what are you going to do?'

'Start my own business!'

Now, that was startling. 'Really? But how can you afford it? What kind of business?'

'Catering.' Perry's voice was sure. 'It's a growing field, you know, because women can't get domestic servants the way they used to. Most houses don't have a cook anymore. They get by with a maid, if they have anyone at all. So when they have parties, they're bringing the food in from outside. I've noticed that, but there was no way of doing it myself. Not in London, when I'm already working. In Yorkshire, though, with George's bakery as my base . . .'

'But can you afford it?'

Perry nodded. 'I know it's old-fashioned, but my grandfather left me – well, a small dowry. I only get it if I get married. Blackmail, really, but it does mean I'll be able to set up for myself. Not be reliant on George.' She had blossomed into happiness and hope in just minutes. Kit envied her, both her certainty about George and her plans for the future. Catering seemed far more likely to succeed than a career in the theatre.

Perry put on a stern look and waggled a finger at her. 'But don't think I've forgotten how this conversation started, young lady. What are you going to do about Zeke?'

Kit could feel herself pout like a kiddie. 'Why do I have to do anything about him? We're friends. We work together.'

'Not for long.' Perry arched an eyebrow at her as they both got up to clear the table.

As she washed the dishes, Kit thought about it. 'He's the only friend I have in the theatre. It's so *reassuring*, having him there. Marguerite and Basil don't like us, because we're young and on the way up. The chorus don't like us because they want to *be* us, and the rest of the crew treat us like children – except Susan. She's lovely. But she's not around much. Zeke is my – my bulwark. If we were more than friends . . .'

'Lovers,' Perry said. 'You'd be lovers. And he could still be your bulwark.'

'What if it went wrong, though? And we were stuck, performing together every night in Charlot's next play?' She shivered. 'It would be horrible.'

'It *could* be wonderful. Loving someone is always a risk. Better Zeke than Henry.'

Exasperated, Kit let the water out of the sink and dried her hands, throwing the tea towel onto the dresser. 'Why does it have to be *anyone*? I'm sick of people trying to push me into a love affair! At least Zeke never does that!'

Perry smiled pityingly at her, and picked up the tea towel to fold it and hang it on the oven door. 'He's no fool. He would if he thought it might work.' She laughed. 'I said it before, and I'll say it again. You're an idiot.'

She was definitely an idiot who didn't know her own mind. But too bad. She wasn't going to moon over a man. She had work to do.

◆

Unfortunately, her work involved pretending to moon over Zeke. That night, after the show, he was her partner to a charity costume ball. The publicist Brett Vickers had set it up, after making sure there'd be photographers and society columnists there.

He'd even organised for them to have costumes from the studio. Zeke got a kilt and sporran, and she was in a medieval-style gown which was surprisingly comfortable. It was figure-hugging to the hips and then flared out into a flowing, floor-length skirt.

No room for a corset of any kind under it; the gown clung to every curve. She'd topped it off with a long blonde wig and a circlet around her brow. Zeke eyed her admiringly as she came out of the dressing room after the performance.

'I'd whistle, but I don't want to get thrown out of the place,' he teased her. She smiled and blushed a little. Whistling was a bad habit for an actor – the stagehands who moved the sets up and down into the flies communicated with whistles, so a misplaced whistle could land a sandbag or flat on your head. Which was why most actors thought whistling was bad luck inside a theatre. It really could be.

She was quite looking forward to the ball; dancing with Zeke was always fun. But she hadn't realised that it was at the Bridlinghams'. They drew up outside in the cab and she froze.

'I can't –' A ball at the Bridlinghams' would be a disaster.

'What's the problem, Miss Linton?' Vickers asked. He was their 'minder' for the night, there to make sure the photographers got the right shots and the reporters the right quotes.

'The woman who owns this house doesn't like me,' Kit said bluntly. 'I don't think she'll let me in.' And wouldn't that be relished by the newspapermen! Yet another scandal with her name on it.

'Lady Sinclair?' Vickers asked, puzzled.

'Lady Bridlingham.'

He shrugged. 'Never heard of her. The Sinclairs organise this. And it *is* a good cause. Chin up, Miss Linton! It'll be fine.'

Zeke took her hand. 'You don't have to go in if you don't want to.' His mouth was firm; he'd back her against Vickers. But it *was* a good cause: the Foundling Hospital. And, after all, they'd invited a lot of actors for tonight. Lady Bridlingham *must* have known she was invited.

Taking a big breath, she followed Zeke out of the cab, holding his hand to alight.

She threw back her shoulders. All her ballet training went into the poise of her head on her neck, tall and elegant.

'That's my girl,' Zeke whispered.

Lady Sinclair was the first in the receiving line, and greeted Kit, subtly managing to imply she had no knowledge of her outside the event.

The other matron in the receiving line was Lady Bridlingham. She glared at Kit all the while she was saying the most polite welcome. But to Kit's relief, the woman's own sense of decorum didn't permit her to actually throw Kit out.

Summoning up her acting skills, Kit dropped a small curtsey and smiled with apparent warmth.

'It's so kind of you to give your house for the ball,' she said.

Lady Sinclair cut in. 'Oh, Beatrice is the most charitable

of women. There are half a dozen causes that would collapse without her!'

Trying to stop herself blinking in disbelief, Kit smiled wider. 'How amazing!'

Lady Bridlingham leaned closer, and hissed, 'You have the hide of a rhinoceros! How dare you!'

Thank God the line moved along then and she curtsied to the man of the house – Bingo. He winked at them, but he called her Miss Linton, not Kit. She shouldn't feel hurt, but she did. Tonight they were in high society, and she was there as a professional, not as Henry's partner. She had to be prepared to be treated like an actress, not like a lady. Fury built in her at the thought, but she made sure it didn't show on her face.

They moved into the ballroom; normally, when she came to a ball, the first glimpse always silenced her with profound pleasure. The sheen of silks, the way the skirts swayed in the dance, the music . . . it set her feet tapping and her spirits soaring. But tonight her stomach was in knots.

Henry was there, in a corner, drinking, along with all his ordinary crowd, and the Prince of Wales and his set: the young princes, the Mountbattens. She had no idea if she should acknowledge them. Would it just start the gossip all over again? She held on to Zeke's arm more tightly, and he patted her hand.

Lady Bridlingham sailed past her with a sideways sneer. What a witch that woman was! And then, inevitably, Henry came over.

He looked Zeke up and down in a most offensive manner.

'Slumming it, Katherine?' Oh no. She wasn't going to take that from anyone.

'My name is Kit. Come on, Zeke. Let's get a drink.'

'A *drink*?' Henry parodied. 'This milksop doesn't drink. Haven't you noticed? He's a pansy boy. Can't hold his liquor.'

She couldn't help laughing, which disconcerted him mightily. He obviously didn't know any of the hard-drinking 'pansy boys' she did.

Zeke's hands were fists, but he chuckled, too, which made Henry see red. He took a step forward and grabbed Kit's arm. She shook his hand off. Before anything else could happen, Lady Sinclair walked up and patted Henry on the back.

'Henry, my dear, the Prince of Wales is looking for you.'

It was the one summons he couldn't refuse. Looking daggers at both of them, he allowed himself to be led away. Lady Sinclair glared frostily at Kit. This was her fault, apparently, not Henry's.

'Pugnacious little puppy,' Zeke remarked lightly, but his eyes were hard. She didn't blame him.

They moved into the ballroom and began to dance, followed by a couple of photographers. Professional smile fixed to her face, she acted as though there were nothing wrong. Nothing at all. She was having a lovely time, dancing with the handsome and charismatic Zeke Gardiner, amidst this glamorous and aristocratic gathering.

If only her stomach wasn't churning so much, she might even believe it herself.

Two dances later, the prince himself asked her to dance. She curtsied, but as they began to waltz, she murmured, 'Is this wise, sir?'

'A charity ball, a sedate waltz. Why not? If we avoided one another, there'd be a different kind of talk. I wanted to have a word about young Henry.'

Startled, she jerked her head up to stare at him. 'Sir?'

'He's in a bad way,' he said. 'Very down. I thought a word in your ear . . .'

'Did he ask you to –'

'Good God, no! No, he wouldn't do that. Suffering in silence, stiff upper lip, that kind of thing. But I've known him since he was at school with Harry . . . he's not himself these days.'

His voice was melancholy. For the first time, she felt she might actually like him. 'He, er, objects to my professional relationship with Mr Gardiner. I've told him that I won't end that.' Should she have betrayed Henry's privacy like that? But the prince only wanted to help.

'Ah. I see. Perhaps not the wisest course of action?' Delicately, he seemed to imply that she would never get a better offer. She had to stop herself rolling her eyes. There seemed to be no man on earth who could imagine that a woman might be better off alone.

'I'd rather not marry without love,' she said.

At that, he looked down at her, slowing in the dance. His eyes were surprised, and soft with a kind of admiration.

'You stick to that,' he said. 'You're lucky to have the choice.'

It sounded heartfelt. As Prince of Wales, he'd no doubt be pressured to marry some European princess he barely knew. She nodded at him, and they swept back into the dance. He deposited her back to Zeke quite neatly.

'Gardiner,' he said, nodding. Quite benevolent. Condescending, perhaps, but polite.

'Sir.' Zeke's face gave nothing away, but his short bow was much better than it had been the first time he'd met royalty. Once the prince had walked away, Zeke guided her to a small side table where he'd put two glasses of lemonade ready for them. 'Was he campaigning on Henry's behalf?' His voice was tight with anger. Surprised, she put her hand over his as it held the stem of his glass.

'A little. But he agreed with me when I said I wanted to marry for love.'

His gaze met hers, and his mouth twisted with wry self-deprecation. 'He must envy us sometimes,' he said. 'Poor bastard.'

She grinned. 'The one thing we can be sure he's not is a bastard!'

They both began to laugh, tension running out. Perhaps this ball wouldn't be so bad after all.

But every older couple who passed them looked straight through her and, apart from Henry's close friends, not one of the people she'd conversed happily with at private parties gave her a single nod. Cecil and Daphne kept to the opposite side of the ballroom at all times, acting as though they'd never seen her before.

She was *persona non grata* in the public arena, despite dancing with the Prince of Wales.

◆

She should feel either crushed or set free, but she felt nothing. A kind of blankness. She wasn't sure what she should do next.

After supper, they went out through French doors onto the terrace for some night air; the smoke in the ballroom, from cigarettes and from the candles in the chandelier, was starting to pall.

It was a cloudy night, with a hint of rain in the air, but it was warm enough, and other couples were strolling up and down the stone-flagged patio.

'Right!' came a voice out of the shadows. Henry advanced into the light from the French doors. She tensed, expecting a confrontation, but Henry stopped a few yards away and stuck his hand out to Zeke.

'I was acting like a boor in there,' he said. 'Please accept my apology.'

They shook, warily on Zeke's part, determined on Henry's. She was impressed as well as surprised. It took courage to admit fault. There was so much good in Henry; if he'd been brought up in a less privileged way, he'd have been a lovely man.

'Sorry, Kit,' he added.

She nodded at him. She wasn't sure what to say: 'Don't call me' didn't seem either polite or kind. She wasn't sure she meant it, anyway. Was it so bad to be loved?

He nodded back and walked away to the ballroom. Perhaps there was a slight wobble in his walk?

'Drunk as a skunk,' Zeke said.

'Oh, Zeke! He wasn't that squiffy.'

'He hides it well. That's a bad sign.'

Zeke's mouth was set. He was so *stubborn* about this! She found herself siding with Henry almost automatically. Zeke didn't understand how things were *done*. She herself and her sisters had all been taught how to drink in polite society from the time they were fifteen. 'Because otherwise these young gels get given champagne and have no idea how to handle it,' her mother had said.

Everyone drank. It was just how society operated.

And if, sometimes, some people went a little too far . . . well, it wasn't admired, but it was hardly cause for ostracism, either. Even among the very religious set her parents mixed in.

She didn't enjoy alcohol much apart from champagne, and as a dancer she needed to be moderate, but there was nothing *wrong* with a drink or two.

'You're such a wowser, Zeke,' she said. 'Come and dance with me.' When they were dancing, they were in perfect harmony.

But he shook his head.

'I've had enough. Home for me.' Brusquely, he led her back to the ballroom. 'Do you want to come with me?'

Across the room she saw Lady Sarah waving at her. Some of her other friends were there, too. Henry was not in sight. But if the girls still wanted to be her friend . . . a warmth in her heart grew at the thought. Not everyone in this room despised her.

'No,' she said. 'I'll stay on.'

He bowed, the same short, correct bow he'd given to the prince, and walked off. The nerve! That really was very rude. As her escort, he ought to stay as long as she wanted. Or, at the very least, escort her across the ballroom to her friends. Henry could do with a bit less arrogance, but Zeke could do with a few more manners, if this was his idea of how to treat one.

Sarah came over and slid an arm through hers. 'Isn't it lovely!' she said happily.

And it *was* lovely. Sarah was prepared to be her friend, despite her mother. *Everything* was lovely. The lights, the music, the beautiful dresses, the scent of jasmine . . . It was gay and frothy, and just what she needed to take her mind off stupid men and their annoyances.

'It is!' Lady Penelope waved them over. In a moment she was in a crowd of Henry's friends, laughing and joking, and for a while, she felt entirely at home.

CHAPTER 29

A wowser. He'd known Kit long enough to understand what that meant. A killjoy. A prosy, preaching bore.

Hell.

He'd like to smash Henry's face in. He almost had. Henry was the cause of all this. Goddammit, why couldn't she *see* that the man was a lush?

Home in Ebury Street, up in his attic room, he got ready for bed by rote.

Think of something else. Money.

Not a happy subject, but sure to occupy his mind. He got out his bankbook and sat on his bed, propped up by pillows, doing some figuring.

He had a solid stash put away. But the nursing home was expensive. He could afford to pay for it for maybe five months. His father wouldn't live for five months, apparently. What was it he had said? A couple of weeks to a couple of months, if he were lucky. And well cared for.

Say three months at the outside. Guilt twinged in Zeke's stomach. It was wrong of him to hope his father went sooner rather than later. A sin, no doubt about it. But he was going to be out of work soon. It wasn't that he wanted his father dead early, so much as he wanted to have more cash behind him.

And any chance of becoming an engineer soon was gone. He hadn't thought much about it, but it was there, the possibility, at the back of his mind. Today, with the threat of unemployment looming, it looked better than ever. A solid job, regular pay packet, and exciting work to do . . . Would he have ever gone into the theatre if he hadn't had to support his mother? Probably not, no matter how much he loved singing.

Not worth thinking about now, not when he wasn't going to have enough money in the bank to do it. When he might have to pay this nursing home for months more.

He ought to get a job as soon as the play folded.

But . . . in two and a half months, there might be another play – if Charlot was offering them auditions so *meaningfully*, he must think they had a very good chance of getting the parts.

He couldn't tie himself into anything major.

That is . . . if he wanted to keep working with Kit.

If not, he could just audition for anything that was going.

He let that idea sit in his gut for a moment.

No.

No. If he had a chance to keep working with her, he'd take it. Maybe that meant he was a sucker, yearning after something he couldn't get. But, you know, he'd never made any real effort in that direction. Once the play was over . . .

Yes. Once the play was over, and before they auditioned for the next one, he'd make his move. That kiss in the third act . . . every night it was harder not to let it get out of hand. He sighed out a long breath. Yes, he'd make a move. Freeze Lord High Muckity-Muck right out.

In the meantime, he had to earn some cash. Maybe he could get some singing work?

Noël was home from France, so Zeke went down to the study on the ground floor where Noël did his writing, and knocked on the door.

'Saved!' Noël exclaimed, throwing up his hands. 'Thank God you came to distract me from this *mis*erable play.'

'It's not that bad, I'm sure.'

'Easy for you to say. Every word is like drawing blood from a stone. Pfft, what a terrible metaphor. Clichéd. Tired, worthless. More like . . .' He screwed up his face in a parody of thinking hard. 'More like sticking a needle into my eyeball and drawing out the fluid.'

'I don't think I'd put that one in a musical revue,' Zeke said. He cocked an eyebrow at Noël and both of them laughed.

'What's the matter, dear heart?' Noël indicated that he should sit on the shabby armchair in the corner, and Zeke duly sat.

'I'll be out of work in a week and I need a short-term job to tide me over until Charlot's next play. He's *asked* us to audition.'

'Oh, well then.' Noël nodded. 'He doesn't do that unless he's pretty sure you'll get the part. Same director?'

'A new fellow, I think. Someone Braithwaite?'

'Ah. Down from Manchester. He's pretty good, they say. But that would be why he hasn't just offered it to you. Doesn't want to put the director's nose out of joint. But he has plenty of pull, don't worry.' Noël sat back and tapped a pencil on his teeth. He was, as always, perfectly groomed, even in the comfort of his own home. It was as though he were always on stage, always playing a part. Maybe men of his persuasion had to be like that. On guard. Just in case.

Noël looked his notes over and frowned. 'You're a singer, aren't you?'

'Song and dance, but I'm a better singer than a dancer.'

'A tenor, yes?'

Zeke nodded.

'Well, I don't like to mention it, it's not *legitimate* theatre. But –'

He was drawing out the suspense deliberately. 'Fish or cut bait, Noël.'

'What a delightful expression! I must remember it. No, but really – it's just a teeny tiny bit tricky.'

'*What?*'

'There's this club I go to . . . they've lost their straight man. Not that he keeps to the straight and narrow, mind you. Very camp indeed, old Jamie. But he can *play* a ladies' man. And he has a lovely voice.'

'What happened to him?'

'Well, that's the thing. He's in quod. A nasty-minded policeman caught him with a young friend of his in a compromising situation. He had a "sympathetic" judge, so he only got three months.'

Zeke shook his head. Poor bastard. And 'sympathetic'? Did that mean that the judge was himself . . . ? Probably.

'So I could perhaps get you the job, because you'll only want it for a couple of months, leaving it open for Jamie when he gets out. *But* . . . the place does get raided, now and then. Are you willing to risk it?'

'What's the pay?'

'No idea, my dear boy. I've never asked. I can carry a tune, but this audience wants someone rather more . . . manly.'

Noël was perfectly manly – but he was on the slight side, Zeke supposed, although tall. Not too *obvious* about it in public, either, unlike some. There was a part of Noël, he'd always thought, that didn't like being homosexual; he certainly didn't parade it.

Was it worth the risk? Not just getting raided, but the gossip that would ensue . . . On the other hand, half the world assumed that any man in the theatre was an invert, anyway. There was truth to that – he didn't know any who weren't, except Fred Astaire.

He could just imagine what this club was like – full of men of Noël's persuasion, all ogling him. He'd be like a chorus girl at an Elks' convention. He laughed.

'Why not?'

'That's the spirit. I'll take you around tomorrow.'

'Thanks. But the money had better be good!'

◆

The money was good. Almost as good as what he earned on the West End. And this was *almost* West End. What Noël called 'Fitzrovia', between the West End and Regent's Park.

'You don't perform here?' he asked Noël as they walked down some steep stairs to the basement club.

The management was waiting for them – a handsome red-headed woman named Mags who dressed like a circus ringmaster, complete with top hat. He wouldn't be at all surprised to know she had a whip hidden somewhere, too. She certainly handled a long cigarette holder with flair.

She smiled at him and pinched his cheek. Perhaps she wasn't a Sapphic after all? Or perhaps she was like Tallulah, and had 'wide' tastes . . .

'Delicious! Our patrons will love him.'

'Our show folds on Saturday. I could start any time after that,' Zeke offered. So soon! The last performance had seemed a long way away, but it was suddenly upon them.

'Monday,' Mags said. 'We get a lot of theatre types in on Mondays, because the *legitimate* theatres are dark.' She said 'legitimate' with the scornful tone of those who had been scorned. 'We can rehearse on Sunday and Monday.'

Zeke nodded. This would be okay. As long as none of those 'theatre types' sold the story to the papers. He felt a qualm, but the money was good, and who knew how long his father would need that nursing home? He couldn't risk him being thrown back out into the poor ward. That would be too cruel.

The club itself was an odd mixture.

Around the small dance floor, it was very genteel. Starched tablecloths with bud vases, each with a single rose. Velvet-upholstered chairs in a pale blue. Rather like that dressmaker's he had taken Kit to once. Behind the long bar, a dark-complexioned man polished glasses. The stage was small, and the tables close together, like in a jazz club. Which this was, in a way. A cabaret.

But the walls . . . the walls were covered with murals that would make a sailor blush. Bold colours, heavy lines, a kind of hard slapping on of the paint that reminded him a bit of how theatrical backgrounds were painted. And the subjects . . . men with men, women with women . . . he turned away before he learned more than he wanted to know.

'Don't you like it?' Noël raised a supercilious eyebrow. 'The Bethnal Green Art Club boys did it. Well, one or two of them. Don't tell the others.' He winked in an exaggerated fashion.

Zeke certainly wasn't going to give him the satisfaction of showing any embarrassment.

'Nice use of line,' he said laconically, and Noël chuckled.

'Come and meet the band.'

The band was a four-piece: drums, bass, trumpet and piano. The other performers, though . . .

'Boys' of all ages surrounded him, assessing his clothes, eyeing his muscles, giving little squeals of appreciation.

'Darlings!' Noël scolded them. 'Don't frighten him away. He's *so* in love with a girl, you'll have no chance with him, so let him be.'

They pouted and one slapped him on the arm as if in reproof. He laughed. That was, apparently, the right thing to do. As one, they dropped the simpering and started to discuss the act like any group of performers might.

It was mostly song and dance, with him being the partner to a succession of female impersonators. Two of them he recognised from the music halls, where they drew a considerable audience.

One of those lived at the Cats' Home.

'Val, isn't it?' Val wasn't one of the boys who'd squealed over him – she dressed and lived as a woman, as far as he knew.

A beautiful woman, too, although a bit tall for his taste. Kit always referred to Val as 'she'. He supposed he should, too.

'Zeke! Lovely to see you. How's Kit?'

He bit back a caustic comment and smiled. 'Living the high life.'

'Lucky girl!'

'Val, why do you perform here when you've already got a good set at the Palladium?'

'Well . . .' She cast down her eyes and half shrugged. 'There, I'm a curiosity. A man dressed as a woman. Here, I'm a woman singer. It's a different feeling.' Her gaze flickered to the man behind the bar, who smiled appreciatively at her. 'A different feeling altogether.'

Zeke grinned. 'I might need a bit of guidance around this place.'

'I'll keep you safe, sweetie.' She smiled back, a gamine smile full of mischief, and he was suddenly very glad he had her on his side. 'For Kit's sake,' she added. 'She's been *such* a love, giving me dresses she can't wear anymore.'

'She's very generous.' This was a side of Kit he'd only realised as they'd worked together. She was always doing things for other people – bringing Sam the stage doorman a sandwich when she came back from lunch, paying for the props boy to have his tooth extracted, and, apparently, giving clothes to someone who would find it very hard to shop.

So many little things, he'd almost stopped noticing. It was just part of who she was. But it was worth remembering – that kindness was why she wouldn't cast Henry off. She'd help any lame dog, and, for some reason, she thought Henry was a lame dog.

That made him feel calmer about the whole thing. He could beat a lame dog any day.

They went through the list of songs he'd be performing. He knew them all; part of this kind of club was familiarity made exotic. Or the exotic made familiar, he wasn't sure which. He'd have no trouble with the actual songs. He'd just need to learn the blocking and 'business' with each partner. It was a return to his music hall days in Victoria; a kind of holiday.

As he and Noël left for their respective theatres, he slapped Noël on the back.

'Thanks, buddy.'

'*Buddy*? Oh, my dear, no. Just no.' But he said it with a twinkle in his eye. 'You dealt with all that rather better than I thought you would.'

'I've been working in theatre, back of stage and on, since I was fourteen. If I had a problem with men of your persuasion, I'd never have made it this far.' He didn't add that a female impersonator had safeguarded him from all the advances those men would have made on him while he was racing around handing out props. Gilbert had been kind to him. Very kind. Even his mother had liked him, although profoundly disapproving of his way of life. But Gil hadn't been like Val. He doffed the dress as the curtain came down and became a dapper man about town, with a wife tucked away in the suburbs. It was a job to him, not a life.

Noël made a soft 'chuff' of agreement. 'We're everywhere in the theatre. You're something of a white whale, my dear. I hope Kit appreciates you!'

'I hope so, too.' Maybe his tone was a little grim, because Noël patted him kindly on the shoulder.

'She'd be a fool not to.'

They parted at Trafalgar Square and Zeke walked to the theatre with a sombre tread. He had to shake himself out of this mood or Kit would accuse him of sulking. Maybe with some justice.

At least he had a job when the show folded. He laughed out loud at the thought, drawing shocked looks from passers-by – respectable men in bowlers and respectable women in silk stockings and high-heeled shoes. It made him grin all the more. He could just imagine what these respectable people would make of the club.

England was so . . . so *polite*. It had been weighing him down without him even realising it. Half an hour in the club and he'd shuck that weight right off. It *would* be like a holiday, and he intended to enjoy it, mugging it for the crowd, playing up to whatever outrageous antics the others got up to. And he was sure they would.

Smiling, he went in the stage door, saying hey to Sam. It would all be fine.

CHAPTER 30

Their last night.

Susan Maxwell was philosophic. 'When you've had as many last nights as I have, dearie, you learn to take it in your stride.'

Kit wished she could. But Susan had all those last nights as a promise there would be others. She'd stayed the course. She might never be a star, but she'd get her next job without auditioning – in fact, she'd already been engaged to play the Nurse in *Romeo and Juliet*.

'I have another five, maybe ten years of best friend roles, and then I'll be reduced to mothers and aunts,' she said matter-of-factly. 'With the occasional go at something like this – a Shakespeare nurse or a Sheridan widow.' She smiled at Kit with genuine calm. 'If the stage is in your blood, that's all that matters. Keeping on acting.' Kit took a deep breath and nodded. 'And,' Susan added, 'sticking away every extra bit of money you can. It's a cold, dreary old age if you don't.'

That made panic rise up in her throat. She had *some* money. Enough to get her through the next two weeks, which was all that was left on the sublet of the flat. Enough to pay her way at the Cats' Home until Charlot's new play came up. If she didn't get the part . . . she half wished she hadn't given all those frocks to Val. She could have sold them if need be.

Girls in her class weren't brought up to think about money. It was assumed they'd have a husband to do that for them. She'd fought so hard to get free of her family's restrictions, without ever realising that some of them might have some practical use. A lack of money might be the greatest restriction of all.

Nonsense. She shook herself out of her mood and put her makeup on. Last time, so it had to be perfect. The whole performance had to be perfect. She and Zeke had to put aside their recent coolness and dance their hearts out.

She went on stage to warm up. Zeke was there, limbering up, stretching, tapping across the stage to an unheard melody. Standing in the wings, she could watch him unawares. He'd improved considerably as a dancer since that first rehearsal. She hoped she'd improved as much as a singer. She'd grown as an actor, she knew.

Zeke did a shuffle and turn, and saw her there. He smiled, as if he couldn't help it, and held out his hand to her. Lightly, she ran onto the stage and took it. Being in his arms felt as natural as sunlight. They went into their second number, the two-step with a tap sequence in the middle, and then she stretched.

'What are you doing *tomorrow* night?' he asked.

'I haven't thought that far.' She didn't *want* to think that far. Besides, it was Sunday tomorrow.

'Come to dinner with me.'

'On a Sunday? Nothing will be open.'

'Come to church, then. And a walk in the park afterwards.' His voice was tense, as though her answer mattered.

'Clear the stage, please!' the stage manager shouted.

They obediently went off on the prompt side and headed towards the dressing rooms.

'Ten minutes, beginners!' the callboy yelled.

'Kit –' Zeke stopped her with a hand on her arm. 'Shall we go to the park tomorrow?'

What an odd way to start a new stage in their relationship. Because she was fairly sure that's what Zeke had in mind. A walk in the park. Reassuring, she supposed. She had no idea how she wanted to respond, but she'd have to face up to it sooner or later.

'All right,' she said softly. He had to bend to hear her. 'I'll see you there.'

◆

A West End last night was, it turned out, a bit of a romp. Marguerite and Basil were sparkling, changing lines and upstaging each other. The audience – who had mostly seen the show at least once before – greeted every new sally with applause and uproarious laughter.

Kit didn't dare be so outrageous, but she and Zeke hammed up their love scenes a little, and put a little more oomph into their dancing. Less sedate, more sex. The audience loved it. In the kiss scene, Zeke bent her back over his arm and gave her a loud smacking buss, which prompted laughs and catcalls.

And, at the end, there were many curtain calls and flowers. Flowers! Bunches of roses and lilies and carnations. Mostly for Marguerite, but Kit got her share – even Basil received one of delicate orchids. He blew a kiss to a couple in a box on the off-prompt side. The man blew one back, and the audience applauded. It was that kind of night.

Jack Bernes, the director, was in Edinburgh, on tour with another show, but Charlot was waiting for them as they came offstage.

'Wonderful, *très admirable, mes amis.*' He'd organised a post-theatre party at a restaurant for the whole cast, and another party at a pub for the backstage staff. The British class system worked even in the theatre, she thought, but shrugged it off. No dark thoughts tonight. Tonight was for celebrating a dazzling West End run.

The uproarious nature of the performance carried over to the party. Marguerite displayed a hitherto-unknown ability as a mimic, and took on every cast member to great applause. Her version of Kit was shamingly recognisable – the too-high voice, the blushing. Kit forced herself to grin and clap along with the others. Her version of Zeke, on the other hand, wasn't all that accurate. He was far more expressive than she made him out to be, and the accent wasn't quite right. But he clapped, all the same, and his hand found hers under the table.

As they rolled out of the restaurant in the early hours of the morning, she said, 'I don't think I'll be in church tomorrow.'

The long, slow notes of Big Ben cut across the night. One, two, three.

'I don't blame you,' he said. 'Gosh, I need some sleep.' He took her hand again, and held it. 'I'll come and take you for a picnic lunch instead.'

'All right.' The group was breaking up, everyone kissing everyone else indiscriminately. Marguerite took her by the shoulders and leaned forward, but instead of kissing Kit's cheek she hissed, 'Grab that one and keep him! And have lots of babies. Don't find yourself like me, in ten years' time, with nothing to show but a bunch of reviews.'

Then she turned away as airily as if she'd said nothing at all.

Gosh. Kit grabbed a cab – her last little luxury – and left them all behind, Zeke standing on the footpath watching as she drove away.

Grab him and keep him. Have lots of babies.

That was tempting. Lord, it was tempting!

Best not to think about it all now. Enjoy the fine summer night, the lights reflecting off the wet London streets, the memory of applause and curtain calls . . .

At the flat, she found that Charlot had organised to have all her bouquets messengered around. Perry had taken them in and put them in vases and jam jars and jugs, so that the whole place was a flower garden. It smelt heavenly.

She sat down heavily on the sofa. Two weeks more here, and then back to the Cats' Home. What a letdown.

What a farce.

Her agent was talking about some radio sessions for which she'd be paid. But other than that . . .

Her days would be empty. Her nights, too.

Three months. Could she bear it?

Perry came, sleepy-eyed, out of the bedroom.

'Well, kid. Your first last night.'

'Not really. I've had last nights in Sydney.'

'Not the same.'

No. It hadn't been. The last nights in Sydney had been stepping stones up to the next thing, all of them leading to London. Now, the possibility of taking a step *down* was all too plausible.

Perry patted her shoulder. 'It'll be all right. You've got what it takes. Not like me. When you're on stage with Marguerite, no one looks at her. That's why she doesn't like you. You have It.'

It. Star quality. An ephemeral, unsteady thing. She'd rather be a magnificent actress. Once, she'd imagined herself as Ophelia, or Portia. Not a musical-comedy star.

But, oh! she did love to dance.

Kit sighed and got up. 'Only two more weeks. We'd better talk to Mrs French about a room.'

Perry cleared her throat and stood awkwardly in the bathroom door.

'Not me, cully. I'm off home to George.'

A kick in the stomach, that felt like. She'd depended on Perry just *being* there when she had to leave this place. Smile. She should smile.

'Do I get invited to the wedding?' She went over and hugged Perry, who clung to her.

'I'm doing the right thing, aren't I?'

'Do you love him?'

'Yes.' Perry stood up straight and tugged her pyjama top into place. 'I really do.'

'Then you're doing the right thing.'

'Sounds so easy,' Perry sighed. She made a face. 'At least he's agreed I should start my own business. I won't be dependent on him.'

'Well, then.' That felt stupid to say, but Perry nodded as though she'd been particularly wise.

'Yes. Yes.'

She brushed her teeth and went to bed. Lying in the darkness, Perry drifting off to sleep beside her, Kit wished it were that easy for her. Love . . . it just seemed too complicated. If only she didn't have to deal with it at all.

Her dreams didn't agree with that. She woke in the morning, drifting out of Zeke's arms into a cold, wet London Sunday, and turned away from Perry's sleeping form to silently cry.

CHAPTER 31

'A *drag* show?'

'Please!' Zeke turned up his nose and looked haughty. 'We are a respectable cabaret of female impersonators.'

Giggling, Kit slipped her arm through his and skipped to keep up with his long legs. He slowed immediately.

'Sorry.'

'I love the idea of you in a cabaret like that. It will be hilarious.'

'Val's in it. She comes in after her show at the Palladium.'

'Oh, lovely! She's so nice.'

They sat on a bench and looked at the Serpentine, snaking its way through Hyde Park. The rainy morning had cleared to what the English thought of as a fine day. Even in August, with the muggy days upon them, she couldn't take this weather seriously as summer. Nothing like a Sydney summer.

It was only at moments like these that homesickness struck her. Perhaps she was cold-hearted, but she didn't miss her family all that much. But the Australian sky and the breeze from the sea, lifting over the masts of the ships in Darling Harbour, rattling their shrouds; the long, low horns as they sailed out the Heads; the curve of a breaking wave, brilliant in the sunshine at Bondi Beach; the golden sandstone of the cliffs . . . she missed those, sometimes, with a sharp and urgent yearning.

England was beautiful, in every weather. She had no intention of going home. But on a 'lovely summer's day' like this one, when the sky had a cast of clouds and the distance was hazy instead of crystal clear, memories of Sydney did tend to crowd her mind.

'Penny for your thoughts,' Zeke said. She shook herself out of the mood.

'Oh, they're not worth a groat! Tell me more about the club. You'll have to watch yourself with all those men.'

'Noël warned them off for me. Said they had no chance because I was too much in love with a girl. He was right.' She stared at her shoes, shocked into silence. She hadn't expected an outright declaration. 'Kit?'

His voice was so tentative, light and worried. She had to look up, to reassure him.

'I didn't expect –'

'The pact was "while we're working together",' he reminded her. He put a gentle hand under her chin, and waited until she tilted her head up. That was so like him. Other men would push so you *had* to look at them, but not Zeke.

'But we might work together again!' She was aware, even as she said it, that it wasn't the main reason she resisted him.

'We'll be saying that for the rest of our lives.'

Underneath all the surface arguments was her fearful suspicion that they didn't really live in the same world. She had come far enough, she thought, to feel guilty about that, to know his background shouldn't matter, but it was there, poisoning any thought of a future with him. It wasn't rational or reasonable or kind. But she couldn't talk herself out of it.

And yet. He was Zeke. There was nothing else solid in the world. Not work, not family, not friends, not a place to live. She didn't belong anywhere, really, but with him that didn't matter. He didn't belong anywhere either.

Was that enough to be involved with him? Or would she be cheating him? And if they began a love affair, and it didn't work, she'd be truly cast adrift, without any anchor.

Perhaps that was the real reason she didn't want to risk it, and all her concerns about manners and etiquette were just a cover for her own cowardice.

She tried to explain how much she valued him, but she must have done it badly, because he sat back, letting his hand drop. He pulled his hat off and ran a hand through his hair.

'All I hear in that is that you want me around.' She nodded, miserable. 'Oh, don't look like that, Kit! I'm not going to start shouting at you or accusing you of anything. But I'll tell you this for free: you can't keep a man waiting for too long.'

He brought out sandwiches in a paper bag and they ate, then walked along to get an ice cream from a cart, trying to recapture the fun of a day out.

An organ-grinder with a monkey was performing for a group of children. The monkey danced along to the music and Kit laughed, imitating him. In a moment, she and Zeke were dancing a Charleston, with the organ-grinder grinning and the crowd swelling second by second.

They finished to a shout of approval and applause as the monkey, perhaps annoyed at being upstaged, jumped on Zeke's head and threw his hat on the ground. Laughing, they pointed the crowd to the organ-grinder's hat on the ground, and put some coins in themselves before moving on.

She was full of – something. Happiness, exhilaration, affection. A sudden swift mood change. Who else would have danced like that in a public park with her?

'I'm not saying "no",' she said as they reached the edge of the park.

'Hmm.' He looked down at her. 'I have to go rehearse. But while you're not saying "no", think about this.' Bending down, slow enough so that she could move away if she wanted to, he kissed her.

So sweet. So long and lingering and warm. Not at all like their stage kisses. Heat started in her middle and spread out to her fingertips and toes. She softened and moved a little closer – but at that, he moved back, his eyes glinting with something other than friendship.

'No more, unless you mean it,' he said. 'Just remember it when you're trying to decide if I'm worth the risk.'

He tipped his hat to her and left her standing there.

Damn him. *Damn* him! He had done that deliberately, got her all stirred up and then just *left*.

◆

Walking home the long way, to get the annoyance out of her system, didn't work.

She put the key in the door of Sicilian Avenue with petulant fury. Blast! Why couldn't men just, just – *stop bothering her*!

Upstairs, Perry was packing her things, getting ready to leave the next day. Kit's emotions got the better of her; she burst into tears.

They sat on the bed and clung to one another.

'I don't even know where you're *going*,' Kit wailed.

'Just to the Midlands, to visit my parents before we get married.'

'I have no idea where the Midlands are.'

'It's not that far.' Perry laughed, half crying herself. 'Not like going to Australia. You can visit.'

She was being ridiculous. This was *England*. Even if you counted in Scotland, you could get from one end of the country to another in a day. She *could* visit Perry any time she wanted. For a weekend, say.

'Make sure you give me your address,' she said, blotting the tears away. A heavy sigh escaped her. 'Everything seems to be ending.'

'Endings are just beginnings,' Perry said briskly. She got up and went back to her packing, pausing with a pair of half-rolled-up stockings in her hand. 'But listen –'

The church bells were ringing for Evensong. They floated out across London, one by one, each of them seeming to call the next into the carillon. St George's, St Margaret's, St Anselm and St Cecilia, St Giles and all the others, the music of their bells rising up to God and calling the faithful to prayer.

She was filled with a desire to answer that call.

'I'm going!' Grabbing her hat, she ran downstairs and out into the street, heading for St George's in Bloomsbury. Not far. She was a dancer; she could run fleet-footed, faster than most men, and she came to the church barely winded, crammed her hat on her head and went in to the pale-walled interior, alight with candles and some pale electric bulbs shining dimly in the corners.

Here was the scent of home: incense, beeswax, old wool and a trace of brass polish. This was childhood and girlhood, boredom and security. She slipped into a pew and took up the hymn book for the first hymn.

This was where she'd learned to sing, in her father's parish church, before he'd been moved to the cathedral. An eagle-eyed choirmaster, a ham-fisted organist, and the wonderful melodies and words of Anglican worship.

How much of religion was faith, and how much this bone-deep familiarity and sense of home?

She didn't care. Lifting up her voice in song, she worshipped.

CHAPTER 32

This was a doubly depressing day.

Kit trailed Perry through Euston Station despondently. She was glad – of *course* she was – that Perry was going home to her George with a light heart.

They stopped at a kiosk and Kit bought her a chocolate bar and some mints for the journey. And a sandwich.

'It's only a few hours!' Perry protested. She had sent her luggage on ahead and was travelling with no more than a handbag. She looked . . . carefree. Kit smiled at her with wholehearted affection.

'Still. You might get hungry.'

The train was waiting on the platform. Perry was travelling third class. It was an odd thought. Kit had never travelled anything other than first class. And wasn't it odd that England didn't have second class? As though the elite wanted to emphasise the difference between them and everyone else. It reinforced her fears that, after today, she and Perry would drift apart, living in different worlds, wanting different things.

'Well, this is me,' Perry said, opening a compartment door. The barely padded seats looked uncomfortable and the compartment was almost full with a large family party, including four children, one already crying. Perry made a face, but the conductor was shouting something indistinguishable and waving a flag, so she hopped on board and turned to hug Kit.

'Come and visit!'

Then she had to slam the door and move back as the train gave a toot and began to move away.

Kit stayed where she was, watching until even the smoke from the engine could no longer be seen.

One hard thing done.

Now, the next.

She'd packed and sent her trunk on to the Cats' Home by the same carter who had taken Perry's gear to the train. It should be there by now. She *could* have stayed a few more days, but the flat would be too quiet and empty without Perry. She'd leave the keys with Barry at the theatre, so all they'd had to do this morning was slam the door shut behind them. All done.

Normally, she'd walk to Charlotte Street from here. It wasn't that far. But she couldn't be bothered, when the Tube was right here at the station, more or less.

The Northern Line ran from Euston and she could get off at Goodge Street, just a couple of blocks from the Cats' Home.

She didn't much like the Tube – it was noisy and smelled faintly of old fruit and ash. But it was quick and cheap.

At Goodge Street she climbed the steps to the street wearily. How could she be so tired at this hour of the morning?

Charlotte Street was the same as ever, but it looked more squalid. Just her state of mind. A few months couldn't have changed it that much. She climbed the steps to the yellow-brick building and took a deep breath before she opened the door, which was left on the latch during the day to facilitate deliveries to the kitchen.

No one in the hall, but her trunk was there – and after she'd paid the carter extra to carry it up the stairs for her! How annoying.

She followed the sound of voices into the kitchen, where Mrs French was chatting to the butcher's boy. A 'boy' of more than forty, by the look of him, and rather keen on Mrs French. It had been a great joke among the girls.

'Kit! There you are. Lovely. I've put you in number ten.' Mrs French went to the board by the back door and took down a key, which she handed over. Kit paid her first month's rent, and that was that. At least Mrs French, well used to the ups and downs of theatre life, took her return for granted.

Number ten was a single room at the front of the house on the first floor. All the street noise. But, she told herself, with a lovely large window that would get the morning sun.

And she could be up early in the morning now, if she wanted to be.

The butcher's boy, perhaps hoping to impress Mrs French, hoisted Kit's trunk on his burly shoulders and carried it up for her. She tipped him as generously as she could. Her *very* last little luxury.

And then she unpacked.

A single bed. Well, that was something, not having to share a bed anymore, especially in the muggy London summer. She sat on it. The springs creaked.

The curtain at the window was a faded cretonne, which would probably let in *all* the morning light. But it was a cheerful yellow.

She pushed up the window, which stuck halfway, and the many sounds of a London street sailed in. A lorry chugging by, a newspaper boy shouting his headlines incomprehensibly on the corner, two rowdies outside a pub down the street banging on the door despite it not being twelve o'clock yet, perambulator wheels on the footpath, a child crying, women talking, pigeons.

Her clothes didn't all fit into the chest of drawers, so she kept the winter ones in the trunk. Fifty or so days until she could audition. What on *earth* could she do with herself in the meantime, in this tiny, drab little room?

Oh, Lord.

No, she wouldn't cry.

Better to go down and help Mrs French with lunch. Much better to keep busy. And she should go out and get *The Stage*. There hadn't been any work she could apply for in it yet, but who could tell? There might be today. She should visit her agent, too. She'd spoken to him when they got the news the show was folding, but it wouldn't hurt to remind him she was available now.

Going to the door, she had to stop as tears welled up out of nowhere. *No!* She would *not* be what Delly called a Moaning Minnie. She would *not*.

Kit straightened her spine and put her chin up. She had the promise of the chance to audition for a new Charlot production. Other girls would give their eye teeth for that chance.

Time to buck up.

She wondered what Zeke was doing. He'd said he had a lot of rehearsing to do. That he'd be busy all day.

Lucky him.

CHAPTER 33

Kit tapped her foot to the band with energy. She couldn't wait to see Zeke on stage being propositioned by a succession of female impersonators. Giggles were waiting, just below the surface – not just for her, but for Delly, too.

Fred and Adele had been delighted to come to the cabaret with her and Noël and Tallulah. And, delightfully, Benny and his wife, a rather beautiful young Indian woman who was dressed with Benny's trademark flair in a stunning pink calf-length gown bordered with sequins.

'I'm Prithi,' she said, shaking Kit's hand.

'She runs things,' Benny said. 'I just create – she's the head of the business, really.'

Noël had disappeared as soon as they arrived, floating from table to table – he apparently knew every single patron. Tallulah's opening night was in four days, but she refused to go home early.

'This is my last chance to drink too much and have loads of fun before I put my nose to the grindstone! Besides, there are some rather yummy menu items here.'

But she wasn't looking at the actual menu. A striking red-haired woman was at the bar, dressed in form-fitting trousers and jacket and tie, assessing her in a meaningful way. Tallulah smiled slowly. 'If y'all will excuse me,' she said in a fake Southern drawl. 'Someone's calling my name.'

She sashayed over to the bar, her red satin dress swishing nicely. The woman lifted a champagne glass in welcome and slid an arm around her waist.

'That girl,' Fred said, shaking his head. 'She'll get into real trouble one of these days.'

'Get *into* trouble?' Delly replied, laughing. 'She *is* trouble!'

The band blew a fanfare and fell into silence. The woman Tallulah had approached appeared at the microphone, having somehow got to the stage in a matter of moments. Her voice was low and vibrant, and her lifted eyebrow decidedly wicked. No wonder Tallulah liked her.

'Ladies, gentlemen and those who can't decide!' A round of chuckles went through the club. 'We're pleased to present our latest talent, standing in for the sadly absent Jamie Carruthers – Zeke Gardiner and his garden of lovelies!'

Zeke appeared in white tie and tails, complete with top hat. 'He's stolen my look!' Fred exclaimed, but he didn't seem to be annoyed. It was, after all, not only 'his' look.

'You only started wearing a top hat because you were shorter than me!' Delly said.

'Well, I was only four and a half,' Fred protested. 'You were all of seven. Of course I was shorter.'

Flowing out from backstage came a half dozen young ladies, dressed in various levels of drag. Some were parodying the look, others were more beautifully presented than Kit herself. Each of them draped herself over some part of Zeke, who began to sing:

Life is not a highway strewn with flowers
Still, it holds a goodly share of bliss
When the sun gives way to April showers
Here is the point you should never miss

Gosh, he could sing! He was also, rather surprisingly, showing a comic side she'd never seen before. Playing up to each of the ladies, parading them around the small stage and off to the wings, until there was only one left – Val.

Though April showers may come your way
They bring the flowers that bloom in May
So if it's raining have no regrets
Because it isn't raining rain you know, it's raining violets

Val smiled up at him, and began to sing along. Good Lord, she was a counter tenor! A high, pure voice. No wonder they loved her at the Palladium. Kit felt rather guilty that she hadn't been along to see Val's act. Mind you, until this Saturday she'd been performing herself, so it would have been tricky. It was an odd circumstance that those people who loved the theatre the most got to see least of it. Unless they were 'resting' as she was now.

If only she had the money to see all the shows in town!

Perhaps she could give up a few shillings and sit up in the gods, the cheapest seats. Standing room only, even. That would give her a project to keep her occupied, and incidentally do her some good. She was sure to learn something from watching the London thespians.

Val was crooning to Zeke as if she were in love with him. Was that what *she* looked like on stage with him? He was so handsome, it was quite believable. Kit wasn't sure how she felt about that.

> . . . *where you see clouds upon the hills*
> *You soon will see crowds of daffodils*
> *So keep on looking for a blue bird*
> *And list'ning for his song*
> *Whenever April showers come along*

It was August, but never mind that. The crowd loved the song, applauding loudly – and laughing and cheering when Val kissed Zeke on the cheek.

He grinned and bowed low, taking off his top hat with a flourish and kissing Val's hand, in his element. A born performer.

The rest of the show was far more risqué and much funnier. The girls took every liberty they could, and Zeke pretended to be oblivious to them all, turning to almost catch them, seeming not to see their lascivious mugging.

'Great timing,' Delly murmured.

'Yeah.' Fred nodded in agreement. 'That boy's wasted in a straight role.'

No, he wasn't! she wanted to say. But Zeke certainly was funny.

'If we get the next show, I might suggest to the director that we build up the funny stuff.'

'Good idea.' Delly laughed again as Zeke, finally, at the end of the last number, raised an eyebrow at a particularly impertinent partner and flounced off the stage, flicking his swallow tails at her in a move reminiscent of can-can dancers and their skirts. The audience shouted with laughter and banged on the tables for an encore.

He and Val came out and sang 'Keep the Home Fires Burning' to calm them all down. It was such a sentimental, nostalgic song, he had them all singing along. A few tears might even have been shed.

Then there was more applause and he and Val came down to join them.

As they got closer, Kit could see the sweat on his brow. She handed him her handkerchief and he took it gratefully, mopping up.

'Whew!' he said. 'That was a hard night's work.' Fred stood to shake his hand.

'You did well,' Fred said. 'There were a couple of things . . .' They fell into a deep discussion of timing and blocking while Kit jumped up and hugged Val.

'You have such a beautiful voice! Twice as good as mine!'

'Oh, you're sweet. A very limited range, though, or I drop into chest voice and sound like a man.'

'That could be funny,' Delly said judiciously, the veteran of years of music halls.

Val flushed. Kit stepped in before she had to say something.

'Val's an *artiste*,' she said, emphasising the French pronunciation, which indicated a female.

'Well, we all have our schtick,' Delly agreed. Tallulah and Noël had long vanished, so Val could have her chair, and Zeke took Noël's.

'All right?' he asked Kit.

'More than all right. You were *very* funny!'

He smiled with relief. 'Gosh, I was nervous! Odd, isn't it, but it's much harder to be up there as Zeke Gardiner than as a character.'

'But you were Zeke Gardiner in the music halls in Canada.'

'No. I had a stage name. Charles Lamont. So my father couldn't find us. I only used my real name when I came to London.'

She was silent, and put her hand over his. It was painful for her to imagine him being so frightened. Not for himself, but for his mother. As if he were following her thoughts, he said, 'My mother loved "Home Fires".'

She lifted his hand and kissed it. 'You're a good man.'

'Oh, Kit. Don't do that if you don't mean it.' He leaned towards her, so close she could feel the heat coming off his body. She was aware, out of the corner of her eye, of Delly looking on with interest. Around them, at tables and in booths, quite a lot of kissing and fondling was going on. What happened in this place was out of time, out of real life – but that was only for those who couldn't take their desires anywhere else. What happened here between her and Zeke was all too real.

Kit wished she knew her own mind.

As she hesitated, he sighed and drew his hand away. 'Never mind. I don't want half-hearted.'

Other people came over once he looked up, to congratulate him. Noël, the woman MC with Tallulah twined around her, men and women who patted Zeke on the back or made blatant offers, which he laughed at in a kindly way.

He seemed happy.

'You like this place.'

His mouth twisted awry. 'England's pretty buttoned-down. I like that you can let your hair down here.'

Frontier life, she supposed, would make you less amenable to the shibboleths. It was something she'd never even considered about him. What else didn't she know?

'You're a success!' Noël put a hand on each of their shoulders. 'Now, Kitty, how about we put you in a swallow-tailed suit and have you belt out a couple of songs?' He turned to the woman MC. 'Mags, how about putting this little firefly up in the spotlight?'

'Wonderful idea,' Mags said, looking her up and down with appreciation.

'If I *could* belt out songs, I might take you up on that. But you know, Val sings much better than I do.' Kit grinned. 'I'll tell you what I will do. Put me in a suit and Zeke and I can do a tap number.'

Mags clapped her hands. 'Wonderful! Let's *do* it!'

A surprisingly short time later, courtesy of a female patron whose clothes had been commandeered by Mags, she and Zeke were on stage tapping to 'Toot Toot Tootsie!' The audience was keen – and, as if they couldn't bear to be offstage, Fred and Delly rushed up to join them.

Fred made up the steps and they followed his lead, light-hearted and dancing for nothing but the joy of it.

They set the place alight.

Afterwards, they collapsed into their chairs and gulped down cold lemonade.

'Gosh, that was fun.' Fred tousled Zeke's hair. 'Thanks, feller.'

'What about me? It was my idea!' Kit protested.

'Yeah, but if I touched you, lover boy here would punch me out.'

Laughing, they all relaxed, letting the exhilaration of the dance flow out of them.

Prithi said yearningly, 'I'd *love* to be able to dance like that.'

'You could learn,' Kit said.

'I don't have time! Maudie, our model, has left – pregnant, would you believe! So I have to model as well as do the books!'

Benny held her hand. 'It's worth it. Soon we'll be able to afford a family.'

'I'd better give that woman back her clothes,' Kit said reluctantly. She'd quite liked being in trousers. An odd feeling on the legs, but so comfortable! She might have to buy herself a pair to wear around the house.

Zeke went backstage with her. Before she went into the dressing room, he put a hand on her arm. 'Now I have this job, if you need money at any time . . .'

The offer didn't offend her. She was too scared of the prospect of poverty. Kissing his cheek, she murmured, 'You *are* a good man.'

Was she a total fool not to jump at the chance to be his girl?

As she came out of the dressing room, it was time for Zeke to get ready for his next set, and somehow there wasn't an opportunity to speak to him for the rest of the night. They went home separately, Delly and Fred giving her a lift in their cab, while Noël and Zeke walked back to Ebury Street.

She floated into the Cats' Home and up the stairs to her tiny room. What a wonderful night. It was only as she was getting ready for bed that she thought about how horrified her parents would be to know how she'd spent her evening.

The house by the cathedral seemed more than half a world away; it seemed like a different century.

She preferred this one.

CHAPTER 34

Her agent had nothing.

'It's August,' he had said. 'Nothing starts in London now. Everyone's away. The Glorious Twelfth and all that.'

Grouse shooting season, which opened on the twelfth of August, wasn't the only reason everyone had left who could.

Kit thought she had a good tolerance for heat – and, certainly, in terms of actual temperatures, London had nothing on Sydney. It never got to one hundred degrees here. But the mugginess! The heat came off the roads and stone houses, mixed with damp air, because it was always mizzling or had just stopped mizzling, and hung heavy and humid.

Five minutes after she stepped outside, she was drenched with sweat – and it *was* sweat, not perspiration or 'glow'.

She was going to run out of money very fast.

There was only one possibility she could think of to earn some more, and the idea made her feel sick.

But what if she didn't get the role Charlot had talked about? Then she'd have used up all her extra emergency money and would have to decide whether to touch the money she'd put aside for a fare home.

Or else go home, a failure.

She'd scrub floors before she'd do that.

So she put on her best silk stockings and her nicest day dress, and went to M. Dernier's.

◆

As she'd hoped, Prithi greeted her when she walked in.

'Kit! How lovely to see you. Are you after an evening gown?'

Kit swallowed hard. 'No. I'm after a job.'

'A job?'

'I'm . . . I'm between engagements. There's a play with Charlot coming up, but in the meantime, I thought, since Maudie had left, perhaps . . .' She was stuttering like a fool, and blushing beet red. This was harder than an audition.

'Ohhh.' In an instant, Prithi's demeanour changed. 'I'm sorry, we've filled that position. But we poached that girl from Savion's, so they're looking for someone. Would you like me to call them and recommend you?'

A mixture of disappointment and hope was really very unpleasant for the stomach. 'Yes, please.'

Prithi disappeared into the office. Kit could hear the murmur of her voice – unlike Benny, Prithi spoke without a Cockney accent, and had the lady's habit of modulating her tone to ensure privacy.

After a few minutes, she came out smiling. 'Deidre Masters at Savion will see you now. But . . . I didn't tell her your name.

If I were you, I'd take an alias. And perhaps wear a wig. You don't want journalists getting hold of the story – it wouldn't be good for your career.'

The lump in her throat could be swallowed. She managed it. 'That's good advice. Where would I get a wig?'

'We can lend you one. We have several, for when clients want to see what their colouring would look like with a dress – you can imagine, *I* was getting a *lot* of complaints about that when I was modelling!' She laughed, but there was an edge to it. Kit had no idea what to say, but she tried to look sympathetic.

'Way of the world,' Prithi said, shrugging. 'But they'll see when Benny makes a knighthood one of these days. Let me get you the wig.'

She brought out a dark brown bob, and helped Kit fit it on – a net first, and then the wig, held on by bobby pins. Kit's own hair was short enough that it looked entirely natural.

'Gosh!' she said, entranced by the difference it made. Her eyes were startlingly bright, but her mouth seemed far too pale; she hadn't worn lipstick today in case there was a rule about it – Kit had never seen Maudie wearing it on any of her trips to the shop.

'Perfect,' Prithi said. 'A loan. Bring it back when you've finished, or pay us for it when you're back in real work.'

'You're so *kind*,' Kit protested, but Prithi laughed.

'We've had a good bit of business through you, Kit. Didn't you realise? Even Lady Sinclair, whom Benny had been angling after for *months*. Good luck at Savion!'

Savion was a shop much like Benny's but on Bond Street, so more expensive, and decorated in jazz pinks and greens.

More fashionable than Benny's; she was likely to meet women she knew here. A horrible thought, but beggars couldn't be choosers.

Deidre Masters turned out to be a tiny woman with dyed black hair and wrinkles *everywhere*, including her hands.

'Name?' she barked.

'Agatha Gardiner.' Oh, Lord, why did she say that? But it was the only surname that had come to mind.

Deidre inspected Kit as though she were a prize ewe at a fair. 'Turn around.'

Kit turned, trying not to blush.

'Walk,' Deidre said.

She knew how to walk. Finally, the debut training paying off! She walked up the shop, she walked back.

'All right,' Deidre said. 'I need you here nine-thirty to four, six days a week. When you come in, you sweep the shop and dust the desk and window display. Make sure you smell nice – no body odour and no cheap perfume! Clean fingernails. No lipstick. No men hanging around the shop. Do what you're told. Two pounds a week. Pay depends on how well you sell the dresses. Sell a lot, there might be a bonus in it for you.'

Two pounds! How little that was. But it wasn't really a full-time job, was it? Six and a half hours a day instead of eight or nine.

'Thank you, Mrs Masters,' she forced herself to say.

'Miss,' Deidre corrected her with a fierce look. 'And make sure you remember it! Can you start tomorrow?'

'Yes.' Kit swallowed again. 'Yes, I can. Thank you.'

Miss Masters sniffed. 'Off you go, then. Don't waste my time.'

Dazed, Kit left the shop and walked back up Bond Street. She had a job. Perhaps, if she convinced herself that showing dresses was just like putting on a show, she might even enjoy it. She did love dressing in nice clothes . . .

Agatha Gardiner. What had *possessed* her to use Zeke's name? Mortifying. She'd never be able to tell him. Agatha Scott would have been a much better choice, but she'd baulked at that, for some silly reason she couldn't quite figure out.

Too close to home, perhaps.

She contented herself with a nice little daydream about frocks and ladies who bought frocks, and the bank balance that would grow no less while she was waiting for Charlot's audition. Because two pounds was not much at all, but it was enough. Just. If she did nothing and went nowhere, and made her own lunches instead of buying them, and darned her stockings instead of getting new ones, and walked everywhere instead of taking the bus or Tube.

Sighing, she started the long walk back to Charlotte Street. At least she wouldn't lose any of her fitness.

CHAPTER 35

'You will address the patrons as "madam",' Miss Masters said.

'Yes, Miss Masters.' Kit stood with hands folded, as she used to stand in front of the principal of her old school.

Miss Masters sniffed.

The store opened at ten. Because rich people, like theatre folk, didn't get out of bed before nine. She had arrived at twenty past nine, waited for ten minutes until Miss Masters came to open up, and then dusted the shop and office and window displays.

She thanked God for Perry's lessons in how to clean their room and the flat. Before London, she'd never cleaned anything in her life. At least she knew how to dust now.

Mary had helped her. She was the second seamstress – the first seamstress, Peg, was too important to clean, apparently. Fair enough. Mary was a spitfire of a girl who laughed at everything Kit said, as though her accent was the funniest thing she'd ever heard. Better than being scowled at, the way Peg looked at her.

And now they were ready to open. And, wonders, there were customers – *patrons* – outside.

Miss Masters snapped, 'Places!'

Mary and Peg scurried behind the velvet curtain that marked the boundaries of their territory. Kit checked her wig in the long mirror, then stood by the side of the curtain, near the white Louis XIV-style desk which was Miss Masters' domain.

Miss Masters ushered in the first patrons: an older woman and a younger. Mother and daughter? Fortunately, no one Kit knew.

After the patrons were seated on a settee and Mary had brought them tea and petit fours, Miss Masters had a murmured conversation with them.

'Agatha, the aquamarine.' She turned back to the customers. 'I think that will suit you beautifully, Miss Cartwright.'

It took Kit a split second to remember that she was Agatha, and Miss Masters glared at her. She slid behind the curtain, where Mary had the aquamarine day dress all ready, and slipped out of her own dress – a grey smock Miss Masters had presented her with.

Two seconds, three, four, and she was through the curtain again, walking that particular walk she'd practised at the Cats' Home the night before, which showed off the sway of the skirt to its best. If she got more pay for selling more frocks, she was going to sell frocks!

She paused, turned. Turned again. She'd seen Maudie do it often enough, at Benny's.

As she turned, she gave a little flick of her finger to the

skirt, to make it flare out – an old ballroom dancing trick. Miss Masters gave the smallest nod of her head.

'Well, it's a lovely cut, but it's a bit . . . ordinary,' the girl complained, in a voice that whined nasally.

'Let's try the green, then, Agatha. An exclusive design from Paris, madam.'

Unlike Benny, who created his own clothes, Miss Masters bought her 'exclusive designs' and had Peg and Mary make them up.

The green, it turned out, wasn't jazz green, that lovely deep shade of Nile green – it was Kelly green, bright and arresting. Horrible. The dress itself was a nice design, but the colour . . . Kit shuddered as she got into it.

Peg laughed at her. 'You wait,' she whispered. 'That nincompoop will love it. All that type wants is to stand out.'

Sure enough, the girl squealed with pleasure at the colour, and ended up buying it *and* the aquamarine – one for her and one to placate her mother. To be delivered in four days, since these were samples. The girl pouted at that, but the mother said, 'You don't want *ready-to-wear*.'

'Good,' Miss Masters said to Kit after they'd left. 'But change faster.'

The next customers walked in five minutes later; Lady Penelope and a friend whose name Kit didn't remember, but to whom she knew she'd been introduced. She stood, frozen, beside the desk.

But they didn't look at her. They looked at a couple of frocks on display and talked to Miss Masters. It was as though she wasn't there.

Miss Masters said, 'Agatha, the pale blue.'

She slid behind the curtain and pulled the smock off over her head, to make it quicker, being careful not to dislodge her wig.

They would be looking at her. Well. It couldn't be helped. If she'd wanted to avoid the rich, she should have taken a job at Woolworths.

She set her jaw, to be ready and smooth-faced when the humiliation kicked in, and went through the curtain in her best walk.

Lady Penelope never even glanced at her face.

Not once.

It was as though she were a store dummy, a mannequin that happened to be able to walk. Not a person at all.

The two women went all around her, even poked at her waist to see how the material sat there, and never once acknowledged her as a human being. She called up all her acting ability, pretending to herself that she *was* that animated mannequin. Miss Masters eyed her narrowly, but apparently was satisfied, because she said nothing.

'Swish the skirt,' Lady Penelope said. Kit swished. Turned. Swished again.

'Yes, I like that,' the other woman said. 'But not in blue. Charcoal grey, with a silver sash.'

'I have just the fabric. Agatha, would you ask Mary to bring out the charcoal jersey, please?'

Going through the curtain felt like an escape. Mary was already getting the charcoal jersey from the shelf. Peg helped Kit out of the dress and she pulled on the smock, taking a moment to smooth her hair and her nerves before she went back out.

Kit took up her position beside the desk and was ignored for the rest of the visit. Anger built up, moment by moment. She had *liked* Penelope. But Penelope, apparently, didn't even *see* people of the 'wrong' class.

For a moment, she wondered rather uncomfortably how she would have treated Maudie if she hadn't been taken to Benny's by Adele Astaire. Would she have been this unknowingly offensive? She hoped not, but a hot bubble of shame was waiting under her breastbone at the thought, which meant she wasn't sure.

She was a servant, now, as far as the upper classes were concerned.

Invisible, irrelevant.

She'd been ready for one humiliation, only to be plunged into another.

◆

She walked back to the Cats' Home in the late afternoon, thoroughly down about the next three months. The whole day had followed the same pattern – women stared at her like a piece of meat in a butcher's window, and ignored her otherwise. Spoke about her as if she weren't in the room, right in front of them. 'It looks fine on her, but she doesn't have much *décolletage*.' 'This girl's colouring is all wrong for me. Don't you have a red-headed model?' 'Her hips are too thin.' 'Her hips are too big.' 'She's much longer in the body than I am, are you sure this will suit me?' Like a prize poodle at a dog show, being assessed by less-than-impartial judges.

The next day was even worse.

The first customer did more than ignore her.

'Put your leg back! Not that one, the other one, you stupid girl!' The woman poked her between the shoulder blades. Hard. 'Stop slumping! Why do these girls all *slump*, Masters?' Miss Masters glanced down at the floor and Kit read in her shoulders how much she hated being treated like a shop assistant.

She caught herself up on that thought. No one should be treated with this disdain. This scorn based on nothing more than money. No one.

The second customer drawled nastily, surveying Kit without actually registering her – although it was a woman she'd met at Lady Patricia's garden party. A Mrs Nestor.

'Rather *outré*,' she said of the first gown, a beautiful tawny silk satin which did, admittedly, have a low back.

'Pedestrian,' she said of the second. 'Girl, how does it feel on?'

'It's beautifully comfortable, madam,' Kit said with truth.

'Oh, *comfortable*.' Mrs Nestor shrugged. 'How bourgeois. No doubt that's important to *you*. But I'm hardly going to catch a bus in it!'

After she left, having bought nothing but having consumed a remarkable quantity of tea and petit fours, Miss Masters scowled after her. 'Scavenger,' she hissed. 'They come in here and eat me out of house and home. Wasting my time because she's lonely and bored.' She sighed. 'But I can't throw her out, because when she gets her quarterly allowance, the shame of sponging on me will bring her back to actually buy something.' Seeing Kit's expression, she grinned. 'You'll see the pattern if you hang around long enough.'

Remembering a ghost of gossip she'd heard at the Cats' Home, she said, 'If it makes you feel better, she's lonely because her husband's having an affair with a chorus boy.'

'Hah!' Miss Masters gasped once with laughter, and then shut her mouth like a trap. 'No gossiping about patrons. It's a rule. Absolute discretion.'

'Yes, Miss Masters.'

That afternoon, opening the front door of the Cats' Home, feeling very much what Zeke would call 'dog-tired', and with aching feet, she found a letter for her on the hall table.

From Henry.

Pick you up at seven on Friday, it said. *Squibs is having a do down at the river house.*

A flicker of annoyance at his presumption was drowned by pleasure. A party on the river! That was just what she needed to cheer her up after this horrible day. And she was pretty sure that the rest of the week would be just as horrible.

Despite her tiredness, Kit spent half an hour in the parlour, stretching and practising. Mrs French let her use the space because all the other girls were out at their theatres. She was on a different schedule now, and it felt lonely. But she had to keep her muscles in good trim, and she had to earn a living.

Afterwards, she went up to soak her feet in a bath. As the water ran, and she poured the last of her nice bath salts in, she wondered if *everyone* who did a job like hers felt the same as she did, or if she felt the lack of manners more keenly because she was used to being treated better.

The water was piping hot, and heavenly, even though the enamel was wearing off the bath in places. Kit rested her head against the rim of the bath, and thought. It didn't matter which answer was right to that question.

If she felt it more, it was only because other people had been ground down into *not* expecting to be treated with courtesy.

If she felt it no more than others, then all around her, for her entire life, other people had been treated badly without her noticing, and had hated it as much as she did.

There was no escaping the shame. It coursed through her, hotter than the bath water.

Inevitably, those thoughts led her to Zeke.

She had thought her response to his lack of 'breeding' instinctive, but of course it wasn't. It had been *learnt*. In the same school which had taught those customers that the shop model was a nothing, barely human.

So really, the question was, could she unlearn that lesson? And did she want to?

She was so tired that she just couldn't think about it anymore. She'd thought she was fit, being a dancer, but standing all day was peculiarly tiring. She forced herself to go down and have some dinner, because she needed to eat, but afterwards she fell into bed and was asleep almost before she could close her eyes.

CHAPTER 36

The horrible girl who had bought the bright Kelly green dress was at Squibs' party.

She was charming to Kit, since Kit was on Henry's arm.

Kit pushed down a strong urge to tell her the colour looked dreadful on her, and said to Henry, 'Let's have a drink. And for God's sake, find me somewhere I can sit down.'

Henry looked at her in surprise, but jumped to obey.

Breaking her normal custom, she had a cocktail instead of wine. She needed something tangy to cut through her mood.

The house was small, as Henry's friends' houses went; a holiday cottage. But the grounds stretched right down to the river, and there was a large patio in front of the jetty there, on which dancing was happening.

This crowd, unlike their parents, didn't care if she were an actress or a bishop; they didn't care about much at all, which suited her mood precisely.

278

How beautiful it was! Chinese lanterns hung in the trees, the moon was full, laying down a silver path on the river, the women's dresses gleamed and shimmered with sequins . . . and the music, even if it was a gramophone, was bright and cheerful and jazzy.

She downed her cocktail and grabbed Henry's hand. 'Let's dance!'

◆

The next morning, she had to be at work early; Saturday opening was at nine.

She dragged herself out of bed and groaned. So this was what a hangover felt like. All those times the other girls had complained and she'd felt superior.

'Eat something,' Mrs French said at breakfast. 'Toast and jam, at least. You need to coat your stomach or you'll be sick all day.'

So it was that obvious.

'Looks like someone had a good night,' Dolly giggled, which started a wave of chaffing, not all of it good-natured.

'Lady Muckamuck's come down off her high horse,' Betty drawled.

She didn't have the energy to be offended. Probably they were right, and she'd been standoffish. Shy of them, but they wouldn't believe that.

Makeup helped, but Miss Masters inspected her closely when she came in, and sniffed.

She'd better not party on a working night again. Not now she had to get up the next morning.

But tonight was Saturday, and tomorrow she could sleep in for as long as she wanted.

◆

Lady Penelope's mother, Marchioness Closter, was having an '*en plein air*' entertainment that night – singers and musicians performing in her rather extensive garden while the guests sat on the terrace.

When she'd come in, the marchioness had managed to peel off from the receiving line just before Kit reached her; a smooth manoeuvre which allowed Kit to be a guest, since she had been invited by Penelope, without being actually welcomed. Old biddy.

Still, Kit got to sit down and listen, which was heaven. The entertainment was passable; too many amateurs, debs who fancied themselves as sopranos, brothers who were sure they could be successful as jazz musicians.

But the champagne was delicious, and so were the quail eggs, and the smoked salmon, and the tiny little mushrooms filled with *brie*, which were served during the interval.

Henry regarded her with amazement. 'My word, I've never seen you put it away like this, Kit!'

'You've never seen me after a day of working for my living!'

She'd told Henry about her job, in confidence, and he thought it 'a lark'. Now, he grinned.

'Have another drink.'

'Not just yet,' she demurred. She didn't want another hangover.

Lady Penelope wandered over and waved genially. 'Kit, darling, so nice to see you again. We must lunch.' She wandered off to greet some other guests. She was wearing the dress she'd bought at Savion and had insisted on taking home immediately. A dress Kit had actually worn. It was such an odd feeling. Like being a spy, perhaps, only more . . . humiliating.

She wanted to stand up and say to Penelope, 'You treat shop models like animals!' And smash her glass and plate on the terrace.

'I will have that drink, Henry,' she said, biting into another mushroom cup. 'Let's hope the next act will be more professional.'

The next act was an earnest young tenor who had atrocious breath control. Kit kept Henry in stitches with a *sotto voce* opinion of his technique. Afterwards, they escaped and headed for St James' Palace.

'Are you sure we should just turn up?' Kit was trying to perform running repairs on her makeup in the intermittent light from the streetlamps as the cab went through the crowded streets.

'Oh, it's fine!' Henry said. 'PW's keeping open house tonight.'

So it proved.

CHAPTER 37

Kit wasn't at the park the next day.

Zeke supposed they hadn't actually made a date, but they'd met up the last two Sundays, and . . .

Best to go to the Cats' Home and see.

Mrs French wouldn't let him past the parlour, but Val saw him, and she offered to go up and tell Kit he was there.

A long five minutes later, Kit came down, dressed in what was clearly a hastily donned cotton frock. The simplest thing he'd ever seen her in, besides rehearsal shorts. No makeup, and her hair mussed.

She looked dreadful. Dark circles, a little shaky.

'Are you ill?' he asked.

'Oh, no,' she said, trying to smile.

One of the other girls (Dolly?) laughed. 'She just needs a hair of the dog. Been out with his lordship two nights running, living the high life.'

Nausea jolted in his gut, and his heart clenched. Actually clenched, as though a fist had closed around it. He'd thought, after that kiss . . . and *liquor*? That wasn't like Kit. She was almost as abstemious as he was.

They couldn't talk here.

'Would you like to come for a walk?' he asked.

'Best get some food into her,' Mrs French advised. 'Hot chips. A bacon butty. She missed breakfast.' In her voice was long experience of girls with hangovers. He winced, and she raised her eyebrows as though amused at his reaction.

'Kit?'

She seemed dazed. 'All right.' Val went to her and fixed her hair, and then Kit found her hat and gloves by the front door – where, apparently, she'd pulled them off the night before – and they went out.

It was a grey day, or he figured she would have flinched at the light. He couldn't believe it.

'It's not like you,' he ventured, 'to drink . . .'

'Oh, don't you start!' she snapped. 'I got enough of that from Val and Miss Masters.'

Cold settled on him. He knew that tone of voice. He'd heard it enough from his father. Best not to engage with that.

'Who is Miss Masters?'

She blinked at him in surprise. 'Oh. You don't know. I've got a job.'

They'd reached the little park in Colville Place, and sat on a bench. It was only a half hour until the pubs opened. He'd get her some food then.

'Tell me about it.'

She sighed, and then it all poured out. The lack of work, the job, the 'patrons' – someone called Penelope was apparently the worst, or at least the most hurtful. He couldn't help a small twitch of the lips. Kit was seeing how the other half lived, by the sounds of it. He wouldn't be human if he hadn't enjoyed the idea of that. And yet, wasn't it like her to simply walk into a job other girls would have killed for?

The benefits of beauty.

'So you went out partying to get over it?' He spoke as gently as he could, but it didn't help.

'Well, *you're* working. Was I supposed to sit at home and bemoan my fate?' He hadn't been prepared for how lonely it was, not to see her every day. Perhaps that could be amended . . .

'You could have come to the club –'

She just stared at him. 'Follow you around? Wait until you have a moment to spare? No, thank you. I was at the Prince of Wales' party.'

And there they were.

She went to the Prince of Wales' – with Henry – and he consorted with female impersonators and people of dubious morals.

But he didn't get drunk.

'Be careful,' he said, not gently at all. 'It's easy to get caught up in a drinking habit.'

She waved it off. 'I can't drink on a working night. No need to worry.'

But he did worry. He couldn't help it.

◆

It was a long week. With every day that she had to smile and say, 'Yes, madam,' no matter how stupid or nasty the customer was, Kit hated the job more. And the 'patrons'. There was the occasional nice woman, but they tended to be suburban matrons buying a mother-of-the-bride outfit. The others treated her . . . not *badly*, most of them. Just with complete lack of interest.

She admitted to herself, somewhat ruefully, that that was harder for an actress than just about anything else. At least, if they were being rude to her, they *noticed* her. Kit was used to being *seen*. And she missed – oh, how she missed! – the camaraderie of the theatre, the music, the dancing, the uplifting zing of audience applause . . . and Zeke. Life seemed flat and boring without all that. Her only relief was partying with Henry when the weekend finally came. At least that was a change from being polite.

On a very warm Wednesday, Henry was waiting for her outside the shop when she got off, complete with an open touring car, a basket from Fortnum & Mason, and an iced bottle of champagne. It was ridiculous. It was charming.

He lifted his hat and put on a funny voice. 'Moddom, would you care for a jaunt in the country?'

What a perfect thing. He could be so kind.

'I'd love one.'

Bourke drove them out to Richmond Park and they had their picnic on the banks of the ponds.

'It's not *exactly* country,' Henry said. 'But it'll do.'

It certainly would. England was so *beautiful*, especially on a clear summer evening. Deer came out of a stand of pines to graze near them and larks were singing overhead. Kit sighed and lay back on the picnic blanket. This was what she'd needed. Some peace and quiet.

'Oh, just a word to the wise. The thing at Carleton Towers – my mama's giving a costume ball. So you'll need a costume. Just thought I'd mention it.' He was telling her because he thought she'd have to save up to rent one. That was rather sensitive of him. It made her feel as though he were genuinely trying to understand her life.

'Lovely.'

Henry propped himself up on one elbow above her and tickled her nose with a blade of grass. She batted it away, but returned his smile.

'You hate that job,' he said.

'I do. But it could be worse. I could be at Woolworths. Or even Harrods.'

'You shouldn't be *anywhere*! You're a lady, goddammit, not some suburban shop girl!'

He sat up, agitated, and she levered herself up as well and sat cross-legged.

'Lady Bridlingham wouldn't agree with you.'

'Damn her and all her old cronies!' he flashed, with genuine anger. 'You're worth three of her!'

'Henry –' She put a hand out to him, touched, and he took it eagerly.

'If you married me, you'd never have to work another day in your life! *And* all those old biddies would have to be polite to you!'

Stillness came over her, as quick as being drenched in water.

'Married?' Was that her voice? How odd she sounded.

'Yes!' He leaned towards her. 'Married. What do you say?'

'But –' It had never occurred to her. Not once. Not for all

his 'you're my girl' and tipsy declarations. She'd thought he wanted to get her into bed, not *marry* her. 'I never thought –'

'Why not?'

'Well, we only started this because of the Palace . . .'

He kissed her hand and held it tightly, eyes bright. 'Oh, Kit. That charade was over weeks ago. The press has long since lost interest. Did you really think I was only seeing you for that?' A long sweep of his free hand indicated the park around them. 'Do you see any reporters lurking? I see you because I care about you.'

She really felt very strange. As though the ground had shaken beneath her feet.

'I – you've taken me by surprise,' she managed. 'I don't know what to say.'

'You'd be Lady Henry,' he said, as if tempting her. That broke some kind of spell, and she laughed heartily.

'Oh, Henry, as if that mattered!'

'That's just it.' He stared earnestly into her eyes. 'That's *just* it. It doesn't matter to you.'

He looked, tonight, like such a perfect gentleman: perfectly tailored, perfectly mannered, perfectly romantic. Handsome, yes. And she was fond of him, but she'd never imagined . . . It was as though she'd never seen him before. Her nerves were shaky. *Could* she think of him that way? She should say something less serious.

'Besides, I only dislike being in a shop. I wouldn't give up my theatre work.'

'I wouldn't want you to!' That was quite a declaration for someone in Henry's shoes. Astonishment made her dizzy.

'This has been quite a day.' She cleared her throat.

'No! Don't say anything!' He held up a hand to stop her. 'I didn't realise you'd get such a surprise. Don't say anything now. Think about it.' The hand lowered and covered hers warmly. 'I'd be a good husband, Katherine. And you'd never have to worry about anything like money, ever again.'

Two months ago, she would have laughed at that. Tonight, it struck an unpleasant chord.

'Just think about it,' he said again.

'All right.' She pulled her hand out from under his, and bit her lip, wishing she had some idea of what else to say. 'I'll think about it.'

His face lit up. Surprise, relief, or actual happiness, she couldn't tell.

'This calls for champagne!' he said, and picked up the bottle.

◆

When she got in, Val was sitting on the sofa, darning a stocking. She must have come straight from the Palladium.

'Henry asked me to marry him!' It came blurting out.

Val dropped her darning in her lap. '*Lord* Henry?' Her voice held a kind of awe. It felt wrong for Val – sensible, kind Val – to sound like that.

'Don't say it like that!'

'But he's money, isn't he? You'd be set for life!' Val got up and did a little celebration dance, but stopped when she saw Kit's face. No doubt she looked totally confused.

'That's what he said.'

'Who'd have thought he'd fall in love with you!'

Good Lord. She hadn't even noticed – he never *had* said he was in love with her.

'I – I don't know he has.'

'Well, of course he has, or he wouldn't have proposed.'

Perhaps she was right. She had to be right. Men like Henry didn't propose to actresses unless they were desperately in love. Yet had Henry ever *acted* like he was in love? What did she know? She wasn't exactly experienced.

Val went into the kitchen to make tea, and Kit trailed after her, irresolute.

The paté and champagne sat heavy in her stomach. Tea might make that worse, but she needed its comfort. They sat, sipping, a ginger biscuit on each saucer. Val cocked a perfectly curved eyebrow at her.

'What d'you think Zeke'll have to say about it?'

The stone under her breastbone hollowed out at the thought.

'I may not tell him,' she said slowly. 'I'm not going to say "yes", anyway . . . at least, not yet.'

'You're a fool if you don't snap Henry up. If I were you I'd be hauling him down the aisle in two shakes. *One* shake!' She put a hand on Kit's knee. 'It's a hard old life, the theatre. You're okay so far, and maybe you always will be. But, once a woman gets too old for romantic roles, there's not much left . . . you have to put your money away and save up for that rainy day, or else you have to get married. Otherwise . . .'

Otherwise one ended up alone and poor. The kindness in Val's eyes, her earnestness, was sincere. It made sense.

She was lucky. By any reasonable standard, she was lucky. She should stop being a Moaning Minnie and buck up.

'Well, it's nice to be asked,' she said, smiling. She had to tell Zeke, though. She just had to.

CHAPTER 38

'He *what*?' Zeke couldn't believe it. How could she even *consider* it? 'You're not thinking about saying yes!'

Kit looked at him as though *he* were being unreasonable. Fortunately, Mrs Coward had gone out to a friend's and left them to their afternoon tea in peace. He'd been sitting alone and uncertain until Kit had arrived, and now he wished she hadn't. The very idea of her marrying that clown made him want to smash something. Preferably Henry. His fists clenched. Kit noticed that, and her expression became mulish.

'I didn't expect you to be so angry about it.'

'Henry's a drunk,' he said brutally. 'And if you marry him, he'll drag you down, too.'

'Oh, Zeke!' She sounded so *sorry* for him. As though he were the one with the problem. She just couldn't see. It was because she'd lived such a sheltered life. She'd never had to face up to the harsh realities. He hoped she never would have to, but if she didn't . . . could she really be duped into marrying that popinjay?

'Honey, I don't know why you reckon so hard on this guy. He's nothing, compared to you!'

She glared hotly at him, her hands balled in her lap. 'You're prejudiced. Just because –'

'Because he's never done a hand's turn in his life, and he spends all his time drinking and carousing? Damn right I'm prejudiced against a man like that!'

'He's a gentleman! You –'. She fulminated without words.

A gentleman. That was a low blow. He could learn and dress well and study his lines and move around in society, but he'd never be a gentleman. Not ever. Hell, he hadn't even finished sixth grade. Everything he knew (and he knew a lot), he'd taught himself. Or his mother had taught him – her and her friend, Mrs Treece. His mother had *wanted* him to be a gentleman, but the best he'd ever be was a copy. People like Kit would always be able to tell the difference.

And clearly she preferred the real thing.

Perhaps he'd have to show her the truth about this 'gentleman'. Yes. He would show her what awaited her if she went down his path.

He put a hand into his pocket. The telegram crinkled against his fingers, the paper flimsy but so powerful.

'I had a telegram an hour ago.' Bringing it out, he laid it on the table for her to pick up. She did so; as she read it, her face paled.

'I'm so sorry! Are you going to him?'

He hadn't intended to. He didn't want to be at his father's deathbed. He'd walked away and never wanted to see him again. But to save Kit, he'd do it.

'Will you come with me?'

'Of course I will!' She put a hand over his.

'There's a train every half hour,' he said.

'I'll just go . . .' She slipped off to the toilet and he mechanically collected his hat.

Marrying Henry . . . he was sucking her back into the life she'd left behind, trying to get her to turn into some Lady. She was a performer, not an aristocrat. No one who'd seen her on stage could doubt that. And more importantly, if Kit married Henry, she'd have just as miserable a life as his own mother had had, even if she'd be financially much better off. Being in the aristocracy didn't protect a woman from a drunken husband – the law was on the man's side no matter how high-born the woman. No. He was the only one who could protect her, and he would, if he had to take her to the deathbed of every drunk in London.

◆

Zeke had been very quiet on the train. No wonder. Despite everything, it had to be hard to contemplate the death of one's father. Kit shivered. She didn't want to even think about her own father's death.

The nursing home at Croydon seemed very nice. The matron led them into Mr Gardiner's room and left, indicating to the nurse sitting beside the bed that she should leave, too.

Mr Gardiner lay on his back, unconscious. His skin was yellow, his belly distended, face and hands so puffy the skin was stretched, pink and shiny, and quite disturbing to look at. She found Zeke's hand and held it. How awful for him this must be! She blinked back tears; he wouldn't want to deal with her distress as well as his own.

They stood by the bed. Mr Gardiner's breath was harsh, with a kind of rasping in his throat. Was that the death rattle she'd read about?

There were large purple and yellow bruises under his eyes and on the skin of his neck. It made her feel faintly sick. How would it make Zeke feel, the poor boy?

'Sit down,' she urged. It might take a long time. Zeke should rest as much as he could. He'd need someone when it was over. Her whole body seemed to be centred on him, on how he felt, on what he needed. No matter how long it took, she'd stay. She wanted to enfold him in the warmth that flooded her. She could pray, at least.

'No.' Zeke dragged his gaze away from the man in the bed and fixed a steely glare on her. What in heaven? 'Look at him. Take a good, long look at him. This is what Henry will come to, eventually. This is what a drunk looks like at the end.'

What?

'Zeke –'

'You have to understand, Kit. Once a drunk, always a drunk. Henry's already on the path. This is what will happen to him, sooner or later. His liver will give out. Maybe his stomach, before that. He'll be a wreck, and you'll be tied to him, lifelong. And Henry has a temper. When you're there, with him, and no way out, he'll take it out on you. I swear, that's how it works. I know you don't understa—'

'Shut up!' She'd never said those words in her life before, but they were needed now. 'This is your father's *deathbed* and, by God, you will show some respect!'

Her eyes were full of angry tears. She hadn't known it was possible to feel such rage. How could he. How *dare* he?

'You will sit in that chair and you will keep vigil. You'll act like a decent human being. Or have you inherited your father's contempt for what's right?'

He paled and was silent.

'Sit down,' she said again. He sat, staring at his father. His hands were shaking. *Good*, she thought. *Good. Face up to it.* 'When we next meet, we'll have a discussion about how you have no right to try to control my life. But for now, you sit there and you pray for your father's soul until it leaves this Earth.'

At the door, she paused. 'I'll let the club know you won't be in tonight.'

'Thank you.' His voice was almost inaudible. She gave a most unladylike snort, and went out.

The matron was waiting for her. She forced herself to seem calm.

'I have to return to London,' Kit told her, astonished that her voice sounded normal. 'I have to let Mr Gardiner's employers know about the situation and organise a locum for him.'

'I understand. It won't be long now. Have . . . arrangements been made?'

'No, I don't think so. Is there a local funeral home? Perhaps you can organise for them to come, when it's time?'

'Certainly. We have a most reliable family firm.'

'Thank you.'

She walked back to the station, marvelling over the power of social expectations. She'd never been so angry in her life, or so shaken, but she and the matron had been able to converse in the most reasonable way because they both understood what was 'done' in these circumstances.

It was a strong and sustaining thing, to know what was done. She should thank her mother, one day, for that knowledge.

As for Zeke . . . rage overtook her again at the thought. How *dare* he! Not only to desecrate his father's deathbed, but to think he had the *right*! To use his own dying father as an object lesson. To, to . . . to *lecture* her!

Goddamn him. God*damn* him. She sat in the ladies' waiting room on the platform, blotting tears from her eyes that were half anger and half desolation.

She'd lost *everyone* now. Zeke had abandoned her as surely as if he'd gone back to Canada. How could they be friends after this? She might even have to rethink auditioning for Charlot's play. Could she work with him? She wasn't sure.

She went to the Gentleman's Relish because she didn't know how else to contact the manager, Mags. In the afternoon light, the club looked, surprisingly, less seedy than most places of entertainment did during the day. Perhaps it was the vibrant murals that made the difference.

'Oh, damn.' Mags put her hands on her hips and scowled. 'What shall we do!' Her eyes, outlined dramatically with kohl, narrowed. 'You. You did that very good tap number. And you can sing. You've been here a couple of times, so you know the general flow of the show. You can fill in for him. We'll get you a tuxedo and a top hat. It'll be positively Shakespearean!'

Yes. Yes, it was just what she needed. Performance would calm her down. She could let all this angry energy out into the dance. And she could afford her silk stockings.

'Perfect,' she said. 'Is there time for a run-through?'

♦

The club was full. She suspected that Mags had put a few calls out to say there was a 'new act', and when Prince George walked in, followed by a couple of his less manly cronies, she was sure of it.

But so what? She'd had time for a basic rehearsal, and she'd always been good at improvisation.

Kit and the 'girls' had a ball, hamming it up, and the audience loved it. When she and Val sang together, Val used her chest voice, and the combination of baritone and soprano, male and female, opposites and harmony, was a showstopper. The handsome Spanish bartender stopped serving drinks altogether to watch – mostly Val, Kit noticed.

Then Tallulah sprang up from the audience and challenged her to a cartwheel contest. Made bold by her trousers, Kit agreed enthusiastically. Tallulah, it turned out, had no knickers on under her brilliantly blue chiffon dress.

They got a standing ovation.

Afterwards, the prince invited them to his table, Kit still in her tuxedo.

'Come back with us to York House,' he said jovially. 'In costume! That would be jolly.'

The invitation brought back memories of the spectacular hangover she'd acquired there last time, and made her flinch

internally. But the remark did give her an idea for her costume
for Henry's birthday.

'Thank you, sir, but I need to return this to its rightful
owner, and I only have my day dress with me.'

'I'll come!' Tallulah said brightly.

Prince George looked her up and down. 'Divine!' he said.
They exchanged a long, meaningful glance.

Mags appeared almost magically at Kit's elbow.

'Sorry, gents –' she winked at Prince George to show she
was pretending not to know who he was, and he winked back,
'– but I need this little darling.'

Mags shepherded her back to the dressing room, where the
owner of her tuxedo was waiting, draped in a bright purple
kimono.

'I'll get that washed for you,' Mags said, taking the damp
shirt from Kit. 'Wear one of mine.'

'Darling, I shall!' the woman said, kissing Mags with some
enthusiasm, which was heartily returned. Kit couldn't help but
smile. There was so much simplicity about life here, because
although people played roles – like Mags' circus impresario
act – the roles revealed who they truly were, once social shackles
had been dispensed with.

That made her think quite hard. If this was a place where
one was, inevitably, oneself, then who was she?

Just a song and dance girl, she supposed.

Once she was back in her own clothes, Mags paid her.
More than she got for three days' work at Savion. Zeke was
onto a good thing here.

'If you ever need me again, I'm at the Cats' Home,' Kit said, tucking the money away in her purse.

'Darling, I love you, but you're too perfectly ladylike for this place,' Mags said. 'Not fair to give you a job when those of other persuasions need work.'

That hurt. Which was ridiculous.

'Mind you, if you ever feel like taking a walk on the other side of the street . . .' Mags flicked back her red hair and smiled, showing her teeth, deliberately over the top. Kit laughed and hugged her.

'If I ever did feel like that, you'd be my first call.'

She left the still-lively club with some regret, and made her weary way to the taxi rank.

As the cab purred across London to Charlotte Street, she finally let herself think about Zeke. Her initial anger was there, ready to be poked into flames, but she was too tired for that. With the best will in the world, she couldn't forgive him for using his own father's death to manipulate her.

Horrible.

She spent the rest of the trip saying prayers for Mr Gardiner. If everything Zeke had said about him was true, he needed them.

CHAPTER 39

Somewhere, a clock was ticking. Not in this room. Down the hall.

As the night drew on, and the nursing home settled into sleep, the tick grew louder. There were no other noises. It was a still night, and out here in the suburbs the ever-present rattle of traffic was missing.

Just the clock, and his father's struggle to breathe.

Kit had told him to pray, so he prayed. The old prayers, the ones his mother had taught him when he was very young. *Our Father which art in Heaven* . . .

Over and over again . . .

He listened to the breathing and tried not to look at his father's face, so horribly distorted.

'His liver is not working,' the matron had said. 'So the fluid isn't leaving his body. It will build up until his heart can't cope with it anymore.'

And then he would die.

A sob wracked him. Not for his father. He couldn't be crying for his father. But this – this deathbed vigil was what he'd missed for his mother. She had gone, flying away to her heaven without a chance to say goodbye. If only he could have sat, as he was now, and held her hand.

Another sob. It *hurt*. Ripped through his chest and out his throat. Blindly, he grabbed for something to hold on to. His father's hand. Puffy under his fingers. This hand had touched his mother; sometimes in kindness, with affection. He bent his head over that hand and cried for everything lost. His mother, the father he'd adored as a little boy, before the drinking had got bad. The farm, which, for all he'd pretended otherwise to his mother, he'd loved with all his heart. Those long, sunny, blue days, the hugs before bedtime, the laughter and the sense that all was well with the world, while his parents were there. The freedom before he'd had to look after his mother and make sure his father was kept away from her.

All the safety and the happiness and the promise of love, and everything else that was gone.

The grief came from deep, deep within, a storm, a whirlwind, thoughts and memories and waves of feeling surfacing and sinking, over and over.

And when it subsided, and he could draw breath and look up, the only sound in the room was the ticking of the clock.

His father lay still.

Zeke held on to his hand for a long moment, tears drying on his face. He wished, desperately, that his father had been awake when he'd arrived. That he'd spoken to him one more time. That his father had *known* that he came.

The matron, as though drawn by the silence, came to the half-open door. Zeke turned to her, unsure what to do or say.

'He didn't know I came.'

She moved into the room and gently took his father's hand from his, laying it back over his father's breast.

'He knew,' she said. 'They always know when they're not alone. They go more peacefully when family are there.'

A wealth of experience in her voice. He let it comfort him.

'I'll organise for the funeral home to come tomorrow morning, as I discussed with Miss Linton. They'll be in contact with you.'

He was expected to leave, apparently. Shakily, he got to his feet and took a last look. No matter what they said, his father didn't look like he was asleep. He looked – empty.

'Thank you, Matron. And . . . thank you for waiting up.'

She smiled, but perfunctorily, as though the idea of *not* waiting for the end was unthinkable.

'Shall I call you a cab? The last train has gone.'

'No. No, thank you. I think I'll walk back a while and pick up a cab closer to the city.'

She picked up his hat and gave it to him. 'Are you sure? It's a long way, and you're very tired.'

He drew a long breath. 'I'm sure.'

He made his way to London Road and set off through the still night. It seemed as though he could breathe deeper; as if something had been constricting his chest for months, and now was gone.

He had no family. His stride faltered at the thought, but then he went on. They were just words. He'd been alone ever since his mother had died, and even before that, he'd had no one to rely on. His mother had tried her best, but society wasn't set up so that a woman with a child could earn enough to keep them both. It just wasn't possible – at least, not in British Columbia.

He'd had to cope, and he had. Left school, worked hard, made sure she was all right. He could be an engineer now, if he wanted. The money he had put away, plus what he'd save from the next show, would be enough to see him through university. Tempting. Very tempting.

But then he remembered the fun he'd had at the Gentleman's Relish, how exhilarating it was to dance with Kit, the wave of applause that lifted you up and pushed you to do better and always better the next time, the sheer *joy* of singing well . . . he didn't think engineers ever felt quite like that. He was where he ought to be. But that was just the beginning of figuring out who he was as a man; as an adult with no one to look after but himself.

Deep in his sternum was a constant pain, which probably would never go away. That was his mother. His father . . . he'd done his duty by his father, and that was good. Kit had been right; how he treated his father was about what kind of man *he* was. And he'd done what was right. More than he'd intended, even.

Although his attempt had failed horribly, trying to help Kit had brought him to that bedside, and to this calm. He was glad he'd been there. Perhaps it was right that he remember the good times with his father. Perhaps the man was owed that much, no matter what came later.

He didn't really think so. What his father had done, and done again and again, had dissolved anything owed to him.

He had not owed him an easy death, or a bedside vigil, or any respect at all.

Evil deserved no respect, and his father had carried evil within him like a cancer. Drink had simply set it free.

No, he was glad for his own sake, not for his father's. He was glad that he could look back on all of this and not be ashamed of a single minute. That he *wasn't* his father's son, out only for what he could get, hurting others to make himself feel stronger. He could hold his head up and go into his future without guilt or shame.

And that was all because of Kit.

He'd hurt her.

Goddammit. He'd think about that tomorrow.

CHAPTER 40

Kit dragged herself out of bed on Saturday morning, wincing. She might have practised regularly, but the cartwheel contest had left her with aches in entirely new places.

Mrs French had made scrambled eggs for breakfast and, miraculously, there were some left, with fresh toast.

'You're too good to me, Mrs French.'

'Mr Coward called. He says the funeral will be on Monday at Croydon Cemetery at noon.' There was a question in her voice. So.

'Mr Gardiner's father died last night.'

'Oh, dear!' Mrs French's face creased in concern. 'I didn't know his father was in London.'

'He's been in a nursing home in Croydon for some weeks. He was . . . ill before he arrived.'

Mrs French nodded. 'And he wanted to be with his son

for the end. How thoughtful of him to come all the way to London, so Mr Gardiner didn't have to leave his employment!'

That was the way it *would* look to outsiders. Good. Zeke wouldn't want the world knowing his business.

'Yes, indeed,' she said. What should she do? Go to Zeke? It would be the – the *noble* thing to do. She wasn't sure she was that noble. It wasn't like he loved his father, anyway. She wasn't even sure he'd be grieving.

'Thank you, Mrs French.' She packed up her dishes and took them into the kitchen, where Val and Sally were washing up. Val greeted her with delight.

'We were sensational! Tell Sally, she doesn't believe me.'

'Oh, we were sensational, all right,' Kit agreed. 'But we were outdone by Tallulah.'

Val described, in graphic detail, how the cartwheel contest had gone.

'Well, I never did!' Mrs French gasped.

'I hope not!' Sally quipped, laughing.

They all laughed. Kit had just a little envy of Tallulah. To be so unafraid, so recklessly free . . . well, good luck to her, even if she was *outrageous*.

She dried the dishes and set off for Savion. Another horrible day. She managed some time off her feet, helping Peg and Mary finish a rush job. One thing she *could* do was hand-roll a hem – sewing was considered a nice, ladylike pursuit at her school. Miss Masters raised her eyebrows, but said nothing; Peg gave her the first smile since she'd started there.

After work, she went over to the New Theatre to find Fred and Adele. Fred was on stage, warming up, waiting for Delly to get back from the hairdresser's.

It was beautifully cool inside. She relished the contrast with the overheated streets. Oh, how she wished she were coming here to work tonight!

'Heya, Kit,' Fred called. He was in loose trousers and shirt, as always.

'I have a favour to ask you, Fred.'

He got that look on his face he sometimes turned to Adele when she wanted something: the suspicious brother look.

'Oh, don't be like that!' she scolded him. 'I have to go to a costume ball, and I thought I'd go in top hat and tails. Can you lend me an outfit for a week?'

'I've got enough,' he said ruefully. 'Delly keeps getting me new ones. I tell her I don't need them, but what can you do? She says the style has changed! How can it? It's classic!'

Kit laughed. 'It's the width of the lapel.'

'That's what she says. You can *have* one of the old ones, if you like.'

So that was organised.

'Noël let us know about Zeke's dad,' Fred told her. 'Monday, right? Where's Croydon?'

'A suburb on the other side of the river. Are you planning to go?'

'Oh yeah. Wouldn't be right not to, would it?' He snapped his fingers in a quick rhythm. 'What's the matter, kid?'

'Oh, I'm just thinking about Zeke. He . . . he and his father didn't get on, you know.'

'So he said.'

'He did?'

Fred put a foot up on a chair and leaned on his knee. 'Zeke and I have a lot in common, Kit. Our father was a drunk, too.

Mom took us to New York and put us in theatre school. That's why we started so young. He helped out, got us contacts in the early days, but we had to put food on the table.'

'I didn't know. I'm sorry to hear that.'

He waved one hand eloquently. 'Oh, it wasn't like Zeke's folks. Dad's a sweet drunk. But he's a drunk. We kept in touch, you know. He visited, we visited. Mom never actually *said* that she'd left him – the official story was that it was all for us kids, because Delly was so talented.'

She huffed in disbelief. 'Just Delly?'

He raised a quizzical eyebrow. 'I was only four, remember.' He stood for a moment, looking out into the empty rows of seats.

'He's been ill, lately,' he said quietly. 'Mom's taking him into the country for a rest cure. It's not like her to spend so much time with him. I wonder . . . she wouldn't let us know if anything were serious. She'd want us not to worry.'

'Let her do that for you, then,' Kit said. 'Even if something were wrong, you couldn't leave here, anyway, under your contract. Trust her to know what's best.'

Fred took a deep breath. 'Parents! They're a trial and a blessing.'

Amen, she thought. Perhaps she'd been luckier in her parents than she'd known.

Fred got her a ticket to see the show and afterwards she went back with them to their apartment to find a set of tails. Delly thought it was a great joke, although she was sad about Zeke's loss.

In the bedroom, she supervised Kit trying on a number of Fred's suits. On impulse, Kit told her what Zeke had done.

'He wanted you to see his dying father as a – a *lesson*?' Delly said, her voice rising.

'That was outrageous, don't you think?'

'Oh, these men who want to protect you!' Delly sighed theatrically. 'They *always* think they know best. And they'll lie and cheat to prove it.'

'I was so *angry*.' Kit tugged the front of the jacket down over her breasts. Unlike the suit she'd worn the night before, which had been tailored for a woman and had made her look like a slight man, this jacket seemed to emphasise her womanliness.

'So you should have been,' Delly agreed. 'Turn around.'

The pants were a bit tight, although fortunately Fred favoured a loose cut. Perhaps she'd be better off with a standard tuxedo jacket, to cover her bottom properly. Adele didn't agree.

'Not for a costume ball. Tails are much better. And if the pants are tight . . .' She wiggled her eyebrows meaningfully. 'So much the better!'

Delly could always make her laugh. But she sobered quickly.

'I should go to the funeral, shouldn't I?'

'Oh yes, honey. Don't kick a man when he's down.'

As she changed back into her street clothes, Kit nodded at herself in the mirror. If Fred and Adele were going, she could go, too, without it looking like she forgave him. Yes. It *was* the right thing to do.

CHAPTER 41

S he was there.

So great a tide of relief flowed through Zeke that he almost stumbled. She had come.

Dressed in sombre black, Kit walked through the lychgate with Fred and Adele, also in funeral clothes. Even Adele was behaving with propriety. He was lucky to have friends. Noël and the Cowards had come with him in a cab, and Mrs Coward had taken his arm as they walked into the churchyard. He hadn't been sure of the etiquette. He'd sung at funerals as a choirboy, but he hadn't been to one before as a member of the family.

'As family, you wait here until the hearse arrives, and then the congregation goes in and then you and the pallbearers bring the coffin in.' She was quite matter-of-fact about it. She must have been to many funerals, he supposed. The War, the Spanish flu – and just life.

Kit came to join them. She smiled quietly at him; not her open-hearted smile, but she was *here*. He could survive it if she were here.

Others came, too. David and Bobbie, Bruce the stage manager, Susan Maxwell, Courtney, even Charlot! How had they all heard? He cast a sideways glance at Noël, who shrugged. 'They would have been offended if they hadn't been told,' he said.

Maybe. But he thought it was one of those proofs of Noël's essential kindness. So that he didn't have to sit in an empty church.

He wasn't prepared, even so, for Noël and Fred and some of the others to stand with him as pallbearers. The thought of carrying his father's coffin was nauseating on one level – it was supposed to be a mark of respect to the dead, wasn't it? On the other, these men had come out of their way to show *him* respect, and he would honour that.

Kit and Mr and Mrs Coward went in with the congregation. The funeral director, at the door of the church, received some signal from inside, and said, 'Ready, gentlemen. On three. One, two, *three*.'

With easy strength, the six of them grasped the coffin handles and hoisted it neatly onto their shoulders. He and Noël were much of a height, just over six feet, so they were paired at the front.

They processed into the church to organ music; he'd put his foot down over 'Oh for the wings of a dove' and so it was a Bach fugue. Intricate and complicated enough, he supposed, to represent his own feelings.

He sat next to Mrs Coward, with Kit and the Astaires behind. He was conscious of her presence, silently supporting him.

The service was mercifully short, since the pastor hadn't known 'our dear brother in the Lord'. The graveyard was attached to the church. It was quite full, but the pastor had found a spot in the corner for 'our Canadian brother'. Zeke wondered if he would have been so accommodating if he'd known how the 'brother' had lived his life.

Well, let God sort that out.

He and the others carried the coffin out and to the grave.

There were chaste white lilies and a bouquet of roses laid on top of it. He had no idea who had sent them. He'd never even thought about flowers.

At the graveside, Mrs Coward moved back and pushed Kit forward, bless her. Kit took his hand as the final words were said, and then they all stirred and shifted away.

'Everyone is welcome back at our house,' Mrs Coward announced, but only a handful accepted the invitation.

'Thank you all for coming,' he said, heartfelt. In Canada, people would have been hugging him and patting his back; in stiff-upper-lip Britain, they just nodded and shook his hand.

Right now, that suited him. The undertaker gave him the cards from the flowers – the Cowards and Charlot. That made sense.

The rest of the day passed in a blur. He was set down in a chair in the living room and every so often someone would give him something to eat or drink. Kit was somewhere around, flitting past, helping Mrs Coward. She didn't come over, except to give him a cup of tea.

'All right?' she asked. He nodded, and she went away.

He *was* all right. Just exhausted.

Then, somehow, the place was empty except for the Cowards. Even Noël had gone, to rehearsal for the new revue, he supposed. Kit came out of the kitchen, fixing her hat onto her head.

'I'll be off, then.' She touched his hair lightly. 'God bless, Zeke.'

That had the air of a final goodbye. He grabbed her hand. 'Don't go.'

'You have to sleep. You're tired out.'

'But I'll see you soon.'

'When we audition, if not before,' she said. If that was meant to be comforting, it failed. She pulled her hand from his and left without a backward glance.

Mr Coward pulled him up out of the chair. 'Go to bed, lad. It'll seem brighter in the morning.'

He hoped so. At this moment, he couldn't think beyond the next action. Foot on staircase. Up. Into the bathroom. Into his bedroom. Pyjamas. Bed.

The ceiling was sloped in this room, and the shadows in the corner were deep. But outside were the perpetual lights and noise of London.

It soothed him to sleep. An orphan. Could you be an orphan if you were fully grown?

He didn't know. He only knew that you could feel like one.

CHAPTER 42

On the next Saturday night, it was a relief to go to a show with Henry. The society parties she had once enjoyed were now like walking a tightrope – would anyone recognise her from Savion and, if they did, what would she say? It had been bad enough to be an actress, but a *shop girl*? All of Henry's friends would turn away as surely as Lady Bridlingham and Lady Penelope's mother. The very thought made her ill.

So much easier to sit beside Henry and laugh at Gertie Lawrence. And envy her, just a bit.

There would be a party, no doubt, at David and Bobbie's flat, but she shied away from bringing Henry into that crowd. They would all take it as a declaration that the relationship was serious, for one thing; and Zeke might be there.

After the show, they had a light supper at Maximilian's, and headed off to St James' Palace. It was becoming almost normal to her, to sail under the archway with its royal crest and through the courtyard to York House. The footman who opened the door greeted her by name, now.

She was wearing an older dress she had gussied up, following Peg's advice; white jersey with silver sequins, which glittered in the lamplight as they passed the wall sconces in the long corridor.

In PW's rooms, there was the usual congregation of interesting people. He had quite a talent for putting together a party. Never a dull moment – and, as always, a lot of liquor.

She had decided that Saturday was the only night she could let her hair down. She couldn't risk her job by socialising during the week. Tomorrow, she didn't even have to get to the park to see Zeke, so she could stay out all night if she wanted to. That gave her a twinge. No time to think about it now.

Plunging into the gathering, she exchanged greetings with Prince George and a few others, and was given a cocktail (something pink) by a footman. She drank it down, and Henry laughed.

'That's the spirit!' He did the same, pulled her into his arms and they danced to the gramophone; a foxtrot. They were dancing better together, now. Either he'd improved, or they'd just become used to each other. That was an odd thought; perhaps the same would happen if they married?

The Prince of Wales was swaying in place with a woman she had not met before.

'Oh, that's Freda,' Prince George whispered in her ear as he passed by. 'Quite middle-class, my dear, but he's totally infatuated. Just as well she's married, or we might be in for it. She's just back from America.'

Not for the first time, she was astonished at what royal princes would confide to almost strangers.

The prince came over to greet her.

'Miss Linton. Divine to see you!'

Behind him, 'Freda' said, 'Parpee, come back to me!' The most beautiful smile broke over the prince's face; the kind of smile a child gives on Christmas morning when he sees the presents under the tree.

'Excuse me. Coming, my angel!' He practically skipped back to his partner and kissed her lavishly, ignoring the onlookers.

She could just imagine Perry saying, 'Well, isn't that sick-making!'

The gramophone wound down while a footman was getting her a drink, and the party settled onto the overstuffed sofas around the fireplace, which had been filled, on this hot evening, with an arrangement of pine cones and dried flowers.

She sat silent, sipping her cocktail, as the party talked politics. Even George got involved.

'I say!' he exclaimed at a remark his brother made. 'I don't think you can hold this Hitler chappie up as an example. He has some rather nasty ideas about people like me.'

The Prince of Wales shot him a look. 'I'm not saying we need adopt *all* his ideas. But he's a strong hand on the tiller in a time of instability, and that's what Britain needs. A bulwark against communism.'

For once, the long nights she'd spent not working came in handy, as she'd had time to read all the news. They were talking about this man in Germany, Hitler, who had just taken over some political party there. She'd read no great good about him. His ideas seemed very . . . extreme.

'Oh, let's dance!' Freda said. She jumped up and went to the gramophone.

Freda's word was law, apparently. They danced.

Kit had somehow lost count of the drinks she'd had. Henry had outpaced her, she thought, but she didn't care. She was happy. Uplifted. She wished the harpies from Savion could see her now, dancing with the Prince of Wales, dancing with Prince George, dancing with Lord Henry Carleton. They'd soon change their tune.

She could imagine the fawning, and smiled.

Henry grinned back at her, and swung her around and away from the small group by the gramophone. There was a balcony she'd never noticed. He led her onto it. The depths of night. No stars in London, just low clouds, faintly orange from the streetlamps. She loved London. What a nice place. What a nice man the prince was.

'Good to be alone, eh?' Henry asked, slurring his words just a little. She smiled sleepily at him. Gently, he pushed her back against the brick wall and kissed her.

It was a nice kiss. He was a nice boy. They were nice together. Henry pushed closer, his body firm against hers. It was a bit like being made prisoner, and she didn't like it. She never liked being constrained. Why didn't he *know* that by now? Zeke knew it. When Zeke touched her, he made sure to leave her room to move away.

Henry's tongue flicked against her lips. All right. She supposed that was all right. He tasted of gin. She wriggled a little, to get him to move away, and he moaned and pressed closer. His hand moved up, over her breast, and squeezed gently.

Her hand came around in a swinging blow against his ear.

'Dammit, Kit!' He fell back, angry and astonished. His eyes were bloodshot and staring.

'How *dare* you!' she said. It was hard to get the words out, and she stumbled over them. 'He-ow d-dare you!' she said again.

'But Kit, we're – we're engaged!' He swayed as he stood there, and she realised he was drunk.

'What? No, we're not!' She, too, was unsteady on her feet. Propping herself up against the wall, she felt nausea rise. 'I didn't say "yes".'

Henry waved that away. 'Oh, I know, but let's face it, you're not going to say "no", are you?'

He had that look: privilege and arrogance and surety he'd get what he wanted. He always did.

Anger roared up out of nowhere, the same rage she'd felt at Mr Gardiner's deathbed: these men who believed they owned her, that they could decide *for* her what she should and shouldn't do.

'Go to hell!' she said.

Walking back into the party, it was astounding that no one seemed to have noticed anything. Except Prince George, who was always alert. He came over to her and took her arm.

'You know, I think I might get a car to take you home,' he said thoughtfully.

'Why?'

'Well, my dear, I think you're a bit the worse for wine. And apart from me and my friends, every man here besides PW is already married, and is here with someone other than his wife.' He winked broadly at her. 'I think this is a little hot for you, especially if you've had a tiff with Henry and lost his protection. And it will get hotter, believe me. They haven't started really drinking yet. No, my sweet little kitten, this is not the party for you.'

Adultery. The future King, neck-deep in it. George's remark about it being lucky Freda was married suddenly struck home. All these people, adulterers. She felt sick. Licentiousness was one thing, but *adultery* – and so openly! Fornication seemed clean in comparison. Her head was swimming. Henry had stayed on the balcony, full of pique, no doubt. Leave him be. The anger had swirled out of her and left a strange dizziness behind.

'Thank you. Should I say goodbye?'

'Oh, I'll do the necessary for you. Just slip away. I'll get Peter to order you a car.' He kissed her cheek. 'And I do thank you for introducing me to Tallulah. What a girl she is!'

Nervous laughter choked her. Of course. It was inevitable that the two of them, so alike, would collide and make sparks.

Peter was, apparently, the footman.

She followed him unsteadily down the corridors, where the electric light gleamed off gilt furniture and dazzled off crystal chandeliers. Too 'hot' a party for her. She wondered about Henry. How hot would his behaviour have become if she hadn't hit him? What had he expected of her? She remembered Prince George, sneaking off somewhere with that girl, and knew the answer.

The Prince of Wales was several years older – twenty-eight or twenty-nine, she believed – while Henry was just about to turn twenty-two. She was only a month off her own twenty-second. Old for a deb. Too young for the prince's set, surely, as Henry was. But he'd been to school with Prince Harry; that was the connection. Harry was off serving with his regiment, but the connection held.

She was still angry with him, but while she waited for a car to be brought around, she fretted over Henry spending too much time with these people. Although perfectly mannered, they were not good influences on him, she was sure. It wasn't just the openly flaunted adultery – they were also somehow *immature*. That was it. The prince acted more like a schoolboy than an almost thirty-year-old. He behaved as though Freda were a special treat. 'Parpee', indeed!

And Tallulah and Prince George . . .

Oh, forget them. Her real problem was going to be getting home without being vilely ill.

◆

She made it, but only just. She was strenuously ill in the downstairs WC. Afterwards, she crept up the stairs to her bedroom and stared at herself in the mirror over the basin.

Her mascara had run, her hair and dress were dishevelled, her lipstick smeared . . . she looked like a tart after a hard night's work. Disgusting.

And the worst – the very *worst* thing – was that Zeke had been right. The bastard.

She was filled up and running over with shame. A drunken scene, a man groping her, and she herself vomiting from too much drink. Like the worst drab. Like . . . like the woman of low repute the Palace had thought her. Desperately, she grabbed the hand towel and scrubbed the makeup from her face. She would *not* become that woman. She would *not*. If she never took another drink again, or went out with another man, she would *not* descend into drink and debauchery.

So help her God.

CHAPTER 43

'Look!' Mrs French was holding out an envelope.

Thick cream paper, a beautifully calligraphed address – and on the back, a red wax seal.

'It has a *crest!*' Mrs French said. The butcher's boy was there, too, sitting with his hip on the dining table – Mrs French must really like him, as she was death on that. 'Hand-delivered by a footman!'

Kit took the envelope with a strong feeling of foreboding. Which was ridiculous. It was probably from Lady Sarah.

She opened it carefully, so red wax didn't go all over the floor.

From Henry's mother.

Dear Miss Scott,

As I believe Henry has told you, we are having a house party to celebrate his birthday.

We would be so pleased if you could join us there on the 23rd inst., and stay for a week or so. We shall be having a costume ball on the 25th. If you cannot arrange for a costume, we shall be glad to supply one.

Your mother and I, as it happens, were at school together, and we have been corresponding lately; I have her permission to invite you.

If you can inform us by which train you will arrive, I shall send a car for you.

Yours, etc.

Clara, Countess Carleton

Oh, God. Her mother had said she and the countess knew each other, but Kit had thought that was all in the past. No wonder her mother had let any mention of Henry lapse in her letters – she'd been planning this. The 'Miss Scott' was a dead giveaway. No one in Henry's world called her that. But why had the countess gone along with it?

Henry had put her up to it. She'd been ignoring his messages and notes since that disastrous party, so he'd called in the big guns. She hadn't even decided for herself if she'd see Henry again, and she didn't like having her hand forced.

Wordlessly, she handed the invitation to Mrs French, who positively squealed in delight as she read it. Kit realised that she'd never told Mrs French about her visit to Barrows; in retrospect, that had been ungenerous of her. The girls and Mrs French took so much pleasure in the good fortune any one of them enjoyed.

'My word!' the butcher's boy said. 'That's the high life and no mistake!'

'We'll have to go over all your things and get them ready!' Mrs French said, handing her back the letter. 'Don't you worry, dear. If you don't have what you need, the other girls will pitch in. I'm sure we can come up with a costume.'

There was no way out. Not only would it be incredibly bad manners to decline the invitation, her mother would never forgive her.

And part of her, Kit had to admit, was longing to get out of London, out to the cool, astonishingly green countryside of England. To a place where no one would treat her as a servant.

'I've organised one,' she said. 'Henry said this might be happening.'

She thrust the letter into her handbag and turned on her heel.

'I'll look at your dresses and make sure they have no spots on them!' Mrs French called after her.

'Thank you!' she said over her shoulder. She had to get out and think about this. She couldn't possibly stay for a whole week. Perhaps just the weekend?

'Wait!' Mrs French said. 'Aren't you going to write your acceptance?'

Almost to the door, Kit stopped dead.

Yes. She had to do that immediately. To delay would be unacceptably rude. She had some notepaper in her room. Her mother had given it to her, so it was the right quality.

But – 'I have to ask Miss Masters if I can have the Saturday off,' she said in a small voice. Another humiliation.

'Bother!' Mrs French said. 'But a job's a job, I suppose. Still, you can always go down on the Saturday afternoon. And here's the train timetable!' Triumphantly, she produced the small booklet from the sideboard drawer.

'Thank you. Everything I need!'

Mrs French beamed.

◆

There was nothing for it – she'd have to come clean with Miss Masters about who she really was, because the woman would, quite fairly, want some evidence of this invitation if she were going to give Kit the weekend off. Maybe even the Friday, too.

Damn it.

On the other hand . . . the countess had written to Katherine Scott, not Kit Linton. Perhaps she didn't have to come *totally* clean.

'My parents would be rather embarrassed,' she said to Miss Masters, 'if it got out that I'd had to take a job. So I used a false name.'

Miss Masters stared up at her from under threatening brows.

'Hmph. So you're going to Carleton Towers.'

'Lord Henry is a friend.'

The sharp grey eyes bored into her for a long moment. 'Is that your real hair?' she demanded.

Unbidden, Kit's hand went to her head. 'No.'

'Come in here and take it off.' Was she going to be fired? She followed Miss Masters behind the curtain and took her wig off, pulled the hairnet free and shook her hair out.

'Oooh,' Mary said. Peg laughed nastily.

Miss Masters glared even harder.

'Whose clothes do you wear?'

'Monsieur Dernier's.'

323

'Hmph. Benny. Might have known.' She clapped her hands together, and Mary and Peg jumped up from their chairs. 'Three-day house party. Costume party, you say?'

Kit nodded dumbly. Miss Masters waved dismissively. 'You'll have to deal with that yourself. Girls, fit her out. As a blonde.' She glared into Kit's eyes. 'Miss Katherine Scott will appear *only* in Savion's creations, and she will *talk* about them, am I clear?'

'Yes, Miss Masters.'

'I expect to get custom from this, girl, and don't you forget it.'

'Yes, Miss Masters.' Was she in Wonderland? How could things turn around so quickly?

The shop bell tinkled.

'Put that thing on and get out there,' Miss Masters ordered, waving at the wig in Kit's hand as she went out through the curtain.

Kit obeyed.

As if to make up for Miss Masters' generosity, if that's what it was, the patrons that day were abominable.

◆

When she got home and told Mrs French and the girls that she'd be able to go for an extended weekend, there was general excitement. She'd never missed Perry so much – planning for the event with her would be more fun than actually going. Leaving her chums from school behind had been much easier than saying goodbye to Perry. Perhaps because her life had been so exciting at that point, sailing off to England . . .

Reluctantly, Kit went upstairs and took her correspondence folder out of her trunk, sitting at the rickety rattan table and drawing up properly black ink into her fountain pen.

The tan leather folder had been a present from her father – it had the notepaper with her name on it that her mother had given her, blotting paper, a place for her sealing wax and for stamps, and a small address book.

'So you won't forget to write to us,' he'd said with a sad face.

Damn. She missed them. Even though they'd never understood or approved of her acting, they hadn't actually forbidden her. Now, having lived through society's censure, she realised how hard it must have been for them to watch her going down the road to social ruin without disowning her. She should thank them one day.

She consulted the train timetable. Carleton, it turned out, had its own station – 'Stop by request to the guard'. That was a demonstration of power, the like of which you'd never see in Australia.

The twenty-third of September was a Thursday, only eight days away.

Dear Countess,

How kind of you to invite me to Henry's birthday celebrations.

I would be delighted to come, although unfortunately I have engagements in Town, which means I will have to return on the Sunday afternoon. I hope that will not inconvenience you.

Thank you for your generous suggestion, but I'm sure I can arrange my own costume.

I shall take the 1.30 train from Town on 23rd inst. If that suits you, I should be at Carleton station at 3.12 p.m.

I am very much looking forward to meeting Henry's family.

Did that sound as though she had expectations? Yes, it did. She screwed up the paper and wrote the first part out again. Better to say nothing that would imply a relationship with Henry.

Yours sincerely,

She hesitated. The countess had addressed her as Miss Scott, but she would surely know of her acting career. How should she sign her name? Kit or Katherine, Scott or Linton? She had a brief hysterical moment of wanting to sign 'Agatha Gardiner', but pulled herself together.

Oh, damn it.

Yours sincerely,
Kit Scott

That was the best compromise she could come up with. It was odd, because that was what she'd been called all through her girlhood. Even at school, the teachers had all called her Kit, because there were three Katherines/Catherines in her class, and it made it easier. Kate, Kit and Cathy, they'd been. Kit Scott. She'd hadn't been that in a long time. It made her feel both much older and quite young.

This party . . . perhaps it was a bad idea to go. But she would get out of London for a few days. Thank God.

She had stamps. She affixed a penny-ha'penny stamp onto the envelope and hesitated. She had her own sealing wax and seal. Would it be thrusting to use it?

Yes. Better to simply seal it the normal way. She licked the flap and closed it down firmly. There. No going back now.

She crammed her hat back on her head and went out to the post box on the corner, sliding the letter through the slot with a sick squirm of her insides. Something about this felt wrong, but she couldn't tell what it was.

Just nerves about seeing Henry after their fight, probably. But if he'd got his mother to invite her, he must have forgiven her.

And she'd forgiven him. Or, at least, she would act as though she had, because that was what a lady did in these circumstances.

She walked on without thinking; ten minutes later she was on Piccadilly and realised she had headed for Ebury Street out of instinct. No. No need for that, not anymore. Instead, she would treat herself to a seat in the gods for Tallulah's play. Maybe some of Tallulah's self-confidence would rub off on her. She needed it desperately.

CHAPTER 44

The train trip down on the Thursday afternoon was quite pleasant, if hot and sticky. Once out of London, though, Kit and the other traveller in her compartment, a nice old lady in an old-fashioned dress, agreed to put down the window, and the country air flowed through, pleasant despite the odd belch of smoke and ash.

She wished it could settle her nerves, although she had no idea why she was so nervous.

A country house party wasn't all that intimidating, even if it were at an Earl's seat. Riding might happen. The men would play billiards and perhaps fish. The girls would play tennis, perhaps croquet, take walks, swim if there was a lake (somehow, she was sure there would be a lake), eat quite a lot, dance with the men after dinner.

Nothing she hadn't done at friends' houses in the past,

including at Barrows. The house might be larger, but the programme would be the same.

Thank God and her mother that she'd brought all her 'sporting' clothes to London. Tennis whites, jodhpurs, a hacking jacket and riding boots, swimming costume. Val had been frankly awestruck by the number and variety of clothes she'd packed. She'd taken it all for granted at Barrows, but now she understood how much labour and money went into such a wardrobe. How many people had worked for days to make these clothes.

'I'll be expected to change at least three times a day,' she'd explained. 'Breakfast clothes, and then something for whatever activity is planned, and then lunch clothes, and then dinner. And perhaps something else in the afternoon, depending on what's happening. But they'll probably lend me a maid, so I won't have to keep track of it all.'

'It's overwhelming,' Val breathed, holding up the Australian-style swimming costume Kit had put on the bed. 'And look at this! It's exactly like a man's! How can you *wear* it, Kit? You're normally so modest!'

'Everyone my age in Australia wears that type of costume. If you want to really swim or surf shoot, it's the only practical option. But, generally, a lady puts on a covering wrap as soon as she gets out of the water.'

Val folded it gently and put it down, shaking her head. 'I'll never learn all the rules about being a lady,' she said ruefully.

Kit put an arm around her shoulders. 'I was trained – *strictly* trained – in those rules for seventeen years straight. You can't expect to know them by instinct.'

'If you hadn't been trained . . .'

Laughing, Kit threw up her hands. 'Oh, I wouldn't have a *chance* of doing it right!'

'Will you train me?'

'You don't need training.' Val's uncertainty hurt Kit's heart. Of all the people she'd met in London, Val was the one she admired the most. 'You're a perfect lady, just as you are. Kind, poised, careful of other people's feelings . . . that's what makes a lady, not some stupid bits of etiquette!'

Val's head tilted to one side as she considered that. Her rich auburn hair hung in a smooth, shiny curtain, her blue eyes shone.

'It's no wonder that bartender at the Gentleman's Relish has his eye on you,' Kit added.

'Oh, more than his eye, honey!' Val winked broadly. 'He's talking about moving in together.'

Goodness me! She was so glad that Val was happy; although it did make her own situation feel even lonelier. Both Perry and Val happily coupled . . .

'He's a lucky man.'

Val grinned, looking at herself in the small mirror. 'You know, you're right. I am a lovely lady!'

'Like a queen!' Kit said.

Val grinned and struck a regal pose. 'Queen Mary, eat your heart out!'

It took ten minutes before they stopped laughing.

◆

On the train, Kit considered what she'd said to Val. Kind, poised, careful of other people's feelings. By that standard, if she were a lady, she would have forgiven Zeke by now, and seen him since his father's funeral. She felt bad that she hadn't – but every time she imagined calling him, rage spiralled up out of nowhere. The way he'd lied to her and used her affection and care for him to get her down into that nursing home – to use his *dying father* that way! It was really beyond the pale.

On Tuesday week, it was auditions for Charlot's new show. She should probably see Zeke before then, just to settle how they were going to work together. Or if they could. That sent a shiver through her. Being on stage without Zeke . . . auditioning without him for other shows . . . it made her feel sick to even think about it. But she had to grow up sometime.

No time like the present.

What would Lady Carleton be like? Her letter had been nice. On the other hand, she was reputedly Lady Bridlingham's best friend, which didn't bode well.

Kit was more anxious than she had thought she would be. She did so hate that feeling of not fitting in, especially when there was a good chance some of the other guests would cut her completely. And Henry . . . oh, she would have to be on good terms with Henry, if only for the sake of the other guests. His last words to her still rankled, though; perhaps because they had a possibility of truth to them.

At the small Carleton Towers station, a car was waiting for her and for one other guest.

'Sarah! Oh, I wish I'd known we were on the same train! We could have travelled together.'

Lady Sarah beamed at her, and tucked her hand through Kit's arm. 'Never mind. We'll have a comfortable coze in the car on the way up to the house. Have you been here before?'

'No.'

'It's jolly.'

The drive to the house was through one of those storybook estates one imagined while reading Jane Austen. Pemberley, perhaps.

Kit still couldn't get over how *green* everything was, even in the height of summer. Remembering the parched paddocks of home, the yellow-grey grass and dust, it was hard to believe she was even on the same planet.

There were deer in the dappled shade of old trees. A pretend little Grecian temple down by – yes, there was a lake. The gravelled road wound sinuously between small hills, revealing vista after vista; a Capability Brown landscape? Or influenced by him.

Then the house. She'd seen photographs of Chatsworth, the Duke and Duchess of Devonshire's house. This was smaller, but of much the same style. Part Baroque, part Italianate, part Palladian – mostly it just looked big and expensive, which was no doubt the intention of its builders.

The car drew up to the front door and the chauffeur ushered them out.

'Thank you,' she said vaguely. She couldn't quite shake the feeling of being in a fairytale. Not 'Cinderella' – 'The Princess and the Pea', perhaps? Which was silly, wasn't it? She hadn't felt quite this way at Barrows.

Sarah once again hooked an arm through hers and led her to the doors, which had been opened by a butler, who greeted Sarah like an uncle.

'Lady Sarah,' he said. 'The countess is in the blue drawing room.'

Which door led to the blue drawing room? There were so many leading out of this panelled hall. Thank God there was no suit of armour. That would have been too storybook for words. But there were portraits on the walls, including a fairly recent one of a bushy-eyebrowed man in a general's uniform. It was like Barrows writ large. But Barrows had made her feel at home; this place overwhelmed her.

'Do I have any smuts on my face, Nelson?' Sarah asked, putting her face up to be inspected. He smiled benignly.

'No, my lady. And Miss Scott . . . would you like to freshen up before meeting her ladyship?'

Kit suspected that meant she *did* have smuts on her face.

'No, no,' Sarah said. 'We'll just pop in first and say hello, and then we'll freshen up.'

'Very good, my lady.'

Nelson led the way to a door to the back left of the hall, opened it, and announced them.

'Lady Sarah, my lady, and Miss Scott.'

This was it. Time to face the music.

The blue drawing room was twice the size of the entire Sicilian Avenue flat, and looked out over a terrace that led to a long, perfectly mown lawn. The brilliance outside the long French doors blinded her for a moment to the room itself.

Which was blue. Blue like Gainsborough's *Blue Boy*. Very blue, and pretty, with delicate French furniture and an intricately carved mantelpiece. Huge.

Around the fireplace, a group of settees and chairs. And there, a woman, rising to greet them.

Thin, elegant, dark-haired, she moved with that perfection of poise that comes on some women as they age, a kind of assurance that no young woman can claim. The actress in Kit observed it closely, with a kind of yearning. To walk like that on stage! That would get the curtain calls.

Unfortunately, Lady Bridlingham was standing beside her, glaring at Kit.

'Sarah. How lovely.' The countess – this must surely be the countess – kissed Sarah on both cheeks, and then turned to Kit as Sarah went to greet her mother. 'You must be Miss Scott.'

◆

'Clara,' Lady Bridlingham said, with malicious satisfaction. 'I think you are under a misapprehension. This is Miss *Linton*. She is an actress.'

Kit froze. Surely her mother had explained . . . oh Lord. It would be just like her to skim over Kit's acting as though it didn't exist. If she were introduced as Kit Scott to people who knew her as Linton, everyone would be sure it was because she was leaving the stage to take up life as Henry's wife.

The countess nodded reassuringly at her and smiled at Lady Bridlingham.

'Beatrice, this is Agatha Scott's daughter. Agatha Dassington, you remember her from school. She's Joseph Dassington's niece. Linton is merely a stage name.'

Lady Bridlingham bit down on her lip so hard Kit thought blood might well. She was both mortified and angry; her complexion darkened with rage but she swallowed it, visibly.

'Agatha Dassington? Then you must be Cecil and Daphne's cousin.'

This old witch would scupper Daphne's reputation with relish. She had to be stopped.

'Countess,' Kit said. 'Most of Henry's friends know me as Kit Linton. Perhaps it would be better to keep it that way.'

The countess gave her a shrewd stare. 'For Daphne's sake? Better to get it all out in the open, my dear. You have nothing to be ashamed of, and neither do the Dassingtons. As far as I can tell, the worst you've done is dance with the Prince of Wales, and that's a fate that's happened to us all!'

The Bridlingham was frothing. 'I'm afraid I disagree, Clara. I think knowledge of the connection might hurt Daphne's chances quite considerably.' Kit suspected she would make sure of it out of pure spite.

'And I don't think my mother would like people knowing,' Kit ventured. Her mother most certainly would not.

Patting Lady Bridlingham on the arm, the countess smiled peaceably at her. 'Very well. I trust you to keep Katherine's secret, then, Beatrice. For now.'

That spiked her guns. Kit felt a spike of her own, of satisfaction. 'Beatrice' bridled as she realised she'd given up the chance to make trouble, but the countess turned away from her serenely.

'In any case, we're very glad to welcome you, for your mother's sake as well as Henry's, Miss *Linton*. Agatha was such a nice girl – so funny!'

Kit blinked at the very idea of her mother being funny.

'I'm sure she'd want me to give you her best,' she said, falling back on manners.

'Oh, no need. We've been corresponding. Henry's just come in from a shoot – he'll be down momentarily. Naughty boy. He should be here to greet you.'

Somehow there was no more talk of freshening up, although Lady Bridlingham, after nodding reluctant agreement, fixed her eyes on a spot on Kit's cheek. A smut from the train, no doubt. Kit refused to rub at it. She wouldn't give her the satisfaction.

'Nelson, tea?'

'On its way, milady.'

'Lovely.'

They sat, she and Sarah, on a settee together, and discussed, inevitably, the weather. And then, as the tea was brought in, and poured by the countess, the party.

'It will be quite the occasion,' Lady Bridlingham said with a smile at the countess. A real smile, too, not just a tilt of the lips! Perhaps they were friends.

'Oh, just a bit of fun,' the countess said. 'The young people like to dress up. You have a costume, Miss Linton?'

'Ye-es.' Now she was here, in these inescapably aristocratic environs, she was unsure about her costume choice. 'I have a man's tail-coat outfit. With a top hat.'

Lady Bridlingham sniffed disapproval. Knowledge of Kit's real parentage seemed to have solidified her disdain, rather than lessened it.

Not a flicker on the countess's face showed any concern. 'Oh, what fun! And so comfortable, I imagine.'

Kit laughed, relieved. 'Well, the trousers are a little tight.'

'Henry should drag up,' Sarah suggested. 'Then you can be a reverse couple!'

The countess did not endorse this suggestion. With the ease of the well bred, she let the idea drop into some well of silence, and went on as if Sarah hadn't spoken, discussing her plans for the party. It sounded tremendously complicated. Lady Carleton seemed to have the logistics skill of an army general.

The tea was very good. The cucumber sandwiches were as horrible as she always found cucumber sandwiches, but she ate one to be polite and then moved on to a scone with jam to get the taste out of her mouth.

Sarah was describing her deb ball to Lady Carleton, who had apologised for not being able to come.

'We were on the Continent, my dear, and Marcus had contracted the most appalling cold. I couldn't ask him to travel in that condition.'

'Oh, don't worry, Annie,' Sarah said. 'I perfectly understand.'

Annie? It was most unusual for a girl Sarah's age to call an older titled lady by her first name. And wasn't the countess's name 'Clara'? The countess saw her confusion.

'Sarah's mother and I have always been more like sisters,' she said, smiling at Lady Bridlingham, who smirked. '"Annie" was her try at saying "Aunty" when she was little.'

The door was flung open with enthusiasm and Henry came in, followed by both Squibs and Bingo, who was carrying a rifle, although they were all in flannel bags and striped jackets. Henry looked well, bursting with health, a golden boy. She *was* fond of him; and still annoyed with him.

'Lawrence, put that thing away!' the countess said. Bingo, looking shamefaced, dropped the rifle into a tall ginger jar standing near the door.

'Sorry, Countess,' he said.

Henry came over and she stood up to greet him.

Time to put on a show of friendly, polite distance. They were no more than friends, and always had been. But he kissed her cheek – right there in front of his mother!

'There you are!' He looked her over and a shade of concern came onto his face. 'Hello, what's this? You're looking tired.'

'Henry! You can't tell a gel she looks tired! It's very rude,' his mother said.

'It's the heat in London,' Kit explained. 'It drags one down so.'

'Well, now you're here,' he said happily. He seemed quite blasé about the other night. Did he even remember what had happened? 'You can rest and recuperate and not do a hand's turn for a week.'

A week? She'd only planned for a few days. She had to get back to work on Monday. And a week and a day later, she was auditioning for *Pretty Maids*. Should she say something now? But Henry had moved on, over to the tea tray, and was organising himself an enormous afternoon tea. Everything felt topsy-turvy, as though Henry's entrance had leached away her own certainty. Did that mean she *did* care for him?

Other people came in – a couple of Sarah's friends, an uncle of Henry's.

'Clara,' Lady Bridlingham said to Lady Carleton, 'do try this pound cake.'

Lady Bridlingham sat next to the countess, making sure she had tea and enough to eat. She *was* thin – perhaps she was one of those people who forget to eat, so her family cosseted her a little.

The afternoon became, well, fun. Lady Bridlingham aside, she did *like* these people. The jokes were, perhaps, a little juvenile, but after two months of being very adult and looking after herself completely, it was rather nice to lapse back into juvenile humour and have someone else organise her.

Very nice, in fact.

'How about tennis?' Squibs suggested, and they all surged off to get into their tennis gear. At the doorway, Kit stopped and looked back.

'Lady Carleton –'

The countess shooed her off as though she were an errant hen. 'Off you go, my dear. Have some fun.'

Kit smiled; she could feel it break over her face. Not a polite smile. She genuinely *liked* Lady Carleton. 'You're so kind, Countess.'

Something changed in Lady Carleton's expression. Surprise? Sorrow? She couldn't tell.

'Go on,' she said softly. 'Go join the youngsters.'

Kit went lightly up the stairs to the room Nelson directed her to and swiftly changed into her tennis clothes with the help of a young maid, Betsy. As the lowest ranked member of the party, no doubt her maid was the least experienced, but that was all right. Her clothes weren't designed with a maid in mind.

She was rather ashamed that she hadn't even bothered to learn the name of the maid who'd waited on her at Barrows. She would make sure she left a good tip for Betsy, even if it cleaned her out.

Working in a dress shop taught you the value of serving.

'Thank you, Betsy,' she said as the girl slid a tennis headband over her bob and fixed it with bobby pins. 'I will need a bath after this, I'm sure.'

'Oh yes, miss! That's the door to the bathroom. You and Lady Sarah are sharing it.'

Thank God for that. She made a quick stop in the bathroom – yes, there was a smut to wipe off – and then began to go downstairs very sedately, only to be overtaken by a posse of the others and swept down in a run.

She was by far the best tennis player of the girls, and outmatched most of the men, including Henry, despite not having played since Barrows. She'd missed it.

'These Australians!' he said, casting himself down in the shade of a tree near the courts, where a footman had laid out a table with cool drinks. 'Is there anything you can't do?'

'I can't draw.' Kit fanned herself with his hat, which he'd thrown on the grass. 'Hopeless. My watercolours look like a five-year-old's efforts.'

He let out a shout of laughter. 'Never understood why gels have to be able to draw, anyway.'

'Nor I.'

She found herself comfortable again with Henry. His unreasonable demands appeared to be a thing of the past, although he did seem to be slightly smug about having her there. Still, what a lovely afternoon and a lovely party! She sipped lemonade and looked out over the ordered and beautiful English countryside.

That feeling she'd had at Barrows came over her again; as though this could be home. Ridiculous. And yet it was hers for the taking.

The footman came back with a new tray of drinks, followed by a tall, surely familiar figure.

'Mr Gardiner, sir.'

She shot a disbelieving look at Henry, who was now *insufferably* smug. Zeke smiled at them all impartially, not even nodding at her specifically.

'Good afternoon,' he said.

Henry bounded up and shook his hand heartily. 'Zeke! Good man. Come and have a drink. I say, Johnson, sun's over the yardarm, bring us some cocktails.'

'Yes, sir.'

She wouldn't ask. She wouldn't give either of them the satisfaction of asking.

'There's lemonade,' she said instead, pouring a glass and handing it to Zeke.

'Thanks.' He took his hat off with his free hand and finally smiled at her. Despite her crossness, she wanted to smile back. The afternoon seemed to rearrange itself around him, like one of those sliding picture-puzzles. No! She wouldn't have that. She was still angry with him. Nodding politely, she went to sit on the soft grass with Sarah.

'Did you know he was coming?' Sarah whispered behind her hat.

'Not a clue. Damn Henry. He just wants to force a scene.'

'Oh no, it's not that. Look at him.'

Henry was watching Zeke with a faint frown. Why? Sarah giggled. 'He thought that Zeke would be overawed by all this grandeur,' she suggested. 'Probably expected him to eat with his knife or something.'

'But –' She could feel herself colouring. She had thought much the same about Zeke herself, after Barrows.

'This is *Carleton*,' Sarah said. 'Henry's been brought up to believe that Carleton is an anteroom to Heaven. Or at least to the Palace. I doubt he could imagine that Zeke would be at home here. He wanted to show you that Zeke isn't a gentleman.'

Now, that was unexpectedly perceptive. Sarah was regarding Henry with amused but slightly scornful affection. Like a sister. Kit felt a swift pang of relief. Thank God Sarah wasn't enamoured of Henry.

Bother Henry. She was angry that Zeke had come without telling her, and at his awful behaviour the night his father died. He had no right to try to make her decisions for her. If he was so disapproving of Henry, then he shouldn't have accepted the invitation. *That* was poor manners – to use someone you didn't like for social gain.

That was *not* the action of a gentleman.

Zeke came to sit beside them on the grass.

'Lady Sarah,' he said. Sarah flopped onto her back in exaggerated fatigue.

'Sarah, for heaven's sake. It's too hot for formality.' She smiled beguilingly up at Zeke. Really, she was a very pretty girl. But . . . No. None of her business. None at all. If Zeke took up with Sarah, that would solve everything. She should try to promote it, despite the hard core of annoyance under her breastbone.

Johnson arrived back with the cocktails, and the group gathered around, only Zeke and Kit not imbibing.

'What's the matter with you, man?' Bingo demanded.

'Someone has to keep a clear head,' Zeke said.

'Can't hold his liquor,' Squibs opined. 'Good job to avoid it, in that case.'

Zeke's mouth tightened, but he didn't rise to the bait. Suggesting he wasn't manly didn't seem to be working; Zeke's height and physique allowed him to simply smile at the aspersions. Kit was impelled to intervene.

'It's too hot for liquor,' she said. 'Hard liquor dries you out.'

That started a lively discussion about the best drinks for a hot day, which took them safely up until the dressing bell went.

'Safely'? What was she afraid of? Kit wasn't sure, but she was afraid of something. All her lovely ease had disappeared. Damn Zeke. And damn Henry for inviting him. Men! Always trying to control the situation.

◆

Maybe he shouldn't have come. But when Henry had invited him, it had seemed like the answer to a prayer. The chance to get Kit alone, to apologise, to sort it all out . . .

He should have realised, after Barrows, that they'd have no chance to talk privately. He went up to dress in a thundercloud of a mood, and washed and dressed like he was preparing for a battle.

Henry had invited him here to show Kit that he wasn't a gentleman. That was clear. Well, the lordling was in for a surprise. Noël had been tutoring him in 'how to go on' since Barrows; just here and there, a comment or a word of advice. He hadn't even had to ask. And it all added up, bit by bit. Whereas at Barrows he'd been uncertain even about which fork to use, now he was settled and comfortable with every last damn bit of silver. Because it was all solid silver here. Naturally.

He glared at himself in the mirror as he arranged his black bow tie. Black tie tonight, white tie tomorrow night, the butler had informed him. Well, he had both of those. He *looked* like a gentleman, and he knew how to act like one.

He even had more than one day suit now, and he'd brought walking shoes and a pair of flannel bags. He was ready for this dog-and-pony show.

Maybe he should look on this weekend as a chance to show Kit that he was up to snuff in the manners department. He was pretty sure he could do that.

Mostly sure.

The real trick would be to get through the weekend without punching Henry right in the mouth.

◆

Dinner was nerve-wracking. It shouldn't have been, but she was afraid Zeke was out of his depth. He would hate being shown up by Henry.

So far, so good. He had coped with them all going into the dining room in order of precedence, which had left him at the end – Kit was two steps above him, apparently, as her uncle's niece, squired in by a friend of the earl's who was the local doctor.

The earl himself, met on their return from tennis, had turned out to be a mousy man; it was hard to believe he was hail-fellow-well-met Henry's father. But on closer inspection, as they'd gathered in the yellow drawing room for sherry before dinner, she realised that the impression was mostly assumed. He was the general in the portrait in the hall; just as tall as Henry, and his eyes bright and sharp beneath brows she suspected he kept bushy as a hedge he could peer out from.

She'd quite liked him, at first. He had peered at her and assessed her blatantly. 'Well. You're the actress, eh?'

'Yes, sir.'

'Hmph. Funny job for a gel.' She'd stared down Charlot. This man, no matter what his title, was only playing at being brusque in comparison.

'I like it,' she said composedly. He barked with laughter and patted her on the shoulder.

'Stupid young thing. You'll ruin yourself.' She had stiffened with outrage, and he'd glanced at her in amusement. 'You'll learn.'

'Ruin only applies if I want to be respectable,' she said, surprised at how vicious she sounded.

He blinked and looked around. 'If you don't want to be respectable, m'dear, why are you here?'

'Unrespectable people have friends, too, Lord Carleton.'

'Not friends in my family.'

He'd moved away, leaving her fuming. The old – she couldn't think of a word bad enough.

Lady Carleton, on the other hand, had been endlessly welcoming and encouraging. She was also endlessly busy – organising, overseeing, managing the dinner service with a lift of her eyebrows and a nod to Nelson.

Bingo and Squibs, on either side of her, did their best to be entertaining, but well before dessert Kit was wishing to be back in her room – her beautiful, rose-pink room – and safely alone.

There was that word again. Safe. What was she afraid of?

Across the table from her, Zeke was managing his manners perfectly. Nothing to fear there. He must have studied up on his etiquette since Barrows. It made her sad that he'd felt the need to do so, but it was proving handy now. There was nothing Henry could use against him.

She drank a glass of riesling with the chicken, and some claret with the beef. It wasn't so much that she chose to, as that she didn't want to refuse when the footman poured it for her – and then it didn't seem polite to not drink.

Bingo and Squibs weren't that bad, really. She laughed at one of Squibs' stories, and turned to give the conversation for the next course to Bingo, as she should. They were less formal, talking across her and expecting her to reply to both of them. Lady Bridlingham, next to Zeke, was staring at them with open annoyance. Kit fell into silence, but the two boys kept talking across her, about some cricket game which was on tomorrow, house party against the village eleven.

Wonderful. Was there anything worse than cricket?

CHAPTER 45

'The breakfast room is this way, miss,' the footman waiting at the bottom of the stairs said.

'Thank you,' she murmured. She was getting better at remembering to murmur – not a skill that came easily to an actress, used to articulating so clearly the back rows could hear. She followed the footman to one of the rooms behind the Great Room. He opened the door and she went in, smiling her thanks at him. For the last day, she had been thankful for her mother's obsessive insistence on the smallest details of etiquette. The thought made her throat close up a little, as if she were in too small a room with the heat turned up.

Straw-yellow morning light blinded her as she came in, and she moved aside from the glare to see the others. But only Lady Carleton was there.

No doubt the rest of the party were nursing sore heads.

There had been more brandy drinking after the older members of the party had gone to bed. Neither she nor Zeke had imbibed.

Lady Carleton was standing by the window, surrounded by damask curtains in a cheerful yellow and white. The whole room was bright with yellow accents and light-toned furniture. Meant to jazz you up at breakfast, no matter what the weather was like.

Going over to the window, Kit joined Lady Carleton in staring out at the perfect day. No rain today: this was what an English summer was supposed to be, although it was more like a nice early spring day in Australia.

Out on the lawn, servants were setting up a croquet course for later.

'Ah,' Lady Carleton said, turning to greet her. 'I'm so glad you've come down. I wanted to have a private chat, Kit, just the two of us.' She nodded to the footman who stood near the sideboard, and he left the room.

'Of course,' Kit said. Meaningless statement, but what else could she say? Nerves suddenly hit her, like on a first night. This wasn't just Lady Carleton – it was Henry's mother, and she'd bet it was as Henry's mother that Lady Carleton wanted to talk. This wasn't going to go well.

For a moment, Lady Carleton stood, one hand on the damask curtains, looking out over the spectacular view: terrace and lawn sloping to the lake, the stands of oak beyond, dark green studded with the lighter green of beech and chestnut. Beautiful. Eternally English. A small twist of something moved in her heart. A part of her would so have loved to become a part of that long history.

'When Henry told me about you, frankly, I was appalled.' Lady Carleton turned now, and looked at her with eyes full of knowing amusement. 'You can imagine what I expected: a thrusting colonial with no manners, all rouge and rhinestones.'

Kit smiled warily, unsurprised.

'Even when I realised you were Agatha Dassington's daughter, I thought . . .' she made a small, expressive movement with her hands, '. . . a gel who chose to go on the stage . . . hardly a *lady*.'

Kit shrugged. What could she say that wouldn't sound self-aggrandising – or, worse, like an excuse, as though she were ashamed of her job?

'Well, my dear, you were a very nice surprise.' She made an expressive gesture with both hands. 'Compared to Henry's last girl!' She shrugged eloquently. 'So I just wanted to tell you that you'd be welcome in the family. In case you were concerned. Now, I must get on. Ring for fresh tea if you need it.'

She sailed out of the room before Kit could gather her thoughts. Numbly, she took a plate and gathered some breakfast from the sideboard, and rang for tea.

As she drank it, something slowly sank in. Acceptance. Lady Carleton had accepted her completely. Her mother would be delighted. Honestly, so was she. Lady Carleton's good opinion was worth having. It eased a tightness in her that had been there since the charity ball. Perhaps it was shallow of her to care. Or perhaps she was more her mother's daughter than she'd realised.

She finished her tea and got up to leave just as the door opened and Lady Bridlingham came in, stopping short just inside the room, clearly displeased to find Kit there. Kit was armoured against her now.

'Lady Bridlingham. Good morning.'

The woman glared at her with real hate.

'So you're still here? You have a great deal of gall.'

Oh, she'd had enough of this!

'Why do you dislike me so much, Lady Bridlingham? I've done nothing to you.'

That face twisted with scorn and anger. 'You're a bad example!'

Kit was filled with a fierce satisfaction. 'Good! I hope I *am* a bad example! I hope Sarah and Penelope and all the rest look at me and think, "Perhaps *I* could do more than my parents expect of me!" And the boys, too. I hope they look at their lives and see how shallow they are, how meaningless!'

'As though *acting* is meaningful! Degrading, more like it.' The older woman's fists clenched at her side as though she wanted to strike out.

'You hate me because you're afraid of me,' Kit said more slowly, thinking it through. 'Because I *am* an example. I prove that there's a way out. To equality.'

'Hah!' Lady Bridlingham smiled with real pleasure. 'But you haven't taken it, have you? Oh, you're playing around with this acting nonsense, but I don't see you marrying that Gardiner boy you consort with. Breeding matters, even to you. You just can't lower yourself to his level, even though you want to. No. Something in you revolts against it. Early training holds true.'

Shame flushed through her. The old biddy was right. And wrong. 'Just because I'm bad at living up to my ideals doesn't mean the ideals are worthless.' She walked towards the door, pausing at Lady Bridlingham's side, trying hard to keep her voice steady. 'Remember, it only takes one generation to reject all this class nonsense, and the whole house of cards collapses.'

Lady Bridlingham's face went white. Good. Kit left her behind without another word.

Walking up the stairs, her legs trembled. To have her own weakness ruthlessly revealed like that . . . she was disgusted with herself. With the pleasure she'd felt when Lady Carleton had accepted her. That was just the other side of the coin.

Privilege was wrong, and based on nothing more than centuries of the oppression of others. Intellectually, she knew it. But without it, there would be no Carleton Towers . . . and oh! there was so much to love about this place. She couldn't help that sense of *belonging*, the way she'd belonged at Barrows.

Or perhaps she just wanted to belong, because of 'early training'. She hated the idea that Lady Bridlingham might be right; but what if she was?

◆

The house eleven – including Zeke, uncomfortable in borrowed whites – lined up in the shade of an oak tree while the local eleven took the field. They had come to a nearby village, called, inevitably, Lower Carleton, and gone up against a rugged crew of young farmhands and older men who eyed them up and down and smiled sourly.

Nothing brought home the reality of war like the absence of men in their twenties and thirties. Whole classes from this village school had been wiped out. Zeke had seen the names on the memorial as they drove to the cricket ground – an almost picture-postcard pitch, surrounded by trees and, honestly, a babbling brook as one boundary. They'd won the toss and Bingo, who was captain, had chosen to bat first.

'I didn't think Yanks played cricket,' Bingo said, assessing where he should go in the line-up.

Zeke let the 'Yank' go past. 'I'm from *British* Columbia. Where the British go, there goes cricket.'

The team laughed.

'Civilising the natives one bat and ball at a time,' Squibs quipped.

'Still, you can go in the tail,' Bingo said, all business. Zeke nodded. It would suit him if he never got to the pitch. He hated cricket. Tiresomely slow.

Bingo and Squibs went out to bat.

'They played for Eton,' Henry said. 'Love the blasted game. I can take it or leave it myself.'

Henry had been friendly today, as though cricket overruled any rivalry between them. It was odd, given his own suspicions about why he'd been invited to Carleton – Henry had wanted him to look bad. No time like the present to confirm that.

'So why *did* you invite me?'

Henry scuffed his heel into the dirt, obliterating a clump of grass.

'I wanted a fair fight.' He shrugged. 'I wanted her to choose between us, fair and square.'

Zeke laughed, tossing a bat up and catching it again. 'A fair fight on home ground, is that it? Where she could see how I was so under-bred and not worthy of her?'

His mouth twisting in a self-deprecating smile, Henry shrugged again. 'It was worth a try.'

'Has it worked?' Zeke tried to keep his face unconcerned, but his stomach twisted in a tight knot.

'I haven't put it to the touch yet,' Henry confessed. 'Whatever she says here, that's it. Done and dusted.'

Done and dusted. As they were, after only a couple of hours. Bingo and Squibs were all the talent the house side had. They made forty and twenty-five respectively. The others had drunk too deep the night before, and were run out in quick succession, so that Zeke stood at the crease for only a matter of minutes, watching someone called Nubs flail unsuccessfully at the ball. At least in baseball you only got three chances to make a fool of yourself.

'Out!' the umpire ruled. Zeke sighed and trudged back to the shade of the oak tree without even facing a ball. A cup of tea was definitely in order before they took the field.

He managed to snatch a moment with Kit, drinking tea under an elm, before Sarah and the other girls collected her and moved off, laughing light-heartedly like nymphs and sprites.

She sent him back an apologetic glance, but soon enough she was caught up in the conversation.

A fair fight . . . maybe it was a fair fight, after all. If she rejected Henry and all he stood for here, on Henry's ground, it was a sure thing that she meant it.

But the nerve of the fellow, serving him up to Kit as a comparison! Anger rose in him, the dreaded thought-annihilating anger which had pushed him to fight his father when he was fourteen. The last time he'd felt angry like this he'd dragged Kit to his father's bedside, and what a disaster that had been.

He beat it down, by sheer will. This was not the place for rage. He was not his father. He refused to be.

◆

Zeke watched Kit as unobtrusively as possible at dinner.

She moved through this extraordinary house – mansion – as though she belonged here. He'd always admired her grace, her poise. At Barrows, he'd seen where it came from, but here that sense was magnified. He knew what to do, how to act, which fork to use, because he'd studied it. She'd absorbed it from her cradle. Like the way she treated the servants. Never haughty, nor unfriendly, but not – not *friendly*. Just matter-of-fact.

And they treated her in exactly the same way they treated Lady Sarah. He remembered Mrs Treece saying, 'The servants can always tell a real lady.'

He didn't want to consider what they thought of him.

There was a lot on Henry's side of the scales.

He didn't think she was at all influenced by the money on display at Carleton Towers. Not for a minute. Not Kit. But the, the *milieu* . . . the sense that this, perhaps, was where she belonged. He didn't know how to fight that.

When the ladies withdrew after dinner, he braced himself for unpleasantness, and he wasn't disappointed. The earl started in on him as soon as the door closed behind the women.

'So, you and that lightskirt are having it off, are you?'

He was an older man, and Zeke's host, so he couldn't punch him. Shouldn't.

'I beg your pardon?' he said in his iciest posh tones.

'Don't try that on with me,' Lord Carleton said. 'I've seen the way you look at her.'

Zeke merely turned his head and looked straight at Henry, who bit his lip but said nothing, taking a swig of brandy instead. *Coward.* Zeke turned back to the earl.

'If you're referring to Miss Linton, Lord Carleton, everyone who sees her must look at her in admiration. But I can assure you that any calumny against her is undeserved and quite false.'

There. Let him put that in his pipe and smoke it.

'Are you calling me a liar?'

Zeke smiled, slowly, and said nothing. This wasn't the kind of thing that spurred him to anger. He could look after himself. Around the table, the younger men were leaning forward, as though wanting to intervene but not sure how. Henry took another drink. The doctor leaned back and laughed.

'Lay off him, Marcus. He's not going to bite.'

The earl sneered and then glared at Henry, who sat back and passed the brandy.

'Port,' his father ordered. A footman brought it forwards, and it was sent round.

Zeke refused. 'My drink not good enough for you?' the earl barked.

'I don't drink liquor,' Zeke said calmly. This was nothing new. He'd been challenged on this by far tougher men than Lord Carleton.

'Pansy, eh?'

Zeke laughed. 'You don't know many of those, do you? The ones I know drink like fish.'

'What are you doing here, eh?'

'You'd have to ask your son that, sir. He invited me.'

Henry paled as his father fixed an arrogant gaze on him.

'Hmph. Time to join the ladies.' They rose together, but the earl held back and stared up at Zeke. 'I don't like you, sir.'

'I don't like you, either.'

The older man blinked, astonished. 'Good Lord, do you always talk to your host like that?'

Damn him. He wanted Zeke to squirm on his hook. That wasn't going to happen. He'd never learned to bow down to fathers. 'Do you always talk to your guests like that?'

'Give as good as you get, is that it? Not appropriate for a younger man. You should show some respect. In the old days –'

Zeke thought of that portrait of the earl in the hall – decked out in general's uniform but almost certainly never facing battle. They didn't send earls in to face the enemy.

'In the old days, men like you sent hundreds of thousands of young men to get killed for no good reason.'

'For King and Country!'

'For your glory. For profit. Nothing there worth respecting. Times are changing, Lord Carleton. Men have to earn respect these days.'

Appalled, Henry almost wrenched him away and out into the hall. An ominous silence lay behind them. He'd feel better about it if the old man had sworn at him.

'I say, you can't talk to Pater like that! I mean, really, you can't.'

'No,' Zeke said. '*You* can't. Do you want me to leave?'

Henry hesitated.

'Fine. I'll go. But I want to say goodbye to Kit first.'

'No.' Henry firmed, shook his head. 'No, don't go. The old man shouldn't have spoken to you like that, goddammit. You're a guest in his house!'

'All right. But if you change your mind, just let me know.'

They paused outside the drawing room door. The women's voices, inside, were raised in amusement. Kit's laugh rang out. Henry's face, damn him, softened into genuine affection.

'M'father's afraid I'll marry her and bring the family into disrepute. He's taking it out on you.'

'*She*'s not the one who'll bring it into disrepute.'

Henry grimaced and shrugged, then walked towards the half-closed door with the absolute confidence that the footman would spring forward to open it for him. Which was exactly what happened.

No wonder the boy didn't know how to stand up for himself.

CHAPTER 46

After only a brief gathering, they all dispersed to get into their costumes.

Kit wasn't sure, anymore, if hers was suitable. Sarah was coming as Marie Antoinette, in a gown 'dug up from grandmama's attic'. Moving down the staircase, Kit was ridiculously relieved to find that the footmen were in livery – their normal dress of tails and white tie was so similar to her costume that she'd been anxious about someone mistaking her for a servant.

Which was silly, given her lack of height and rather obvious curves. It just showed how nervous she was.

They were to assemble in the blue drawing room, all other rooms in the house having been taken over for card rooms, smoking rooms, supper rooms, and so forth.

She'd hardly had a moment with Zeke all day. She'd gotten over her miff at him coming at all; that had been Henry's doing. Her anger at his behaviour over his father, though . . .

On impulse, she'd told Sarah about it, and Sarah had said, 'Oh, men don't like to say that they need anything,' quite carelessly, as if it were something everyone knew. 'He probably really wanted to go, and you gave him the excuse.'

That rang uncomfortably true. Yes. She could see Zeke secretly wanting to go to his father's deathbed, but not acknowledging it, even to himself. Which didn't excuse his conduct, but did somewhat remove her complete puzzlement over it. It had been curiously unlike him, to force her into a confrontation like that.

So she was prepared, if he was properly repentant, to forgive him. But she hadn't had the opportunity to tell him so.

Zeke strode in, dressed as a matador. The costume suited him, showing off his dancer's legs and his broad shoulders. The red cape swirled.

As he saw her, he stopped. Admiration and affection spread across his face. He laughed, his head going back with genuine amusement. 'I think I know where you got that idea!'

She couldn't help but smile at him, remembering that riotous night at the Gentleman's Relish. 'It's one of Fred's.' Twisting around, she showed him her back. 'Is it too tight? Honestly?'

'You look wonderful.'

The moment was interrupted as Sarah and the other girls came in, laughing as they tried to get Sarah's enormous skirt through the doorway. She waved her handkerchief and pronounced, 'Let zem eat cake!' with a strong French accent.

The young men came next – there were, inevitably, a couple of Pierrots, a Nelson, a Napoleon, a Caesar, a clown. Henry was a cowboy, complete with ten-gallon hat and sidearms.

'I hope those are cap guns,' Zeke said to her. Oh, Lord, so did she! She could just imagine what the boys would get up to with real six-shooters.

Squibs and Sarah had apparently coordinated – he was in a Louis XVI costume, which made him oddly authoritative. Perhaps a romance was blooming there?

'Come on, you blighters,' Henry said, brandishing a pistol, 'to the ballroom!'

'Not you.' His mother took his arm and led him to the Hall, to join the receiving line. He cast an imploring look at Kit, but she just laughed. It was his birthday, after all.

Lord and Lady Carleton were dressed as Cleopatra and Mark Antony. While she was stunning, he looked rather ridiculous. But Lady Carleton gazed at him with affection. How odd love was! Impossible to understand from the outside.

Kit went to the ballroom arm in arm with a couple of the other girls. She wasn't exactly avoiding Zeke, but it was nice to be in the group, and she didn't feel quite up to dealing with the intensity of his gaze right now.

The Carletons had done nothing by halves. A ballroom full of flowers, a good modern band on the dais playing soft preparatory music, the parquetry floor gleaming under the lights . . . the room began to fill up, the costumes vivid and colourful. Ostrich feathers, sequins, velvets and silks glistened and sparkled as the guests moved under the chandeliers.

The sober-hued footmen, in dark green livery, moved among them with trays of champagne, weaving a practical note into the finery.

'Shall we dance?' Zeke asked her.

'Oh, no,' she said, startled. 'We can't until Henry gets here. It's his ball. He has to lead off.'

'Do they really stick to all that still? It's like something from Victoria's time.'

'Yes. They still do.' She wanted to defend the Carletons, but she didn't. Zeke was right, and yet . . . there was still a place for formality and etiquette in the world, wasn't there? To make things run smoothly, the way they should.

'All these rules,' he said, leaning comfortably against the wall and watching the crowd with shrewd eyes. 'They're just to make sure you can exclude people who aren't your class. That's all etiquette is.'

There was truth to that. But surely there was more to it?

'No place for grace and politeness? Etiquette is a good way of stopping people fighting, too. Of smoothing over differences. You and Henry have got along fine so far, haven't you?'

Laughing, Zeke took her hand and swung it gently. It was a move so familiar to her, from the second act of *Dance Crazy*, she wondered if he even realised he was doing it.

'So far. Ah, there he is.'

Since it was Henry's ball, he had to lead off. But the other side of etiquette was having to stick to the rules; he had to dance with the highest-ranked young woman there, who was some European princess. From Serbia? Somewhere like that. She was pudding-faced but very vivacious, keeping Henry in laughter as they made their first circuit of the room.

'Now,' Kit said. She and Zeke were about to take the floor when Lady Carleton intercepted them.

'Ah! I've been looking forward to a waltz with a real dancer, Mr Gardiner.'

He bowed, very correctly. 'I'm the most fortunate of men.'
Kit bit back a smile as they moved onto the dance floor. She
strongly suspected that Zeke was playing a role – that of the
charming upper-class man about town. He was doing it well.
But it was rather odd of the countess to have danced with him
instead of some lord.

Bingo grabbed her hand. 'C'mon, Kit, before that Gladys
girl gets to me!'

It was three dances before Zeke found her again. She moved
into his arms with relief. Bingo and his friends, despite all
having had lessons since they were almost in the cradle, were
terrible dancers.

But they'd hardly taken a few gliding steps before Henry
tapped Zeke on the shoulder.

'May I?'

Kit made a mock-annoyed face, for Zeke's benefit. 'It's his
birthday. He's allowed.'

Zeke said nothing, but his expression was stony.

Henry grinned at her, tipping his cowboy hat back on his
head. 'I'm quite enjoying myself!' After dancing with Zeke, she
was freshly aware of how she had to adjust her steps to Henry's.

They made a circuit of the room with Henry uncharacteristi-
cally silent. Kit simply enjoyed the music and lights and the
freedom of dancing in flat shoes. It was both harder and easier;
harder to get the dip and flow, but with no fear of overbalancing
or turning an ankle. She could get used to it.

'Have you had a nice time, Kit?'

Oh, she hated that sinking feeling. His voice had that *tone*
men took on when they wanted to be serious with a woman.

'Very nice, thank you,' she said primly. She looked at his middle shirt stud. No eye contact. Not now.

'You know what I mean.'

'Yes, I do, and I'd rather not discuss it now.'

'Well, that's an answer in itself, isn't it? I'd hoped we could announce our engagement tonight.'

Despite herself, she looked up. Part of her was still surprised that he was serious about marriage. 'Henry, no . . . I wouldn't have accepted an engagement so soon even if I, if I . . .'

'If you loved me.' His voice was almost a whisper, and his eyes were full of genuine pain.

And yet they kept dancing, because that was what one did.

She said nothing; whatever she said would be wrong.

'It's Gardiner, I suppose, is it?'

'No,' she said. 'It's no one.' She'd thought he'd be pleased at that, but he scowled.

'So it's better to be alone than with me?' Oh, Lord. Now his pride was hurt, as well as his feelings.

'Zeke . . . perhaps . . .' she murmured. Oddly, he relaxed.

'Gardiner's all right,' he said. 'But you'll get tired of slumming sooner or later, and then I'll be here.'

Oh, the arrogance of it! But she still kept dancing, because that was what one did. And probably half a dozen older women here tonight had gone to school with her mother, and would send a full account of her actions, so walking away from Henry in the middle of the dance was not a good idea.

Besides, it was a lovely party. She didn't want to spoil it for anyone.

It was odd, really. Although she'd never been properly in love with Henry, she had rather fallen in love with Carleton

Towers, as she had with Barrows. She understood why Lady
Carleton devoted her life to it. And she had fallen into the
rhythms of this kind of life without a blink, as though her
own landed ancestors were guiding her. There was something
magnificent about it; the links to the past, the long line of
ancestors, the beautiful spacious rooms and the perfectly
groomed, well-mannered people. There was a large part of
her that cherished it, as she cherished the Anglican service
and the sound of choristers sending their voices up to Heaven.

She disagreed with Zeke; etiquette *mattered*. It created
this place and its beauty. She was on its side. But that beauty
wasn't maintained by people like Henry. It was maintained by
the Betsys of this world, who never got to enjoy it.

Was it wrong of her to feel sad that she'd never look at a
place like this the same way again? That, now she'd *been* one
of the serving class, she'd always be too conscious of the hard
work that went into making it seem effortless? Perhaps she
was just growing up.

◆

In the early hours of the morning, as the older guests left,
the younger people slid onto the terrace, to dance across the
stone flags in the cool night air, the music floating out from
the long doors.

The champagne was flowing. She deserved a glass or two.
What a night! And there was Zeke, listening too attentively to
a girl dressed as a gypsy. Kit slid up next to them and leaned
on the terrace balustrade in a parody of a male stance.

'Hello, my sweet,' she said to the girl, twirling an imaginary
moustache.

The girl, whom she'd never seen before, grinned. 'Why hello there! Come on, we're going down to the lake.' She grabbed both Kit and Zeke's hands and towed them along, following Henry who was waving his pistols over his head, and chanting, 'Swim! Swim!' The others took up the chant.

'Swim! Swim!'

Henry had a bottle in his hands. Not champagne – some kind of spirits. Too late, Kit realised that almost all the group had similar bottles. Where had they got them from? Instead of walking, they were stumbling along, weaving from side to side.

They were drunk. She had been enjoying the dancing too much to notice how much Henry had put away.

'Zeke –' she said. The girl swung them around roughly, so that they were sent spinning in opposite directions. Thank God she had flat shoes on! She still landed on her rump in the grass next to the lake, but she hadn't twisted an ankle. A week out from the audition, she couldn't afford that.

Zeke pulled her to her feet. 'Let's get out of here,' he said.

'Yes.'

'No!' Henry shouted. 'No one leaves, espesshly *you*, Katherine!' He put his pistol up and aimed it at Zeke.

Around them, the others whooped with approval.

'Shoot! Shoot!'

Henry gestured with the pistol. 'Into the water with him!' he shouted. The crowd yelled and surged forward, seizing Zeke by the arms and torso.

'No, Henry! Stop it!'

'One, two, THREE,' they chanted, and they all swung Zeke out, into the air and over the lake.

She caught a glimpse of his face; bored and annoyed. With a small gasp of relief, she went down to the shoreline to help him back up out of the water. His matador's cap was gone, somewhere under the surface.

'No!' Henry said, and this time there was something nasty in the way he levelled the handgun. 'Let him stay in.'

'Don't be ridiculous,' she snapped.

'Let. Him. Stay. In.' Around them, the group was cheering and yelling encouragement. Even Sarah, who was flushed and leaning against Squibs.

'Henry –'

'Do what I tell you.' Henry had lost his hat. In the moonlight, his blond hair shone like silver, and his eyes were in shadow. Zeke stood up slowly, his hands out by his sides, up to his knees in lake water and reeds.

She put out a hand to help him out of the reeds, and Henry fired. The report was so loud she froze in shock. A murmur went up from the crowd. Had that been a cap gun or a real round? She couldn't tell.

'Steady on, Hal, he's unarmed,' Bingo protested.

'Oh. Right.' Nodding as though recalled to some rule he had forgotten, Henry handed Squibs the pistol and squared up to Zeke, fists clenched in the approved position. Now the gun was gone, her anger began to rise, pushing out that icy fear the shot had plunged her into.

'Sober up, pal,' Zeke said, shaking water off his legs. He didn't even bother to look at Henry.

'You don't deserve her!' Henry said through his teeth. Oh, how she hated men and all their posturing! Their constant *pushing* at her – they were all the same, all trying to put a cage around her and keep her *safe*. Keep her obediently safe.

Zeke looked up at that; first at her, and then at Henry. 'Kit is not a boxing trophy. She can decide for herself what she deserves. And who.'

The cage opened up and she could breathe clean, fresh air. Her whole body calmed immediately.

She moved a pace towards him and Zeke came closer. Henry stepped into their path and slapped Zeke across the face.

'You're a coward, sir!'

The crowd stirred. 'Now we're for it!' Bingo said. He rubbed his hands together and motioned the others back, leaving a clear space for Zeke and Henry to fight in. Zeke wouldn't be stupid enough to, would he? But honour . . .

Zeke took off his cape. The excitement in the group built, but then Zeke wrung it out and flicked it back over his shoulder, one finger hooked into it. Only she was close enough to see that his hands were shaking. He wanted to hit Henry; she could tell. More than hit him. His free hand was a fist.

'This isn't a Victorian melodrama.' With a long-suffering look, Zeke made shooing motions with his cape, as though Henry was a hen who had to be guided back to the flock.

'I say!' Squibs said. 'You can't *not* fight him.' The group murmured agreement.

'It's not done!' a girl said, and various others repeated it.

'What makes you think I care about what's done and what's not done?' Zeke *seemed* amused. He straightened, and let his hand loosen from the fist it had made.

He stood there, that hand casually at his side, balanced easily, ready for anything but not ready to start something.

His dark hair was curling from the lake water, and his shirt clung to his back. He was so . . . so himself.

'*Kit* cares,' Sarah said. He flinched at that, the first sign he'd shown of any stress. Slowly, he turned to look at her, his shoulders tight.

'Do you?' They all leaned forwards for her reply, the whole group silent, poised, waiting. Eager for her to set the violence loose. Henry took a step back, as though giving her room to display her loyalty. Not to him. To them.

There they were, the cream of British society, the *ton*, the elite. As hungry for a fistfight as any East End rabble. Relying on a kind of etiquette; on what was *done* and *not done*. Relying on the carefree days, the good service, the delicious food and drink, all the things that came with *belonging*.

'No,' she said, to Zeke, not to them. 'No. I don't give a damn.'

She took his hand and flicked a scornful glance over the lot of them. She wanted to spit in their faces. Maybe it showed, because Sarah took a step back, her brow furrowed with puzzlement.

As they moved off, she took the gun from Squibs' loose hold, and threw it in the lake.

'Kit!' Henry whined. 'That was rented! I have to give it back!' A cap gun, then. Thank God for that. At least Henry hadn't been genuinely murderous.

'Go in and get it, then,' she said, and the group immediately started to chant, 'In! In!'

Kit and Zeke walked up to the house together, slowly enough that it was clear they weren't running away.

'Oh, leave them be!' Sarah said. 'Let's *all* go swimming!'

A shout of approval went up and, as they crossed the terrace, they heard a loud series of splashes as the group jumped in.

'Keep an eye on them,' Zeke said to the footman standing by the door, still holding a tray of drinks. 'Some of those costumes will drag them down, and they're a bit far gone to save each other.'

'Very good, sir,' the footman replied, wooden-faced.

The ballroom was empty; even the staff had gone, leaving behind nothing but flowers and the scent of liquor.

'You'd better go and change,' Kit said. 'You don't want to catch cold before our audition.' He tightened his grip on her hand.

'I'm going to get changed, pack my bag, and then walk down to the pub. If I can't find someone to let me in, I'll go to the station and wait there.'

Out on the hills beyond the terrace, the sky was lightening in that odd English way. So early, well before any reasonable person would get up. The air was scented with roses and lilacs, and that deep earth smell, which was so evocative of England. She paused and looked back through the French doors. The pre-dawn light made it all seem unreal, like a stage set with blues on it.

Another footman was outside the ballroom door, in the corridor that led to the Hall.

'Has the countess retired?' she asked him.

'Yes, miss. Some time ago.'

She freed her hand from Zeke's so she could tuck her arm into his as they went up the stairs. 'I'll say goodbye for us both to the countess in the morning and meet you at the station,' she said. 'It might not be the first train.'

'Do you have to?'

'Yes,' she said firmly. She wished she could pack up and leave with him, but, she smiled wryly to herself, some things were not *done*. And leaving without saying goodbye to one's hostess, who had been nothing but polite to her, was one of them. It was a rule she didn't want to break.

She let go of Zeke's arm with reluctance, and he disappeared into his room.

In her own room, the poor little maid had fallen asleep in a chair. Kit left her there. There was the other side of all that comfort and pleasure – a kiddie staying up to unlace some witless fool of a woman, like her. Too easy to be seduced into thinking it was all perfectly normal; but it was profoundly abnormal, for some people to be catered to by others, for some people to be at permanent leisure while others toiled for them.

She might as well have a bath – the countess wouldn't be up for a while yet.

A long bath, a change of clothes, and she was ready to pack. She filled her trunk swiftly, put a few things she would need that day into a large handbag, and laid a big tip for Betsy on the bed. She had to push the trunk closed with a snap, and the maid woke up.

'Oh miss!' she said, flustered, straightening her cap. 'I'm ever so sorry!'

'Never mind, Betsy. I'll be leaving today. You can go to bed. I won't be needing you.'

'Oh, thank you, miss. But I'm sorry to hear you're going.' Oddly, she did seem sorry. Without Kit to look after, perhaps Betsy would have to go back down in the pecking order. Back to a simple housemaid, perhaps.

It was still early, but the countess was an early riser, and Kit suspected today would be no different.

That sense of being suspended, clarified, which so often accompanied a sleepless night, came over her as she came down the stairs. The house was quiet. Too early even for servants.

The breakfast room had none of the dazzle of the day before; not only was the sun not fully up, but the horizon was rimmed with clouds. She stood at the window and watched as the clouds were outlined in rose and red and orange; as the grey was washed over with pink, and the pale sky above deepened into blue.

She couldn't remember when she had last felt this free. Had she ever? Perhaps when she was a child, rolling down that hill near their house. She let her thoughts drift. She'd decided all the important things. Now all she had to do was be polite.

A footman brought her tea and toast, and was followed by other staff who began to stock the sideboard with all the appurtenances of breakfast: bacon, scrambled eggs, kippers, kedgeree. The smell made her slightly sick. But the tea was grand.

'All well, Nelson?' The countess came in and cast a swift eye over the sideboard before she saw Kit.

'My dear! You're up early.' She smiled, a lovely, welcoming smile.

'I'm afraid I'm up because I'll be leaving. Zeke Gardiner has already gone. He would want me to give you his apologies. There was an . . . altercation.'

The happiness drained out of the countess's face. Kit felt like a murderer. To have guests leave so precipitously because of Henry's bad behaviour must be like a knife to this woman's heart.

'I don't think Henry will want me to stay,' she added.

'I think you were his last hope,' his mother said. Her voice was quiet and full of despair.

'Send him to Australia,' Kit said. 'Or Canada. Give him some real work to do. It's idleness that's destroying him.'

Lady Carleton smiled with dark wryness. 'My dear, our kind don't work.'

'Then may I speak frankly?'

'Yes.' A lifted chin. Ready for anything.

'Keep him away from the Prince of Wales' set.'

Lady Carleton blinked and stepped back a half pace. 'That bad?'

That last night in York House. Adultery, drinking, drugs, the willingness to accept someone so much younger into their set . . .

'They are not people of good character,' Kit said. She stepped forward and looked the other woman in the eyes. 'A bad influence. If you want him to control himself, give him something to do and get him out of London.'

Lady Carleton's mouth trembled, and she sighed. 'I hope I can.'

'I can't help him.'

'No. No, I understand that.' She looked up, straight into Kit's eyes. 'You're the only one who *sees* what's happening to him. At least I can talk to you about it.'

'You can always talk to me, Lady Carleton. I will always listen,' she said gently.

Lady Carleton stood straighter. Compassion wasn't the answer. It could only be met by dignity.

'Now, let's not be overdramatic. Do you need a maid to help you pack?'

'I've already packed.' Kit went to the door and turned. 'I'll speak to Henry before I go. Perhaps someone could drive me to the station?'

The simple question seemed to shake Lady Carleton back into her role as lady of the manor.

'Certainly,' she said, quite civilly, voice even. 'I'll tell Benjamin to bring the car around. There's a train at seven-thirty. An all-stops, I'm afraid, but . . .'

'That will do fine.' Kit hesitated. 'Lady Carleton, thank you for your hospitality.'

That little tremble of the lips again. 'My dear, you're welcome. I wish you could have stayed longer.'

'I wish so, too.'

They stared at each other for a moment in perfect understanding, and then Kit went out, her heart beating fast and her feet not quite seeming to come into contact with the floor, as though her surroundings were only a dream.

Or a nightmare. Here was Lady Bridlingham, up early once again. She stared at Kit with an odd expression. How much had she heard of what had happened last night? Damn her.

'Well, Lady Bridlingham, I'm leaving. And I won't be back. You can be happy now.'

'Leaving?'

Kit smiled, letting a little spite show through. 'It turns out that early training didn't hold true enough. I'm leaving with Mr Gardiner.'

That stunned her. The woman couldn't believe that Kit would give up Henry for a commoner. She just stood there, staring.

Hah! Kit thought, and turned her back before Lady Bridlingham could speak again.

The ubiquitous footman, from earlier in the night, was standing near the front door, looking very tired.

'Is Lord Henry up, do you know?'

'Not yet, I don't think, miss.' The footman was carefully not looking at her. The servants knew everything, Henry always said. No wonder. Well, this fellow would have a lot to talk about in the servants' hall today.

'Thank you,' she said, and went up the stairs.

Henry's room was three down from hers. She knocked firmly on the door and entered at his 'Come in!'

He was sitting in an armchair, still in his cowboy costume, sipping coffee.

'Hello, old girl!'

He looked shocking, and he seemed to have completely forgotten what had happened by the lake. He looked at her as though he were happy to see her, his eyes unfocused and his hand unsteady. Whatever he'd drunk at the ball, he'd added to it after she'd left.

'Henry.' She went across the big room to the foot of the bed, and held on to one of the bedposts. Henry slept in a four-poster, hung with beautiful tapestries. Naturally. 'I've packed my things.'

He threw the coffee cup against the wall.

'Fuck off, then. You're an ungrateful jade and I'm better off without you.'

All the emotions she'd pushed down in her conversation with Lady Carleton surged up.

'Ungrateful? For being courted by a drunkard? For being paraded around in front of your family like a performing monkey? You think too highly of yourself, mate. In the end, you're just a younger son who can't do anything or make anything of himself, who's drinking himself to death from sheer boredom!'

A gasp of breath. Maybe no one had ever spoken to him like that in his entire life. He stared at her, struck dumb. But she wouldn't be tricked into gentleness. That wasn't what he needed, and she cared enough about him to try her best.

'If you don't pull yourself up, you'll kill yourself. Maybe in that car of yours. Maybe your liver'll give out. Maybe you'll just fall over in the street and hit your head. But you're heading for the graveyard. Give it up. Give them up. Strike out on your own and do something worth doing.'

His lip curled. 'When I want a lecture, I'll take it from a peer, not from some jumped-up colonial who can't appreciate when she's being raised above her station. Not from some little whore of an actress.'

Well, she'd tried.

'Goodbye, Henry.'

She walked away, and the saucer of the coffee cup sped past her head and cracked against the doorjamb.

'Good fucking riddance!' he yelled.

Yes, she thought, closing the door behind her. *Good fucking riddance*.

◆

Zeke walked down the long road to the station with something very like pleasure. No sleep gave him that clear, uplifted feeling; and Kit would be along soon. They'd go home together.

It wasn't only that.

Ever since he was fourteen, he'd believed he was like his father. Rough, rage-filled, capable of beating a man to death. Untrustworthy as a husband; as a father. It was why he'd never *really* tried his hardest with Kit, he finally realised. Part of him had been afraid she'd say 'yes', and then what would be revealed about himself?

But if he could refrain from beating the dickens out of Lord Henry Bloody Carleton last night, despite the provocation . . . now he came to think about it, that rage only filled him when he wanted to protect someone else. His mother. Kit.

He could live with that.

Whistling, he strode off into the English dawn, gravel crunching under his perfectly heeled shoes.

CHAPTER 47

There he was. Sitting in the station waiting room, his long legs stretched out before him, leaning back against the wall, his hat tipped over his face. Kit stopped in the open doorway, just looking. The first time she'd seen him, she'd thought he was dishy. And he *was*. Enough to make her tremble, now she was looking at him without any barriers between them. Kind, poised, and careful of others . . . a gentleman.

She moved into the room; hearing her, he sat up and took off his hat, and smiled. She waved a paper bag at him.

'I have pasties from the bakery!'

Getting up, he took them from her.

'You are the best woman in the world,' he said lightly, but his eyes were saying something much more profound.

They sat in a first-class compartment and devoured them as the train slid through station after station on its way to Kings Cross.

After they'd licked up every crumb and wiped their fingers, Zeke took her hand, rubbing his thumb across the back of it.

'Are you all right?'

'I should be asking you that. You're the one who was treated badly.'

'Oh, I'm all right. Better than all right.'

The outline of a big house like Carleton Towers slid past the window. Lady Carleton had wanted her to be happy there. When had she last been happy? Really happy? She smiled. That was easy – on stage with Val and the others at the Gentleman's Relish. What fun they'd had!

If she looked back, all the best moments of her life had been on stage. Last night, it had felt like she had to choose between what Henry represented, and Zeke. But she didn't. She could choose for herself; choose what *she* loved and enjoyed. *Take* that freedom instead of waiting for someone else to give it to her.

She might not know what social group she should be in. There might not be a single group of people she felt completely at ease with. But she knew where she belonged. She'd always known.

Did Zeke? She felt impelled to ask. Today was the day for getting everything sorted out. Everything.

'Are you still thinking about being an engineer?'

He looked surprised, and then thoughtful.

'You know, once we do this show, I'll have enough for university, if I want to go.'

She couldn't quite take a breath. 'Do you?'

He looked out the window for a moment, his eyes unfocused. Then he turned and smiled at her. 'I don't think someone who was meant to be an engineer would have enjoyed performing at the Gentleman's Relish quite so much.'

She laughed, out of sheer relief.

'No. No, I can't quite see an engineer there.'

'Except in the audience.' They laughed together, a little sadly, knowing how many engineers and doctors and lawyers had to hide their desires in that little basement club. She couldn't let it sober her, though. She and Zeke could keep on performing together.

'I'm sorry,' Zeke said. 'About my father, and all that.'

Kit smiled at him out of a vast sense of relief. It was as though her life was opening up again, when it had been closing in around her since the play folded.

'You were trying to do the best you could for me. Not a good way to go about it, though. Don't try to control me in future.'

He held up both his hands in surrender. 'Not a chance. Never.'

'All right, then,' she said, mock-stern.

'So,' he said. 'Does this mean I have a chance?'

She had known this was coming, and she hadn't known what to say, but the answer burst out of her.

'I'm only twenty-one! Twenty-two next month. I don't want to marry *anyone*. I just want to, to work and live and have some fun.'

He bit his lip as though she were funny. 'I'm only twenty-three myself, you know. I'm happy not to get married.' His voice deepened. 'But I would like to be allowed to love you.'

'It's a risk. We'll be working together again. If it goes wrong . . .'

He took both her hands, and her whole body flared alight.

'It is a risk,' he said. 'I'm ready to take it. Are you?'

As he'd done once before, he bent his head and kissed her knuckles, his mouth warm and exciting.

'Oh.' Her hand went up to touch his hair without her intending it. 'Well.' This was it. She didn't really need courage, though, when she felt like this. He was worth any risk. 'Yes. Yes. I am.'

He straightened and pulled her across and into his lap. Gracious! She almost laughed: how Lady Bridlingham would disapprove. But she didn't care about what was 'done'. Not now. Not with Zeke . . . she let her head fall back onto his shoulder and as his lips touched hers she shuddered with pleasure. His arms, warm around her; his mouth, hot, tasting her delicately; his hand on her back, holding her close to him. Happiness and desire surged in time with her heart. She kissed him, nothing held back.

After a long while, she drew a shaky breath and touched his cheek. He turned his head to press a kiss into her palm. Tremors went through her, a mixture of nerves and desire. Time to take the next step into being a modern young woman. How bold could she be?

'If we get this job with Charlot,' she said, 'one of us should get a flat. So we have somewhere to be private.'

His hands tightened on her and he swallowed. '*I* will.' He kissed her again, gently, and rested his face against hers as though gathering strength. 'I can afford it.'

They gazed at each other while her heart bumped strangely in her chest and her whole body grew warm. She slid her hand up his cheek and leaned in to kiss him again, just as the train jolted. Their noses bumped, hard, and they pulled away, laughing. She rubbed his nose for him.

'So much for romance,' he said ruefully, touching hers.

'We don't need romance,' she said. 'We have love.'

A smile broke across his face; one she'd never seen before, full of joy.

'So we do,' he said. 'So we do.'

EPILOGUE

Noël introduced them, his rounded tones particularly upper-class tonight. 'Ladies and gentlemen, please welcome Miss Kit Linton and Mr Zeke Gardiner, soon to be appearing in André Charlot's new production, *Pretty Maids*!'

The audience burst into applause as they ran onto the stage, Kit's silver dress swirling around her ankles.

This was an exhibition dance, for a children's charity gala. She and Fred had worked out the choreography, in between rehearsals for the new show. That was going to be wonderful – a much bigger production, with a full orchestra and a complete bevy of chorus girls. Charlot was pleased with them so far.

Zeke swung her out as they bowed, and then back in again as they moved into the dance.

She was conscious of the audience; they were a big cuddly animal, breathing and reacting as one, making the space alive as it never was during rehearsal.

The music, the lights, the audience . . . oh, how she loved being out on stage, moving to the rhythm, hearing the rustle and sigh in the stalls as Zeke swept her into a dip, relishing the applause as they segued into a tap number and she flipped her long skirt right off to reveal a shorter tap skirt.

She laughed up at Zeke and they held hands as they went through an intricate series of steps, to much applause. He grinned back at her, as alive as she was, as happy and solidly *there*, wishing to be nowhere else in the world.

She kicked and stepped and twirled, and felt joy and love spiral up and out of her to infect and encompass the entire audience, who gave it all back with interest.

In the end, where else could she belong, but here? Right here. Right now.

They finished and took two bows before running off into the wings, hand in hand.

'Very nice,' Charlot said, nodding to them. 'But don't be late for rehearsal tomorrow. We have a technical bump-in and we need to get the lighting right.'

'Yessir,' they both said.

Fred and Delly came up. They were the closers before curtain, the star turn. 'Nice job,' Fred said. 'I like that double you did to start.'

'We should go out for supper afterwards,' Delly added, standing back for the next act, a performing dog troupe, to move onto the stage. It made Kit laugh.

That's all she and Zeke were, so far, a prelude to the performing dogs, but that was all right.

That was perfectly all right with her.

ACKNOWLEDGEMENTS

Many thanks to:
  My husband, Stephen, who is not only my first reader, but who also wrote the lyrics for the *Dance Crazy* songs. When you ask someone for the lyrics to a 1920s love song and he hands them over half an hour later, you know you're a very lucky woman. They got cut out in the developmental draft, but we're planning to record the songs, anyway!

  Mike Cullen and Margaret Morgan, sensitivity readers most generous.

  Everardo Miranda, manager of Wyndham's Theatre, which is the model for the theatre in this book, who was kind enough to not only show me around backstage, but let me on the stage itself to get a sense of what it might feel like to the actors. Many thanks also to the other London theatre staff who answered questions and let me take a lot of photos of theatre lobbies and corridors and doors. (As an aside, Wyndham's Theatre was the place where Talullah Bankhead made her British stage debut in 1923, and if I hadn't seen a photo of her in the lobby, she would never have appeared in this book!)

Jane Alison Stutley (aka Jaz Stutley) for her invaluable help in finding 1920s songs that were out of copyright – you'd be amazed at how long most songwriters seem to live!

Colin Utley, volunteer guide at the London Transport Museum, for clarifying exactly what kind of train/Tube carriages Kit and Zeke would have been riding in.

And, as always, my thanks go to the team at Hachette Australia, especially Rebecca Saunders, my long-suffering editors Alex Craig and Dianne Blacklock, and the wonderful Karen Ward.